GUNBOAT JACK

Also by Timeri N. Murari

Fiction
The Marriage
The Oblivion Tapes
Lovers are Not People
Field of Honor (re-titled) Gunboat Jack: A Novel
The Shooter
TAJ, a Story of Mughal India
The Imperial Agent
The Last Victory
Enduring Affairs
Four Steps from Paradise
The Arrangements of Love
The Small House
The Taliban Cricket Club
Chanakya Returns: A Novel

Non-fiction
The New Savages
Goin' Home, a Black Family Returns South
My Temporary Son
Limping to the Centre of the World
Empress of the TAJ, in Search of Mumtaz Mahal

Young Adult
Children of the Enchanted Jungle
Axxiss and the Magic Medallions
Axxiss and the Undersea Kingdom
Axxiss and the Parallel Universe
Harvey and Melville, Detectives

Film and Television
The Square Circle (Daayra)
The Only Thing
Television Trilogy: Only in America

Plays
The Inquisitor
Hey Hero!
Lovers are Not People
The Square Circle (also directed)
The Assasination of an Unknown Writer
Killing Time
Enter Queen Lear

Editor
The Evil Within

GUNBOAT JACK

a novel

TIMERI N. MURARI

ALEPH BOOK COMPANY
An independent publishing firm
promoted by *Rupa Publications India*

Published in India in 2019
by Aleph Book Company
7/16 Ansari Road, Daryaganj
New Delhi 110 002

Copyright © Timeri N. Murari 2019

All rights reserved.

The author has asserted his moral rights.

This is a work of fiction. Names, characters, places and incidents are either the product of the author's imagination or are used fictitiously and any resemblance to any actual persons, living or dead, events or locales is entirely coincidental.

No part of this publication may be reproduced, transmitted, or stored in a retrieval system, in any form or by any means, without permission in writing from Aleph Book Company.

ISBN: 978-93-88292-90-0

1 3 5 7 9 10 8 6 4 2

For sale in the Indian subcontinent only.
Printed and bound in India by Replika Press Pvt. Ltd.

This book is sold subject to the condition that it shall not, by way of trade or otherwise, be lent, resold, hired out, or otherwise circulated without the publisher's prior consent in any form of binding or cover other than that in which it is published.

*To Waris and Cecilia
And to the luck of having
Such great friends.*

A Prince ought to inspire fear in such a way that,
if he does not win love, he avoids hatred.
—MACHIAVELLI

Float like a butterfly
Sting like a bee.
—MUHAMMAD ALI, Former World Heavyweight Boxing Champion

For God's sake, let us sit upon the ground,
And tell sad stories of the death of kings:
How some have been depos'd; some slain in war;
Some haunted by the ghosts they have depos'd;
Some poison'd by their wives; some sleeping kill'd;
All murder'd.
—SHAKESPEARE, *Richard II*

PART I

ONE

It was hot. The brown dry earth seared the feet and the large granite boulders scattered over the hillside burned the palms of hands. The sky was a malevolent blue and achingly bright. Far overhead, almost near the sun, kites circled and circled and circled.

There were two people climbing the hill. The tall, thickset man was a few yards ahead of the woman, and he stopped to rest and wait for the woman to catch up. He wiped the sweat off his forehead and flicked the moisture at a boulder. It sizzled and evaporated. He tugged at his shirt, but the sweat sucked it back against his skin. If there had been shade, even a small tree or a bush, he would have liked to rest under it. There was little except these vast boulders that seemed to have tumbled down from nowhere to rest on the side of the hill.

A couple of hundred yards below him, pulled off the narrow tarmac road, was their car. It glittered. The road curved and wound through the landscape, passing now and then a hill such as the one he stood on, until he could no longer see where it went. There was no traffic, although now and then he sensed the movement of people in the distance.

The woman reached his side. Her face was the colour of the earth and her make-up cut by rivulets of sweat. She started to lean against the boulder and then leaped away.

'Damn,' she said. There was no vehemence. She was too breathless for that.

'You're sure dressed wrong for this.'

'I couldn't wear trousers,' she answered with irritation. 'And I wasn't going to dress like a native.'

She patted her face with a tiny cotton handkerchief. The powder came off in patches, making her skin look afflicted. She wore a flowered cotton dress that pinched in on her narrow waist and then abruptly flowed out over her stiff petticoats. She had a thin gold chain around her neck, a brooch of a butterfly made of metal and cheap stones above her left breast. On her right wrist she wore two gold bangles.

She was nearly as tall as he, and was certainly pretty. Her face was small, oval, with high cheekbones, a wide mouth, and large brown eyes. Her hair had been carefully permed, but the morning's walk up the hillside had dampened and flattened it around her forehead and the back of her neck.

'C'mon.'

He began to climb again. The path they followed was narrow and well worn. It wound around the boulders and was edged on either side by tufts of spare grass. A stone cut his foot, and Gunboat Jack hopped.

'Did we have to be barefoot?'

'Yes. This is supposed to be a holy hill,' Gertrude said and giggled as Gunboat hopped some more. 'At least that's what the natives say because of him.'

Gunboat peered upwards. They had another two hundred yards to go. He caught a glimpse of a thatched roof.

'He better be good.'

'He's supposed to be very holy.'

They reached the top. The thatch he had seen was only a roof held up by bamboo poles. It was about twenty feet square, and twenty people were sitting in its shade. They looked up with open curiosity at Gunboat and Gertrude, and two women shifted away, giving them room to sit. Gunboat moved forward, grateful for the shade.

'You shouldn't sit with them,' Gertrude said.

'I sure as hell ain't standin' out there in the sun,' Gunboat said, and sat heavily down on the flat earth. There was a slight breeze on the hilltop, and with the shading it felt quite cool. When he craned around, he could see nearly the whole countryside: flat with small patches of bright emerald-green rice fields and shining squares of water tanks. There was a village in the distance he hadn't noticed before, and women, brightly clothed in reds and blues, working in the fields.

Gertrude sat. It was difficult with her starched petticoats. They billowed up and out, revealing her thighs, and she tried to hold the skirt down as if it were a blowing parachute. The women giggled, and Gertrude glared at them. She finally settled to rest in a kneeling position.

'Where is he?' Gunboat Jack asked.

Gertrude shrugged. There was a small cave at the top of a slight slope. There were a few fresh flowers, bits of coconut, and some fruit outside the entrance. Otherwise it looked bare and uninhabited. The others under the thatched roof were squatting facing the open mouth of the cave.

It was quiet and calm on the hilltop. Gunboat could hear only the breeze whispering through the thatch and the occasional clink of a bangle or an anklet. Once or twice the kites high in the sky called: a long, lonely sound. They keened, as if mourning their solitude. Even Gerty, and he was grateful for that, remained silent, though he could sense her glaring at any of the natives who turned to meet her eye.

Gunboat turned when he heard voices. A couple came over the rim of the hill. They were in their late twenties, and the woman carried a child in her arms. The child appeared asleep, but the tender way in which they handled him made Gunboat suspect he was sick. He made room for them. The husband held the child until the woman was settled, cross-legged, and then laid it gently on her lap. She was beautiful. Her face was heart-shaped with a sensual mouth and liquid brown eyes, tinged with sadness, that filled the face. There was a diamond in her nose and silver rings on her toes. She kept her head down as if sheltering the child from his look.

'What's wrong?' Gunboat asked.

The woman made no answer. The husband, sensing the meaning, turned his palms up and looked skywards.

'They think that sadhu can cure him?' he asked Gertrude.

She hesitated, wavering between contempt and belief. 'Possibly. He is supposed to have many powers.'

A youth came out of the mouth of the cave. He wasn't more than fourteen. His head was shaven, and he stood straight. He wore only a flimsy cotton cloth around his waist. He came straight to Gunboat and beckoned them both.

'No,' Gunboat said. 'He should see this couple.'

'He knows we're more important than them,' Gertrude said and scrambled to her feet.

'How does he know we're here?'

'He knows,' she said. 'And he knows about the child too.'

The youth turned, and they followed.

It was gloomy and cool in the cave. They smelled incense and fresh water. Gunboat waited until his eyes had adjusted. There was very little in the cave. A few earthenware pots, and a fireplace made of mud. The cave was a dozen feet deep, and the roof of uneven height.

A man sat cross-legged on a worn deerskin at the farthest end. His eyes were closed; his beard, black streaked grey, began just below his cheekbones and fell to his chest. He was slim and straight and his skin, the colour of old gold, appeared to shine in the light from the single oil lamp. It was a dry shine.

The youth gestured; they sat. Gertrude knelt, trying to appear as if she were not in front of this man in a loincloth.

'Does he speak English?' Gunboat whispered.

Gertrude shrugged. The youth withdrew to the opening of the cave. The sadhu appeared unaware of their presence. Gunboat noticed he hardly seemed to breathe.

'Yes,' he finally said, though his eyes remained closed.

'Shouldn't you have seen that sick child?'

'I already have.' It was an accentless voice, so soft they had to bend forward to hear.

'Were we more important than them?'

'No.' He chuckled. 'An American boxer and an Anglo lady are as important as everyone else.'

'How do you know who I am?' Gunboat Jack asked, and strained for the reply.

'I know.'

Gunboat wished the man would open his eyes. It was disconcerting talking to him. Gertrude rustled uneasily.

'You seen me fight?'

'No.'

'You disapprove?'

The man chuckled again. 'Why should I? It is an honourable profession. Here we have wrestlers.'

'Back home too,' Gunboat said and found he was enjoying the man's company. 'I used to be pretty good. Boxer I mean. I didn't win no championship...but I was good.' He wished now he had won a title back home. He wasn't given the breaks.

'Only one man at a time can be champion. It was not your time.' He paused. 'You are a man of honour?'

'You bet I am. I didn't take no dives. I made my money straight.'

Without warning, the sadhu opened his eyes. They looked directly at Gunboat Jack. The eyes were pale brown, almost the colour of beach sand. They appeared not to look, yet they saw everything of him.

'You are also a man of courage.' It was a statement.

'Yes.'

'Then what you have come to ask for depends on a test of these two qualities in you.'

'They won't give,' Gunboat said.

'If you hold to them, you will be victorious; if you let go of them you will be defeated.' The sadhu hadn't blinked once.

'What the hell does that mean?' Gunboat considered his own question in the long silence. 'So if I want to get home,' he finally replied to himself, 'I will have to be true to myself.'

'That depends on you. It is going to be difficult.'

'What will this test be?' Gunboat asked. If he knew ahead of time, he could be careful.

'It will happen soon. In your profession.'

'I haven't fought for years.'

'You will not need to fight.' His eyelids began to lower slowly. It seemed as if a door was closing.

'What about me?' Gertrude asked quickly. The lids were half closed, considering her.

'You will leave your home to be forever a stranger, for that is your wish.'

'With Gunboat?' She glanced at Gunboat and smiled shyly.

'You love him?'

'Yes.'

The sadhu chuckled. It sounded pleasant, benevolent. He had been sitting, arms outstretched, with his wrists resting on his crossed knees and the palms facing upwards. The thumbs and forefingers touched to form circles. Now he closed one hand, and opened it a few moments later. There was a small pile of white ash in the centre of the palm. He lifted his hand up to his face and blew. The ash was fine as dust and delicately perfumed.

'Love is like this vibudhi. Visible one moment, invisible the next,' he said. 'Your love will depend on his actions.'

Gertrude snorted and shifted as if to rise. She wished she hadn't asked. Nor come to see this fakir.

'How'd you do that?' Gunboat asked. He stared at the empty palm.

'That was a trick,' Gertrude said.

'Isn't everything?' the sadhu said gently. He then addressed Gunboat although there was no perceptible movement to his head or to the last peep of his eyes. Only his voice appeared to shift direction. 'You will meet a woman of your own race. Be careful. She holds your destiny.' He paused. 'And a prince. If you wish it, he will change your life.'

'I don't know any prince.' Gunboat spoke only to a silent image.

The sadhu's eyes closed. They sat awhile, but the man appeared to have withdrawn from them. Gunboat leaned forward and reached out.

'Gunboat.' There was panic in Gertrude's voice.

Gunboat touched the palm on which the ash had materialized. Delicately he drew his finger across the palm. The sadhu did not stir. Gunboat drew back. The ash was on his fingertip. He smelled. It was sweet and dry.

TWO

'It was real,' Gunboat said.

'It was a trick,' Gertrude said stubbornly. She had lost her nervousness. 'He admitted it himself. They're all full of tricks.' Her contempt was returning. 'Who's this woman?'

He caught her glance; it was fully of worry. 'I don't know any woman either.'

They reached the car and climbed in gingerly. The seat stung their backs, and the wheel burned Gunboat's palms. The car was an Austin Cowley with a canvas top. It was a few years old, but it ran well, though not fast. Gunboat pulled the starter. The engine turned over after several tries and he put it in gear. He drove down the centre of the road, since there was no room to keep to the left-hand side. There'd be little traffic: an occasional car, a truck, many bullock carts.

'You want the top down?'

'No. It blows my hair,' Gertrude said, and dabbed at her forehead. The handkerchief was soaked and mopped nothing. Only smeared the perspiration.

'You must have met her,' Gertrude said.

'Not that I know of.' Gunboat slowed to pass half a dozen bullock carts.

The right wheels of the car spun on the earth, kicking up dust, and bumped when he got back on the road.

In spite of dark glasses, Gertrude had to screw up her eyes to peer through the glare. The landscape changed little: the boulders, the hard dry earth, the scrub grass, the stubby lantana bushes remained the same. There were a few gentle hills and sharp curves in the road.

Now and then they passed small rice fields, each field divided by a narrow ridge of the earth. The green of these fields looked like emeralds and the men and women working them stopped to watch the car. The children darted after it, and pariah dogs snapped at its wheels. But they would soon be left behind in the dust. They passed a grove of mango trees and the deep, dark shade, in which a small group of peasants were resting, looked inviting.

'This is your home,' Gunboat said.

'It was,' Gertrude said stubbornly. She gestured. 'Would you want to live here?'

'I'm stuck here,' Gunboat said. 'It ain't the Bronx, but it ain't that bad.'

'Would I like the Bronx?' Gertrude asked this question often, like a child being promised a special treat.

'You bet. It's a great place to have grown up in. That's where I learned my fightin'.' His answer, too, was the same. 'There's a bar, just on my block, called The Garden of Roses. It's cool, and dark, and the beer is always cold. Real cold. And they have a jukebox by the door. I used to drink there a lot, a long time back.' He paused. 'Maybe it ain't there anymore.'

He had spoken of it before, and Gertrude could nearly imagine it. The owner's wife was called Rose, and she was a pretty, cheerful Irish girl. The owner was John, an ex-cop.

She glanced at Gunboat. He looked as if he were dreaming. He had clear blue eyes and stubby lashes. His face was bony: not broken, just very bony. There was a slight ridge above his left eye. It was difficult to see but she had felt the long bump. He had a stubby nose and a small mouth. A couple of teeth were missing, and that could be noticed only when he laughed. It was a strong, not particularly handsome, face. His short brown hair was thinning.

'Would you do anything to leave?' Gertrude broke the silence. She didn't like silences.

'Would I?' Gunboat reflected: Jesus, at times I figure I'd sell my own mother and my sisters to get home. I'd fight Joe Louis himself, with one hand behind my back, and let that Negro pound me to pulp to get home. And then again, it depends, doesn't it? The holy guy said I'd have to hold my honour and my courage. I got nothing else. I can't fight. I'm too slow now. Sure I think I could match up pretty good against one of these Indian boxers. They got the weight, but not the punch or the technique. No, Jesus, I couldn't go through that again. Not after that last fight in Calcutta, and what I did to the Tiger...

'Depends,' Gunboat said. He fumbled in the glove compartment and pulled out an orange pack of Charminar cigarettes. 'Would you?'

'Yes. I want to go home.'

At first, when they had met, he had not known what she meant. Home was not the town they were motoring back to. It was a mythical kingdom called England. Though she had not been there, she was as familiar with it as he was with his street block. Her family spoke of places and streets and things as if they'd seen them with their own eyes, and not read of them or heard about them in conversations. It had puzzled Gunboat at first. As an Anglo-Indian, the descendant of mixed parentage—English or Welsh and Indian—she had a clearly defined identity in India. It was, visually, British with all those familiar tics and mannerisms—European clothes, tea in the afternoon, the jolly slang, and those haunting English names—but below, the souls of the Anglo-Indian were wholly Indian for they could not escape the past or the colour of their skin. With India's independence in 1947 they became a lost people—never Indian enough to remain, nor British enough to leave. Now Gunboat felt a deep sadness for Gerty. She had exiled herself from this country. Physically she remained trapped; mentally she was over the seas.

'That sure ain't the Bronx,' Gunboat said, and squeezed the bulb horn. Two small grizzled men stepped off the road and watched the car pass them.

'No. And it isn't here either.' She wanted to change the subject. The longing had become a dull ache. Its only cure was money, enough for the whole family, not just for herself. 'You coming to the dance at the Bowring this evening?'

'I'll think about it,' Gunboat said. He wasn't particularly fond of dancing.

'What else can you do?'

'Shoot some pool. Snooker,' he added to correct himself. He felt her studying him and glanced at her. She was chewing her lower lip, worried.

'I do love you, you know,' she finally said.

'I know.'

'I didn't want you to believe what that sadhu said about me.'

'He didn't say anything about you, baby,' Gunboat said and patted her knee. 'He just made a remark about loving.'

'It was meant about me,' she insisted. 'Old…' She didn't complete the sentence, as if in fear the sadhu might overhear her even from this great distance. 'He talked more about you than me, didn't he?'

'Not much more.'

'Have you met any American girls?'

'Not recently. I told you. Besides,' he hesitated and tried to recall the exact words, 'he didn't mean American. He said race. That's a different ball game.'

'I suppose it could mean English as well,' Gerty said sullenly.

'Or French or Swedish or Italian.' Gunboat laughed and Gerty saw the gaps in his mouth. He grinned at her. 'I was also warned to be careful of her.'

'I wonder who the prince will be?' she asked wistfully, wishing he was for her, as in all the fairy tales.

Gunboat shrugged; he didn't quite believe the sadhu. He slowed the car. They were approaching a village, and few, if any, villagers had road sense. They were quite liable to dart in front of the car.

'I'm hungry,' Gunboat said. 'It's been a long time since breakfast.'

They had left an hour past dawn when it had been cool. It had been pleasurable then, the soft breeze just touching the skin and the sun giving out only the hint of warmth. The sun had been pale gold and its edges so clear. The sky had been a gentle blue. By nine it had become hot, and the very nerves buckled under the almost physical weight of the heat.

'Well, I don't want to eat in one of these places. You shouldn't either. You'll catch something, Gunboat.'

'I've had the lot,' Gunboat said and slowed.

The village was only a row of small brick and mud and thatch huts on either side of the road. There was a tiny provisions stall, a tea and coffee stall, blacksmiths, and a shrine. He stopped at the coffee stall and climbed out. Immediately he found himself surrounded by a dozen children and an equal number of adults. They stared at him with curiosity, examining him as they would any alien visitor. The children touched the car and ran their fingers through the dust on its metallic sides, delighting in the smudges and marks they left.

'You sure?' Gunboat asked Gerty.

She sat sunk in her seat. 'Sure,' she said, and then shouted in deliberately bad Kannada, 'Ho-go, ho-go' to the boys, who only giggled.

The stall owner was a young man. He scrambled to stand as Gunboat approached. There was little in the stall: a few glasses for the coffee and tea, a kettle, a few large bottles of biscuits, and a stack of paan leaves.

'Coffee,' Gunboat said, and pointed also to some biscuits.

The young man hurried to fill his order. He was slim, dark, and obviously awed by Gunboat's patronage. He wiped the glass carefully and poured the coffee into it. The coffee was too hot, and Gunboat handed it back. He watched while the youth cooled the coffee by pouring it from one glass into another. He had seen it done before, but it still held his attention. The youth began to pour with the glasses inches from each other. Then he lifted one glass higher and higher until the two glasses were a couple of feet apart and the coffee was a slim falling stream. He did it half a dozen times and gave Gunboat a much cooler coffee.

Gunboat offered to pay for the coffee and biscuits but the youth insisted he didn't.

'You really should take the money,' Gunboat said. It wasn't much, but neither was the stall. The youth only shook his head and grinned. Gunboat knew few places where his patronage was so honoured. 'Okay. Thanks, fella.'

He turned. He was still being studied by the villagers. The crowd had grown some, and Gunboat had to push his way gently back to the car. He was a good head and shoulders taller than the tallest man in the crowd.

Gertrude was sulking behind her glasses. She had given up shooing the little boys away, and they now stood on the running board watching Gunboat start the car. It fired almost immediately, and he slowly eased it back on the road.

'I hate the way they stare,' Gertrude said vehemently, as the car picked up speed, 'as if they've never seen a European man and a woman.'

'Ah,' Gunboat said. 'Not such a pretty-lookin' woman.' He leaned over and kissed her cheek. She wanted to resist, then melted and smiled.

They passed a waist-high stone marker. Bangalore was another thirty miles.

THREE

Gunboat had borrowed the car from one of Gertrude's friends, the Shortworths. They ran a small family garage on Wellington Street in Bangalore cantonment.

'Shall I drop you off first?' Gunboat asked as they neared the outskirts of the city.

Gertrude thought of the half-hour walk back to her house in the heat. She was already tired, and she needed to be fresh for the dance. What she wanted was a good cup of tea, a rest, and a bath. 'Yes,' she said. They were nearing a fork in the road. One fork ran near her house. 'Why can't you keep the car for tonight?' It would be pleasant to be driven to and from the dance instead of taking a rickshaw or a carriage.'

'I told Henry I'd drop it back when we returned.'

The traffic had increased. There were trucks beginning the run down to Madras, two hundred miles southeast on the coast. Many more cars. And bullock carts returning to the villages. There was a large factory building going up on their right, and further on, to their left, another. There was still a lot of open space between the houses, and here and there a mansion set well back from the road. The whitewash on the brick walls was turning grey from the rain, like the fading of an old photograph.

Gunboat liked these old houses. They reminded him of a visit he'd made down south in the U. S. of A. They looked alike: pillars and porticoes and porches and high-ceilinged rooms and spacious gardens. Even here there was an air of neglect. One, the Cavendish, was empty. An English judge had lived there eight years ago. It had been his home for forty years, and then he'd returned home for good. It had been rented out, but now it was too big and expensive.

The traffic became heavier: rickshaws, tongas, cyclists, countless pedestrians, and cows. Gunboat used the horn a lot. Bangalore was full of hills and the little car strained up one now, paused at the top, and coasted down. Bangalore was on the edge of the Nilgiri Hills and was pleasantly cool two thirds of the year. In winter it occasionally even became cold. The British had used it as an army base and divided the city in two: the cantonment and the city. The cantonment was liberally scattered with army barracks and every street name had a military ring to it. The streets here were spacious and wide and tree-lined. The city, to the west of the cantonment, was more crowded; the streets were narrower and bore Indian names.

Gunboat turned off South Parade. It was the main street in the cantonment, and the longest. It had been renamed Mahatma Gandhi Road, but no one ever called it that. Gertrude lived on Walker Street. The house was small; it had a tiled roof, a narrow trellised porch, and a little garden.

'You coming in?'

Gunboat peered past her. He saw her father, Patrick Nailer, sitting on the porch. They waved to each other. Her father was a signalman with the railways. He was a pleasant, quiet-spoken man. He'd been a bit of a boxer in his younger days—strictly amateur, a lightweight who'd fought for Southern Railways—so he and Gunboat had a common interest.

'No,' Gunboat said. 'I'd like to get the car back.'

'Am I seeing you this evening?' Gertrude asked and kissed him swiftly on the cheek. She was a chaste woman in her father's presence.

'I guess so. I'll catch up with you at the dance.'

She settled for that, though he sensed her wanting to argue. 'If you're good, I'll drop you back home.'

'Okay.'

He watched her open the small gate, shut it carefully to prevent wandering cows from eating her mother's roses, and kiss her father. Gunboat turned the car around in the narrow lane, careful not to fall into the culverts on the sides of the lane, waved once more to Mr Nailer, and accelerated.

It was a ten-minute drive to the Shortworth garage. Wellington Street was a narrow road, off Richmond Road. Many of the Anglo-Indian families lived in the area. It was called Richmond Town. All the houses had gardens and were individualistic in their architecture. All were single-storied and sprawled, with porches running alongside the rooms. The Shortworth garage was about a third of the way down the street. Gunboat turned in and parked the car next to a DeSoto. It was new, maroon, and made him faintly homesick. One of the Shortworths' sons, a tall blond youth, slid out from under a car. His face was streaked with grease.

'Back on time,' Gunboat said and tossed the keys over. 'Thanks a lot for the loan.'

'Ran okay?' Stephen asked. He spoke with the same accent as Gerty, somewhat singsong.

'Like a bird. Henry in?'

'No. He's out testing a car.' For a minute they both admired the DeSoto together. 'Belongs to an Indian family up the road. Their driver doesn't know how to use the Fluid Drive, and he's messed it up. Stupid bugger.'

'A real beauty.'

Gunboat looked around. There were a couple of other old cars, British-made, in the compound. The garage was only a sloping tin roof, filled with tools and junk. The family, three grown sons in all, lived in a small cottage.

'We're going home soon,' Stephen said. 'Maybe in four months.'

'Yeah. Where to?'

'Near Reading. Dad's got a cousin there. He's helping us out.'

'How far's that from London?'

Stephen hesitated, then shrugged. He was a handsome boy, almost nineteen, so Anglo-Saxon looking, yet not a European. Gunboat himself couldn't distinguish the subtle difference; he had had to be told by Gertrude.

'I don't know,' Stephen said. 'But not far I hope. I'd like to live there.'

'Tell your father I'll drop by in a couple of days to say hi.'

Gunboat walked up Wellington Street. He passed a couple of pretty women in frocks, sitting on a parapet. They giggled and nodded at him, flirtatiously tossing their heads. He smiled, vaguely recognizing them. He was a familiar figure, and the territory he lived in, the cantonment, was small. He trudged up the hill of Richmond Road, his shoes scuffing the dust. It had grown cooler, and once the sun set the evening would turn chill. He waved to another acquaintance and turned onto Brigade Road.

Gunboat strolled in the shade of an avenue of gold mohur trees. They bore flowers as bright as flames, and he thought of the harsh Bronx sidewalks: less exotic; more familiar. It had been eight years since he'd walked them. Just my goddamn luck, Gunboat muttered to himself. I figure to make my fortune and have a good time, and I end up here for life. Still, it was good while it lasted. Mona and I had some real good times; if it hadn't been for my meeting her I'd be a broken-down bum in the Bronx. A goddamn punchbag for any fighter who needed practise.

Gunboat had met Mona Gugala at a party on Charlotte Street, thrown by Pete Culley. She was a pretty woman, with blond hair, blue eyes, and a child's face and body. She was a few years older than Gunboat. It turned out she was a widow. Nothing rare in the winter of '47. Her husband hadn't died in the war; he'd been stepped on by an elephant. Gunboat had laughed; Mona didn't. Her husband had owned a small circus and travelling show. She was the bareback rider and accountant. Mona needed a man to look after her and the circus.

Gunboat knew by now he was no champion fighter. He didn't have the weight to be a heavy and in his few years he'd only made a couple of grand. Most of his earnings ended up in the pocket of his manager, Frankie Grosse. A week after meeting Mona he told Frankie he was no contender for no title.

He couldn't completely quit the fight game. It was, he joked, his raison d'être. So he added a sideshow. Step into the ring with the Great Gunboat Jack for a hundred bucks. Gunboat picked his opponents carefully. None too fit or strong. He preferred them with bellies and braggadocio. That way they split at the seams easily.

For the first year the circus travelled the United States. Then Mona decided to try the world. They spent a few months in Europe and then caught a boat east, meaning to head for Singapore, Australia, and back home. They stopped in Bombay for a break and to make some money.

That was their big mistake, Gunboat thought. If they had kept going, nothing would have happened. I'd be back in the U. S. of A. by now; maybe even married to Mona and with a couple of kids.

They had put on a few shows on a large maidan outside the Gymkhana Club. Third week in, Mona had fallen sick. She had cholera, and a week later she died. It happened so fast. Like that, Gunboat would click his fingers and say to himself. Just like that. He buried her in a Bombay cemetery, this pretty girl from the Bronx. He still wasn't sure whether he loved her. They had been together a few years, and had gotten on well. Her death hurt; not bad, but he ached. He missed her. Gunboat wanted nothing more to do with the circus. He kept a few bucks for himself and handed the whole shebang to the clown.

He did some heavy drinking after that and lost most of his money. He knew little about the country he was in, except that he was in the wrong place at the wrong time. A change was taking place. The English were leaving. He saw them come into Bombay from all over the country: parents, children, tonnes of baggage, servants. They boarded the magnificently white P & O steamers moored at the docks, sang songs of farewell from the safety of the deck, and sailed slowly west towards the setting sun. On the surface they appeared cheerful, bustling, relieved; yet beneath, Gunboat sensed their bewilderment and their loss. Some wept; even the stiff, arrogant women shed tears. Gunboat wished he could go with them, but he'd lost his money and no one had time to lend him the fare.

Gunboat reached the bottom of Brigade Road. There was a small traffic circle not far from the gate to his compound. Beyond it, Brigade Road rose steeply to South Parade. There were two movie houses at the corner. One, the Rex, showed American movies; the other, the Rajkumar, showed Hindi. The Rex had been running *High Noon* for the last four weeks.

Just opposite his gate was a small open space. There was shade only around its fringes, and during the day rickshaw-wallahs, travellers, and beggars rested in it. Sometimes he would find a small impromptu market for itinerant salesmen selling new plastic buckets, wooden toys, and tin saucepans; at others, itinerant magicians. Once he came across a youth lying in suspended animation five feet above the hard earth. In the past, he would have sworn it to be a trick. He'd seen all things in his circus. But here, in this open space, with no equipment, he could not understand how it had been done. Strangely enough, he found himself accepting it as magic.

Today the small square was empty. Gunboat turned into the compound. There was a long low cottage to his right. An Australian trainer, his wife, and his son lived in it. Jockey Rosen also owned a couple of horses, and frequently when they had a drink together in the evening, he gave Gunboat a hot tip for the Sunday races. The horse always won. This, Gunboat knew, was no magic.

The house at the rear was quite large, and old. The whitewash was patchy and yellowed from the rains. The pillars supporting the porch roof looked as if they'd collapse at a punch. They appeared to depend on the bougainvillea creeper for a scaffolding support. There was a small jackfruit tree to one side, and Gunboat brushed past its branches and went around towards the back of the house. Here grass and weeds grew beside the tiny path.

He needed no lock for his door. There was little to steal in the room. A bed, a table with two chairs, an almirah, and a dresser. Even that was too much. A small suitcase was tucked under the bed. The room had a high ceiling. It soared above him like a cathedral, and there were a couple of windows in the walls near the tiling. String hung from each shutter so he could close it during the monsoon season. His bed was unmade, and Gunboat gathered up the mosquito net and flipped it over the railing above the bed.

Gunboat took a small pint bottle of MacDougals Whiskey from the dresser drawer, took a pull, winced, and put it back. He wished for a cold beer once more. A Bud would do.

He lay back. Sounds: crickets beginning for the evening, voices from other parts of the house, car horns, the leaves of the jackfruit tree shivering against each other. He heard Mrs D'Souza's voice, then her daughters' voices. The Carters from behind him arguing. It was a small enclave of exiles.

Fear. Gunboat remembered those white faces rushing for the P & O liner. He knew it, he sensed it: taut skin, the stink of fright. A decade in the ring had taught him, if nothing else, to recognize it. Smell, gestures, the flicker of the eye, bursts of sweat. He'd been afraid; his opponents had been afraid. They were all lonely in a ring, vulnerable to pain, hurt, nausea, their own blood. Those people had lived two, three centuries in fear. They embraced brown friends, brown servants; quickly, relieved, they hurried up gangplanks. Weeping, waving, watching the sombre mass drift farther and farther back. It was difficult to understand why they had remained so long, and hated for so long. And now these half-caste dependents remained, cast off as quickly as the moorings of the liners.

◆

Gunboat slept. He woke an hour later. It was pitch dark; night came swiftly. The crickets were loud, the voices muted, hushed by the night and the walls. Gunboat switched on the light and sat up in bed.

He shared a bathroom and the latrine with the other families. He bathed in lukewarm water, pouring the water over his body with a tin mug. He looked down at himself as he dried. He was still strong, somewhat flat-bellied. The legs looked good, but Gunboat knew how deceptive the appearance was. In a ring they'd turn to jelly in two rounds.

He dressed in clean cotton trousers and a shirt, took another pull on the Indian whisky, and went out. The evening was so cool. It was difficult to remember the heat of the day now. He strolled towards the traffic island and began up Brigade Road.

The sidewalk up Brigade Road was crowded with young people. They were college students and some schoolboys and girls. During the day the sidewalks were nearly empty. Once the sun set they came in groups, the boys in one, the girls in another. They looked at each other, talked aloud, giggled, even exchanged jokes with the other group, but never quite met. When they tired they adjourned to Koshy's, a small coffeehouse. It served good coffee, excellent masala dosais, and it had the only jukebox in town. Gunboat could hear the juke now. The song drifting across the streets with the café lights was 'Blue Suede Shoes'.

A few doors further up, and across the street, was Gunboat's. The signboard needed a coat of paint and was dimly lit. Gunboat turned in, climbed the narrow steps, and entered the billiards saloon. There were four tables, stagnant green in the shielded lights, and a bar at the far end with stools for the patrons.

Alongside three walls were raised-wood and cane-bottomed benches and overhead a slow-moving fan. The walls were bare and needed a whitewash; the coir carpet was frayed.

Only one of the tables was taken. A boy was playing by himself and, Gunboat noticed, he was good. Three men Gunboat didn't know stood to one side, watching with deference and admiration. They appeared to be witnessing a miracle. Gunboat took the cold beer left for him on the counter by Krishnan the bartender, and settled himself on the stool.

The boy was tall, nearly five nine. He was thickset, well muscled for an Indian, and stood very straight. He moved like an athlete, surely, confidently, around the table. His eyebrows were startlingly thick: A little finger of black hair arched above his eyes and joined above his nose. He had a full woman's mouth and a firm jaw. There was a scar on his cheek, just above the line of the jawbone.

He didn't look at Gunboat but continued playing, firmly stroking the cue and spinning one ball against the other. He finally missed, and the three men sighed in sympathy. The boy shrugged. Gunboat guessed him to be fifteen or sixteen. One of them stepped forward and took the cue, as if it were a gift.

'Are you Gunboat Jack?' The boy spoke from where he stood, across the length of the room.

'Yeah.'

The boy considered the reply. It hung in the silence between them, which gave the reply a reverberation of meanings. The three men, having once glanced in his direction, now stood a few feet back, arms behind their backs, studying the boy. They looked alike: slim, dark, servile. They dressed alike too: white dhotis, long white open-neck shirts, and slippers.

The boy said, 'You killed a man once I am told.'

FOUR

Gunboat decided he did not like the boy. He was too confident, too much an adult for a child his age. There was little doubt he expected an answer; his bearing was that of someone used to giving commands. Gunboat considered throwing him out, but suspected it would not be a judicial move. There would be endless trouble. The boy suggested ripples of unseen power, which made Gunboat dislike him that much more.

'Yeah.'

The boy nodded, as if this expanded his understanding. He had been solemn until now. He smiled. It made him boyish for the first time; gave him a vulnerability he had not had before. He also had dimples. 'I would like you to teach me how you did that.'

'Oh Jesus!' Gunboat uttered under his breath.

He turned his back on the boy. Remembering...

He knew he could never forget the Tiger. The man's face was still so clear and that long fall, a moment after Gunboat's punch, would never end. A man had died and the blame lay heavy on his soul. He had no wish to be constantly reminded.

'Go to hell,' Gunboat said and turned from the boy.

The three men looked worried, frightened even. The boy nodded solemnly but didn't move away. Gunboat felt his back studied. The beer tasted bitter and bad. He pushed it away.

'It couldn't be helped,' the boy said.

'For Christ's sake, why do you all say that?' Gunboat shoved the glass. It fell and smashed. The liquid turned the faded coir carpet red. Blood-coloured.

The boy would have turned, except he sensed the expectations of his retainers. He felt trapped between the white man's hostile back, embarrassed and unsure how to handle that spurt of anger, and the eyes of Swami, Kanni, and Vikrant. One was his valet, the other his chauffeur, the third his father's aide-de-camp. He was also unused to rejection.

He gestured to his men to wait and walked over to the bar. Gunboat ignored him. The boy didn't notice the barman who snapped to attention and poured Gunboat a new beer at the boy's gesture.

'I am Nataraj,' he announced formally. It sounded like an edict. He relented. 'But I was given a nickname. Nicky. I am sorry I offended you.' His accent was immaculately British.

'You want to kill a man?'

'Not particularly.' He smiled. 'I said it more as a compliment. I thought a fighter would take that as praise.'

'It ain't.'

'I have apologized.' Nicky spoke stiffly.

'Okay, I accept it. What do you want me for?'

'I'd like to learn to box.' He corrected himself: 'I need to.'

'A guy like you doesn't need to do anything.' Gunboat felt the boy's assurance, like mail armour.

'That's true.' He hadn't expected that power of observation in Gunboat. Boxers were not intelligent men. 'My needs are my own. No one is forcing me.'

'Have you ever boxed before?'

'Never. I am athletic and play nearly every sport well.' He said this simply; an accepted gift of life.

'Things come easily, huh?'

'Yes, I play cricket, hockey, football, polo, squash, and tennis.'

'I haven't heard of half of those games,' Gunboat joked.

'I didn't expect you would have,' he said it seriously, and then laughed.

Gunboat wasn't sure whether to take offence or not. It could be his sense of humour. 'Okay, why do you need to then?' He turned and nodded to the three men standing patiently by the door. 'You could get those guys to do your fighting.'

'I want to enter a boxing match in school, and I must defeat my opponent.'

'Does he know how to fight?'

'Yes,' the boy said impatiently. 'Otherwise I wouldn't need to learn. We would be equal and I could beat him. He learned in school. The one I used to attend didn't have it.'

'That's tough. Sounds like an expensive kind of place.'

Nicky made no reply. He had only a vague notion of the cost because it failed to interest him. He had been raised not to care about it. However, he was aware that money could purchase the integrity of men. And women, for far less. He eyed Gunboat, trying to calculate this man's worth. He noticed the clothes: frayed, cheaply tailored, but clean. The billiards parlour he knew to be not Gunboat's but a Muslim's, and it looked a shabby place. The air was stale and warm. The fan made little difference to the strong odours of tobacco and spilled beer. Nicky also knew where Gunboat lived. Swami had investigated and told him the rent, the size of the room, and the quality of Gunboat's neighbours.

At this point in his life, Nicky accepted poverty equably. It surrounded him, as natural as breath, fire, water. He noticed it occasionally: in the ribs of a man, the squalor of a child, the cost of men's honour. For the most part, however, he ignored it. It was the luck of a man to be a prince, his ill luck to be a pauper.

Gunboat noted the silence. It amused him. The boy behaved like a lord. Money could be discussed at his convenience, not Gunboat's.

'How long do I have?'

'The match is in four weeks. That should be enough time.'

'You must be joking. It took me a couple of years just to learn how to use my feet.'

'I'm a quick learner,' Nicky said, not quite contemptuously but near enough.

'You'll learn all right, when you get your head pounded in.' Gunboat revealed his own edge. A fighter needed to be arrogant, but not cocky. That could be fatal in the ring. 'How good is this guy you're fighting?'

Nicky considered. 'Good,' he finally conceded reluctantly. 'He is his school's champion.'

Gunboat considered asking why Nicky wanted to fight this boy and decided against it. He would learn in time. Nicky, he noticed, was not given to being questioned closely.

Gunboat still wasn't sure he liked Nicky. He was undoubtedly spoilt but, he conceded in his turn, there was little question of his courage.

'What are you?' Gunboat asked.

'A Kshatriya.'

The warrior caste. He was bred for battles though not for the ring. Gunboat had seen delicate paintings of turbaned men, dressed in light armour, mounted on caparisoned elephants, and carrying wickedly curved swords. The battle scenes had been fierce, yet so delicately elegant, as if the men portrayed were more concerned with the art of war than the actual brutality of it.

It took little to imagine the boy so intricately costumed. He had the face: fine, proud, finally cold and self-contained. He would fight well, not out of hunger or for the possession of money, but out of his honour. Gunboat knew few fighters who fought for honour. All those he knew did it for a buck. The bigger it was, the harder they fought. The physical pain was infinitely preferable to the hollow ache in the centre of a man's belly. The boy would know nothing of that.

'What will happen if you lose the fight?'

'I will not lose.' The softness was fierce. 'You will teach me only to win.'

Gunboat listened. He heard the passion. So it wasn't mere honour or an exercise in the mastery of an art. There was hatred as well. The boy he was to fight was not an opponent, he was an enemy. That was another kind of hunger.

'Listen, I can teach you a little about fighting. I can't guarantee the win,' Gunboat said. 'Is the other guy Indian?'

'No. English.' Nicky then added calmly, 'A friend.'

'Yeah?'

'Yes,' Nicky said. For a boxer Gunboat was more astute than he'd expected. 'So you will teach me!'

Gunboat considered. Since Tiger he had not been near a ring. Killing a man, even accidentally, left an odour that could never be erased. It stank one's whole life out for there was not the forgiveness of forgetfulness. It remained. More than a mere wound, it was an irretrievable loss. It had been his life, his only skill, and he had wandered this subcontinent half a decade with emptiness. This chance would be a sly return, a preparation for the time when he returned home and taught others his skill.

'How much?' Gunboat asked.

'Five thousand rupees.' Nicky paused. 'If I win!'

Gunboat had expected much less. Enough only to support him a little longer and make him less dependent on the saloon. Five thousand! It was enough for the ticket; enough to live a few days in New York until he found work. With that kind of money at his disposal, the boy must be a rich man's son—more, perhaps, a prince. Gunboat hesitated.

The sadhu had predicted this. He felt the unease of men when they cannot understand an event. How the hell had he known? 'You understand, in four weeks I can't teach you everything.'

'I understand.'

Nicky slid off the stool and stood beside it. He put out his hand. There was a return to his stiff formality. Gunboat was also expected to rise. He did, and stood a head higher than the boy. They shook hands.

'I will send a car to pick you up,' Nicky said. 'It will be a six-hour drive.'

'Six hours? Where the hell am I going?'

'To my state.' He added apologetically: 'What was.'

'I can't do that drive daily.'

'No, you can't. Which is why you will be my guest for three weeks. My school has closed for the holidays. The remaining week we can train at my place here.'

Gunboat wasn't sure he liked that arrangement. Six hours was certainly the sticks. He corrected himself. It was more than that. Once he left the familiarity of this city, he would be entering another world: India. It would be alien, incomprehensible; the nearest community to the boy's home would be a village. He had passed through the country often on train journeys. The cities in which he had begun and ended these journeys were not so much physical boundaries as time zones. They were the present, the future; they were not so much a part of India but of his own civilization. The landscape beyond was the past, the permanent. Fields and forests and mountains and countless small villages; a kaleidoscope of colours baking in the heat and bright sunlight. He had seen the women at the wells, the bullocks drawing the stick plough, the children riding the water buffaloes, ancient temples rising in the distance behind trees. Sometimes the train would halt for an hour or two or three, waiting for an unseen signal, and the silence would be pervasive. The distant call of a boy, the breeze bringing in the snatches of a woman's song, the hum of flies. Beyond that, nothing. And at night, when the moon was full, he could see the land stretch away to the horizon, seemingly uninhabited, remote.

'I need time to think,' Gunboat said, wanting somehow to break the spell, to defy the unseen wires that so easily manipulated him.

'How long?'

'Couple of days.'

Nicky considered and nodded. 'It is possible. You have until Monday to decide.'

'Sure, I'll do that.'

'Good. Then you will be picked up at nine. If you do not want the job, dismiss the driver.'

'Make it ten.'

'Nine. It is a six-hour drive.' He was firm on that. He turned to leave. 'You must take an advance.'

'No thanks.'

'To prove my good faith,' he insisted softly and snapped his fingers.

Swami came forward quickly. He was shorter than the boy and much older. He was bald, except for a fringe of hair that was touched with white. His face was round, almost blandly so, and his eyes were expressionless raisins stuck in that pudding face. From the deep pockets of his jiba he carefully extracted an envelope and handed it to the boy. Nicky gave it to Gunboat. Gunboat opened the envelope. There were ten one-hundred-rupee notes.

'What happens if you lose?'

'Then that is all you will get. Agreed?'

'What is the alternative?'

They both looked at the envelope.

'None,' Nicky said. 'It is what you Americans call incentive?' He turned. 'If you don't want the work, return all the money to my driver.'

'Yeah. Okay.' And he felt trapped by the envelope of money. He remembered a word that bothered him. 'What...state?'

'Tandhapur,' Nicky said.

Gunboat watched them leave: the boy first, the retainers a few steps behind. He had met his prince, and he uneasily awaited the impending menace of the European woman.

FIVE

'How was the holy guy?'

Johnny slid onto the next stool. He was a slim, dark young man with heavy spectacles and a pencil-line moustache. He was the manager and part-owner of Gunboat's. Gunboat himself had only ten per cent of the action. Johnny and Abdul Hassan had put up all the money to buy out old man Greene when he'd gone home to England. The ten per cent, and a couple of free beers a day, was the royalty for allowing them to use his name.

'He didn't say too much,' Gunboat said cautiously. 'Somethin' about me having to do something in the fight game if I'm to ever get back home.' He needed time to mull over the events.

'He's supposed to be pretty hot,' Johnny said. He liked using American expressions and if he couldn't pick up enough from Gunboat, he'd get them out of the movies. Johnny's real name was Jaganathan Swaminathan, and he was a Brahmin. 'People say that his predictions are accurate.'

'You ever been to him?'

'Nah,' Johnny drawled. He adjusted his glasses and peered owlishly at Gunboat. 'I got a guy in Basvanguidi who is real hot.'

'Listen, you might know,' Gunboat said. 'This guy closed his list, and when he opened it he had this fine kind of dust in it.'

'Vibudhi,' Johnny said. He tried to sound casual, but Gunboat knew he was impressed. 'Only very holy men can do that. It's a holy ash.'

'Was it a trick? I mean a sleight of hand?'

'No. Some very holy men have the powers to materialize objects,'

Johnny said. 'These powers are called Siddhis. And you only get them after years and years of prayer and meditation.'

'Yeah,' Gunboat said, only half believing.

'Yeah,' Johnny mimicked him, trying to catch the same drawl and intonation. He invariably failed. 'Tapas.'

'What's that?'

'These prayers. I learned all that when I was a kid,' and waved his hand dismissively. 'My old man stuffed it down my throat. I even read Sanskrit. Who the hell's gonna give a guy a job with Sanskrit?'

'You got your degree.'

'A third in chemistry.' Johnny laughed. 'That's why I'm running this place.' He sat upright and snapped his fingers. 'I forgot. There was this guy looking for you. Young, five eight. He had a couple of henchmen, he wouldn't tell me who he was. I would think he's a rajah's son. Or something.'

'Yeah. He is.'

Gunboat still held the opened envelope, and Johnny plucked it from his hand, riffled the notes, and whistled.

'He give you this?'

'Yeah.'

'Why?'

'Mind your own business, Johnny.' Gunboat ordered a fresh beer.

'Come on,' Johnny persisted, 'you know I'll find out one way or another.' He took a stool and settled on it.

'Yeah,' and Gunboat told him. 'What's Tandhapur?' he asked when he'd finished.

'Tandhapur,' Johnny shrugged it away. 'It's a small state, and they are small rajahs.'

'Big enough for me.' Gunboat waved the envelope.

'I mean compared to Mysore or Jaipur or Baroda. Those are maharajahs. Not that it makes that much difference now. They all had to accede to India when we became independent. The only one who gave problems was the nizam of Hyderabad. We had to invade his state.' Johnny took a small sip of Gunboat's beer. 'Damn good thing too. A few of them were okay, but most were real bastards.'

'Tandhapur too?'

'I don't know. I think they were okay.' He sighed. 'They all still have an easy life. The government gives them all a privy purse.'

'You don't approve?'

'No. They should be treated the same as us, but as this isn't a democracy what can one expect.'

'I figured it was. Nehru was elected to his office.'

'Sure.' Johnny waved away the reality. 'But you don't change India overnight. Nehru is the biggest maharajah of them all. But one day his time will come too. We need to change faster.'

'To what?' Gunboat had not seen Johnny so impassioned.

'To a socialist state, where everyone has an equal opportunity. Look at me. The educated jobless. There are millions of us. We are the seeds of the revolution.' He paused, softened. 'You know the only way I can get a job. Through influence. Some rich man talking to another rich man. He'll say "Give that Swaminathan a job." And I get a job.' He blinked at Gunboat, eyes large and calculating. "I need a job. You can get it for me."

'Jesus man, even I don't have a job, and I don't know any rich guy—'

'You do…now.'

Johnny baffled him. He could switch his thinking like a flipped coin and Gunboat was never sure which of the many faces would land up.

'What about the revolution?'

Johnny chuckled. 'What better way to subvert revolution than give a hungry man food? Gandhi once said that God had no right to reveal himself to man other than in the form of bread. Talk to the prince or his father. You'll meet him too. They have extensive mines, and they could give me a job.'

'I'll try' was all that Gunboat could promise though he doubted he could do anything.

'You place the bets?'

'Yeah. I laid them off with my bookie. Pretty good odds too. You want to bet some of that?'

'No.' Gunboat carefully tucked the envelope into his back pocket. 'Why don't you settle our tab?'

'Okay.' And he watched Johnny calculate his debt to the saloon. 'One hundred and eighty-five rupees.'

Gunboat checked the figure carefully and paid out. Money never remained long in his hands. On Monday he would have to enter the car.

'You talked to Jockey Rosen?' Johnny asked.

'He's a trainer.'

'He used to be a jockey,' Johnny said. 'And we always call him that. What did he say for the Sunday Gold Cup?'

'I didn't get to speak to him.'

'The race is tomorrow,' Johnny realized in horror. 'I gotta hustle the money for the bet.'

'So hustle. He'll give me the name in the morning. And you can put one hundred rupees for me. To win.' If he won, he could return the money intact.

Gunboat looked at the old clock above the entrance. It had a round, large, simple face with Roman numerals. Ten. The dance finished at midnight. As always, he thought of not going. There was a dance every Saturday night. The same orchestra, the same dancers, the same music. Gunboat knew he would think about not going for a while, and then go. He sipped his beer. It had begun to turn warm, and he had Krishnan drop a couple of chunks of ice in it. He stirred the beer with his finger.

'When are you going to the dance?' Johnny asked.

'You reading my mind or something?'

'Shit. Every Saturday it's the same.'

'Then why ask?'

'You know I hate silences. That's why I'd never make a sadhu.

Sitting alone and meditating would drive me nuts.'

'You shouldn't do that,' Gunboat said. 'Keep hittin' at what you are. It don't help you at all. Just makes things worse. You can't be me; I can't be you.' Gunboat finished the beer and stood up. 'You never hear me hitting the U. S. of A.'

'No,' Johnny said. He sat silent awhile and Gunboat would have moved off, but he sensed Johnny wanted to say something. He expected a wisecrack. 'Two hundred years of white rule makes you want to be someone else,' Johnny said quietly. 'Anything but this.' He pinched at his dark forearms, 'and this.' He opened his shirt and tugged at the thread that ran diagonally across his chest.

'Well, I'm not one of them. So you don't have to put on that kind of a show.'

'Yeah?'

'Yeah.'

They shook hands. By the time Gunboat reached the door and glanced back, Johnny had recovered. He was joking with one of his friends.

Gunboat turned right on Brigade Road and began downhill. The sidewalks were emptying; the promenaders were going home. The shops had closed, and the little paan shop on the corner was doing brisk business with the after-dinner crowds. Gunboat remembered he'd not eaten. He followed the curve of the road and stepped into a small restaurant opposite the Imperial cinema. *Executive Suite* with William Holden was being shown.

The meal he ate was simple and cheap: a small plate of curried mutton and a paratha. The interior was a peculiar green, and in the purple neon light Gunboat had trouble focusing on the food. The other small tables were occupied by Indians, and some, those who were strangers, stared at him. Europeans never ate in such establishments. Gunboat ignored the stares. The food was good, and he had a second helping. When he finished, he washed his hands and lit a cigarette. And belched. There was comfort in that gesture.

'On the slate,' he said on his way out, and the pudgy old man behind the small marble-top desk grinned and nodded. He opened a grubby book and made a note.

The Bowring Club was half a mile up the road that ran adjacent to the Imperial cinema. Gunboat strolled somewhat near the centre of the road. The sidewalk was of uneven granite slabs and full of holes, rodents, and occasional snakes. It was dark. Every fifty yards a small bulb high above the road, made a sad attempt to illuminate the night. Its glow was so weak that Gunboat cast no shadow as he passed under.

It was cool, and Gunboat smelled the night: jasmine and the sweeter odour of Queen-of-the-night. He could also detect smoke from wood fires, faint yet pungent. He liked India at night: it became calm, simple. The complexity of the people and the country were stilled. He understood little. At first he had made an effort, but each explanation drew him only deeper into an intellectual maze from which he could not extricate himself. God was simple; yet not. Men were simple; yet not. People here, Gunboat said to himself, thought in paradoxes. There was no yes or a no. Only explanations that explained nothing to a man like him. He looked up. The sky was so clear. Nearly every star could be seen, a steady pinpoint of white light. There was little moon; only a sliver drawn by a god's thumbnail. It was the same sky, the same universe that enclosed the Bronx. There it was the sun and moon and stars; here it was cosmic theology.

He thought of the day: the old man with that ash. Johnny accepted that materialization absolutely. It was as natural to him as his own breath that a man could produce vidbudhi. 'Vidbudhi,' Gunboat said aloud, testing his pronunciation.

Yet how could he? Gunboat needed an explanation. Something more than just the mere repetition of prayers. If he prayed, could he do the same trick? Jesus, he thought, when I get back to the U. S. of A. I could make a bundle doing something like that. Get a booth at a fair and show them hicks all the ash they'd ever see in their goddamn lives. He stopped, not wanting to be blasphemous.

He'd been here too long for easy blasphemy now; he felt the same sense of unease that Gertrude had shown when he reached out to touch the sadhu's hand.

And the prince? Gunboat felt chilled once more. He had been materialized, like the ash, and Gunboat had no explanation. He didn't want to think about it: the labyrinth threatened. He had deliberately not mentioned the prediction to Johnny. Nor did he want to relate the materialization of the prince to Gertrude, for a while anyway, until he'd made up his mind. Despite the holy man's prediction, he still felt he had enough free will to refuse the prince.

The road curved around St Joseph's School, then straightened. Ahead was St Mark's Road. It was brighter. Across the road was the Bowring Club. It was set back in a deep garden and was full of lights and the faint strains of music. Outside the railings were parked countless rickshaws and old hansom carriages. The rickshaw-wallahs slept on the road, by the side of the vehicles; the horses dozed between their shafts. Both men and beasts were emaciated. The men looked as if they'd been melted down to dark skin stretched over the bone frame: ribs were to be counted and the muscles were mere hardened flesh. Gunboat had seen them pull fat ladies up and down the hills and had wondered from where they drew the strength. Like the beasts, they now slept, huddled in foetal positions against the chill, between the shafts of their vehicles. The horses were no better. Their hipbones jutted sharply and from there the skin dipped to form a deep hollow by the side of the rib cage. They slept fitfully, jangling bits and stamping hooves. Their drivers slept on the passenger seat.

Gunboat looked away quickly, hurrying towards the lights and the music. Too late. On the gravel pathway he felt the despair of having brushed too close to such poverty. He had learned early after his arrival not to look directly on it, otherwise it touched one with terror. The terror was one of luck, of destiny, of the flip of the coin, that one was not part of that condemned and luckless tribe that slept on the pavements and scavenged the garbage heaps. For Gunboat the pavements were a tiny room away, and the good chance of friends and his own wits.

The gravel road led straight to the steps of the club. On either side were the lawns and flower beds; to the rear he could see a couple of tennis courts and the children's playground.

The club was a one-storey building. The central hall was used as a ballroom in the evenings, and during the day as a members' lounge. On either side, in the wings, were a billiards room to the right, and to the left a card room. All the doors were open, and the lights threw long white patches onto the lawns. Gunboat could hear the voices more distinctly, and the music was louder and off-key.

The Bowring wasn't *the* club in Bangalore. Eight years ago its patrons had been the enlisted men in the British army, box-wallahs—Englishmen working for companies—a few of the richer Anglo-Indians, and those anglicized Indians who were permitted to pass by the committees. The enlisted men were no longer around, and the club had opened its membership to more of the Anglo-Indians and richer Indians.

The club in Bangalore was the Bangalore United Services—the BUS—club. It was a mile up Residency Road. It was vast and elegant. Gunboat had visited it only once. There was a separate ballroom, a high-ceilinged dining room, a members' lounge with comfortable leather armchairs, half a dozen bars, a swimming pool, a squash court, and a few tennis courts. At the rear of the main building were furnished rooms for out-of-station members.

The BUS members had been the officers of the regiments and the civil servants. And an occasional Indian who had attended Oxford and received his blue in cricket. It had no box-wallahs. Since Independence, the BUS had had to open its doors to the box-wallahs who had stayed on in India, German technicians working on collaboration projects, and, of course, many more wealthy Indians—even those without a blue from Oxford. The tone, Gunboat heard, had certainly fallen although an old English brigadier who still remained as the secretary tried his best to retain the standards.

Gunboat stood at the edge of the dance floor. The Goanese band at the far end—a sax, drums, bass, and guitar—was playing a Presley tune with a curious waltz rhythm, and the dancers were jiving. Some were good. The girls in their stiff petticoats and brightly coloured dresses whirled and jumped and twisted; the men wore suits and narrow trousers. Gertrude was dancing with a young man with brilliantined hair and a tight-fitting cotton suit. When she saw Gunboat, she immediately broke off the dance and threaded her way towards him. She looked enormously pretty: flushed, happy, swaying to the music.

'Come and dance.' She grabbed his hand after they kissed. She was surprisingly bold, and Gunboat presumed her parents were not in the room.

'I need a drink first,' Gunboat said. He'd not yet recovered from that moment of vulnerability near the gate.

He couldn't talk to her or anyone else about it. He knew none of them saw the poor anymore. He understood that need for self-preservation.

'I'll have a beer too,' Gertrude said, and when she noticed him raise an eyebrow in surprise, added: 'I had one earlier on with Malcolm. You know him.'

'The guy you were dancing with.'

'Yes. He's Patty's cousin. He says he will be going home in a few months,' she sighed. 'Lucky guy.'

'Is that why you had the drink?'

'It was a celebration.'

They skirted the dance floor. The bar was at the rear in a small comfortable room. It was crowded. The men sat on stools, the ladies sat at the tables. Some of the men appeared drunk and occasionally slipped off their stools. It was noisy and boisterous. As Gertrude was the member, she ordered him a whiskey and soda, and a beer for herself. The waiter brought it across to their table. 'You comin' back with me?' Gunboat asked and studied Gertrude over the rim of his glass.

She shrugged, as she always did. It was a ritual for her; the game of distance. He wished she would be more honest. She enjoyed herself in his bed, but each time it was a new seduction and he wasn't up to it. It drained him.

'I'll think about it,' Gertrude said. 'It depends on whether Daddy and Mummy want me to go home with them.'

'They know their own way home. And Jill can go with them if they need the company.' Jill was her younger sister. 'Come on.' He reached and squeezed her hand. He was horny.

'You do love me?' This was ritual.

'Sure I do,' Gunboat answered, and added: 'You told the sadhu you loved me too.'

'Yes,' but she appeared distracted, as if her mind, even her heart, was listening to another, more subtle voice. He strained forward, as if wanting to hear that. Only the drunken voices from the bar and that band playing another jive number, this time to a foxtrot rhythm, could be heard. She moved her hand to pick up the glass of beer, and Gunboat caught her eye watching someone else. He glanced up and saw Malcolm coming towards the table.

'Hi, Gunboat,' he said, and sat.

Gunboat nodded. Malcolm was a sallow, thin young man, only a couple of years younger than Gertrude. His hair was long and shiny, and he exuded the appearance of being threadbare. His fingers were yellow from nicotine. He was handsome in a pretty-boy way.

'It's hot in there,' Malcolm said when Gunboat didn't say anything. He pulled out a white handkerchief and dabbed at his face. Gunboat smelled the cologne through the smoke and liquor. 'You don't like dancing much, do you?'

'Don't have the rhythm,' Gunboat said and chuckled at his own private joke. The other two glanced at each other, unsure, and then smiled as if wanting to please him. He knew they didn't understand.

He wished Malcolm would leave so he could continue the pursuit. It made him restless, waiting for Gertrude to decide. Mona had never played games. Bed to her was a place of abandon, not manoeuvre.

Their table slowly began to fill. Chairs were drawn up, drinks bought, jokes exchanged, backs slapped. He only half listened to the talk: it was gossip, complaints, nostalgia for the immediate past when their rulers were the English. They were not fond of Nehru, not fond of Dr Rajendra Prasad, not fond of any of their new officials and superiors. Gunboat could almost taste the bitterness of their abandonment and betrayal. Yet it was not focused on the English who had left, but on the Indians whose country they had suddenly begun to live in.

The subject bored Gunboat. Each Saturday it was the same. They found little new to discuss; not even any good jokes he could laugh at. He wished now he hadn't come but had remained with Johnny in the bar.

By twelve-thirty the dance began to break up. One by one the people drifted away, some just barely able to keep their balance. Gunboat had drunk all evening, but he felt little of the effects.

Patrick Nailer came in search of Gertrude. He was a tall, handsome man with greying hair and a strong straight mouth. He always looked awkward in a suit.

He had hands as big and strong as Gunboat's. 'We're going home, Gerty,' Nailer said. 'I guess Gunboat will walk you back?'

'Yes,' Gertrude said.

She smiled sweetly at Gunboat, knowing how he would now begin to relax and not act so morose. She disliked being taken for granted each Saturday night and the occasional weeknight. He would not understand how difficult it was for her. She had been raised to remain the virgin, or else behave as one to be more accurate, until her wedding night.

'You win anything tonight?' Gunboat asked.

'A few chips,' Nailer said and pulled out a small wad of one-rupee notes. He counted. 'Fifteen. Not bad.' He laughed at the simple pleasure. 'That'll keep me in cigarettes for a week. Until next time anyway.' He stretched and yawned.

'I've got to get my sleep. Midday shift.'

'Sure don't want you to pull the wrong levers tomorrow,' Gunboat said.

'God no, man. Otherwise there'll be a God Almighty crash.'

He shook Gunboat's hand and kissed his daughter on the forehead. Waiting at the door was his wife Sheila. She was a plump, dark woman wearing a green silk dress. She waved good night to him, and Gunboat was glad she'd remained at that distance. Once she began talking, there was no stopping her. He could understand why Mr Nailer kept so silent. He'd probably lost the use of his tongue.

It was cool outside. Gertrude shivered and drew the shawl around her shoulders. They could hear the crunch of gravel. The music had long since stopped and the bearers were clearing up the glasses and bottles.

'I can't stay long,' Gertrude began.

'A while then,' Gunboat said quickly and took her hand.

It seemed to satisfy her for the moment. He knew she would begin again, possibly even change her mind. They reached the gate. Only one or two rickshaws were left, and none of the carriages. The men scrambled to their feet. Both were old, weary. The stubble on their chins was white; their faces were gouged with malnutrition and lost hopes. Gunboat shook his head to their entreaties.

'Vanda, vanda,' Gertrude said abruptly.

The men stopped at her implacable harshness and sank back to the ground to resume their sleep. They appeared so defeated that Gunboat handed them half a rupee each and they gratefully accepted it.

'You shouldn't have done that,' Gertrude said crossly. 'Even if you ride the rickshaws it only costs four annas. Now they'll start getting ideas.'

'Best of luck to them,' Gunboat said. 'I just felt they needed it.'

'Now each time they see you they'll ask for money. You've got to stop doing that, Gunboat.'

'I'll try,' he said meekly, not wanting the argument at this time of the night.

She tried to free her hand, but he only tightened his grip. They walked in silence to the corner and turned off Residency Road on to McGrath. It was dark. He felt Gertrude relax and move closer to him, so that he could release her hand and place his arm around her waist. He liked her smell. Not the perfume she wore, but the odour of her skin. It was different with every woman. Mona had been faintly pungent and had easily aroused him. One woman he remembered had been clinical: of hospitals and surgeons' rooms, and that had been very unsatisfactory. Gertrude smelled as if her skin had been brushed with a small flower: elusive, clean, sweet.

'What will you do when you get back to America?' Gertrude asked.

He knew what she meant. What would she be doing? Working? A housewife? She wanted him to tell of her future.

'I'll go back into the fight game,' Gunboat said, and felt her sway away. 'Not as a boxer. There are other things to do in it. Trainer, second, road manager. Yeah. I'll look up Grosse…if the son of a bitch is still alive…and see what he can get me. Help out with one of his fighters.'

'Does it pay well?'

'Not bad.'

'How much?'

'Fifty-sixty bucks a week. It ain't much but enough to live on well.'

'That's…,' she calculated into rupees, 'a lot. Where?'

'The Bronx,' Gunboat replied promptly. 'Once I get back, I sure ain't goin' anywhere else. Maybe an apartment on Bruckner Boulevard. They got some great places there, and it's fifteen minutes from midtown Manhattan.'

'Manhattan.' Gertrude savoured the word. She wasn't sure she liked it. 'Why can't you live in London? You could do the same things there.'

'It isn't home. For me.'

Gunboat sensed a movement to his left. Gertrude started and yelped. In the gloom of the street light, they saw a mongoose scurry across the road. They laughed and relaxed. Gertrude allowed Gunboat to kiss her on the mouth before they continued walking. That taste was also inside her mouth, and it lingered in his for a while.

SIX

They passed the Imperial cinema. The late show had long been over, and it was dark and quiet. William Holden, his face slightly askew, stared down at them.

'I like him,' Gertrude said. 'But I didn't like this picture much. Next week there's a Robert Taylor picture I want to see so much. I heard it was terrific.'

She prattled on about her movie stars and their pictures. Gunboat was comforted slightly by that. It would be the same at home. Taking out a date and talking about the stars. Eating popcorn, and then after, maybe having a soda or a dinner somewhere.

The compound was very dark, and they both cautiously picked their way down the drive. It was pitted and uneven, and it would be easy to twist an ankle. She held tightly to his hand as he guided her past the jackfruit tree. Her palm was damp.

'Don't put on the light,' she whispered as he opened the door.

Only once had she allowed him to keep the light on. They kissed passionately. She was frail, almost a wisp, in his arms: tall as he, liquid flesh that fitted so well to his form. He felt her nails gently scratching his back. They would eventually become harder, hurting. He unbuttoned her blouse, and she stepped away. She was still unused to having him undress her. She searched in the dark for the chair and he heard her clothes: the soft brush of cotton, and the harsher sound of the starched petticoat. As his eye grew used to the darkness he saw her more clearly: a slight graceful shape that seemed an image floating across his retina. The whiteness of her brassiere and panties lingered long after she'd slipped them off and brushed past him to the bed. She dropped the mosquito net, and was lost behind the opaqueness.

He undressed and sensed her watching. His whiteness glowed in the night, and for a moment he felt vulnerable. He dipped under the net and lay beside her. He wished he could see her: the movement of her hands down his body, the shyness of her fingers on his cock. Her reticence wouldn't last long. Some women believed the dark hid the contortions of their faces and bodies. In the light they would remain still, passionless, as if to be seen in enjoyment was a mortal sin. The one time he had made love to Gertrude in candlelight, she had lain with her face averted and her eyes closed, so that by not seeing him she did not see herself.

Gunboat kissed her small breasts. They were so perfectly round, as if a child had spent hours patting a perfect mound of smooth golden sand. Her nipples were surprisingly large for such small breasts and he enjoyed kissing and sucking on them. He moved his hand down her belly, brushed the sparse hairs, and slipped his fingers inside. She immediately moaned and pressed against him, wanting him deeper.

'Have you got a rubber?' she whispered after a moment.

Gunboat reached down and under the bed. He found the package and slipped a condom on.

'Sit on it,' Gunboat commanded.

She scrambled up and did as he ordered. In bed she was so compliant, willing, at times. It was getting her there that took up his patience. She sat, rocking above him, head back, digging in her nails. He caressed her body; it felt like silk, warm, so smooth, as if the tips of his fingers were sliding on air. They both came at the same time, and she collapsed on top of him, nestling her head in the hollow of his shoulder. He held her, whispering and crooning, and she appeared so still, as if she were asleep. Finally, she moved and rolled to lie beside him.

'I could do this all night long.' She kissed his ear.

'Let's?'

Silence. He had expected that. She would doze awhile, then suddenly become alert, as if a signal had been received that the exterior world was silent and still. She would jump up, dress, and wait impatiently while he protested but eventually did the same and walked her home. No one would see her return.

Gunboat lit a cigarette. In the glow he caught a glimpse of his woman's serene profile. In repose she strangely reminded him of those carved statues he saw in temples. He had mentioned that once and she'd vehemently denied any resemblance. She thought she was closer to Ava Gardner than to a native carving. It was fairly true. Awake, Gertrude changed. A transfiguration, as if her English thoughts and her longings changed the surface planes of her face and reclaimed her from India.

Loneliness. It would descend, suddenly, oppressive as a summer's night, bringing out the sweat. It became more frequent, and remained longer as if wanting his heart. It bewildered him at first. He'd not experienced much in his life in America. It had grown only over the last couple of years, and only time could dislodge the stone laid in his chest. He resolved to go to a movie the next day, an American movie, possibly *High Noon* again. He could identify with Gary Cooper; here there was nothing he could even remotely recognize as a part of him. Sounds, odours, sights were all of such strangeness as to be continually unrecognizable.

Like this. Gertrude came awake, sat up abruptly, lifted the net, and stepped out and away from him. What woke her? He had made no sound, no movement. Another woman would have slept well into the dawn. He glanced to the window. The light was faint, enough to distinguish the shape of the jackfruit tree. How could that have awakened her?

'Come on, Gunboat,' she whispered. He only sensed her beyond the blur of the mosquito net. She was about ready. It took women long to unclothe, quick to clothe when they needed.

He got out and dressed. He embraced her, and felt her impatience as she buttoned her blouse and stepped into her shoes.

It was damp outside. He felt the early dew on the leaves of the jackfruit tree brush his forearm and leave the cold moisture. He took Gertrude's hand. In the early dawn they could see the unevenness in the lane.

'You gonna make the races today?'

'No. We're having some friends over to lunch.'

'And I'm not invited.'

'Of course you are.' She tugged his hand playfully. He sensed her defence. 'But you go to the races every Sunday with Johnny.'

'Maybe one Sunday I won't.'

'Are you?'

He considered. Her father would be at work. Only the women would be entertaining.

'Yes. Who's coming?'

'Friends.'

He didn't press her to elaborate. He knew she was hiding something and felt too tired to explore. He would learn of her guests eventually, either from her or from gossip.

He felt an even greater loss. In the cool calm dawn he had wanted to confide in her about the prince, share her opinion: to escape the trap of destiny, or to ride with it? But he couldn't and they continued in silence.

It was a twenty-minute walk to her home. No one else was to be seen out at this hour. Awake. They passed sleeping people, a family—father, wife, four children—huddled together under a tree. Their covering a piece of worn blanket. The air was cold enough to see their soft breaths. A pie-dog opened its eyes at the sound of their steps, growled, and watched them pass warily.

'Good night,' Gertrude whispered at her front gate.

They kissed. He watched her cautiously open the iron gate, slowly replace the latch. She waved and crept back to the house.

Gunboat hurried back to his own bed. He would get a few hours' sleep before the heat woke him.

◆

He was awakened earlier. Johnny stood outside the window, pushing a stick at the netting.

'Jesus, what time is it?'

'Nine. Let me in.'

'Go away.' He turned over. The stick was persistent. It rattled against the bars.

'It's not my fault if you spend half the night fucking,' Johnny said. 'Lucky bastard. I got to pay for mine, and I never have enough for the whole night.'

'That's because you're such a goddamn adolescent.'

'I know. All Indian men are. We never get any sex unless we get married. That's why we get married eventually. To any bloody woman. Just to get laid. Listen, I got this joke—'

'I'll let you in if you don't tell me a joke.'

'I don't know whether it's worth that much.' He considered gravely, looking owlish. 'Okay.'

Gunboat opened the door and returned to the bed. Johnny had brought coffee and a masala dosai wrapped in a plantain leaf. He found a plate and handed it to Gunboat, and watched him eat the spicy potato wrapped in a rice pancake with the watchfulness of a mother.

'Good?'

'Great,' Gunboat said. He wished he could eat a large plate of eggs, bacon, home fries, and toast and jelly. He was handed the coffee and then a cigarette. He knew why Johnny was so considerate.

'Is Jockey Rosen awake?'

'I saw him sitting on the porch. He looked hung-over.'

'He always does at this time of the morning. The same way I do. Except he's lucky. He doesn't have some bastard wake him up at the crack of dawn.'

'Crack.' Johnny giggled. It was a delightful obscenity to him.

'A cunt of dawn. That's what I dream of. What's she like?'

'None of your business.'

'How do you expect me to learn anything if you don't teach me? The prostitutes just let you put it in, and out.'

'Get married then, for Christ's sake.' Gunboat rolled out of the bed and wrapped a white dhoti around his waist. 'At least that'll keep you from bugging me.'

'Who'll have me?' Johnny looked mournful, and down. 'I'm a B.Sc. third class, and I can't get a job.'

'You have one.'

'My family don't think that's a job. A Brahmin boy managing a billiards saloon. Gunboat, by a job they mean working for Parry's, or ICI, or in government service. Safe jobs. With security, pension, and retirement at fifty-five. Until I get one of those, they refuse to look for a girl for me.'

'Go look yourself.'

Johnny glanced up, surprised. He only shook his head, not trying to explain. He appeared in distress.

'Is that what you want?'

'To please my family? Yes.' He stood up and shouted, 'Anything to stop them driving me round the fucking bend, man.' He chuckled at his fair imitation of Gunboat and then added, 'I wouldn't survive if I left my family.'

'Why?'

'Because I'm weak. I was raised to be dependent on my family system. On my cousins and uncles and aunts and grandmother. Jesus, we all live in the same house. I couldn't live too far away from them.'

'Least you're honest.'

Johnny laughed. 'In India honesty is only a temporary insanity. It passes quickly. We don't have the moral courage to be honest.' He brooded. 'Or noble. I envy you. Because you do.'

'Why not?' Gunboat asked. He gathered up his towel, his shaving mug and brush and cake of soap. He searched in the dresser and found a clean shirt and a pair of cotton trousers. Johnny followed him around the small room, as if sitting in the centre was too uncomfortable.

'Because as a people we have an allegiance—social and moral—only to God. Our obligations are to the heavens, not to our fellowman.'

'That's not a bad thing.'

'Not in the U. S. of A. A Christian god can tell the difference between right and wrong. Ours can't. Everything—murder, theft, corruption—is permissible if it is to be your karma.' He sat and lit one of Gunboat's cigarettes.

'You don't like your religion then?'

'No. Just because I question it doesn't mean I despise it.' He blew smoke and handed the cigarette to Gunboat. 'Do you pray in the morning?'

'No. I wasn't brought up religious,' Gunboat said.

'I pray every morning.' He closed his eyes: 'Tat Savitur vareniam bhargo devasya dhimahi dhiuo yo nah pracodayat.' The chant ended. Johnny opened his eyes. 'Let our meditation be on the glorious light of Savitri. May this light illumine our minds! What the hell does that mean? Yours goes "Our Father which art in heaven."... Precise, to the point.'

'Simple.'

'Yes. We are too complex for our own good.' He saw the bottle in the open drawer and poured himself a shot of whiskey.

'This early?'

'Discussing God this early always makes me thirsty.' He looked at his watch. 'I got to place the bets.'

Gunboat went out to the rear of the house. The bathroom was small and gloomy. There were a big brass container of cold water and a small brass bucket of steaming water. The toilet was primitive, an aluminum container set in a wooden seat.

Life is like closing your fist on a handful of molasses. It's all there when you begin, and then it's gone, seeped through your fingers.

Fighting makes you honest. In the ring you gotta be honest: to yourself, to your body, to your opponent. You can't lie or juggle with thoughts when you're in there. Straight. Hit, move out, block, jab. That's all I am. I was never a dirty fighter, never.

Johnny was studying his racing form when Gunboat returned. His concentration was total until Gunboat spoke.

'You know damn well you can't trust that sheet.'

'I know that but one day they might let the horses run to form, and I'll clean up a fortune.' He inked a horse's name and folded the book carefully and stuck it in his back pocket. 'I'll wait here.'

SEVEN

Gunboat strolled out into the bright sunlight. The Rosen bungalow had a tiny, lovingly cultivated garden in front of it. The garden was all of two strides wide. There were, as always on a Sunday, two or three punters standing in the garden. They waited patiently in the increasing heat as supplicants would for the miracle to be handed down from the mountaintop. Gunboat opened the little gate and knocked on the door.

Mrs Rosen let him in. She was a plump and pretty woman in her thirties. Her skin was as white as the most expensive porcelain, and in spite of her years in the country there wasn't the faintest suspicion of a tan.

'Hi, Anne.' The door closed and they kissed each other's cheeks lightly.

'Where's the oracle?'

'Trying to shake a hangover. Coffee?'

She went in to fetch one. The hall was the sitting room. The walls were covered with racing photographs. Jockey Rosen had ridden quite a few winners, both in India and Australia; and since then, trained a few too. A small glass cupboard against the wall held the silver cups, some flecked green with age, and rosettes. On a table beside it were family photographs. They had only one child, a son, Jackie. There was a rattan couch against another wall and a couple of rattan chairs.

Anne returned with the coffee at the same time as Jockey Rosen padded out wearing a terry cloth dressing gown. Jockey reached to Anne's shoulder, and mid-chest to Gunboat. His hair was sparse, and on his chest it had begun to grey. He had sharp, well-defined features:

a straight nose like a cutting edge, prominent cheekbones, and bushy eyebrows. His eyes should have been grey, but the red was more dominant.

He growled and took the coffee.

'That's Gunboat's.'

'Get him another.' He drank, sighed, and lit a cigarette.

Gunboat always thought in surprise of their similarities. They were both ex-athletes, professionals in their fields, living in an alien country. Yet Rosen was so small, like a toy, except for his abrasive tongue. They also remained outside the pale of respectable society in the town.

They sat in silence awhile. Anne brought out another coffee and he sipped his and waited. He glanced out through the trellis: two more punters had collected outside. They stood apart, though obviously knowing each other. If they were to be chosen to be given the winners they didn't want to spoil their chances with Jockey Rosen by associating with the wrong person. He chose randomly and took a percentage of the winnings. Except from Gunboat. 'Which girl was that?' Jockey asked, staring out at the punters. He spoke with a clipped Australian accent.

'The same one.'

'I saw you both leaving. I think I did, can't see too well when I'm smashed.' He reached into the pocket of the gown and pulled out black, horn-rimmed glasses. They almost hid his face. 'You're her ticket out.'

'Out where? I'm not goin' nowhere.'

'One day you will. And she'll be wanting to leave too.'

'I know. And you?'

'Pretty soon. Don't mistake me. I love this country. I've been coming here since before the war, and have lived here since '50. But the kid's grown now, and he needs to get to know his own country and people. Also Anne wants him to do his college there.' He put the cup down abruptly.

'Jesus, I need a drink. Anne! Anne!'

'What?' She stood in the doorway.

'I need a drink. The hair of the dog or whatever.' She went back in and returned with two fingers of neat scotch.

'Gunboat?' she asked.

'Yeah. It seems to be a growing habit round here.'

It burned, and he was glad for the breakfast. Jockey Rosen finished his with one throw, shook his head like a terrier, and settled back in the chair.

'Got paper?'

'No.'

He was given a pad and a pencil. 'In the first—Dark Sun. The second—King Vijay. And in the fifth Princess Padmini. That's it.'

'The Gold Cup?'

Rosen shook his head. 'That bastard N. A. N. has three of his horses in it, and you never know which one he's going to let win. I wouldn't bet a handful of shit in that race.'

N. A. N. was a wealthy businessman. He devoted all his time and money to his huge string of racehorses, and through this had come to control the racing on the major courses in the south—Bangalore, Madras, and Ooty. Gunboat knew Jockey Rosen hated N. A. N. He had ridden for N. A. N. before the war, but they had fallen out with each other and remained enemies since.

'It's the same in the fight game. Some guy owns a stable of fighters, and he tells you which one to take a dive to. Then he cleans up a fortune from the bookies.'

'You ever do that?' The eyes had cleared. The grey was dark, steady.

'No. I never did. That's why I didn't amount to much.'

'You should've. I pulled a few horses in my lifetime.'

'Get much out of it?'

'A little.'

'It's never worth it. Not for me. I wanted to win or lose on my account. Not because some guy tells me to do it. Then you own nothing of yourself. In racing I guess it don't matter much. There are a half dozen of you and a tug on a rein doesn't get seen. In fighting, you're alone, under the lights, and when you dive you take your pride, your honour down onto the canvas with you. And your courage. Then there's no getting up, ever.'

'That's a hard way to earn a living. If I was a boxer, I'd take that dive. Anything from getting hurt.'

'On the canvas you get hurt worse. Hurt inside, where no one ever sees it.' Gunboat studied Jockey Rosen. He saw a strong, wiry man. Like him, going to seed. The booze marked his cheeks: The blood vessels were rising, red, broken, to the surface.

Jockey Rosen nodded, as if in agreement. It was a token gesture. He saw a big man, the whiskey tumbler hidden in those bony fists, sitting calmly, squinting out at the sunlight. He liked Gunboat, not because he was a fellow white man. That would have been a sorry reason. In India there were enough Limeys still left that he detested, and scrupulously avoided. No. He liked Gunboat because he was an innocent. Gunboat was certainly not a stupid man. He was intelligent though, like himself, not college educated. Innocence was rare; here, non-existent. Possible in the smallest child, before it could speak, think, learn the moral ambiguities of its elders. Gunboat would never learn deception and would forever retain that innocence. He felt sorry for him too. The tiny room in that old house, the dependence on the favours of others, the long, long loneliness of an exile that could possibly never end. If he ever made that much money, Jockey Rosen swore he would buy Gunboat the passage to New York City.

'Will I be seeing you there?'

'Yeah. I don't like racing too much, but what else to do on a Sunday afternoon.' He grinned, likeably. 'And I can look at all the pretty girls I want. Thanks for the tips.'

They shook hands, like strangers. Gunboat passed the punters. Two wore cheap cotton jackets, shapeless, awkward on their bodies. He sensed it was a mark of sophistication. The others were dressed in open-neck shirts, slacks, and chappals. Gunboat heard Jockey Rosen call and turned to see one of the men, the one in a green coat, hurry in. The others stepped back, as if to turn away. When Gunboat looked back again, they had not moved. Even though they knew only one was ever called.

◆

Johnny studied the three names and compared them against the form book. He looked up in delight.

'Long odds. We'll clean up a small fortune.'

'If they win.'

'He's only let us down a couple of times.'

'All right.' Gunboat considered as Johnny stood up, eager to leave now. He held out his hand. Gunboat took a hundred from the envelope, hesitated, and handed it over. The prince was buying him bit by bit. Smart little bastard. He already knew the value of men.

'I'll pick you up from the saloon in an hour's time.'

Gunboat lay back on the bed, wanting to doze. He was not given long. He heard the timid knock, and opened the door. Sita, the cleaning girl, stood outside. Her head was bowed, her broom of reeds in one hand and a Dalda tin of disinfectant water in the other. He stepped aside and she entered, eyes averted.

She was a small, beautiful woman in her early twenties. She was quite dark, almost black, but the contours of her face could have mesmerized an Italian Renaissance painter. Her face was round, her eyes large and shy, and her mouth very red from betel nut. She never spoke to him. He had tried, but she seemed shy, and surprised he should make the effort. He didn't know Kannada; she had no English. That, Gunboat admitted, could be the problem.

Sita worked quickly. Back bent she swept efficiently. Poured water, and swept that out into the yard. She took his laundry in a neat bundle and was gone in ten minutes.

Once Johnny had bumped into her in the doorway. Gunboat had

not seen such panic in either. She fled. Johnny had stood, shaken, and then abruptly turned and left. When he returned an hour later, Gunboat noticed he'd changed, and bathed, and perfumed himself.

'Why?'

'She's a *panchama.*'

Gunboat had remained puzzled.

'A sweeper. I am a Brahmin. We cannot touch.'

'I thought you were a modern guy.'

Johnny had laughed self-consciously. He was embarrassed and ashamed, near to tears, as if Gunboat had touched a deep and suppurating wound that he knew would never heal.

Gunboat waited for the stone floor to dry and then went out. He would shoot a rack or two waiting for Johnny. It was preferable to the silence of his room.

The punters had left, and Jockey Rosen's house was silent. It would stir by one, in time to catch a taxi to the racecourse.

The door to the convent was open. It was Sunday, and the worshippers were streaming out from St Patrick's Cathedral. It stood well back in the huge compound; the tip of its spire could be seen just above the tops of the rain trees. Gunboat had entered once. Not to worship, but to be immersed in the familiar. He wanted to imagine he was in St Patrick's on Fifth Avenue, a cathedral he'd never entered.

The vast interior had been cool and gloomy. The sunlight muted by the stained glass fell like rich satin on the wooden benches and the coir-carpeted floor. It had smelled of incense, not lightly, heavy and perfumed as in a temple. Gunboat had sat and stared at the altar and the statues in their many niches around him. It seemed as it should be, and yet there had been a subtle transformation that was difficult for him to pinpoint. It was, he thought, not austere as he'd imagined, but flamboyant and too colourful, as if the worshippers had somehow perceived St Patrick as the avatar of a Rama or a Krishna.

Gunboat turned away and joined the worshippers moving up Brigade Road. The women wore their fine dresses and black veiling on their heads; the men wore suits. There were a few Indians too, the women in saris. Their faces were all uniformly self-righteous. Gunboat crossed the road to separate himself from them and to check the times of *High Noon*. He could make the late evening show if his mood persisted.

◆

The Bangalore Race Club, on Racecourse Road, was a mile past Cubbon Park and north of South Parade. It was a small course, elegant, neat. The track was velvet green, a violent contrast to the dull brown earth in the centre. The concrete stand was an open jaw: private boxes above, the folding seats sloping below. At the rear, shading the clubhouse and bar and the winner's circle, were two widespread gold mohur trees.

There were many familiar faces, hands to be shaken, and quick jokes exchanged. Only here and there the bright glimpse of saris. The rich carried binoculars, wore heavy gold rings, and jackets and ties. The poor clutched racing forms and wore their dreams on their faces.

Gunboat strolled with Johnny and Abdul. Of the three, Abdul was the most elegant in a silk shirt, white silk trousers, and snakeskin loafers. He was Gunboat's height, but slimmer and startlingly handsome. He looked like a hawk. He was Muslim, and shaded quite different from Johnny. Gunboat couldn't quite call him arrogant—perhaps it was self-assurance. It could be his riches. Apart from owning Gunboat Jack's, he also ran a few racehorses, a coffee estate, and a couple of commercial buildings on Commercial Street, the Bangalore shopping centre.

They had all bet on Jockey Rosen's tips. Jockey Rosen could be seen only in glimpses, as he moved importantly in the trainer's enclosure, conferred with owners, and advised his jockeys. Abdul had placed the most money.

The horses gleamed richly in the sunlight: mahogany, rippling black, an occasional grey. They were small, crossbred between Indian and Arab, and capable only of short distances. The track ran anticlockwise.

The first race began on time. Abdul had money on that and lost it. In between races they gathered in the bar, discussed form, gossiped. In the second race Dark Sun won, and Gunboat was pleased. There were no winnings to collect as they had bet off the track. Jockey Rosen was good as his word. Princess Padmini won her race, and King Vijay his. Gunboat and Johnny scribbled out their winnings. Five hundred rupees, and they were pleased. Money could be made if the source was right, and the golden chain of the prince's money had been broken. Gunboat felt the confidence of control.

Gunboat would have left after his horse had won, but Johnny wanted him to remain for the Gold Cup. The prize money was fifty thousand rupees; a rich but uncertain race. N. A. N., who bustled around in a white raw silk suit, a silk shirt and necktie, and very dark glasses, had three of his horses running in it. There were eight in all, and the distance was three quarters of a mile. Only a fool would bet on a horse in this one, as N. A. N. invariably played a shell game with his horses. He was a plump, short man with a round face and receding hair, smelling strongly of lavender water. A year previously, when he'd had his jockey pull the favourite, the crowd from the stands had tried to lynch him. Fortunately, the police rescued him in time, but that had failed to teach him a lesson.

Gunboat waited impatiently for the race to begin. If he could leave early, he could persuade Gertrude to join him for dinner, a drink, and possibly half a night with him.

The race began at four-thirty. There were two favourites, Golden Boy and Shakuntala, and both belonged to N. A. N. 'I'd bet on his other one, Grand Moghul,' Johnny said. They sat in Abdul's box and looked around the racetrack. There were no high buildings in view; only houses and gold mohur trees and gardens.

'Yeah? What happens if he lets one of his favourites win?'

'He won't do that. The odds on Grand Moghul are seven to two. I've bet all our winnings on him.'

'Every rupee we just made?'

'Yes. Don't worry. I know we'll win.'

'Oh Jesus.' Gunboat felt his stomach heave.

He glanced at Abdul who only shrugged and leaned towards the English girl sitting by him. Her name was Rosemary, and she had bright carrot-coloured hair, and a remoteness that allowed only Abdul to approach her. She acutely sensed his wealth and the poverty of his companions.

Abdul said, 'Johnny's greedy. He wants to win everything.' The race began. Feverishly, Johnny held his binoculars to his eyes. Gunboat shut his eyes. Grand Moghul led for the first three furlongs, and then, inexplicably, began to lose ground. By the fourth furlong he was lying third, with Shakuntala first and an unknown, Mountbatten, second. By the two-furlong post Mountbatten had begun his front run. Johnny lowered his binoculars; his face was comical in disbelief. He scrambled through his form book. 'The bastard. Mountbatten's giving eleven to two against.' He looked towards the public enclosure. The crowd was silent; none cheered as the horse passed the finishing line two lengths ahead.

'I hope they lynch him,' Johnny said bitterly. 'I'm sorry.'

'So am I.' Johnny appeared near to tears, and Gunboat sighed. 'So what the hell. You win a few and lose a few.' He knew that when the car arrived he would have to step into it.

As he passed through the ground to the exit, he noticed the crowd. They were bunched, moving towards the winner's enclosure. A few policemen dressed in khaki and an inspector were nervously standing between them and the enclosure. Gunboat suspected that reinforcements were already on the way.

◆

Gertrude, her mother informed him, was just waking from her nap. She would join him soon. Gunboat and her mother sat out in cane chairs in the shade of a mango tree. Balanced on the morah between them was a tray of tea and biscuits. They discussed the day's racing and she clucked, unsympathetically, about his loss. Gunboat sensed she looked on him with mixed feelings. On the one hand, she was proud her daughter's boyfriend, in spite of his age, was a European. He had corrected her—'American'—the first few times, but she appeared to be unable to make this fine distinction. However, she remained uneasy over his lack of riches. Now Gunboat told her about his envelope full of money.

'Gerty…Gerty,' she craned her neck and called. 'Come and hear Gunboat's news.' There was a murmur from a curtained window. 'Gerty…come out.'

In the evening sun Gertrude looked even prettier. She had rested and bathed, and as she leaned to kiss his forehead, he smelled the Pears soap mingled with her perfume and powders. Gunboat told her about the prince, and she clapped her hands. 'That's just what the sadhu said.' She told her mother the prediction. The older woman nearly crossed herself in protection.

'Are you going to be staying in the palace?' Gertrude asked excitedly.

'I don't know.'

'Oh, you must take me with you then. I've never stayed in a palace. I haven't even been inside one.'

'It won't be big,' her mother said. 'They are only rajahs. You should see the maharajah of Mysore's palace in Mysore. It's huge, and it has such a beautiful garden. What a pity he's so fat.'

Gunboat had caught a glimpse of the maharajah. He led the Dussehra festival procession annually, sitting in a gold-and-jewelled howdah on top of an elephant. He was fat.

'How old is the prince?' Gertrude asked offhandedly.

'Only a boy.' And Gunboat smiled at her disappointment. 'How was your lunch?'

Gertrude's mood changed. She became cautious. 'Okay. Just friends. We had a pulao, and I ate too much.' She glanced at her mother. Their eyes held a moment, then both looked away. Gunboat felt the unease, as if he'd trespassed.

'So will you be leaving in four weeks?' Gertrude asked. She leaned towards him as if she were not able to hear.

'Depends,' he said, and wished her mother would leave. But she remained, stubbornly imprinted in the cane chair, studying them both. Her eyes, however, remained mostly on her daughter, as if she were willing her to make their considered reply.

'On what?' Gertrude laughed coquettishly, wanting him to step further.

'On many things.' He had also learned how to be evasive and it saddened him. 'I'll tell you over dinner. We could go to the Blue Fox.'

'Oh, I'd love to, Gunboat.' She looked at her mother. 'But I'm still full from that lunch. And I promised Mummy I'd stay home and help her with her new frock.'

'A drink?'

'Have one here. I'm sure Daddy's got some left.' She shot into the house before he could demur and returned with a whiskey, no ice, and a Spencer's soda.

Gunboat sipped the warm liquid. Without the ice it appeared to have lost all sweetness. It was so bitter. 'I won't be seeing you for a whole week.' Her mother rose at that signal. Gunboat stood and watched her roll wearily into the house.

They sat in fading light. Night came fast and soon the darkness would be on them. The mosquitoes buzzed, nipped, and they slapped their faces and forearms too late.

'I'll miss you.'

'You'll be too busy,' she countered.

Gunboat felt her sliding away. He wasn't sure why or how. A year had passed in their relationship, and if they had not been totally at ease with each other, they had been lovers and companions. Now she had become distant, and it was recent. Over the last few days only, and it puzzled Gunboat. In fact, since that sadhu. He brooded over what he'd told her—about living with a stranger all her life—and thought it applied to her coming with him. Now, he wasn't sure.

'You'll come with me, won't you?' he offered.

'To Tandhapur? I said I'd like to see their palace.'

'I don't mean there. When I get the money, I'm going to buy the tickets.'

'I want to think about it, Gunboat.'

'I thought you were sure.'

'America is so different from home.'

'Which home are you talking about?' he asked wearily, as if listening to a past conversation they'd had.

'England,' she said indignantly. 'It's not England.'

He finished the whiskey. 'Let me know,' and he walked out of the small garden.

PART II

EIGHT

The car came precisely at nine, and the punctuality impressed Gunboat. Nothing ever occurred on time in India. It was a white Rover 3.8, and he guessed a 1948 model. Its bodywork shone in the sun. The large headlights mounted on either side of the bonnet glittered like searchlights. It was certainly a regal machine. It had no ordinary number plate. Instead there was a red plate with silver crest—a tiger's head and a sword. It stood high off the road; the body was square and swept down and back abruptly. The chauffeur was a plump little man, dressed impeccably in a white coat, white trousers, and white hat. He wore chappals on his feet.

'I am Lakshman, sir,' he said when Gunboat opened the door. He took the small suitcase and carried it to the car. He placed it on the seat beside him and opened the rear door for Gunboat.

The interior was spacious, and the seats were real leather. Gunboat sank back and stretched his legs out. There was a window between him and the chauffeur.

The car turned left out of the gate, past the cathedral and up the slope of Brigade Road. The driver enjoyed his horn. He kept his thumb on it, a klaxon sound, and accelerated down the straight stretch of road. Gunboat swayed in his seat. He knew they were heading west. St Andrew's Church had just been passed, and soon they were nearing one of the army barracks. Beyond the barbed-wire fence Gunboat glimpsed neat squares, hockey fields, long, low, well-maintained buildings, ancient cannons placed in front of the unit's flagpole, and clean drives. The army was impressively neat. Soon they were out in the country.

Villagers walked in the centre of the road and jumped aside hurriedly at the sound of the horn. As usual they returned to the centre when the car passed. Gunboat fell asleep.

◆

When the car stopped, Gunboat woke from his doze. They were parked by a Burmah Shell petrol bunk in a village. It was an oasis of modernity encircled by the medieval. A couple of old, vividly painted Bedford trucks were being worked on by a swarm of chokras. An old unshaven man wearing greasy clothes supervised them from the shade of the peepul tree.

He rose, saluted Lakshman, and shrilly ordered two of the chokras to attend to the rajah's car. The boys looked no older than ten. The petrol pump was hand-driven and they laboured with surprising energy, pushing the pump handle from one to the other.

'Would sir like to eat?'

'Just coffee.' Gunboat pulled out a couple of rupees. Lakshman hesitated fractionally and then took them. He ordered one of the chokras to fetch the coffees, and some food for himself. Gunboat watched the boy sprint down the road to the coffee stall. Power, Gunboat considered, could be proportioned out. As the rajah's representative, Lakshman behaved as if he were him.

'How much longer?'

'Three, four hours, sir.' He waited for a further question. None came and he added, 'It will become cooler soon.'

Gunboat watched the shadows of the ancient hills stretch out across the miniature rice fields. In the distance he caught glimpses of small, neat villages and straggling lines of peasants, some balancing the plows on their shoulders, slowly winding their way home. Dung smoke rose straight in the air, hovered, and dispersed.

It did become cooler. Gunboat wound up the window as the car began the climb into the hills. There was little to see in the valleys on either side except thick jungle. The road was deserted.

'You get any animals round here?'

'Tiger, elephants, sambar, jackals. Sir. You like shooting, sir?'

'Never tried it.'

'The rajah does not permit it, too.'

'How much longer?'

'Soon, sir.'

Two curves later Gunboat caught a quick glimpse of the small town. It was little bigger than a village, except the buildings were of brick, whitewashed, and had more than a single road. The town spread out to include a few narrow streets. The palace stood a mile farther along. In the evening sunlight it was washed pink. There were archways, a dome, a minaret on each corner, a delicacy of whitewashed brick set in a vast garden. There were a few smaller buildings within the walls. Then it was lost to sight. 'Am I staying in the palace?'

Lakshman hesitated. 'Yes, sir.'

It took ten minutes to cross from one end of the town to the other. The main street was wide, semi-deserted. It looked like a long marketplace, with the central building, all of two stories and set back, dominating. The signboard read Tandhapur Mining Co. (Pvt.) Ltd. There wasn't even a movie house. He could smell the odours of food and wood smoke and fresh night air rising from the valley.

There were two uniformed guards outside the palace gates. They carried only lathis and immediately saluted the car. The gravel driveway was long, ran beneath the constant canopy of trees, and wound past the stables, servants' quarters, a large octagonal fountain, and a cricket pitch. Beyond it Gunboat saw a tennis court.

The road branched. The car swept to the left and Gunboat craned his head. He saw the palace receding.

'I thought you said I was staying in the palace?'

'This is the palace, sir.'

The car pulled up in front of a smaller building. The stone steps led up to a large veranda, divided by graceful arches. Beyond, French doors led into the main drawing room.

'The guest palace, sir.'

Lakshman opened the door. Two bearers came down the steps. Gunboat looked up. The guest palace, if not compared to the main one, was big. It rose three stories, and trellised balconies ran the breadth and length of the building. Tall, massive pillars supported the roof above the veranda.

One bearer had taken Gunboat's suitcase, the other waited to lead him in. Gunboat followed him. The drawing room was formal. French chairs and sofas, their silk coverings worn and faded, were grouped around a marble-topped table. Above them, an old chandelier dripped fine blue glass. The room smelled of dust and was cold. Standing against the walls were teak cabinets filled with a jumble of things. The floor was half covered by a faded Indian carpet.

The bearers mounted the curving wooden staircase to the left. Gunboat slid his hand along the smooth mahogany. Looking down, he felt the drawing room was never used. It was a stage set.

'Is there anyone else staying here?'

'No, sir.' The bearer without the case answered. The other remained mute. 'I am Mohan.'

The stone floor of the corridor was covered with coir carpet. Even so Gunboat heard his footsteps. The bearers were barefoot. The corridor ran straight for three doorways, then branched left and right. He followed the bearers right and guessed he was heading to the front of the building. A door at the end was open.

The bedroom was large. The bed was a four-poster, with the mosquito netting tucked above. The sheets were folded back and a thin blanket covered the foot. To one side were a couch and two straight-back chairs grouped around a marble-top table. On the table was a cold beer and a bucket of ice and a glass. Beyond the bed was the bathroom. It had a tile floor, a modern toilet, a bulbous hot-water tank, and a shower; French doors led out onto a balcony, and Gunboat saw the palace opposite. It stood a hundred yards away, surrounded by trees. A servant or two moved down its corridors, but otherwise it looked deserted.

◆

He was awakened at six by Mohan.

'Chota hazri, sir,' he said, and placed a silver tray on the marble-top table. On the tray was a pot of tea and a plantain.

It was chilly and the light looked autumnal. Mohan wore an old army pullover and made a lot of noise. Gunboat heard him in the bathroom drawing water, banging on a tin mug, rattling his razor. He sat up, weary.

The evening had been long and silent. After the cold beer, Mohan had served whiskey and sodas, and Gunboat had wandered around the small palace. There were half a dozen reception rooms below, all furnished alike. Stiff chairs, marble tables, teak cabinets. Some of the cabinets contained cheap junk, souvenirs of travels, but here and there, as if the owner were not aware of the value, were carved ivory statues, jade Buddhas, elaborate wooden carvings. The dining room was to the rear. There was a long mahogany table, enough to seat twelve, two paintings of princely men on the walls, and little else. A place had been set at the top of the table.

Gunboat sat down to dinner at nine. Three courses were served: tomato soup, mutton cutlets with potatoes and green beans, and burned custard. At the end, Mohan served brandy.

'When do I see Nicky?'

'The yuvaraj said he will be joining you for breakfast, sir.' He waited. 'Will there be anything else?'

'No.' Gunboat could almost smell the silence of abandonment.

'You speak pretty good English.'

'Thank you, sir.' Mohan considered elaborating. 'I learned it in England when I was with the yuvaraj.'

Gunboat tried to guess his age. It wasn't possible. The man was wiry, his face unseamed. The eyes were watchful.

'You been here long?'

'Since I was born.'

'Do you know why I'm here?'

'No, sir.'

He did, but knew of no reason why Gunboat should know. Gunboat was a 'boxer', whatever that meant. He was awkward in his surroundings and had chosen the wrong knives and spoons to eat with. He was not used to being waited on. His clothes were cheap, and badly made, and few. If Mohan had not visited England with the yuvaraj, he would not have believed there were poor Europeans. The ones he'd seen in India made him believe they were all rich.

'I'm a fighter,' Gunboat said. Mohan stepped forward and filled the empty glass. They both listened to the brandy falling into the crystal glass.

'I've come to teach Nicky how to fight.'

'He knows, sir.'

'Not boxing.'

'What is that, sir?' His curiosity prevailed.

'Fighting with your fists in a ring.'

'Wrestling?'

'No,' and Gunboat tried to explain. He finally added, 'When I teach Nicky, you'll see what I mean.'

The other bearer entered. He cleared the table quietly, leaving the brandy and the glass. Mohan poured another.

'Will I get to meet the rajah?'

'I believe so, sir. He is also a great sportsman. He played cricket for Oxford.' He made it sound like a personal triumph.

'And the rani?' And Gunboat felt Mohan withdraw.

'She is no longer alive, sir,' and the sadness also sounded personal.

'I'm sorry. Was it recent?'

'A year after the yuvaraj's birth.'

'And the rajah didn't marry again?' The brandy made him

loquacious. Mohan was better company than the silence.

Mohan took his time to answer. He corked the bottle first, moved it fractionally out of reach. French brandy was expensive and not to be poured down a boxer's throat.

'Not yet, sir. Will that be all, sir?'

Gunboat nodded, swallowed the remainder of the brandy, and rose. Mohan saw him to the foot of the stairs.

Gunboat winced at the sunlight. His eyes and head ached, but he stepped out onto the terrace. A glass-topped table was set for two. Two cane chairs were placed opposite each other. Gunboat sipped the ice water, poured some more, and emptied the glass.

The terrace stepped down to a small lawn. To one side was the building, on the other sides, mango trees. Beyond was only a dense foliage of trees and undergrowth. A mali was slowly watering the lawn. He held a large metal pot and scooped water out with one hand.

Gunboat sat. As if on that signal, Nicky came into view from the far end of the lawn. He was dressed in riding breeches. Mohan was a step behind, carrying his riding crop and hat.

'And what else did he ask?' Nicky enquired.

'Whether he would meet the rajah, your highness. I said it was possible. And then he wanted to meet the rani.'

'And?'

'I told him she was not alive.' Mohan paused, wanting to gauge the yuvaraj's mood. 'He then asked had the rajah remarried. I said no.' He decided not to correct himself. His answer had been close enough.

'You mentioned nothing about *her?*'

'No, your highness.'

'He will find out for himself. There is little I can do.'

He waved to Gunboat. 'So he drank a lot?'

'Half the whiskey, and three brandies. And the beer.' Mohan gave an accurate count.

'Did he go to bed immediately?'

'No. He sat on his balcony and looked at the sky a long time.

Is he an astrologer?'

Nicky chuckled. 'No. Only a boxer. Do you have the men ready?'

'Yes, your highness.'

They climbed the steps. Gunboat stood to shake hands and was surprised that Nicky wasn't bigger. He gave the impression of height and girth, yet was a slim boy. It was the authority of his position that created that impression.

'I hope you're comfortable?'

'You bet. Quite a place you got here, Nicky.' Gunboat spoke the name deliberately, wanting not to be awed.

'Thank you.'

The bearer served freshly cut papaya slices. Mohan stood a few feet away, watching, as they began breakfast. Three dogs trotted across the lawn. In the lead was an alert black-and-white fox terrier. Its two companions were a gold and a black Labrador. The fox terrier sniffed Gunboat's shoe and eyed him inquisitively; the other two sat waiting for morsels from the table and completely ignored Gunboat.

'How long has your family ruled here?'

'Two, three hundred years,' Nicky said. 'I'm afraid we're always a bit vague on the exact date. Unlike the Europeans, we Indians have no concept of the past. One of my ancestors made a fortunate choice. He fought with Clive against Dupleix and won. So we got to keep our state. If he'd fought for the French, the British would have taken away the throne.' The bearer brought out bacon and eggs and toast and marmalade. 'You must tell me what we have to do.'

'How fit are you?'

'Fit.'

'In a fight that's never enough. You have to build up strength in your legs and stomach. So you gotta do a lot of roadwork.'

Nicky frowned. 'Roadwork?'

'I mean running,' Gunboat said. Nicky's face cleared. 'And a lot of exercises for your stomach and arms. How many rounds?'

'Five three-minute rounds. It isn't much, is it?'

'If you're losing, that's an eternity. In a ring, time stops. I don't know why or how, but three minutes there feels half an hour. You got things like punchbags, skipping ropes, or a ring?'

'I don't have a punchbag, but the men are waiting to build a ring. You will instruct them how.'

Gunboat sketched out their work programme for the coming weeks. Nicky listened closely and finally nodded in approval.

Gunboat figured Nicky would learn quickly, but still four weeks wasn't quite enough. He had not mentioned his opponent again, but Gunboat sensed the boy's presence in the way Nicky revealed his determination. Victory was important.

They finished breakfast and strolled across the lawn. Mohan and the terrier accompanied them. The dog darted ahead; Mohan remained a few feet behind.

They passed the line of trees. From afar the undergrowth had looked unruly; closer it was orderly and controlled. There was a miniature canal system that carried water from some source, and the grounds were dotted with small tanks that were filled with water. Malis constantly laboured, pruning, watering, cutting, to keep the grounds tended. Gunboat counted a dozen.

They reached a clearing of about twenty square feet. The ground was level and hard and was surrounded by clumps of bamboo. The trees were tall and canopied the clearing, filtering the light through their slender leaves and pale yellow trunks. Half a dozen men had been squatting on the edge of the clearing. Now they stood, close together.

'I thought we could build the ring here,' Nicky said.

'Looks okay. There's enough space for a nine-foot ring.' Gunboat paced it. 'We can make it a foot high. Okay?'

'Whatever you say. If you draw it, Mohan can explain it to the men.'

Gunboat knelt and sketched the ring on the earth. Mohan bowed over him, listening; then he beckoned to one of the men. The one who came forward was old, stooped, with a calm, proud face. He namasted, to Nicky who spoke to him briefly. Gunboat didn't understand a word, but the old man was obviously pleased.

'I'll leave you to it then,' Nicky said. 'I will have my bath and return.'

◆

He turned, whistled to the terrier, and strode back the way they'd come. Nicky felt pleased. Gunboat knew what he was doing. In a way he was sorry he had to hire a European. The recent past could not be easily shaken; two centuries of foreign rule had instilled a belief that the European was superior. Nicky had no illusion on that, but Gunboat was the best he could hire.

He also felt excited. He would learn everything that Gunboat could teach, and in four weeks he'd beat Ian in the fight. He had to.

He passed the guest palace and saw the three women approaching. One was his grandmother, the other two his sisters. The old rani was small and plump with fierce black eyes. A heavy nose stud, holding a large diamond, glittered on her face. Her hair was grey and drawn tightly back in a bun. On each wrist she wore four heavy gold bangles, and around her neck hung an intricately plaited gold chain. From the chain hung the small symbol of marriage: twin breasts of gold with diamond nipples; and on her toes the other symbol: silver rings. Her sari was an exuberant red interwoven with fine gold thread that joined to form heavy gold squares every foot or so. The border was also of gold thread and measured at least four inches wide.

His sisters were pretty. The elder, by four years, had an oval face, a straight nose, and the same sensual mouth as his. She wore her hair like her grandmother's, but woven into the heavy black strands were small, delicate white flowers. They were still fresh and smelled sweet and soft. Her sari was of that bright yellow seen in the heart of a flame. It had silver thread running through it and the heavy border, instead of forming squares, traced the curving shape of the mango. In her nose was an emerald-and-gold stud, and from her ears, small and frail, hung emerald earrings. She wore a gold chain and from it hung the same symbol of marriage, except the nipples were emeralds. On her wrists were gold bangles studded with emeralds, and on her toes simple silver rings.

His other sister, three years his senior, had a heart-shaped face, a firm jaw, high cheekbones, and the same familial mouth. Her toes were ringless, and instead of a gold chain she wore a necklace of rubies set in gold claws. Her nose held a ruby stud and in her ears were even larger stones. Her hair was cut fashionably short. Her sari had the pale fine greenness of a newly planted rice field. It was threaded with gold and the pattern was of leaves. She wore two gold bangles on each wrist with rubies set half an inch apart. On the third finger of her right hand was a ruby ring. The stone was about the size of a pebble and it nestled in a cluster of diamonds.

'Where's this boxer?' his grandmother asked.

'Showing the carpenters how to build a ring.'

Nicky was deferential, almost subdued. He was in awe of his grandmother. Her temper was quick and sharp, and she was stubbornly eccentric. As a widow, she should have been dressed in white, hair shorn, jewelless, withdrawn from public gaze. Her vanity and character were too strong to be suffocated by this Hindu rite.

'Did he really kill a man boxing?' Sushila, the elder sister, asked.

'So I'm told.'

'I don't believe it,' Rukmani, said. 'You can't kill a man by just hitting him.'

'Of course you can,' Sushila insisted.

'The other boxer had a brain tumour.'

'See!' they both chorused.

His sisters bickered as a matter of course. They had inherited their strength from their grandmother and alternated between loving Nicky and intimidating him. Towards each other their moods fluctuated, and Nicky was never sure whether they loved or hated each other. He tried to play the conciliator but was seldom successful.

'Is he English?' his grandmother asked.

'American. There is a difference.'

'How can you tell the difference? I suppose only *she* can,' and his grandmother glanced back at the palace.

'I suppose so.' Nicky was uneasy, unsure where she was leading.

'Maybe she'll run away with him…for good,' his grandmother cackled. Her false teeth clicked.

'That would be good,' Sushila said.

'We can mention it to him,' Rukmani suggested. 'Are you going to beat Ian?'

'I will,' Nicky said.

'You better,' his grandmother said. 'It will teach them all a bloody good lesson.'

◆

The palace had many entrances, and sprawled somewhat haphazardly. Parts differed in age. The oldest was two hundred years, the newest less than a decade. Each rajah had built and subtracted, squandered or saved. There were forty or fifty rooms, possibly more, possibly less. Many were closed off, opened only for functions. Running the length and breadth all around was a veranda. Pillars, ten feet apart, were joined by carved marble arches.

Nicky entered by the north entrance. It was nearest his room. The terrier stopped following and wandered away. Nicky took the stairs and entered a corridor. On either side paintings, European and Indian, hung in recessed shadows. Familiar and unseen.

He had a suite. The living room was comfortable: cane armchairs, a tiger skin on the carpet, shelves of books, and a refrigerator. His bedroom was large. One wall was taken up by enormous cupboards; on the others were paintings and photographs of sportsmen and sport scenes. Swami waited and took his clothes as he stripped. His clean clothes were neatly laid out on the bed.

'Your father wishes to see you after you bathe,' Swami said.
'Where will he be?'
'In his office.'

◆

Gunboat sat in the shade of a tree, smoking. Two men were digging holes for the posts, the carpenter and his helpers had gone to fetch the lumber, and Mohan sat on his haunches a respectable distance away.

It was pleasant to be idle; to watch men work and listen to the crows above, and the constant scold of squirrels. It could be a good life: a full belly, a palace to live in, some work, and enough liquor. Gunboat decided he could get used to it very easily. For the first time also he was to be of some use.

He saw Mohan abruptly scramble to his feet. The men stopped digging and stood away. Gunboat caught a glimpse of bright colours, the flash of gold, and rose to his feet. The three women who stepped into the clearing studied him as if he were a curio in one of the palace cabinets. Frank, uninvolved. The old one spoke to Mohan. He bowed and explained. She strolled around the clearing, as if imagining what would rise there. She studied his crude sketch. The two girls were a step behind, almost in imitation.

The younger girl turned. 'Why are you called Gunboat Jack?'

'Rukmani,' the old woman spoke sharply, but was ignored.

'Don't you have a real name?'

'Like Peter or Paul,' Sushila added.

'Or Matthew, Mark, or Luke, or John?' Rukmani chanted.

They laughed together. Gunboat felt himself gently mocked, yet at the same time from their glances he felt they were flirting with him.

'No, ma'am. I had a name, but I never used it much so now everyone calls me Gunboat Jack.'

'Were you born on a gunboat?'

'Nope. In the Bronx.'

'Sushila...Rukmani.' The old woman bustled between them,

buffeting them across the clearing. She scolded them, but whatever she said appeared to have little effect.

'I've never seen a boxing match,' Rukmani said. 'How do you fight?'

'With fists.'

'Just like that.' Sushila raised her hands, looking incongruous, and both girls laughed.

'Yes. Like that.' Gunboat demonstrated. 'We wear gloves on our hands, too.'

'Are you a champion?' Sushila asked.

Gunboat hesitated. This was no place for modesty.

'Yes, back in the States I won some big fights. A lot of people knew me.'

'And you killed a man here?'

'Yes, ma'am,' suppressing his growing irritation. The questions were too abrupt, too fast. They were not expected to answer any of his. 'It was an accident. It's not something I want to talk about either.'

He had been gentle. They took it harshly. He almost felt the chill of their glare. It was as if he'd admonished two small, spoilt children.

'Are you married?' the older woman enquired.

'No.'

'Why not?' she studied him. 'You are old enough. Too old in fact. But you'll do. I don't suppose it will make a difference though,' and she and the girls clung to each other laughing.

'Do for what?' He was irritated, puzzled. He didn't like such private jokes. They left, still laughing, and for some time he could hear their voices drifting back. Musical, enchanting, almost a part of the garden sounds.

'Who were they?'

'The yuvaraj's grandmother and sisters,' Mohan said. He'd returned to his haunches and lit a beedi. The men returned to work.

'She looks a tough bird.'

Mohan glanced around, uneasy. 'Yes, sir, but quite kind underneath. She is his grandmother on his mother's side,' he added as if this clarified everything.

Gunboat returned to the tree. They'd resembled each other; not fully, only by a nose, a mouth, a gesture, the eyes. Parts were Nicky, others not. Gunboat never had imagined what princesses looked like. He had had no call for that. Now he knew. Regal, aloof, perennial children dwelling in beautiful gardens. Decked in silks and gold and precious stones.

'Hey, we need a punchbag, Mohan.'

'What is that, sir?'

'Something heavy to hit, so Nicky can build up his muscles,' Gunboat said. Mohan only cocked his head uncomprehendingly.

'It's heavy, about the thickness of a man's body, and hangs from the ceiling. It's usually canvas and filled with sand.' Mohan still remained puzzled. He drew it on the ground.

'We can have it made from gunny bags sir, and the carpenter can build something to hang it on.'

'Good. Tell him then.'

◆

The rajah of Tandhapur's office was immense. It was the size of a tennis court, marble-floored, scattered with Persian rugs. One wall was bookshelves from floor to ceiling. The books were leather-bound, old, many first editions of great English authors. On the opposite wall were paintings. There were two Ravi Varmas, a Rembrandt self-portrait, and a Da Vinci sketch of a man's hand. Behind the leather-top desk, between the marble-latticed windows, were photographs of the rajah— in Oxford, with Donald Bradman, the great cricketer, with Pataudi and other princes, with Nehru, with Mountbatten, with the Emperor of India, with George VI, with his polo ponies, with his cricket teams.

The office had two entrances: one into the palace, the other into the grounds. Outside this door was a small circular lawn, and benches shaded by a neem tree. Men, some with their wives, waited here. They were businessmen, merchants, farmers, landless peasants, mendicants, minstrels, politicians, the jobless. They came each morning and waited to be granted an audience. None waited too long, but yet the lines never appeared to diminish.

The rajah was a thickset man, balding, neatly bearded, slim-nosed, and with eyebrows as thick as his son's. He was an inch or so shorter than his son. He wore no rings, no touch of gold on his person. Around his wrist was only a religious amulet. He wore European clothes, and his open-neck shirt revealed a thick matting of hair. He gave the impression of an ascetic, rather than a prince.

Nicky sat in the leather armchair across from his father. The two visitors immediately bowed. He acknowledged them perfunctorily and waited until they'd completed their business. The two were father and son. The father had come to ask the rajah's help in obtaining a job for his son. Nicky's father promised help, and then they withdrew, grateful. The liveried peon was ordered not to show in new visitors for fifteen minutes.

'How is the boxer?' His voice was soft Oxonian, difficult to hear.

Nicky sat forward. 'He's building the ring. It should be ready this evening. Tomorrow I'll start training.'

His father nodded, appearing not to hear. He was a distant, aloof man at times.

He touched the amulet, glanced at Nicky, then away.

'I've been thinking. I've decided not to allow Rukmani to marry Prithivi.'

'I thought it was already arranged. She likes him.'

'They aren't rajahs.'

'Neither are we...anymore.'

'But we were,' his father spoke sharply, 'and we mustn't forget that.'

'How long are we to remember? You are the last rajah.'

'Just because they have taken away our titles doesn't mean we have to lower our standards. His family are business people.' It was flicked sharply.

'I know. But they are well off.'

Timeri N. Murari

'That is not enough,' he said dismissively.

'Then who will she marry?'

'I've been approached by the rajah of Chittandra for Rukmani. They are rich and will be of use.'

'Fat Gopi?' Nicky showed his disgust. 'She hates him.'

'In which case she doesn't marry.'

'But you like Prithivi. So do I.'

'No.' The sharpness softened suddenly. 'I discussed this with Pamela. She feels if Rukmani married Prithivi, it could threaten your inheritance. They would take over the mines and the land.'

'How can they?'

'Because they are business people. They have no honour.'

'What about Ava?' Nicky tried a new tack.

'Your grandmother has nothing to do with my decision.'

'She approved of the family.'

'She has no right to interfere. She's a widow and should stop meddling in the family affairs.'

'Have you told Rukmani?' Nicky felt sad for his sister.

'Not yet. I will at dinner.'

They talked for half an hour. The rajah's gentleness could be deceptive; he was stubborn. By the end Nicky had gained nothing. The decision had been made. He knew his sister would not accept it. Nicky rose.

'Ah, if only your mother were alive,' the rajah sighed.

Nicky went out. He had no memory of his mother; his father constantly thought of her. She was a ghost, and he was haunted. Thirteen years had passed since the rani's death, and he still appeared as bewildered as if it had happened a day before. She had not been old, thirty-one, but had been a diabetic. He had loved his wife too deeply and believed her death a punishment for sins committed in a previous life. There were paintings and photographs of her in the palace: in the family dining room, the library, and, naturally, the prayer room. She had been a beautiful woman.

'How's it coming?'

Gunboat glanced up at Nicky. Two of the holes had been dug, and posts fitted. The carpenter and his assistant had returned with their ancient implements and enough lumber to construct a small house.

'Just fine,' Gunboat said. Nicky looked distracted, restless. He watched the men for a few moments. 'You got gloves I guess?'

'Yes, yes. Four pairs.' He fidgeted, then spoke sharply to Mohan. Mohan stuttered a reply and pointed. 'If you will excuse me...' He turned and left. Mohan trotted after him.

Gunboat stood, uneasy, lonely. He felt himself drifting in undercurrents he could not see. He followed and caught glimpses. Mohan ran ahead, and Nicky was hurrying up the drive to the gate. He hadn't gone twenty yards when a jeep swung round the curve, stopped, and picked him up. The dust drifted back towards Gunboat and he waved it away.

Its sound faded; the garden's silence returned. He turned and caught a glimpse of movement from a second-storey balcony of the palace. It was a white woman. Too far to distinguish features, then she was gone, receding, as if an illusion, into the palace.

NINE

The jeep sped towards the town. The driver kept his hand on the horn, scattering villagers and pie-dogs and scaring bullocks pulling carts.

The town only appeared small. Once the jeep had turned off the main road, it bumped along narrow lanes that wound behind and up the slope of the hillside. The town had once been a village: a few homes huddled together near the palace. It had grown slowly, haphazardly. Now it crept up and down the hillside: small mud houses, here and there a brick one, single-storeyed, crowding either side of the lanes.

From a distance this part of the town could not be seen. The peepul and neem trees camouflaged the houses well; the sunlight on the earth was speckled and faint below them. The earth was also squishy with the tiny fruit spilled by the neem.

The jeep kept climbing. So did the warren of little houses. There was something inexorable in their advance; they appeared to eat into the earth daily and would not stop until they'd crested the hill. The jeep swung left. Here there was a small marketplace: open stalls selling fruit, vegetables, grains, spices. They were huddled against the ochre-and-white striped walls of a temple.

Nicky shed his slippers. The earth was hot, but he didn't feel the burn. Two beggars squatted outside the massive wooden doors. They whined; he ignored them.

The courtyard was no cooler. The temple sat in the centre. It was small, a Vishnuite, and very old. It had been there long before his family, and the priests murmured about the Pandavas and the Pallavas, and Ashoka and Gupta, such a confusion of ages, as the builders. Its vimana rose a mere fifty, sixty feet; the carvings on it were of granite, smooth and blunted by time and wind and rains. The gods were frozen in perpetual dance. Granite steps led up to the deep shade of the inner courtyard and then to the darkness of the temple itself. From the courtyard little could be seen of the god inside the sanctum sanctorum. Once in the shade, the devout could catch a glimpse of the monolithic black carving and the glitter of gold and diamonds and silks.

To the right of the temple was the tank. It was in proportion to the temple, about twenty feet square, ten feet below the stone steps. The water was fresh from the underground springs.

His grandmother and sisters sat in the shade of the inner courtyard on a stone bench. Squatting at their feet and around them were a few women. All chattered, with his grandmother orchestrating the conversation. She loved gossip. Here she felt the pulse of the state; listening to complaints, quarrels, births, deaths, infidelities, thefts, marriages.

The squatting women fell silent and shuffled aside to let Nicky through. A few were old, but one or two were young and pretty. He caught their eye in a glance, sensing the supple smoothness of their bodies beyond the folds of their saris.

'Here,' his grandmother held out her hand. In her palm, on a scrap of paper, was a small heap of vibudhi. Nicky took a pinch, placed a fingerprint of white on his forehead and a smear at the base of his throat. 'Go and worship.'

'I—'

'Go,' his grandmother commanded.

The priest sitting by the door appeared older than the temple. He rose creakily, adjusted his dhoti, slowly manoeuvred himself over the granite doorjamb, and entered the sanctum sanctorum. Nicky remained a few feet away. The priest lit a lump of camphor; the god was illumined in swoops of light as the brass tray was circled in front of him. The light not only caught his riches, but also the serenity of his carved face. The priest finished the Vedic chant and came out slowly. Nicky placed his palms over the flame, then carried them to his face. The priest passed the holy water, which was drunk, and more vibudhi.

'Your father should also visit the temple,' his grandmother scolded. 'Instead he mocks. I knew we shouldn't have sent him to Oxford. He learned all those foreign ways, and now he's passing them on to his children.' She spoke in English so only a few of her listeners could understand. His sisters laughed against him, glad not to find themselves at the end of their grandmother's tongue.

'I went, didn't I?'

'Because I told you.' Her logic was always irrefutable. 'Now what did you want to tell me?'

Nicky glanced at Rukmani. 'I just saw Father. He says he will not give her permission to marry Prithivi.'

Rukmani wept. The tears trickled down, staining her cheeks with kohl. Each time she rubbed her face, the black smeared. Nicky thought how even though grown, his sister still cried as she did as a child. All three comforted her; the squatting women, though they did not understand, clicked their tongues in sympathy.

'Why has he changed his mind?' his grandmother asked. Then to Rukmani: 'Stop bawling.'

'Prithivi isn't from a royal family.'

'I should be the one objecting to the match, not him. I know they are not royal, but they are the same caste.' Her eyes glittered; she looked a predator.

'Did she put him up to it?' she asked.

'He said he discussed it with her.'

His grandmother nodded in satisfaction.

'Who does he suggest then?'

'Fat Gopi.'

This stopped Rukmani's crying.

'I refuse.' She stood and glared at Nicky.

'I had nothing to do with that.'

Gunboat Jack

'Of course she expects you to refuse,' his grandmother said.

'I will not even see that fat idiot,' Rukmani shouted. She stamped, and her anklet jingled. 'I'd prefer...suicide.'

'Stop being a child,' his grandmother commanded. 'Sit down. With you shouting I can't think.'

'What can I do?' Nicky asked.

'Nothing. You are a still a boy.'

He waited, arms folded. His grandmother hunched, brooding. Without the anger she looked older, frailer. She was in her sixties. Her husband had died just after Independence and five years after her only child. His sisters sat, shoulders touching. Sushila whispered to Rukmani, who listened and sniffled. Sushila had been married off at sixteen to a neighbouring prince and appeared moderately happy.

'If only your mother were alive,' his grandmother broke the silence.

'That's what he also said.'

'I have to discuss this with your aunt. You will come with me, Nicky.'

Nicky was confused. His father and his aunt had quarrelled bitterly over the state and hadn't spoken to each other for some years. Nicky had been commanded never to see his aunt. He was fond of her still but couldn't disobey his father.

'I can't,' he said. His grandmother glared at him; he held her eye until she dropped hers. At times he was as stubborn as his father.

'Very well, I will see her alone. Order a car.'

His aunt now lived in Bangalore. Once, and it seemed a long time ago, the whole family lived in the palace. Cousins, aunts, grand-aunts, but over the years they'd left, one by one, and now only his grandmother remained in residence. She refused to be moved, though she and the rajah seldom spoke to each other. He had quarrelled with most of them, minor differences that somehow escalated.

'You will go and stay with Sushila a few days,' his grandmother told Rukmani, 'until we sort this out.'

'I still refuse to marry Fat Gopi.'

'I know,' his grandmother spoke wearily. 'I know. I wish he wouldn't keep doing these things.'

She rose; all rose. She bobbed in front of the open door of the sanctum sanctorum, walked on out. Nicky remained by her side.

'Your father is a good man,' she said. 'I have known him since a boy, but I wish I understood him. He wishes to be westernized, but is not. He wishes to be Indian, but is not. He wishes to be an ascetic, but is not. He wishes to be the prince, but is not. He confuses me. I am old, and I cannot keep fighting him.' She paused, then added: 'And her.' His grandmother leaned on him as she clambered over the threshold of the temple door. 'And you are not old enough or wise enough to assist me. Your sisters cannot.'

The jeep and the car drew up. His grandmother and sisters climbed into the Ford, and Nicky followed in the jeep.

◆

Gunboat studied himself in the mirror. He looked neat. His clothes had been washed and ironed, and he wished he owned a tie. Mohan eyed him critically.

'Give me your shoes. I will have them polished,' he finally pronounced.

They were dusty. Gunboat unlaced them and stood in his socks.

The day had not been entirely wasted. The ring had been built; the punchbag made and hung. Gunboat had tested the gloves; they were brand new Everlasts. The smell had been sickeningly familiar. However, he had not seen Nicky for the rest of the day.

'Should I wear a tie?' Gunboat worried when Mohan returned with the shoes shining.

'Not necessary, sir. The rajah likes informality at dinner. It is only on state occasions that dinner jackets are required.'

'I sure don't have one.'

'Yes, sir,' he said as if he doubted Gunboat would anyway be invited.

'Who will be at dinner?'
'The rajah and the yuvaraj.'
'What about his grandmother and sisters?'
'They are out-of-station, sir.'
'Anyone else?'
Mohan hesitated. 'Madam.'
'Who is she?'
'Madam,' Mohan said stolidly. He glanced at his watch. 'It is time, sir,' and waited until Gunboat finished his drink.

TEN

The floors were teak, inlaid with a lighter-coloured wood. From the ceilings hung Venetian chandeliers, unlit. On the walls were paintings: portraits of fierce men, battle scenes, and gods. For the size of the rooms, the furnishings were sparse: marble-topped tables, straight-backed chairs and sofas, side tables and glass cabinets; occasionally a richly tapestried carpet broke the monotony of the floor.

Gunboat counted half a dozen rooms. They varied only in size and led one into the other. The air was musty and damp. There were peeling patches on the walls, only briefly glimpsed in the dim light as he hurried after Mohan. Here and there the bare brick lay revealed.

The rooms felt dispossessed. They had been transported from another time and lay like old beached galleons, waiting for the tide to carry them away. Gunboat looked back, expecting to see his footprints in the dust. There were none, but he wished he were barefoot for his footsteps echoed.

Mohan slowed, glanced at his watch.

'Would you like to see the armoury?'

'Why not?'

Mohan veered towards an oak door. He pushed and it swung slowly open. They stepped into a large hall lit by the faintest wisp of moonlight. Ghostly shields and swords and lances covered the walls, breastplates and helmets, suspended one above the other, dark with rust and disuse. Muskets cast weak shadows over the bare floor. The door closed and echoed. Mohan fumbled along the wall and threw the switch.

There was no chandelier. Brass wall lamps, yellow and dusty, threw weak patches of light up the walls and down to the floor. The gloom remained in the centre of the hall.

There was no vacant space on the walls. The weapons ranged from curved and cruel swords to daggers and metal-tipped lances with small tattered flags attached to them. The shields varied in size, if not design. They were all circular with spikes jutting from their centres. Long ancient muskets, some nearly ten feet in length, covered one wall, and on the floor below them two Gatling guns pointed towards the door.

Down the centre were three display cabinets. Two were flat; the third, in the centre, rose to six feet. The weapons in the two flat cabinets were of gold: curved swords with jeweled handles, daggers encrusted with emeralds and rubies, shields with gold spikes decorated intricately with precious stones. In the centre cabinet were a saddle, spurs, stirrups, and a bit. Except for the leather in the saddle, the rest was gold, including the bit. The crop had a diamond on its head and rubies on the grip.

'Jesus,' Gunboat whispered. His breath fogged the glass, and he wiped away a layer of dust.

'When the yuvaraj becomes rajah, he will wear these at the ceremony,' Mohan said.

'Will Nicky?'

'No. His father is the last rajah.' He peered in, his face a dark shadow on the glass. 'I was a young man when the rajah was crowned.'

'When was that?'

'Nineteen thirty-five. The yuvaraj had to return from playing cricket for Glamorgan. He was doing well for the county, sir.' He sighed and turned. 'Many princes came, and the governor, and the viceroy sent his vicereine. He was ill.'

'What happened to the old rajah? I mean his father.'

Mohan hesitated, sighed. 'He was removed from the throne.'

'Why?'

'Politics. He hated the British and took part in the freedom movement. They are clever. They took away his title. The present rajah was a follower of Gandhi, and he was also nearly removed, but the times had changed. Instead, the British were removed.' He chuckled and moved to the door.

The library was wood-panelled. Floor to ceiling books lined all the walls. Half a dozen deep leather armchairs circled a brass table. It was a cool and comfortable room. Nicky sprawled in a chair, reading. He stood immediately and came across to Gunboat. 'I'm sorry I couldn't return, but tomorrow we definitely start work. Okay?'

'That's fine by me. You're the boss.'

Nicky mixed him a Scotch and soda with ice and handed it to him. 'Is that right?'

'Looks good.'

They sat, and Gunboat was pleased to notice the shine on his shoes. 'Mohan showed me the armoury. It's pretty impressive.'

'Yes. It's a private tourist attraction. Mohan always likes to impress people.'

'You know how to use any of them?'

'I learned to fence a bit in school.'

'Like in the movies?'

'Yes,' he laughed. 'Like that. It's very good exercise and not as easy as Errol Flynn makes it look.'

'Only an expert can make a sport look easy and graceful,' Gunboat said. The Scotch was too strong, and he sipped cautiously.

'That is true.'

The door opened and Nicky stood. Gunboat struggled out of the chair as the rajah approached. Nicky made the introduction and Gunboat felt the softness of the rajah's hand.

Gunboat recognized the resemblance. Nicky and the rajah looked alike, stood in the same posture, and radiated the same aloof charm. However, he sensed a fractional hardness in Nicky that was missing in the rajah. The prince should have been the ruler.

'I boxed when I was Nicky's age.' The rajah gestured to the chair. Gunboat sat on the edge, for he found it difficult to hear. 'I didn't like it much. I preferred cricket.'

'I gather you played for Oxford,' Gunboat said, parroting Mohan.

'Oh, you know the game.' He brightened.

'I've seen it played on the maidans. In America we play baseball.'

'Yes, I saw it played when I was there.' He fell silent and appeared to be savouring the memory.

'Who was playing, sir?' Gunboat asked. 'The Yankees?'

'I don't remember. I was taken to it by a state department official.' He had a habit of absentmindedly stroking his fingers. 'I'm hoping Nicky will get his blue at Oxford too. In cricket, I mean, not boxing.'

'If I win the fight, who knows?' Nicky spoke quietly.

'It isn't a gentleman's sport,' the rajah said abruptly, and then apologetically, 'I know it used to be at one time, but then professionals took over.'

'We have to make a living,' Gunboat said defensively.

'Of course,' as if he wasn't sure what Gunboat meant. Then abruptly to Nicky: 'Where is Rukmani?'

'She went with Ava and Sushila.'

'Where?' Gunboat sensed the impatience.

'To Sushila's, I suppose.' Nicky shrugged. 'Gunboat, would you like another drink?'

'No, thank you.' He sipped and put his glass down. Gunboat sensed a loneliness between the two, as if suddenly they had moved far apart and couldn't reach each other. 'Your daughters are very pretty girls, sir.'

'Thank you.' The glance measured him as a new opponent would. 'Why did she go there?'

'Sushila asked her.'

'And your grandmother too, I suppose. I wish she would stop interfering.' He turned abruptly: 'Do you have children, Mr...Jack?'

'Gunboat. Nope. I never married.'

'That doesn't prevent children.' He quietened, withdrew, as if he'd overstepped propriety. 'Their mother died and it has been difficult raising them.'

'I'm sure.'

'Shall we have dinner?' Nicky spoke and rose.

The rajah hesitated, glanced at the drink still unfinished, and stood.

'You must be hungry.'

'Yes, I am,' he said for want of another answer, and followed them out of the library.

The gleaming mahogany table sat twelve. It was set for four. Bearers stood behind each chair and pulled them back for the men to sit. The fourth was unmoved, and the bearer waited. The dining room was small, and so was the chandelier. Half a dozen paintings. Four were watercolours, Gunboat suspected by famous painters. A huge, intricately carved sideboard held the gold-rimmed plates that had been laid on the table. The room was, in contrast to the palace, intimate.

The rajah sat at the head, Nicky to his right. The seat to his left was empty, and then came Gunboat.

'Beer?' Nicky asked.

'Yeah,' Gunboat said, and the bearer poured out a chilled bottle. The rajah and Nicky sipped ice water.

The bearers waited. The rajah and Nicky remained silent, preoccupied. Gunboat felt they were battling and wished he'd dined in the guest palace with Mohan's chattering company. His seat creaked. The chairs were old, ornately carved; the table reflected the pale blue glow of the chandelier.

The woman entered. She was white, tall, and thickset. She wore a pink sari, gold bangles on her wrist, and a gold chain round her neck. An emerald ring glittered on her finger. She wore makeup: lipstick, rouge, and powder, and French perfume. She could have been pretty once, but Gunboat thought the weight had rolled out the outlines of the prettiness. She had watchful grey eyes.

The men rose. 'This is Miss Hobbs,' the rajah said.

They shook hands. She was near to eye level with Gunboat; possibly a fraction shorter than Gertrude.

'Why are you all so quiet? Please sit down, Gunboat. You don't mind if I call you that, do you? I presume you prefer that to your real name, whatever that is. Boxers always have such colourful names, I think.' She spoke quickly, at the same time with gestures springing the bearers into action. Her voice was harsh and resonant, and she appeared to be straining to imitate the accents of the rajah and Nicky. Occasionally she slipped, and she sounded like Gertrude or Johnny. The sing-song Indian accent. 'I saw you box...I suppose the term is... fight...once. It was in Bombay. I lived there for a few years. Oh, I do certainly miss it at times. It is such a lively city, isn't it, Gunboat?'

'I guess so. I was too busy earning a living then to enjoy it much.'

'Oh, I assure you it is. I was fortunate that I had so much time to enjoy myself. This was, of course, before we left India. The officers were such good fun. We had parties nearly every day, and there were always balls.' She stopped abruptly, the graciousness shed. 'Look at the coat. Go and change.' The bearer stiffened and went. 'They are so sloppy. Trying to keep them clean is such a problem.'

'He looked fine,' Nicky said, spooning the soup. His tone was quiet, yet provocative.

Gunboat sensed her stiffen, then relax. She laughed, amused.

'Of course, he looked fine,' she said. 'Bearer. Tell the man not to change. The yuvaraj wishes him as he is.' She spooned the soup, a finger crooked as if it were tea. 'You agree with him, don't you?' softly and cruelly demanding.

The rajah carefully put his spoon down. He sat back, as if wishing he were so far away that his presence wasn't noted. The yuvaraj and Miss Hobbs stared at him.

'It makes no difference,' he finally spoke, and pushed the plate away. The bearer scooped it up.

Gunboat noticed the reprimanded bearer had returned, still buttoning his white coat. The red piping was faded.

'This is *your* household,' still so gentle. 'Bearer! Come here.'

The man came. He was old, shaking.

'Look at that coat. It's got stains all over it. I think you should be proud of *your* household, and I am trying my very best, you know,' she spoke as if addressing a child. It was tutorial, basic manners of etiquette imparted from one who was an expert.

'It isn't important,' the rajah said, still trying to keep out.

'It doesn't look stained,' the yuvaraj said. 'It's just an old coat.'

Gunboat sat back quietly, still the chair creaked. He wasn't noticed, and wished not to be. The three were absorbed in the struggle. It wasn't, he realized, trivial. The bearer was a mere outpost in the empire; his capture or release meant victory. Gunboat waited.

'Go change,' the rajah suddenly ordered and then placatingly to the yuvaraj, 'Miss Hobbs runs the household, Nicky. You shouldn't bother about such things.'

'You are too important for that.' Miss Hobbs was softly triumphant.

Nicky didn't flinch; he only withdrew into silence. Gunboat suddenly saw that he was only a boy, and the facade of authority and power had been shelled too swiftly for him to build his defences.

'I am so glad you're teaching Nicky how to box,' Miss Hobbs continued. 'You have such a great reputation here, and you are the best boxer in India. I told Nicky to get the best. None of the Indians are any good.'

'They aren't bad,' Gunboat said.

She didn't hear. 'They don't like getting themselves hurt. I used to watch a lot of boxing up north in the cantonments. It was so exciting seeing the big sergeants fighting.' She spoke with relish.

Gunboat knew he had seen her before. She attended the ringside of every fight in every country in the world. She sat in the front row, wishing for men to be broken pleasurably.

'You must be careful with Nicky. He isn't as strong as he looks.'

'He looks fine,' Gunboat said and helped himself to the biryani that the bearer held before him.

'He was sickly as a child,' Miss Hobbs said. 'And he tires easily. Doesn't he?' to the rajah. He only nodded.

'So was I,' Gunboat lied. 'And he looks as if he's sure gotten over that.'

For the first time she turned to look at him fully. Her face was fleshy, yet beneath were the spare outlines of hunger. The flesh was mere mask; the eyes reflected the hidden stalker.

'You are a different kind of a man,' she said and turned away. Gunboat sensed she had gauged him as finely as any human could another in so short a time. 'You are a European—'

'American.'

'...and there's a difference in character as well. Of course I am sure with your training Nicky will do well. You must make sure of that, Gunboat.'

'He will,' Gunboat said and meant it.

'Of course he will.' She spoke flatly as if he doubted her judgement. Nicky rose. 'If you will excuse me,' he said to his father.

'You must build up your strength for the training, Nicky,' Miss Hobbs said.

'I've eaten enough. Gunboat, I shall see you in the morning.'

He left. The rajah watched him until the bearer closed the door. The boy seemed to puzzle him, and he didn't appear to understand the reason.

Miss Hobbs carried the conversation. She spoke of the family, the state, the vastness of holdings; possessively, as if she were a part of the same heritage. The rajah was the arbitrator on the facts and figures and lineage, when he was consulted. She appeared to want Gunboat to understand not only the wealth but also the power of this family. It amused him at first, until he realized that she was indirectly informing him of her power and wealth.

Gunboat remembered: 'You will meet a woman of your own race. Be careful. She holds your destiny.'

He could almost feel the coolness of the cave, smell the subtle sweet odour of the vibudhi, hear the old sadhu's amusement. The man awed him. He had known of this woman; pierced time and space with a glance and reported the meeting to come. Gunboat now understood fatality: if the future was marked so clearly, how could a man carve his own life? He could only sway to the left or right, like a fighter avoiding punches, but the inevitability of triumph and defeat had already been recorded.

Miss Hobbs was speaking softly to the rajah. She held his still hand, covering it with her own. He was listening, watching, mesmerized.

Gunboat overheard 'Rukmani...Ava...your authority...' and turned away, not wishing to be seen eavesdropping.

She sensed his restlessness. 'Would you like some brandy, Gunboat?'

'No, thank you, Miss Hobbs.' He rose. 'I think I'll call it an early night. Good night, sir.'

The rajah nodded. 'The bearer will lead you back. Even I get lost in the palace at times.'

The bearer walked ahead. He held a hurricane lantern, and its pale glow barely lit the night around him. The moon slid between clouds, alternately brightening and darkening the landscape. Gunboat smelled the night, the perfumes so much more distinct than in the city that he could almost pinpoint their sources. He heard a rustle to his left.

'Pambu,' the bearer whispered, and halted.

He saw Gunboat didn't understand and gestured rapidly, imitating a snake moving swiftly. Gunboat froze. The rustle continued, and from a bush he saw a black-and-white form emerge.

'Sally,' the bearer reprimanded the fox terrier for scaring them.

Gunboat was relieved to have the alert dog trot beside them. It darted occasionally in pursuit but returned as if it had been sent to protect his person.

Mohan had been thoughtful. Beside the bed was a bottle of whiskey, soda, and a bucket of melting ice. Gunboat fixed a drink, chose a paperback from the stack he'd discovered in a cupboard, and lay down. He wasn't a reader, but a Mickey Spillane was preferable to the silence.

He must have dozed, for when he started awake, Miss Hobbs was standing at the foot of the bed.

ELEVEN

She was still, shapeless in the dim light. And she appeared as if she'd been there for some time, looming above, watching and waiting.

'Don't get up,' she whispered.

'I wasn't,' Gunboat said and dropped the book from his chest.

'In the old days,' she spoke conversationally as if they still sat at the dining table, 'the women and children lived in this palace. The men in the other. There were hundreds—cousins, aunts, nieces, cousins of cousins. I had them all thrown out. They were just parasites living off the rajah.'

'Many Indian families live like that,' Gunboat said, paraphrasing Johnny's information. 'Joint families, isn't it?'

'The only joint is money here. It took a few years, but I got rid of them. It cut the household expenses in half, and now guests like you can stay here in comfort. It is comfortable, isn't it?'

'Sure.' Gunboat decided to be noncommittal. She had come for a purpose.

'You are a handsome man,' she swerved in conversation, and studied him. He couldn't see her eyes, only she appeared to lean downwards. Then straightened. 'I know you'd like to seduce me but…'

'Sure,' Gunboat said and wished he had stood. He could move out of reach quicker, if the occasion arose.

'…it wouldn't be safe. Not now. I used to have such a marvellous time in Bombay. Especially just after the war when all the soldiers were there. I met quite a few Yanks. They were all pilots. I really loved them. They were such generous men, and full of jokes.' She brooded. 'I love gaiety—drinks, dancing, flirtation. There is nothing here.'

'Why stay?' Gunboat cautiously wriggled himself upright. He still wasn't sure the swift proposal and dismissal had occurred.

'Where can I go?'

'Home,' he said vaguely.

'Like all the others?' She remained standing as if it were a fresh thought. 'I've got no place there. I don't have a grandmother or uncle or brothers living there. They are all here, like me.' In her confession, her accent had lapsed and she no longer made an effort to speak in the same tones as the rajah. 'I'm not an Anglo-Indian, you know,' she said fiercely. 'I'm pure European. My great-great-grandfather was the governor-general of Punjab. He was an Irish earl, and we have always been aristocrats. I have a painting of him in my room. I'll show it to you. Then my great-grandmother was Lady Mereswoth. I come from a very aristocratic family. Much older than this one. They only remained rulers because we allowed them to.'

'Sure,' Gunboat said. She didn't notice he was completely upright.

'But we've lived in India so long that we lost contact with the rest of our family.'

'Are your parents still alive?'

'No, my father was a surgeon in Delhi. He was quite famous, you know. He was a consultant for the viceroy, and I knew the viceroy when I was a little girl. I used to play with his children in the palace.'

She was silent, possibly remembering her childhood. Gunboat suspected it was a more remote past that she really clung to, full of imaginary honours, titles, and immense riches. The present had come too swiftly for people like her. Years can become mere minutes. The midnight hour had struck, and an empire had vanished, leaving countless stranded on a once familiar shore.

'I have a fifteen-year-old son in boarding school.' Miss Hobbs veered off again.

'Where's your husband?'

'We're divorced and I reverted to my maiden name. He's a tea planter up in Assam. I married so beneath me. I just wanted to get away from home, and he had been so dashing and handsome. Men become so dull once they marry. I suppose that's why you never married. A fighter can't afford an emotional relationship.'

'I don't see why not,' Gunboat countered. 'It just wasn't my luck.'

'If you had, we'd never have met.' She moved to perch on the edge of the bed. 'I am a very straightforward person, as you know. I like you.'

She noticed his position suddenly and burst out laughing. It was loud, coarse, and trickled to a giggle.

'You really thought I would seduce you, didn't you?' she asked playfully. 'How vain. Just because you are handsome and a European.'

'Listen, Miss Hobbs,' Gunboat said. 'I think there's a misunderstanding and possibly you shouldn't be here at this time of night.'

'I can be where I want,' she snapped. 'This is my home as much as theirs. I brought those children up as if they were my own, and do you think I'm appreciated? Not one jot.'

'How did you come to be here?' Gunboat was relieved the conversation had changed direction.

'The rajah advertised for the position of housekeeper and I got the job. He wanted his household to be European rather than Indian. But with that…grandmother here it is impossible to get them to change much. She is a bad influence.' Miss Hobbs held out her hand. 'May I have a sip?' she asked shyly.

Gunboat gave her the tumbler. She sipped, made a polite face, and handed it back. He poured himself another, wondering how much longer she would keep him waiting.

'I'm a straightforward woman, Gunboat,' she continued where she'd left off. 'I know you're not a rich man. You're poor and that's not good for a European in this country. How much is Nicky paying you?'

'I thought you'd know,' Gunboat said.

She laughed. 'A discreet man. Of course I do. Five thousand rupees, isn't it?'

'Yes. It's enough for my needs,' he added, suddenly realizing the tone of the conversation.

'But that's only if he wins. If he loses you get nothing more. I'll give you ten thousand rupees.'

'Five thousand's fine,' Gunboat stalled. 'And he'll win.'

'Don't be silly, he hasn't a chance,' she commanded abruptly. 'You're a bigger fool than I thought. I suppose that happens to a boxer: brain damage.'

'I don't have any brain damage, Miss Hobbs,' Gunboat spoke quietly, barely revealing anger.

'Pamela,' she corrected. 'I think you should call me that.' She stared out of the French windows, as if trying to read the shadows beyond. 'You know what the ten thousand is for?'

'Sure,' Gunboat said and stood up. 'I've been in the fight game long enough. When an offer is doubled it isn't for the same deal. Usually the opposite.'

'Yes,' and she waited.

He opened the doors. The night was cool, fresh, but not silent. The huge garden was noisy with crickets, frogs, mysterious rustles in thickets, the call of jackals in the distance. Farther up in the hills the cough of a larger animal, hunting.

'What exactly do I do?' Gunboat asked.

'Nothing. You don't teach Nicky anything.'

'He'll figure that one out.'

'You can be subtle.'

'Why?' And he heard her shift on the bed.

'If Nicky wins he could get to like boxing,' she said. 'And his father would be very unhappy with that. He hates boxing—'

'Cut the crap.' Gunboat spoke mildly.

She stopped, her breath sharp, and hissed, 'You Yanks can be so crude.'

'That's us all over,' Gunboat said. 'We weren't brought up subtle. If Nicky's so precious, why do you want him to lose?'

'Would you like an Indian to beat a European?'

'I don't give a shit,' Gunboat said.

'You're a stranger to this country.' She was fierce in her passion. 'We ruled them for centuries and—'

'That's past,' Gunboat interrupted.

'Nothing is past,' she said. 'Why do you think Nicky wants to win so badly? Because of the past. By beating Ian. He wants to prove he's as good as an Englishman.'

'And that won't do?'

'No.'

'What happens if I prefer to take the five?' Gunboat broke the silence.

'You don't get either,' Miss Hobbs said. 'Nicky is a minor and he has to get permission from his father to pay you the rest of the money. I'll make sure it's never granted.' Her features were implacable for a moment, and then deliberately softened. 'But you aren't a stupid man.'

'No, ma'am, but I would like to consider your proposition,' Gunboat stalled.

'Of course,' she said pleasantly and rose. 'Until tomorrow night.' She paused, frowned, 'I don't understand you. Another man would have taken the ten without a second thought.'

'I'm not another man.'

She smiled, disbelieving him, and moved to the door. For her size she was light, and Gunboat thought she would make a good boxer. She had, if not weight, the right instinct: killer.

If he thought to see her pass through the grounds below, he was mistaken. He waited for a glimpse of whiteness, but fifteen minutes later he gave up. There must have been another route.

◆

He was awakened at four-thirty by Mohan. It was dark and chilly, as if it were the very beginning of the earth. The tea steamed; he sipped gratefully. Mohan shivered and tucked his hands under his armpits.

'You slept well, sir?' Not meaning the question. He glanced around, and his eyes settled on the bed deliberately.

'No. I feel godawful. Is Nicky up?' he asked hopefully.

'Yes, sir. He will meet you outside in five minutes.'

Nicky wore a red tracksuit with white piping. The terrier and the black Labrador sat by his feet. Thin streaks of light had begun to crack the darkness. Gunboat knew an Indian dawn. The sun would rise suddenly, impatient to scorch the earth.

'Let's do some roadwork first.' Gunboat, wearing old trousers and tennis shoes, jogged up the driveway.

Nicky and the dogs followed. They reached the gate; Gunboat saw a pathway running parallel to the wall and turned up it. The earth was soft, dusty, so unlike the hard New York sidewalks he had run on so often. It felt good to work once again, to waken the natural instincts of his body. The legs, now, could dance and he whipped his arms into short jabs. The pain would come later; it was always waiting. He turned. Nicky was doing the same; jabbing, skipping, hopping. The dogs loped on either side. Overhead, parrots called and crows, black and big, peered down.

They passed servants. The men and women immediately stepped aside, bowed, though their eyes peeped questioningly at the yuvaraj. Gunboat hadn't realized the size of the palace garden. The path stretched as far as his eye could see; it was lost in the shadows of the trees.

'How are you feeling?' Gunboat called back after fifteen minutes.

'Fine.'

Gunboat wasn't. Age stole the speed and the quickness and the strength. Disuse burned his lungs and ached his calves. He steadied his breathing: inhaling slowly, exhaling, wanting to control the stamina. He could hear himself panting; felt the sweat trickle down his face. The sun was halfway over a hill, white and watchable only at this moment of dawn. He could sense its heat, so gentle now, soon unbearable.

Gunboat checked the time. 'Okay, that's fine for the first day.'

He heaved, pressing against a chest muscle that threatened to cramp. Nicky was also sweating and panting; it was some consolation. The Labrador lolled its tongue out; only the terrier was unaffected. It fidgeted and then trotted away.

Two men stood by the ring: Mohan and Swami. They had ice water and towels. Gunboat and Nicky drank greedily and wiped off the sweat.

For twenty minutes they worked out in the ring. Gunboat enjoyed teaching his craft: the feet spread, the body balanced, the guard raised, the left snaking out. Nicky was awkward; it was natural. It was unfamiliar to him; only with practice came the grace and ease that Gunboat revealed.

'How are your arms?'

'Aching,' Nicky said and let them fall. Swami leaped in the ring, practised as any second, and wiped the sweat from the yuvaraj's face and body as tenderly as if he were still a child.

'Now you know why fifteen minutes in the ring is a very long time.' Gunboat climbed out and took the towel.

'How am I doing?'

'It's too early yet.'

He glared, imperious. Both Mohan and Swami shuffled their feet. Gunboat stood his ground.

'Listen, Nicky,' Gunboat spoke shortly. 'I'm not one of your aides. When you get good, I'll tell you. And when you're bad, I'll tell you, too.'

For a minute, the glance didn't soften. Gunboat met it. His blue: stubborn. The prince's brown: narrowed. In another age, Gunboat knew, the cruelty would have had him torn and crushed.

Nicky laughed, delighted and charming. 'You are right; and I am somewhat spoilt.' He held out his arms; Swami immediately unlaced the gloves. 'I shan't ask again. I will wait until you tell me I'm good. I assure you, one day you will, too.'

'So will I.'

Breakfast waited on the terrace. The bearer poured ice water, and they drank greedily and sat down. The table had been moved under a striped awning, and Gunboat was grateful to sit in its shade. The sun was already too hot. The bearer served fresh melon.

'Why did Miss Hobbs go to your room last night?' Nicky asked as Gunboat began to eat.

Gunboat had expected the question. For half an hour after she left, he had lain awake considering. In a palace midnight visitations did not go unnoticed. He could lie: pretend they were two exiles exchanging nostalgia for their distant lands.

Gunboat took his time. He finished the fruit, looked up. Nicky appeared disinterested. He sat back, staring out at the lawn. The malis laboured, their backs bent and black.

'She offered me ten thousand rupees not to teach you,' Gunboat said.

Nicky appeared not to hear. Gradually he shifted to look at Gunboat.

'You are an honest man,' with some surprise in his voice.

'So I've been told,' Gunboat said dryly.

'It is a dangerous trait.'

'Depends for whom. You seem to have expected her to have done that.'

'Something of that nature,' he said and fell silent.

He had the same gesture as his father: stroking his fingers. He looked sad, as if he did not wish for the burden of intrigues at so early an age. A childhood had slipped away too quickly and he was once more the prince calculating his moves.

'And you have accepted it?' he said suddenly, as Gunboat forked a puree into his mouth.

'She gave me until tonight to consider the offer.'

'You are considering?' Nicky was shocked. 'That must have taken her aback.'

'I think it did.'

'And have you?'

'Yes,' Gunboat said and finished breakfast. 'It's gonna be a no.'

Nicky studied him, suddenly wary. 'You are more dangerous than I thought. Why have you turned down twice the amount of money? And it's guaranteed, and doesn't depend on my winning. Do you want me to offer you still more?'

'Have I asked you?' Gunboat spoke softly, concealing contempt.

'No,' and Nicky only bowed his head in brief apology.

'And I shan't. I agreed on a deal and promised to teach you what I could.'

'And that is reason enough to turn down that money?'

'For me, yes. Five thousand—if you win—is enough to get me out of here.' He looked speculative. 'If you can guarantee that amount.'

'What does that mean? I made a promise, too,' Nicky answered sharply.

'She said you had to ask the rajah, and she'd make sure you'd not get the money.'

Nicky appreciated the point, but not as Gunboat expected. She had revealed a confidence in her influence over his father. If he took up that direct challenge, he could possibly lose. He wasn't sure whether his father would back him.

'If you can't get the money ...' Gunboat began.

Nicky started, blinked, and carefully slipped off a ring. Gunboat had noticed it: gold with a single rectangular clear stone.

'Keep this. I will redeem it for five thousand when the time comes. If not, it is yours.'

Gunboat examined it. It shone with internal colours like a kaleidoscope. The stone was the size of a fingernail.

'It looks like glass.'

'It is a diamond.'

Gunboat held it between his fingers. Its touch was cool, its edges and planes sharp. Never before had he held such riches. He suspected it could buy him a city block back in the Bronx. He returned it.

'You shouldn't buy men so easily.' He sounded foolish as he thought of the gold spurs and stirrups and bit.

'It's they who make it easy for people like me.' Nicky took it back, slipped it on to his finger. 'They want what I can grant them and crush their own souls. Am I to blame? I've thought often about that, but I've never found an answer.'

'You can help without having to buy them.'

'One,' Nicky said softly, 'becomes the other. They are both debts; both incur enmity.'

Gunboat would not understand. He had never been in a position to grant favours to men; never realized the sweetness of magnanimity. Princes could change destinies; greater princes, greater destinies.

'I am not saying I dislike my position,' Nicky continued. 'The puzzle is somewhat like the chicken or the egg. Which comes first? Do I corrupt men; or do they corrupt themselves? I offered, and you refused the ring; she offered and you refused the money. Have we affected you?'

'Yes. I feel a damned fool.'

'I am sorry.' Nicky looked genuinely concerned.

Gunboat laughed. 'Why? You tried. I failed.'

'Honest men are a constant moral puzzle,' Nicky said.

'So I'm told,' Gunboat said. 'But we all have our prices. You paid mine. Another time it would have been greater, and not within your power.'

'What was that?'

'The life of a woman. And a crack at the title.'

'Crack at what?'

'The title. I would have liked to have been a contender for the heavyweight championship of the world. I was never given the chance.'

'And the woman?'

'She died in Bombay.' Gunboat stopped, not wishing to mourn again. 'I miss her,' he added.

'You are fortunate to have known her,' Nicky said.

They fell silent. The sun crept up, its heat uncomfortable and its light almost unbearable. Crows flapped by, intermittently cawing, but even they had begun to fall silent. Flies buzzed, angrily energetic, while all around, creatures sought the shade, preparing for a noon that would still life briefly. Nicky squinted. His face, half-lit, appeared remote and distorted. He shifted so the face was fully shaded.

'I never knew my mother,' forcing himself to confide.

'You must remember something.'

'Nothing,' and he appeared puzzled. 'Yet I miss her. The woman's death changed your life. My mother's death changed the life of this whole family. Some deaths destroy those that remain alive.'

'Your father?'

'Partially.' He was about to go on, but he abruptly changed his mind as if he'd confided too much of his own vulnerability.

'You must take up her offer,' he said.

'Whose?'

'Miss Hobbs's.'

'I said I wouldn't,' Gunboat said.

'It would be wiser. Otherwise, she might…uh…make it difficult for you to remain. If I win you can turn down the money.'

'If you lose?'

Nicky rose. 'You take it. That was the price…for my defeat.' And left.

TWELVE

Gunboat swore. He had been pincered. Nicky's defeat or victory depended entirely on him. Either meant betrayal, of Nicky or Miss Hobbs. The one was more precious to him than the other, and yet the choice wasn't his to make. Nicky was the fighter in the ring. He could win if he wanted, lose if it was expedient. Gunboat had no idea what would occur. He was determined to teach Nicky all he knew, sweat his skill, his courage into the boy, determine him to win. Finally, a fighter depends on his heart. If it is clear and clean, he can bludgeon his way to victory. No one can impart that to him. He must have it in himself and snatch his victory whatever the consequences.

He had seen fighters defeated, not by themselves but by others: managers, fixers, wives, sweethearts, even money. They climbed in the ring with the fighter and hobbled him into defeat.

Gunboat bathed. For a while he lay on the bed, watching the fan spinning a warm breeze over his body. The palace imprisoned him: silent rooms, decaying riches, vague perfumes of palace women.

He dozed; he dreamed.

Calcutta. The night had been hot, humid. Sweat did not dry; it ran in rivulets to the ground. There was little breeze, and when it came it was warm, carrying the odours of the city: foods, sweat, dust, excrement, perfumes. Beyond the huge pressure kerosene lanterns the people moved in the shadows like fish through water. Quick, whispering, sparkling. The whites and the colours of their clothes, the teeth in the darkness of their faces, the gold on their fingers and around their necks, could only be glimpsed.

The sky was clear. The moon appeared to race across the sky, so white and full it lit the city with touches of silver. Smoke from cooking fires twisted into that light, like spirits rising up to meet the moon.

The ring was frail, shoddy. It was makeshift, and didn't appear it would hold the weight of two men. The posts were raw trunks, badly stripped and padded with jute bags tied with twine. They would hurt. The ropes were raw, unbound. They would burn. The planking was uneven, creaky. There would be no firm footing. The canvas, stretched over the planks, wasn't tight enough and gathered thick wrinkles. A tin bucket of tepid water and three bottles of ice water sweating in the heat stood beside the two stools in opposite corners of the ring.

Gunboat had moved through the crowd and now stood before the wooden steps that led up the ring. He had felt the pats on his back from the crowd through the flimsy terry cotton dressing gown. It had his name, hastily stitched, on his back. Calcutta was a sporting city. The crowd looked big: twenty thousand, possibly thirty thousand. The folding seats near the ring were all taken; the crowd stretched back across the maidan to standing room.

He heard the familiar murmur, then the roar. The local hero was making his way through the mob. He led a phalanx of supporters: trainers, managers, seconds. Gunboat's following had been smaller: a couple of seconds. His opponent wore a silk robe, bright red, trimmed with gold. He held his arms aloft often as he moved, and the roar rose each time. He reached the opposite corner, glanced at Gunboat, then away, responding to the crowd. He was two inches shorter than Gunboat and ten pounds lighter. His reach was two inches shorter, too. He was a good-looking man: a pencil moustache, wavy black hair, and a sharp clean face. He was in his early twenties. Gunboat was nearing forty.

Both men climbed into the ring. The lamps threw a fierce glare that lit the ring and the first two ringside rows. Beside each light a man dressed in a loincloth, his dark skin shining with perspiration from the added heat, squatted ready to pump up the fierce light if it should wane.

The fight was to be ten rounds. Gunboat stood still. He could not afford to expend the energy to dance. He had never fought in such heat, or smells. And he could feel his age.

Gunboat's second, an ex-havildar, Shiv Singh, took his dressing gown reverently. He fitted in the gum shield and towelled Gunboat's sweating body. Gunboat turned. Tiger knelt, praying. The crowd was mute in sympathy. Gunboat would have prayed if he'd been younger. Now he needed a miracle, and in imitation of his youth, he crossed himself. This was appreciated by the crowd. It gave the battle the necessary sanctity that crowds need before they observe the destruction of two men.

Gunboat had a simple strategy: Stay out of trouble. He stepped out, arms cocked, his left ready to jab out to keep Tiger at a distance.

It was in the fourth round that Gunboat saw the opening. He moved his right, quick and short. He felt the blow down his forearm, and Tiger's head snapped back. Gunboat followed with two quick lefts. Tiger's arms were down. He was looking tired, the eyes were closing. Gunboat threw a right to the heart.

The referee pulled him away. They stood back and watched Tiger fall. It was slow. His knees bent, one arm entangled in the ropes, held the body for a second, and then let it slide to the canvas. The crowd was silent.

The referee counted Tiger out, turned, and lifted Gunboat's hand. The crowd remained mute for a moment, then cheered half-heartedly.

Tiger's seconds jumped into the ring, and Gunboat turned to watch them try to revive Tiger. Shiv helped him on with his dressing gown and removed his gloves. The referee knelt now, and the managers climbed in. Gunboat saw them whispering.

'Get the doctor,' the referee ordered.

Gunboat felt a chill. He shivered. The air grew cold. He went to the gathering and knelt too. He saw the blood seeping from the ears.

'Oh Jesus.'

◆

He awoke, sweating, needing to escape.

The town offered little. The evening lamps were being lit. Men and women prayed briefly, quickly, to the light, and continued with their chores. Most lamps were simple: a wick stuck in coconut oil contained in an earthen holder. Others were hurricane, two or three were pressure lanterns.

The air was rich: spices, frying, jasmine, attar, offal, wood and dung smoke. The blends were continually changed by the subtle breeze.

Gunboat strolled past shops. They were spare rooms: some filled with jute sacks of rice and dal and pulses and wheat; others with spices; one or two sold cloth. On the footpath women sat in front of tiny piles of fresh vegetables and fruits; others squatted before them, haggling. Men grouped at tea stalls, sipping and smoking beedis. There was also a surprisingly large school; the compound was now empty of children.

Gunboat appeared to be known. He was smiled at often, invited in to sample tea or a spicy snack, talked to in a language he did not know. They accepted his ignorance good-naturedly. The women smiled or giggled depending on their age. Children trailed him, large-eyed in awe. Bullocks trudged in their cruel yokes; a few, old and neglected, nosed at the garbage in the company of pie-dogs. He turned off the main road, passing small houses. The men sat out, smoking, gossiping, resting from the day's labour.

He felt stiff from his own. He had worked out with Nicky for another hour in the evening. Twenty minutes of roadwork, twenty of the punchbag, and twenty in the ring. He had thought Nicky would have also been in pain, but he'd forgotten the resilience of youth. The prince had remembered his morning lessons: his guard remained up, his balance was strong, his right, however, still lopped. They had talked little except on the technicalities of the sport. The prince was insatiably curious about fighters, styles, footwork, clinches. He wanted not only the skill, but also the secret knowledge of the foul.

'You don't need it at this level,' Gunboat said.

'I want to win,' he said simply. 'In every sport there is a foul which can go unnoticed. In cricket you don't walk until the umpire raises his finger; in hockey you can maim a player by sliding your stick up his stick and breaking his knuckles; in polo you kick your opponent's feet out of his stirrups; in football you elbow him as he goes up to head; in—'

'I get the picture,' Gunboat said shortly. 'Is that what you've been taught?'

'No. I absorbed it with experience. I don't practice the foul, except in retaliation. I need to know when it is being done to me. Without it, one is helpless in any sport.'

'Okay,' Gunboat said. 'But first you learn the Queensberry rules. Then the Bronx rules.'

'Bronx?' he puzzled.

'Street fighting. You survive only by being faster and dirtier than the other bastard.'

'Ahhh…' He smiled, pleased with the simplicity.

Gunboat walked up the slope. The houses on either side buzzed with life: children, women, dogs. There were two cycle repair shops, and chokras worked in the dim light repairing the few machines. Further along a tailor hummed at his ancient machine, peering down at the stitches.

He missed Gertrude. He had not expected it; but over the year she had become habit. The familiar language they spoke in, the smoothness of her body on his, the child's gaiety and inquisitiveness. He yearned for her physically and emotionally. On the coming Saturday, after the dance, he'd take her home and make love savagely; possibly have her also the following afternoon after a lunch and a few beers. Her odour seemed real, the skin already under his fingertips, the erection poking deep into her.

The jeep honked. Gunboat stepped aside, but it didn't pass. Nicky sat at the wheel, Swami and an old man behind.

'Get in.'

Nicky spun the jeep around, scattering chickens, children, and dogs. He raced down to the highway, turned onto it, and accelerated away from the palace. Beyond the town was deep night.

'Where are we going?'

'To a homam.'

'Fine.'

The lights cut blackness: lit trees, culverts, the narrow road. Ahead, beyond their beam, eyes appeared like emerald stars out of the night. The lights caught the bullocks heading to town and were doused so as not to shine in their eyes as they swept past.

'What is that?' Gunboat asked.

'It is a ceremony of fire,' Nicky said. 'It is to protect us from evil. It will be performed by a priest in a village, and will take some time.'

'Where's the evil?'

'I don't know. I had a message from my grandmother to attend the homam with you. She thinks we both could need protection. It is an ancient ceremony that has been inscribed in the Vedas. When it has been done, we cannot be harmed.'

'Who's going to do the harming?'

Nicky didn't reply. His profile was impassive. He turned briefly to check their directions with the old villager, and then stared ahead.

'I don't know,' he finally said, as if he did know. 'I have many enemies. My grandmother would have taken me herself but she couldn't return in time.'

'I got no enemies,' Gunboat said. He was unsure. It had happened quickly, and he had not adjusted to the mystical direction of their journey. 'Maybe I'll watch.'

Nicky shrugged. 'It is up to you,' he said, but with enough

foreboding that Gunboat almost sensed creatures in pursuit.

'You believe in all that...?'

'In spite of my English schooling,' Nicky completed, and stopped.

Gunboat was American. America was a land of automobiles and toasters, pastel-coloured foods, and film stars. Magic was attributed only to their machines and motion pictures; both easily dismantled, examined, explained. If this could not be done it did not exist. Their world had been made simple. Their minds had followed. Gunboat would not understand: Beyond earth lay a universe, and some men could conjure with its swirling energies and materialize gods and demons to do their will.

'Try me,' Gunboat read the prince's silence.

Silence. Finally: 'Yes. I believe...' He searched, knowing words were inadequate.

'My thinking is in direct opposition to yours. You believe only in that which can be proved; I believe in that which will never be proved.'

'God?'

'A benevolent power, let's say,' Nicky said. 'Not a white man with a flowing beard.'

'Of course.'

'To balance, there must be a malevolent power. Both exist; both can be called upon to influence our actions.'

'I think I understand,' Gunboat said. 'I saw vibudhi materialize.' He saw the prince's surprise and chuckled. 'I couldn't explain, but I think I've finally believed it happened.'

'Who was the man?'

'A sadhu called Rajaram. He lives up in the hills.'

'I've heard of him,' Nicky said. 'He could just as easily materialize a vial of poison.'

The villager spoke. Nicky slowed and turned onto a dirt track. It wound through thick undergrowth. Eyes belonging to unseen creatures gleamed and passed. The old man became voluble. Nicky listened and spoke to him.

'He knew my grandfather well,' Nicky said in a lull. 'And once saw my great-grandfather. He has worked for the family three generations, and before that his father for three. He is the headman of the village we are going to.' The man spoke more; Nicky saddened. 'He also knew my mother.' The void would remain all his life.

The village was small, barely discernible. Oil lamps flickered. There were a dozen huts, a small shrine, and a simple brick house at the end. They walked to it. Gunboat noticed Swami held a heavy bag. An old woman stood at the entrance, silent, reverential to the prince. He shed his slippers, entered. Gunboat followed after removing his shoes.

A plump man, with the breasts of a woman, sat on a stool. In front was a three-foot brick-built square reaching knee height. Beside it were pots containing rice and ghee. A youth piled a flickering fire in the square with wood. In the shadows were three or four others, cross-legged, intent on the flames. Swami spilled his bag: coconuts, betel leaves, fruits, rice.

The prince sat; Gunboat, Swami, and the villager sat beside him. The Brahmin didn't look up: The spiritual was equal to the temporal. The flames leaped and hissed as ghee was poured. The Brahmin murmured to the fire. Nicky stared at the flames. An hour passed, then another. Once or twice, they were handed rice to throw into the fire; otherwise the Brahmin kept up the constant, soothing murmur.

The fire dwindled. All the ghee and the rice and coconut had been fed to the flames. The Brahmin rose stiffly and shambled out. The old woman brought the prince a brass plate. On it burned a lump of camphor. He took it and walked thrice around the fire and handed it to Gunboat. Gunboat did the same.

'Now I'm protected?' Gunboat said as Nicky turned the jeep.

'Yes.' He listened to Swami and added: 'We will have to return later for him to tie the thayethu. It is a…charm.'

'Sure. Like a rabbit's foot.'

'You can call it that.' The jeep bucked along the track and finally reached the highway. 'You must not mention this to my father or Miss Hobbs.'

'Doesn't the rajah believe?'

'He does but...' How could he disbelieve Miss Hobbs? She had got too close. 'Hungry?'

'Starved.' It was eleven. The night was quiet except for the hum of the jeep.

◆

Miss Hobbs waited. Gunboat knew that before he entered. Mohan had told Nicky; Nicky told him. They had eaten in the town, a meal had been prepared. To eat in the palace would have alerted Miss Hobbs, for the cooks would have had to explain.

She sat in a straight-back chair, reading a paperback. She didn't look up and put the book down only when Gunboat reached the bed.

She smiled. 'Where have you been?'

'With Nicky,' Gunboat said. They had rehearsed a story.

'I'm so glad he has you for company. He is a lonely boy.'

'Seems okay to me,' Gunboat said, pouring a whiskey. He offered, she refused.

'It's a bit late at night.'

'He was just showing me round the state,' he laughed. 'Bits of it, I should say.'

'It is the size of an English county,' Miss Hobbs said. 'Only a few square miles smaller than Somerset. What did you see?'

'He showed me the mines, and then we went into the hills to see whether we could spot any tigers. We hung around there...just by the waterhole near the old temple...' She nodded. 'But nothing showed, so we called it a night.'

'The rajah doesn't permit hunting,' Miss Hobbs said, as if it were a fatal weakness. 'I've shot tiger, and sambar and chital. I nearly got a panther once. Do you shoot?'

'Nope. I've never been invited on a shikar.'

'You're missing a great experience.'

'That's the story of my life.'

'It's so exciting,' not hearing him. 'Sitting up on a machan at night, waiting for a tiger to find the bait. The first time there were three of us. Two officers of the Khyber Rifles and me. We had a flask of brandy to keep us warm. In Kamoun it's very cold at night. We sat there for three hours, cuddled together for warmth. Of course they were both absolute gentlemen, you understand. Then it came. It was such a magnificent creature; so beautiful I nearly cried. It stood there sniffing. The goat was bawling away and the tiger slowly padded up to it. Jim got it first shot, thank God.'

'Why?' Gunboat was mesmerized. Her eyes were alight, hair almost bristling from memory.

'If you wound a tiger, you have to go after it. Otherwise it turns into a man-eater.' She slumped, the memory fading.

'You had a good time in India then.'

'Yes,' softly to herself. 'We enjoyed ourselves.' Then sharply: 'But we earned the right to. We worked damned hard to build this country into one nation. It used to be a lot of squabbling princes once, fighting against each other. It won't last as one nation for long. You see, it will break up. We gave our lives for India,' she finished bitterly.

Graves: stained marble and granite headstones. The inscriptions faded, worn by heat and rain. Almost smooth to touch, barely legible. The deaths were not magnificent. Plunder and glory and the sword. They were sad and wretched—cholera, chickenpox, malaria, jaundice, sunstroke. India had claimed them softly and cruelly.

Gunboat had visited the cemeteries. They were high-walled, neglected, lonely. Gertrude had a grandfather buried in the one just off Hosur Road in Bangalore. Once in a while the family would remember. The grave was layered with leaves and dust. They would order the chowkidar to sweep it, and for a day it would look as a memory preserved. But the flowers would fade and rot. Soon it would be completely forgotten.

'Have you decided?' she asked abruptly.

'Yes.' Gunboat swirled the drink. 'I'll take up your offer.'

She smiled. 'You're no different from us.' Then warily, 'Why?'

'I guess I need the money,' Gunboat said. 'Ten goes a lot further than five.'

'Twice as,' she said. She fumbled in the folds of her sari and brought out a bundle of notes. 'Here's five.' She held out the money, watching him. 'For betraying the yuvaraj.'

'I trust you.' Gunboat didn't move. 'Give it to me after the fight.'

'I don't trust you,' she came over, arms brushing. 'I like to own what I buy. Take it.'

Gunboat did, dropping it on the bed. The notes scattered, some blown to the floor by the fan. They appeared to sting his hand, and he glanced down at his palm. It was damp.

'I have to admit I am surprised,' Miss Hobbs said, watching the large notes float, ripple, fall. 'I thought you were like the rajah. He doesn't compromise his principles, and that can be impossible at times.' She remained close. Her odour was French perfume and perspiration.

'Yeah,' Gunboat said, and stepped away.

'You like me, don't you?' she asked.

'Sure,' he lied.

'That means you don't,' she chuckled. 'Never mind. I think we can be friends of circumstance.' Then in realization, she laughed. 'Such vanity. You think I might want to have an affair. Why give up a rajah for a fighter?'

'No reason at all.' Gunboat was relieved.

Suddenly, as if she could no longer bear the sight, she stooped and gathered up the notes. Carefully, she bundled them and tucked them under his pillow.

'The servants might steal the money,' she explained, and went to the door. 'Isn't it a pity the whole wall of that temple has collapsed?'

Gunboat stiffened. Nicky had given no details. She waited.

'Yeah,' he said. 'But I couldn't see too much.'

'Of course,' she acknowledged the lie so that he knew it and left.

THIRTEEN

The rajah's car was a Silver Cloud. Gunboat sat next to him, in the back. He admired the Rolls-Royce: the seats were leather stamped with crests, the wood polished walnut. A small pennant fluttered on the bonnet. It rode the uneven highway smoothly.

'This is all that remains of our power,' the rajah said. 'A car with a flag. Soon they will not even allow us that. Once we were given gun salutes.'

'You don't like the changes?'

'No, but I suppose princes must fall. It is history. If an emperor has, why not a mere prince? The title passes away with me, you know. Nicky will have to be a mister.'

'He doesn't appear to object.'

'What does that matter? He has no choice. It will be difficult for him to adjust. He was raised as the yuvaraj, but he must live as an ordinary man.'

The golden Labrador lay curled at their feet. The rajah fell silent, dreamy in thought. Gunboat felt comfortable with him. He spoke only when the rajah woke from his reveries. That was seldom, and the journey was only two hours long. By seven that evening they would reach Bangalore.

Gunboat was grateful that Nicky had released him early Friday afternoon to hitch a ride with the rajah.

Nicky and Gunboat had worked hard. They'd run each morning and evening, sparred for fifteen minutes daily, and talked strategy for an hour. Swami, Mohan, and two other retainers had kept watch. If any of Miss Hobbs's informers approached, they signalled. Gunboat and Nicky would stop and sit until the person had passed. The only report Miss Hobbs received was they talked a lot and did little.

The prince admired Joe Louis. He wanted to emulate the ex-heavyweight champion of the world, to understand the ingredients that made him so exalted.

'There are a number of reasons,' Gunboat explained. 'Skill, luck, strength, hunger.'

'Hunger?'

Gunboat sighed. 'Not just belly hunger. That's important, but hunger to win. Victory must taste like a steak in a starved man's mouth. It must also be the single most important thing in your life. Once you lose that, you lose. Period.'

'I want to win.'

'Only one fight. It is an indulgence on your part.' They climbed into the ring, circled.

'I wouldn't make a professional?' Nicky jabbed, his guard dropped a fraction.

'No way. You got other things in life. Boxing is pain. Physical and emotional. You get yourself hurt, bad: cut mouths, eyebrows, noses, cheeks, ribs, heart. And it's very lonely in the ring.'

'I can stand pain,' Nicky said, circling. He jabbed. Gunboat blocked.

'Crouch more,' Gunboat ordered. 'If you stand upright, you got no balance. You're dropping your guard. Keep circling, keep coming. Jab, jab, jab, jab.'

'I can stand pain,' Nicky repeated, defiant.

'Sure,' Gunboat humoured him and took a jab on his forearm.

'Try me,' Nicky ordered. 'You've never come at me. All you do is keep blocking everything I throw.'

'You first got to learn to throw 'em.' He moved away. 'Besides, I'm too strong for you.'

'How will I understand then?'

Gunboat complied. For a minute they circled, jabbed, feinted.

There were many openings. He needed to be accurate and sure. The prince dropped his guard an inch. Gunboat snaked out his left, firmly, yet gently, judging it to a nicety. It caught Nicky on the side of his nose; it stung more than hurt.

The reaction was as expected. A moment of surprise, and then a terrible fury. Nicky came at him swinging, cursing. Arms and legs trying to damage, wound, kill. Gunboat stood, parried easily, until the prince tired. The anger was not spent, only the body. He glared at Gunboat, pouring sweat, heaving, readying for another assault.

'And you got to have discipline,' Gunboat said. 'I could have taken you out a dozen times. You have to take the pain and hold it inside you.'

The eyes held their glitter, then the cruelty slowly subsided. The veneer was thin; he had been bred too long as a ruler. Arrogance took a couple of generations to die.

'You are right.' Nicky spoke conversationally. 'Try me again.'

'Another day.'

'No,' he commanded. 'Now.'

He crouched, circled. His guard remained up when he jabbed. He came forward, unafraid, watchful. They feinted, ducked, weaved, jabbed. Nicky threw a sudden right, catching Gunboat's cheek. Gunboat covered, stepped back quickly as if hurt, and Nicky followed fast. His guard dropped, Gunboat threw a left, catching him on the mouth. It hurt. Nicky didn't flinch. The blood seeped from his lip. Momentarily, he nearly reverted to his fury; then, tightly in control, he came forward.

'That's better,' Gunboat said.

He didn't come out from behind his guard. Nicky jabbed twice more: at his head, then the belly. Both were blocked.

'I kept control,' he said and relaxed.

Swami hurried. He muttered furiously at Gunboat and gently dabbed the prince's mouth. It had begun to swell.

'You're not afraid,' Gunboat said.

'No.'

That Friday morning, after their workout, Nicky had driven Gunboat back to the priest. In daytime the land was harsh, spare. The heat broiled the rocks and brown hard earth, deep stands of timber, and tough lantana bushes. Miniature fields—green, swampy, busy—were cut between these ungiving boundaries. Bullocks pulled stick plows through the standing water; women planted green shoots of rice. Boys and bullocks worked the deep wells, pouring the glistening water down neat canals cut in the earth.

The priest waited. Gunboat had not noticed the room on his previous visit. It led off the hall. The room was crammed with innumerable objects of worship: Vishnu, Shiva, Krishna, Rama, Ganesh, Parvati, Venkateswara.

The priest had been sitting in front of his altar. Now he rose and sat on a small stool by the door. From a scrap of paper he picked two silver cylinders two inches long, pencil thick. He tied a black thread to one, held it to his breath for over five minutes, murmuring prayers, and then tied it around the prince's neck. He repeated himself for Gunboat, except his prayer was brief, almost perfunctory.

'What's in it?' Gunboat asked. The cylinder was hollow.

'A prayer,' Nicky said.

'I sure didn't get too many of his,' Gunboat joked. Nicky didn't smile.

◆

'Children are difficult,' the rajah said.

'Yes.' Gunboat was noncommittal.

The silence had lasted awhile. Warm breeze and dust whipped in through the open windows. He wound his half up to hear the rajah.

'If the rani were alive, my children would do what they were told,' he continued. 'They don't now. My daughter is refusing to marry the man I've chosen.'

'Back in the U. S. of A., the girl usually makes her own choice,' Gunboat said softly.

'Yes, yes, I know that. This isn't America. We have different traditions here.' He paused, sighed. 'But those are being changed.' He smiled wryly. 'We are the cause of our own self-destruction. I thought the western values I learned in England would enlighten. But they also change. They release spirits we cannot control.'

'Why didn't you remarry, sir?'

The rajah looked bleak, lonely. 'There is no one I wish to.' He turned to Gunboat. 'Wealth and power are the two major defects in our society. They are insatiable cravings which have to be fulfilled. The woman I marry will conspire to get her share of what we have, and this would be detrimental to my children.'

'Isn't that a cynical point of view? Maybe she will just love you.'

'I know my countrymen,' the rajah said. 'And women. We have been born to intrigue.' He stopped, and finally added as if he'd stood in judgement a moment, 'I was not.'

Gunboat thought, Nor was I.

Miss Hobbs's money lay in his tin case, back in the palace. He had not touched or looked at it since the night it had been given. It would be returned one day, complete. The rajah was indeed innocent. He appeared to be unaware of Miss Hobbs's power, or her manipulations. It was as if all had agreed to keep him uninvolved. Possibly he had made that demand himself. Yet, because of his very stillness, the one closest to him drew his power as if it were honey, to suck and strengthen.

Gunboat began cautiously: 'Do the children like Miss Hobbs, sir?'

'Of course they do,' the rajah said abruptly. 'She has worked very hard for them, and tried to be a mother.'

'It must be difficult...on a salary.'

'Yes, it is, but she devotes herself entirely to the family.'

'And the state?'

'Naturally. Both are one. It is the old rani that causes so many problems.'

'I met her,' Gunboat said. 'She appeared a...fine woman.'

The rajah's glance was hard, intolerant. 'It is only appearance.'

The rajah held his stare, then softened. 'I hear you met an interesting sadhu?' he continued conversationally.

Gunboat was relieved. He recounted his experience and the rajah was delighted. He laughed, as if finally a pagan had attained enlightenment. The rest of the journey was swift. The rajah recounted his mystical experiences, and Gunboat listened. The rajah's detachment, Gunboat understood, was not indifference; it was spiritual. He had been miscast as a ruler. He would have preferred to have been a sanyasi.

'You must come to lunch on Sunday,' the rajah said. The Rolls had stopped on Brigade Road, in front of his compound. 'About noon.'

'Thank you, sir.'

'And do bring a friend if you wish. The palace is on Palace Road, halfway down.'

◆

The city was familiar. He listened to the scooters and cars and cycle bells. Brigade Road shone with lights and movement. The odours here were the same: petrol fumes, frying foods, the fainter smells of flowers.

Jockey Rosen sat on his veranda. He wore a shirt and tie, a cigar in his mouth, and glass in his hand.

'It's Gunboat,' he called out to his wife. 'Bring another glass and ice.' They shook hands. 'How was Tandhapur?'

'Great,' Gunboat said, and sat. 'But it's good to be back. Kind of strange living in a palace.'

'I wouldn't mind that,' Jockey Rosen said. 'I've always dreamed of that.'

'We made a killing at Wednesday's races,' Anne said. 'Over twenty thousand rupees.'

'Which horse?'

'Dark Sun. Won by a length in the Maharajah's Gold Cup.' He laughed. 'I told Johnny, but of course he didn't listen.'

'He never does.' Gunboat smiled. 'Always believes he's got the inside track. How is he?'

'Fine. Still unemployed, and missing you.' Jockey Rosen studied him speculatively. 'You meet Miss Hobbs?'

'You know of her?'

'Certainly. She behaves as if she were a maharani.'

'I've seen her in Spencer's,' Anne said. 'Buying up the whole store. She is a very superior lady.'

'Yeah. I met her.' He thought of recounting the meetings, but stopped. 'Sure seemed in charge there.'

'Believe me, she is,' Jockey Rosen said. 'I met her once up in Bombay when I was riding for the maharajah of Baroda. She had a few admirers then, and she was very pretty.'

'Put on a lot of weight I guess. The good life.'

'No,' Anne said. 'She fell ill, I heard, and something went wrong.'

'India's really a small town,' Jockey Rosen said. 'Especially when it is about Europeans. You get to know just about everyone if you move around enough. It's the same with the upper-class Indians. They're such a small group, they live in each other's pockets. And we got nothing much else to do except gossip.'

◆

His room was claustrophobic. The familiar was mean, shabby, eloquent of his distress. He had once been, if not happy, satisfied with this existence. Now it only revealed his inadequacy. Nicky had been truthful: Princes corrupted without intention. They were a constant reminder that men were flawed, and weak, and purchased for their loose change.

The room was clean, however. Sita had swept and washed it daily, and untidily made his bed. He sat, aware of its hardness. It appeared so small, and he thought of him and Gertrude squeezed against each other under the thin sheets. God, how he wanted her. To kiss, to touch, to feel love; in bed, the directness of sex would erase the recent intricacies of his life.

Gunboat's was busy. He heard the click of balls from the bottom of the stairs. It was satisfying; it always reminded him of the pool halls on Simpson Street. He expected to see his friends, once he entered: Jimmy, Sanchez, Billy, Sticks, Tony. The homesickness nearly made Gunboat puke.

He made it inside. The hall was smoky, noisy. A dozen men waited on the benches.

'Gunboat.' Johnny was excited at his return. It helped erase part of the pain. He was embraced; almost carried to his stool. The beer was chilled; little changed in spite of one's efforts. 'Okay. Now tell me all what you've been doing?'

'Nothing much,' Gunboat said. 'I've been teaching Nicky the art of pugilism.'

'How is H. H. doing then?'

'Coming along well. Why the interest?'

Johnny grimaced. 'Not good. It's five to one against him.' He nearly wept. 'I tried to get better odds, but no one gave him a chance.'

'You seen this other guy fight?'

'Not exactly,' Johnny said. 'But we've heard he's good. He's bigger than H. H., and he is school champion.' He leaned close. 'What do you figure are H. H.'s chances?'

'Good,' Gunboat said. 'But it depends on how much better this English guy is.'

'Would you put money on H. H.?'

'Depends,' Gunboat said cautiously, not wanting to elaborate. At five to one, if he put up a thousand, he'd make a fortune. 'Anyone put money on him?'

'Only me,' Johnny said shyly. 'You know I always back losers.'

'So I heard. Why the faith in Nicky?'

'I want to see an Indian beat a white guy,' Johnny said bluntly. 'I don't mean you. You're not the same as them. And,' he added slyly, 'if H. H. wins, look at the fortune I clear up.'

'How much you put on?'

'Two hundred. If you lend me another two, I could put that on for you.'

'Sure, why not? I've got to show faith in my fighter. How much am I owed?'

Johnny reached for the accounts book. Studied it carefully, calculated, and announced: 'Hundred and fifty.'

'That will do for starters.'

Gunboat stood. 'I gotta go.'

'To see Gertrude?' Johnny sounded worried.

'What's wrong?'

Johnny looked apologetic, 'I've seen her around with that fellow Malcolm.'

FOURTEEN

Gertrude's mother peered from behind the veranda lattice.

'Who is that?'

'Me,' Gunboat said, and stepped into the light.

He stopped, entered, filling the veranda. There was a portrait of the Queen of England above the door, framed photographs of the English countryside on the walls, family photographs on the tables. He sat opposite her.

'What a shock you gave me! Were you standing out there long?'

'No. I just got here. Is Gertrude in?'

'Oh, she's out,' the mother said too quickly. 'What a pity. If only she'd known you were going to call.'

'I did tell her,' Gunboat said flatly. 'She knew I'd be back Friday night.'

'I think she just went to the pictures with her sister.'

'Not Malcolm?'

Gertrude's mother shifted uneasily. He sensed her unhappiness at having been left to deal with him. The chair creaked. Gunboat did nothing to ease her discomfort.

'He's just a friend, Gunboat. She does miss you. All she ever did was mope around the house until—'

'I bet.'

He was angry now; the grief at his loss would come later. It would not be as painful as the loss of Mona; each had its own measure of bitterness.

'She is only a child, my son,' her mother coaxed. 'You must remember that. You are so much older, and wiser. She likes dancing and pictures, and…' She paused delicately. 'You don't.'

She studied him. His face was down and looked impenetrable. She was truly fond of him. He was a good man, always so friendly with her and her husband, not aloof like the other Europeans. He was admittedly not from their class. He behaved a gentleman, but wasn't.

She suspected Gertrude and he were lovers, and that made her uneasy. This was a small town, and though Gertrude was discreet, it could become common knowledge. It wouldn't do for a girl to be considered easy. Gunboat was wrong for Gertrude. His advantages were white; his disadvantages, age and exhausted future. She did not want her child to go to America. It was a strange and distant country.

Malcolm was of her age, her culture, and he would be going home soon. They could go together, settle in London near her relatives, comfortable in a country they knew of so well. She wasn't sure she wanted to leave. All her friends had, many cousins as well, and they wrote glowingly of home. Yet it wasn't home. This was. Yet too, it wasn't. They had been abandoned, and forgotten, but they still had a place here. Warm, familiar, not uncomfortable. There was little future for the young unless they adapted to India. Became Indians. Wore saris and tilak marks and behaved like them. She knew she couldn't; her past was too deeply ingrained. The children could; or leave. For Gertrude and her sister, it was best they left. Maybe she and her husband would follow.

'I'll call in tomorrow.' Gunboat stood. 'Lunchtime. Tell her to be here.' He was restless, wanting to escape this rejection.

'I'll tell her,' her mother said gently. 'I know she will want to see you.'

Gunboat strode out. He needed a drink bad. It had been some time since he'd gotten roaring, fighting drunk, and this was a worthy occasion.

◆

Nicky climbed the steps of his sister's Bangalore home. The house was grand and set deep within a garden. The driveway was lit by carriage lamps and curved round an ornate fountain to the steps.

The house was old, solid Georgian and had been in her husband's family over a hundred years. It was almost a palace and contained many rooms that led intricately one into another. A servant met him and led him through the vast reception hall and down the many corridors. His sister and husband lived in one small wing; she found it more manageable. Relatives and grandparents lived in the other rooms, most of which were sparsely furnished.

The wing his sister inhabited was cosy. She had it decorated as an apartment, a living room filled with paintings, a dining room for a dozen guests, a book-lined study, a bedroom, and a veranda.

The women sat out on the veranda. His grandmother sat between his sisters; in the shadows he noticed a fourth. He stopped. His aunt rose.

'How are you, Nicky?'

'I didn't know you were here.'

'Why? Wouldn't you have come?'

He hesitated, then stepped out in the veranda and took a chair. His aunt had luminous eyes: large, gentle, in a small face that had a prominent front tooth. She reached his shoulder and was slim and pliant.

'Yes, I would have,' he said defiantly. It was natural for them to gather. 'How have you been keeping?'

'Not well,' she said. 'My hip keeps giving me trouble.'

As a child Rukmani had jumped on her and fractured her right hip. He realized it had been some years since he'd seen her. She had aged, grown frailer. There were pain marks round her mouth.

As a boy he had seen her often. He and his sisters had visited her house in Bangalore twice, thrice a month. They played in her garden and explored the exotic storerooms: She had a marvellous collection of gadgets and antiques and sheer junk. Then, inexplicably, when Miss

Hobbs came, the visits grew less frequent. He had been sent to school in England, and he had not seen her since his return. His father did not discuss her; she had been banished.

'And Nandu?' Her husband.

'He's well, and very busy.' She measured him. 'You've grown just like your father.'

'Did you do what I told you?' his grandmother interrupted brusquely. She reached out, bared his chest, and saw her answer.

'Why?' Nicky asked.

'A precaution,' she began cautiously. At times it was difficult to judge Nicky's allegiance. He was close to his father.

'Tell him,' Sushila said abruptly. 'He should know. At least it will show him what kind of woman she is.'

'Your aunt...' his grandmother began.

'I'll tell him.' She brought her chair closer. The light caught the emerald stud in her nostril; it was cold green. Around her neck and her wrists were matching necklace and bangles. 'A month ago, I went to see this sadhu, Vishvanath. I'd heard about him from some friends, and they told me he was a wonderful man. It was to consult him about some of my problems. I didn't tell him I was coming but when I got to see his house I had been expected and he was waiting. He advised me about my problems...mostly to do with property... then he added that a spell had been put on our family. I told him he was talking nonsense. He insisted that it was the truth, and that if I allowed him to do a special puja he would reveal who cast the spell. I thought he was just trying to get some money out of me and at first I refused. Then my husband insisted that I should perform the puja. So I returned, and he did the puja. It was quite long. At the end, a chatty that had been hanging from a hook fell and shattered. Do you know what was in it?'

The others did. They nodded, eager once more for the revelation. Nicky shook his head.

'You remember that gold-bordered green sari of mine?'

'No.'

'You must,' Rukmani said. 'She wore it for Sushila's wedding. The one with the gold threads running right through it.' Nicky shrugged, impatient for the point.

'A piece had been cut from it,' his aunt continued, 'and placed in that chatty. You know, I told you that sari was missing, and I thought it had been stolen by one of the servants and...' She would have wandered off.

'So?'

'What do you mean, "so"?' His aunt was amazed. She looked at the others and laughed. They joined, conspiratorial. 'Don't you understand? Someone had used it to cast a spell against me and others.'

'Which others?'

'There was a piece from your grandmother's choli and...' She dived into her small purse and pulled out a silver and gold medallion, 'this.' She placed it in his palm. 'You remember it?'

They watched Nicky turn it over. It was a thin gold coin: Lord Ganesh on one side, on the other an inscription.

'It is yours, isn't it?' his grandmother demanded.

'Yes.' He had lost it some time back; it was a gift from his grand-aunt on his return from England. It had been in his dresser drawer. 'And this was in the chatty as well?'

'Yes.'

'How did he get hold of the chatty? Did he cast the spell?'

'No. It's a duplicate.' His aunt leaned back and raised a fist in question. 'Who do you think the sadhu described as the person who had the spells cast?'

'Miss Hobbs.'

'How did you know?' She was deflated.

'I presumed,' Nicky said loftily.

'But it wasn't only her,' Sushila said. 'It was also that servant woman, Valli. He described her as well, didn't he?'

'Yes,', his grandmother said. 'But she isn't important.'

'Nothing of father's?'

'No. Why should she? He is important to her.'

He fingered the medallion. It felt real. It was worn quite smooth, possibly a century old. It had hung on the chain of an ancestor. Strangely, he wasn't surprised by Miss Hobbs's actions. It was a familiar strategy, not only in the courts of princes, but in the villages and towns. The need to defeat by summoning gods and demons to take sides in the battles was ingrained deep in mythology.

'Is this enough?' Nicky fingered the silver cylinder.

'Yes,' his grandmother said. 'You must wear it all the time. Never remove it.'

'Never?' He tried to be humorous.

'Never,' she spoke sharply.

'Why did Gunboat have to attend the ceremony as well?'

'Because he will be close to you for some time. He must also protect you.'

He believed his grandmother. She was used to the falseness of people. Her husband had held court in those old days, delicately manoeuvring between the British and his own desires. He had overstepped, and lost; removed with the single stroke of a pen, and she had been reduced from a rani to a mere mortal. He had been betrayed, not by friends but by family. The old rajah had been a philosopher prince, a Sanskrit scholar versed in the Vedas, and a social reformer. A tour of Europe had influenced his thinking, and on his return he had opened a dozen schools around the state for the education of boys and girls, this in itself revolutionary. He had also given three scholarships for a schoolboy or girl to attend an Indian university to study science or economics. However, carried away by his zeal he had then preached sedition to his schoolchildren: refusing to allow them to study British history and making heroes of Indian revolutionaries. An uncle had informed the authorities, and instead of receiving the throne as a reward, he was passed over by the British for Nicky's father.

Familial vendettas were more common than attack from exterior enemies, and Miss Hobbs was, Nicky realized, family. She knew it well: studied its rise, met all the characters, their weaknesses and strengths, and worked from within.

Nicky glanced at Rukmani. She was subdued, an unusual state. At nineteen she already had a wounded heart and expected never to recover from that sickness.

'You're not still carrying on, are you?' Nicky demanded with the exasperation of a younger brother.

'What would you know about that?' she snapped.

'She's always liked Prithivi,' Sushila came to her defence. 'Even in school.'

Both sisters had attended school in Bangalore. Sushila had left early to marry; Rukmani had remained. She had done her Senior Cambridge and was now a student in Maharani College, studying for a B. A. It was a formal pattern: school, B. A., marriage, children. She had not expected to deviate, was quite content to settle down with Prithivi. Now her life had been tilted, and she was deeply unhappy.

'She wants to go abroad,' Sushila announced.

'What for?' Nicky asked.

'To study. I want to join a college there. Maybe Oxford like father.'

'You don't want to do that,' Nicky said abruptly. 'I'm sure you'll find someone else.'

'There's no one else. And I've got as much right to go abroad as you have.'

'I'm not going,' Nicky said. 'Least not for a while. I have to finish school first.'

'You mustn't,' his grandmother added to Rukmani. 'You get all these silly ideas in your head. And you'll never come back.'

'Anything's better than Fat Gopi,' Rukmani said stubbornly. She was expected any moment to throw a tantrum. They waited. She noticed the expectation and instead beguiled: 'Atha did higher studies, so why can't I?'

'I never went abroad,' her aunt said, and then added with harboured bitterness: 'My parents sent your father, but they wouldn't send me. I wanted to do my doctorate there, but in those days women were not expected to do all that.'

She had been an exception. Of her generation, Nicky's aunt had not only taken an engineering degree but had also completed a master's and doctorate at Mysore University. She was a professor now, a specialist in structural problems. Her independence had surprised the family and won the admiration of the women, but few had followed. They had preferred the security of the family.

'Who put this idea in your head?' his grandmother asked.

She'd been listening, studying Rukmani through narrowed eyes.

'No one,' Rukmani said, avoiding her grandmother's stare.

'I see.' Taking this as an answer, her grandmother fell silent.

In repose her face could be melancholy: Deep lines formed on either side of her mouth, and her skin appeared to pit and pucker. Nicky thought she did not look well.

'Miss Hobbs,' Sushila said triumphantly. 'You are a fool to listen to her.'

'I'm not, and don't you dare call me that.'

They would have fought, but their grandmother silenced them. They sat back, glaring at each other, and for a moment Nicky thought how much alike the four women could suddenly be. Age faded, revealing similarities rather than differences.

'Rukmani, think carefully,' her grandmother said softly. 'You don't want to go abroad. Not until you are married.'

'I have thought about it,' she said. 'In the west all the girls go to college and take higher studies.'

'You are not a western girl.' Her grandmother spoke sadly as if not quite believing herself. 'You are a Hindu woman.'

'And marry whom my father chooses?' Rukmani spat. 'Never Fat Gopi. I'd—I'd—prefer to kill myself,' she finished dramatically.

'Good,' Sushila said with satisfaction. 'That will solve the problem.'

His grandmother and aunt were silent, preoccupied. Nicky thought of the simplicity: Miss Hobbs knew his father's pride. Only a prince could marry his daughter, not a well-off commoner. Fat Gopi was ideal. He suited the requirements, yet insulted Rukmani's beauty. A mere suggestion to Rukmani was enough. Miss Hobbs knew how stubborn his sister could be; once an idea had taken root she would cling to it and not rest until she'd achieved her ends. She would go abroad, whatever the cost. And when she left, Nicky would be alone. Sushila, as a married girl, had her own household to care for; his father was already hostile to his grandmother. Nicky wondered how long it would take for Miss Hobbs to turn his father against him.

They dined, quiet and subdued. The bearers moved softly, trying not to disturb the mood and incur their mistresses' wrath. Sushila's husband was out-of-station, touring his state.

'Gunboat told me she'd offered him ten thousand not to teach me to box,' Nicky said abruptly.

His grandmother paused, a neat, small ball of rice held delicately in her fingers. Nicky admired the precise way in which she ate and tried to emulate her.

'Where did she get the money?' she asked.

'Her salary,' his aunt said.

'Not enough,' his grandmother said. 'She has to support her child in school. Has she given him it?'

'Yes. Five thousand.'

'She must have sold something,' his grandmother said. 'What?'

They deliberated. It had to be a single item to fetch that amount. They had not noticed missing paintings; besides those were difficult and too visible. She could not sell property; she had none.

'Jewellery,' Sushila announced.

'She has none,' his grandmother said. 'Nothing worthwhile anyway.' She stopped. 'Not hers. Ours.'

The silence returned. The jewellery was kept in a palace vault. Banks were not to be trusted, and government tax officials remained in ignorance. The vault was of concrete, lined with steel almirahs, each locked, and the keys kept in a safe with the vault key. Only the immediate family could visit the vault.

'We must find out which piece has been taken,' his grandmother said, 'and to which moneylender it was sold.' A bearer took her silver thali, and she moved to the small basin in a corner of the room to wash her hands. 'When we have the proof we can show it to your father. That will finish her,' she added with satisfaction. She appeared to have changed. The enemy was now more visible, more vulnerable.

'Nicky, make Gunboat ask her for more money.'

'I don't think I can. He's a difficult man.'

'No one is difficult,' his grandmother said. She carefully made a paan—three heart-shaped leaves filled with betel nut—and popped it in her mouth. 'Tell him I will give him as much as she does.'

'I'll try.'

'But don't let him know what it's about.'

'How are we going to find out which moneylender?' Sushila asked. 'There are so many.'

'We know the commissioner of police. He will give me a list.'

Nicky's room in the Bangalore palace was cluttered. He kept his sports equipment in town: cricket bats, saddles, hockey sticks, squash and tennis racquets, schoolbooks. It was late by the time he reached home, and Swami waited up to undress him and put him into bed. He had slept an hour when Swami woke him gently.

'It is the police,' Swami said. 'They wish to talk to you now. I told them…' He trailed away, apologetic.

FIFTEEN

A constable, armed with an Enfield .303, stood at the entrance of Shoolay police station. He looked tired and glanced incuriously at Nicky, Swami, and the chauffeur. The interior was simple: a washed granite floor, a sergeant's desk, a rack of rifles chained and locked, and closed doors.

The sergeant at the desk had grey hair, an unlined face, and wary, watchful eyes. Nicky sensed the man knew who he was, though at first he made no effort to rise until Swami announced: 'This is the yuvaraj.'

The hesitation was fractional, enough to allow him to know that the sergeant no longer held yuvarajs in high esteem, but not enough to reveal any contempt. He rose. Then Nicky smiled, waved him down. The gesture, Nicky knew, softened the man. He remained standing, even unbent to bow his head quickly. The lifetime habit of deferring to feudal princes—white and Indian—was impossible to change completely.

'What is your name?' Nicky asked.

'Lekhraj, sir,' the sergeant answered. The boy at least revealed some interest and treated him with courtesy.

'Sergeant Lekhraj,' Nicky said. 'I was called here because a friend of mine is in your cell.'

'Yes, sir. I made the call.' He studied his old, worn ledger. It looked like a school attendance book, with neatly drawn lines dividing the page.

'Two friends in fact, sir.'

'Two.' Nicky turned to Swami as if possibly he knew the other. Swami shook his head. 'I was told it was a gentleman called Gunboat Jack.'

'Yes, sir. The other is…Jaganathan Swaminathan.'

'I don't know him,' Nicky frowned. 'They are together?'

'Yes, sir.' He cleared his throat and recited: 'We were summoned to a disturbance in Murray's Bar on Mahatma Gandhi Road at approximately twelve twenty-five a.m. I sent two constables to investigate the disturbance. The man, Gunboat Jack, was intoxicated on liquor and had caused some damage to the premises. His companion, Swaminathan, aided and abetted him in the damage. My constables arrested them both and brought them back here, sir. Mr Jack then insisted I wake you, sir, and request you to bail him out. And his friend. The owner of Murray's Bar, Mr Sam Owen, informed my constable that the damage to his bar ran to over two hundred fifty rupees, sir.' He glanced away, hesitated, and added: 'I would think it was an excess sum, sir. Only a few glasses were broken and an old clock. Mr Jack threw the glasses at the clock. He did not resist arrest.'

'What is the bail?'

'Only the magistrate can set bail, sir. He will do that in the morning.' He tugged at his loose-fitting khaki shirt. The material was faded, frayed at the edges. 'We have not yet pressed charges, sir. The sub-inspector thought it best you be informed immediately.'

'Is he in?'

The sergeant picked up his cap. It was a foot high, narrow, striped red and black, and bore his rank in a brass badge. He adjusted it and marched to one of the doors. He knew what would occur inside the room. The sub-inspector would do the prince a favour. Mr Jack and Swaminathan would be released; the matter forgotten. He had seen it happen often, even in far more serious cases, murder included. The rich were released, the poor condemned.

He knocked, opened the door, and announced: 'The yuvaraj, sir.'

Nicky entered. Swami would have followed, but the sergeant firmly shut the door and marched back to his desk.

The sub-inspector was a youth. He looked in his early twenties and wore a curled moustache that was the only noteworthy feature in an otherwise round and pleasant face. He rose immediately and offered a chair.

'I am sorry to disturb you so late, sir,' he began.

'I've been told,' Nicky said abruptly. He appeared to have changed, for he sat stiffly, watched coldly. 'May I see them?'

If the sub-inspector had revealed the same weary anger as the sergeant, Nicky would have unbent. He had, with little effort, made the sergeant believe that possibly they were both equals. With the sub-inspector that wasn't necessary. The man was willing to fawn.

'Certainly, sir.' The sub-inspector immediately opened the door. Nicky stood slowly and walked out, past the sergeant and Swami.

The cell was at the rear. It was as simple as the building: a granite room with bars, and an immensely heavy lock. Gunboat Jack sat on the granite bench, singing 'Summertime.' He appeared content. He looked distant, as if only his physical remains were held in this cell; his memory and soul had travelled a great distance. He didn't notice Nicky. His eyes were closed.

Nicky examined Swaminathan. He was dark and appeared to blend into the shadows of the dimly-lit cell. His glasses caught the occasional glare. Both looked neat, though there was the strong and bitter odour of whiskey. Swaminathan turned, blinked owlishly at Nicky, then trying to lean, slid down the side of the wall.

'Your prince has come,' he announced to Gunboat, and giggled.

'Please be quiet,' the sub-inspector shouted at Swaminathan, and then, softly to Nicky: 'I am most sorry, sir.'

'Hey,' Gunboat said. 'You think I'm gonna turn into a pumpkin now.'

'We have no pumpkins here,' Swaminathan laughed. 'Mangoes. You turn into a mango.'

Gunboat rose, helped Swaminathan to his feet. Gunboat was a head taller than the Indian and held him easily as if he were so much straw. He also appeared to be protective of his companion, for he was enormously gentle.

'Hey, Prince, how you doing?' Gunboat leaned against the bars, exhaled, and drove Nicky back a pace.

'Fine, thank you.'

Gunboat studied Nicky, head cocked, as if trying to get him into focus. Suddenly he laughed. He realized that for the first time Nicky was genuinely unsure of how he should behave. He was unaccustomed to drunks and jails and was struggling to maintain his dignity.

'Hey, Prince, you ever had a drink?' Gunboat asked. He reached to touch Nicky; the sub-inspector stepped brusquely between.

'It is all right,' Nicky said. 'He will not harm me. No, I've only tasted Scotch. I don't like it.'

'Jeez. I love the stuff. It does you a lot of good, you know. Helps the liver, puts some pizzazz in your blood. You gotta try it.'

'Possibly when I'm older,' he said, trying to placate Gunboat.

'You gotta try it now, Prince. Be corrupted now; later it's too late. You get control, you get used to it.' Gunboat remembered and pushed Johnny forward. 'This is my buddy, Jaganathan Swaminathan.' He stopped, surprised. 'Hey, I said it right didn't I, Johnny?'

'You did, first time.'

'Shake hands,' Gunboat commanded.

Neither Johnny nor Nicky moved. Johnny appeared to be sober, slightly, under Nicky's incurious stare. He also seemed to have lost his original boldness. It was as if the cell, Gunboat, the heady drunkenness were not real. But Nicky was conscious.

Nicky frowned. He felt uneasy and uncomfortable. He didn't like Swaminathan; drunk, the young man was intolerable. In another circumstance they would never have met. He saw Swaminathan—a Brahmin, poor, possibly a degree-holder, unemployed.

'You puritan?' Gunboat asked softly.

'No,' Nicky said, and added, 'Hello, Swaminathan.'

'Hello,' Johnny said quietly.

Neither touched hands; they nodded in bare recognition of each other. Johnny knew also he would not have met the yuvaraj so informally under normal circumstances. Gunboat considered forcing them to shake hands, then decided not to. He sensed they both would have to cross barriers that they considered insurmountable, and he did not want to damage Johnny's chances of using the prince's influence to get him a good job. He thought that Nicky appeared to react almost exactly the way Johnny had when he had bumped into Sita, the cleaning girl. A certain invisible stain that needed to be erased.

'Can they be released?' Nicky asked the sub-inspector.

'Certainly, sir.' He called, 'Sergeant!'

The sergeant marched stiffly in. He had the key already in his hands and wordless, he unlocked the door. Gunboat and Johnny stepped out, Johnny still supported by Gunboat though he appeared to be able to stand on his own two feet.

'Thank you,' Nicky said to the sub-inspector.

The sub-inspector was immensely pleased. His smile was ear to ear.

'It's my pleasure, sir. My name is Chandrasekhar, sir.' He followed Nicky out. 'If there is anything further I can do, please do not hesitate to let me know.'

'I will,' Nicky said. 'Thank you, Sergeant Lekhraj.'

The older man smiled briefly, nodded. He took it as his due and offered the prince nothing.

◆

Both men breathed deep. The night was cool, silent. Brigade Road was deserted except for a lone cyclist and the palace car. There was a new moon, a sliver of silver, and a sky bright with stars.

'I am going home,' Johnny announced and began to walk up the road without saying anything further. He swayed every third step.

'We'll drop you,' Nicky said.

'Let your chauffeur drop him,' Gunboat said. 'We'll walk back to my place and wait. I need the air.'

Nicky gestured. Swami ran after Johnny, steered him around, and led him back to the car. He stepped in meekly. The chauffeur drove off.

The shops were shuttered. On the small wooden platforms on which during the day sweetmeats, grains, fresh vegetables, and household needs were stacked, men huddled in thin covering, slept, and shivered. As Gunboat, Nicky, and Swami passed, Swami a few steps behind the two, the sleeping men turned and tossed, haunted by their nightmares.

'They ever bother you?' Gunboat asked.

'Yes,' Nicky said, though he did not look at them. 'Does that surprise you?'

'Yeah.' Gunboat considered and added, 'The rich here appear blind to me at times. Most times. You live in big houses, drive big cars, spend more money in an hour than these people make in a year.'

Nicky glanced at Gunboat. He looked serious, though not totally sober. Now and then he swayed against him, bumping him towards the edge of the road.

Nicky chuckled. 'Conscience isn't the special privilege of white men. Princes, and a few politicians, have also been lucky enough to have been granted one. I see them, Gunboat. Their poverty is our poverty. As long as they remain poor, the country does as well.'

Gunboat looked at Nicky in surprise. He felt unsure. The tone of voice appeared to patronize him, yet Nicky held his glance steadily.

'Are you a Marxist?'

'No. I have tried to read him but found him difficult. Possibly I'm too young. I am a feudal socialist. That is a special Indian hybrid, not to be found in any other part of the world. We cannot change what we are, nor what we must become.'

They had covered half the distance and were mid-slope to Gunboat's compound. Gunboat's hard heels were the only night sounds. Nicky and Swami walked softly in their chappals.

'Why did you get drunk?' Nicky asked. He had a boy's curiosity suddenly for an adult's actions.

'A woman,' Gunboat said quietly, and the question revived a part of the pain.

Whiskey was no balm, ever. Neither did it grant forgetfulness. Instead, it touched the source of the ache, the humiliation of rejection, and only made it more acute.

'What did she do?' Nicky could be irritatingly persistent, Gunboat discovered.

'Took up with another guy while I was in Tandhapur.'

'I am sorry,' Nicky said, as if it were his fault. 'Why don't you go and beat him up?'

'That never does any good. It's not him, it's her.'

'Beat her then,' Nicky suggested. 'I had a driver once who regularly beat his wife. We had to sack him.'

'I did feel like that,' Gunboat said. 'That's why I decided to get drunk.' He sighed, shook his head. 'There'd always be another guy to take her from me. She's younger than I am and I guess I was a curiosity to her.'

'You love her then?'

Gunboat thought about that awhile. It puzzled him. He didn't consider himself in love with her, yet could not understand the deep rage he felt at her rejection. Other women had not affected him when it came time to break off. He had expected the same indifference. Possibly it was the habit of Gertrude he missed. The companionship, the physical need, the family in which he'd found some comfort. They had all been suddenly removed, and he'd been gripped by a desolate loneliness.

'I don't think so,' Gunboat said as Nicky was expecting an answer. 'I just...' he hesitated fractionally, then gave in to the weakness, 'needed her.' He wanted to stop picking at the wound. It was still raw; he could taste the blood.

'You ever had a woman?'

'No,' Nicky said. He remained silent a few steps. 'I've always wondered what it is like. We talk about it often in school, as if we all know what it means. One of my friends says he's slept with a woman. His cousin. They were at a wedding, and she was about ten years older than him. So he says.'

Gunboat laughed. He felt somewhat better at the thought already. 'Why don't we get ourselves laid, Prince? I know the exact person for you.'

'Laid?' He half understood but needed to be reassured.

'Sleep with a woman. I mean go to bed with one. Come on. You'll love it.'

SIXTEEN

Nicky glanced back. Swami plodded, almost asleep, after them. He felt excited, dismayed, eager, yet strangely afraid. He had imagined and wondered often, increasingly so of late, what exactly occurred with a woman. He was not ignorant of a woman's body. As a child, as a youth, he had seen many women unclothed from the waist up. village women working in the rice fields, others bathing in temple tanks or in rivers. The mystery of them lay below the sari knotted at the waist.

'I've danced with them,' Nicky admitted softly as if this were in itself a lewd revelation.

'Yeah?' Gunboat laughed. 'I know what you mean. I remember the first time I held a girl. It was Susie Murphy. Everyone had kissed her, and I figure I was the last guy on the block. She was so soft, so warm, Jeez, I had an erection for a week.'

'I felt like that,' Nicky said. 'Except I've never kissed a girl. Even dancing with one was bad enough. My grandmother heard about it and she became very angry with me.'

He had begun the conversation to give himself time to think. He wanted to accompany Gunboat to this woman, but still he held back. He had a position to keep, not only for Gunboat but for any strangers he met at this place. They would know he was the yuvaraj, and gossip would eventually reach his grandmother. He had little doubt of that. She had countless eyes and ears, one of them trailing a few feet behind him.

'I don't think I can,' Nicky said.

'Because of him? Listen, he'll fall asleep the moment he sits down, and you can tell him we're just taking a stroll'.

'Is it a discreet place?'

'You bet it is.'

Nicky waited for Swami to reach them, then spoke softly. Swami appeared to protest, but sleep appeared more paramount than looking after Nicky. He yawned, agreed, and ambled into the compound to find a comfortable place to await the car and driver.

'He has been with me all my life,' Nicky explained as they walked on. 'When I was a child, he bathed me; when I grew older, he came everywhere.'

'But not England?'

'No. He had a family here and didn't want to. Mohan came instead. They are brothers you know. Is it far?'

'Nope.'

It was a small darkened bungalow down a barely lit lane off Walker Street. The gate squeaked, alerting crickets and small quick shadows in the tiny garden. Gunboat tapped on the door, softly first then louder. A grunt finally answered and an old man materialized from his sleep on the floor. He peered at Gunboat, recognized him, and fumbled with the door latch.

Once inside the tiny veranda, Nicky noticed that lights were on behind the tightly closed doors. The old man a chowkidar, opened the door and they stepped into a sparsely furnished room. There were two or three chairs and a table untidily piled with newspapers. It seemed a waiting room. A couple of empty beer bottles rested on the floor. The room was empty.

'Now what happens?' Nicky asked. He felt nervous. So much light, and obviously other men were also visiting.

'Just wait.'

Finally, although it was only a few moments, a woman appeared. She was in her forties, decked in jewels and a richly coloured sari. Her mouth was red-stained with paan, and the perfume was strong, quite suffocating.

'Gunboat. It has been a long time.'

'Yeah. I had other sources. This is a friend of mine. Is Gita available?'

The woman examined Nicky closely. She sensed, if not knew, who he was. The boy stood straight, arrogant, stared back coldly. It took time, and her experienced eye, to realize he was embarrassed, ashamed to be in her presence in this shabby room, undergoing inspection. He was about to turn away.

'Yes, she is,' the woman said and smiled at Nicky. Her teeth too, were stained, and the smile didn't quite touch her eyes. She had calculated his worth and set the price. 'A hundred rupees.'

Gunboat laughed. 'Drop the act, Kamala. I know the price and besides...he glanced at Nicky, 'it's my treat. So try again.'

'No, I shall,' Nicky began and realized he had no money.

Swami carried it all.

The woman grumbled and settled to bargain. Gunboat took her aside. 'Listen. It's a favour to me. Fifty, and that's it.'

She glanced past him at Nicky. Finally she nodded and took the money.

'Who is he?'

Gunboat shook a finger under her nose. 'Never ask questions like that.' He counted another twenty-five. 'And I'll have one of the other girls.'

The room was tiny, a mere cell with a wooden cot and a thin mattress. In the weak light the sheet looked grey and infested. Nicky sat on the edge, miserable, unsure of what he should do. He wished he had not come. He felt a disgust for himself, for the mean room in which he appeared to be trapped. Yet he did not move. He wanted a woman, to experience her body, to consider himself a man.

The woman entered. She was slim, dark, not much older than himself, it seemed, and quite pretty. She had large gentle eyes and a small nose. Her hair hung to her waist.

'I am Gita,' she said haltingly. She spoke Telugu, and Nicky understood it vaguely. She crossed the room, dimmed the light, and slowly began to unwrap her sari. She watched him watching her. 'Have you slept with a woman before?'

Nicky considered lying but knew it would not be possible. She would discover that soon. 'No.'

Her sari fell from her shoulders, loose around her waist; it trailed her as she moved to sit by him. Her choli was small, tight, and her breasts, a size too large, smooth, silk-like, half spilled out. She smelled of sandalwood soap and attar. She sat awhile, allowing him to look at her. When he looked away, she undid her choli and slipped it off. Her breasts were full, heavy with large dark nipples. She took his hand and placed it on one.

Nicky had never touched anything so smooth, so perfectly round and soft. His palms were almost mesmerized by the sensation. He reached for the other, held them both, almost as if weighing them and choosing which he preferred.

She undid his shirt buttons, and when she tried to slip the shirt off, he appeared not to notice. His palms held her breasts so lovingly. She giggled, moved away, and took off his shirt.

'What is your name?' she asked.

'Na…rayan,' Nicky lied.

She knew he had, sighed, and allowed him to slip his hand down her belly and tug at the folds in her sari. It came undone, and she stood so it slid down to the floor. She wore a cheap cotton bodice, tied by a frayed string. Carefully she undid it and let that fall too.

Nicky was awed by the simplicity of a woman's body. The curve of flesh, dipping between her legs, flowing out to her thighs, down to her ankles. Her pubic hair was sparse, and he could glimpse the folds of skin, the thin line of division that ran to the top of the hairline and disappeared. He touched her hips, her slim thighs, but not her pubic area. She moved away when his hand strayed.

She knelt and undid his trousers, pulling them off as he sat giggling. He had no need of help. His erection was hard, so visible. She touched it, almost felt the impact it had on him. Eager, embarrassed, electric.

'Don't worry,' she said. 'Now lie back.'

Docile, he did as she instructed. She straddled him, and slowly, carefully, guiding him with her hand, let him enter. She was hot and wet, and Nicky could not ever imagine a more pleasurable sensation. She only sat, not moving, allowing him to savouir the experience. She knelt forward slightly so he could also fondle her breasts.

'Are you ready?'

'Yes.'

She moved slowly, up and down, knowing it would not be long for him.

Each time she rose, she appeared to suck his strength, his senses out, each fall gave nothing back, only held him poised, waiting for her to rise again and take him far away. He came, suddenly, unexpectedly, painfully yet exquisitely so. He heard himself cry out, she comforted him with her breasts, and he sank into the thin mattress. She lay pressed beside him, saying nothing, caressing him as if wanting to remember who he had been. When he came erect once more, she allowed him to get on top, always guiding. Boys become men quickly, once they learn the power of their cock. The shyness was almost gone. Nicky knelt, thrusting, curious as to the feel of the woman inside, experimenting with their bodies. He pushed in harder, and harder, making her cry out, but he noticed she made no attempt to dislodge him and understood what he was doing to her.

When he had come, he lay for a moment beside her, touching still with a boy's curiosity, yet already a man's experience. The palms had lost their tenderness and their awe.

He dressed. 'Where do you come from?'

'Andhra,' she said and watched. 'A village near Kurnool.'

'You like this?'

She shrugged a shoulder. 'I don't know anything else. I was stolen as a girl.'

'Stolen?' Yet it came as no surprise. In his own state a villager would report a child, son or daughter, missing. It was always impossible to trace. 'Why don't you return now?'

'To what? My family will not have me after this. What man will want to be my husband? And I don't want to return to the fields. I am saving money. One day I might open a small tea *kadai.*' She appeared indifferent to her fate.

Nicky searched his pockets. There was nothing. 'I will come back and ask for you,' he said.

'Of course you will.' She rose, not believing, and began to dress.

◆

Gunboat was weary. Booze and sex took their toll. Each year it took longer to recover. It had been the same in the ring. The punches grew harder, hurt more, remained embedded in the body that much longer. He was glad he no longer fought.

It was a few minutes before noon. He trudged up the small gravel lane to Gertrude's door, knocked, and waited. She peered past the curtain and came out smiling, unbelievably happy at seeing him. He did not understand even when she hugged him.

'Oh, I'm so happy at seeing you, Gunboat,' she said and pulled him into the veranda. 'I really missed you.'

'Yeah?'

'Don't be so unbelieving. I did.'

'What about Malcolm?'

'He's a friend,' she said it so dismissively he would have believed, if he had not known his Gertrude. She was the child, the possessor of lovely smiles; quite willful in her need to hold onto him at her convenience.

Gunboat wished he could disentangle her, rise from the chair, and walk away. He knew he would never do that, he had no strength for that effort. He was only glad she saw him, held him, and chattered away like a sparrow about all her doings over the past week. She held a tremendous amount of trivial information, but he listened and smiled.

'How would you like to lunch in a rajah's palace?' he asked when she stopped.

'You're pulling my leg?'

'Nope. I got invited to lunch and the rajah said to bring a friend.'

'Oh God, I've got to get ready then.' She got off his lap, excited. 'What time is it for?'

'Twelve-thirty,' he said.

'Why didn't you tell me?' she wailed and dashed inside.

'We can always skip it,' he called after her.

'No,' she shouted vehemently, and Gunboat was glad he had played that card. She was a snob.

They arrived by taxi ten minutes late. The town palace was an ornate building, smaller than the palace in the country. There was an ornamental pond, long and rectangular, that ran the breadth of the garden. The garden was small, but still big enough to hold a well-maintained tennis court and a cricket net practice pitch.

Gertrude was nervous and excited. Gunboat behaved as if this was a daily occurrence in his life. A bearer led them through the main hallway, quite similar in size and decor to the other palace: an elegant chandelier, pearl-inlaid tables, silk-upholstered chairs, and mahogany paneling.

'It's beautiful,' Gertrude whispered.

There were other guests. A dozen or so men and women milled around in a small and informal reception room that opened out onto the garden. Bearers moved among them, carrying silver trays with drinks. Gunboat took a beer.

All the people, apart from Miss Hobbs and a boy of around sixteen, blond, grey-eyed, tall, were Indian. The women wore saris, jewellery, and talked incessantly of shopping in Harrods and Fortnum and Masons, while the men, dressed far more casually in bush shirts and slacks, discussed the price of Scotch or else gossiped about their political leaders. Nicky stood in a corner, talking to a young Indian girl with waist-length hair and a simple, yet enormously beautiful face. She looked a couple of years younger than he. He saw Gunboat and left her side.

'How are you, Gunboat?' he asked formally, politely. He had reverted to a prince.

The night before, when they had left, he had talked at length of his experience with Gita. Fucking, he had concluded, was the best sport discovered. Gunboat laughed at the stars. If nothing else, the prince would remember him all his life. He had been responsible for the prince losing his cherry.

'Fine,' Gunboat said, and introduced Gertrude.

They shook hands, and Gunboat noticed a distance in Nicky as if he wasn't sure how to handle Gertrude's presence.

'Come. I'll introduce you to people.'

Gunboat and Gertrude made the rounds, shaking hands, exchanging polite, meaningless platitudes. Finally Nicky approached the English boy who stood apart and watched the party. He appeared to be at ease with the strangers, and yet distant, as if he were not sure exactly why he had been invited. 'This is Ian Potter,' Nicky said.

It took Gunboat a moment before he realized that the boy was to be Nicky's opponent in the fight. His practiced eye measured him. Ian was fractionally taller than Nicky, and thicker. His forearms also had a couple of inches on Nicky, and it looked as if, possibly, he would have greater stamina. He was strong. Nicky was slim, supple, not strong, but wiry. Nicky could have the edge on speed and quickness; both worthwhile qualities, if the fighters were equally experienced.

'I have heard of you,' Gunboat said.

'Same here,' Ian said. 'I used to read about your fights over here, and I heard a lot about you from Sergeant Anderson.'

'Anderson? Yeah. He refereed that Calcutta fight.' Gunboat stopped, not wishing to remember more. 'What's he doing?'

'He's in my school. He's the sports master. Tough, too. He really gets us chaps working hard.'

'I bet. Have you boxed much?'

'Since I was this high.' He cut himself off at the hip.

'You're training Nicky, I hear.'

'Yeah.'

Ian grinned. It was impudent, and he feinted a playful punch at Nicky. 'Waste of time, isn't it, Nicky? These prince-wallahs are too debauched.'

'I've given up wine, women, and song for the big fight,' Nicky said.

He feinted. Ian blocked easily, and for a while they fooled around. There was a contained hostility between them, like strange children forced to tolerate each other's company in the presence of their adults.

'Stop it, Ian,' Miss Hobbs said sharply. The boys drew apart. She said nothing to Nicky. 'This is a lunch, not a playground.'

'I'm sorry,' Ian said, subdued. He straightened himself and tucked in his shirt. Nicky followed suit. They stood apart, suddenly quite distant; yet both equally uncomfortable.

'You have met my son?' she said, and Gunboat suddenly understood why it was so important to her for Nicky to lose the fight.

'And this young lady is…?' Miss Hobbs turned to Gertrude.

'Gertrude,' Gunboat said, nearly having forgotten her.

'Oh, you must feel very left out,' Miss Hobbs said. 'Why don't we find a quiet spot and chat?'

She took Gertrude's arm and guided her to a sofa. Gunboat watched a while. Their heads were close together, as if they were old friends who had not seen each other for some time. He realized that both looked quite comfortable in each other's company.

A few minutes before lunch was announced the rajah made his appearance. He made the rounds, greeting each guest warmly, apologizing, holding to their hands as if it were a political rally. Finally, he reached Gunboat and the two boys.

'I am glad you have come, Gunboat,' he said. 'I thought that tomorrow on our way back to Tandhapur, we could visit your sadhu, Rajaram.'

'Not quite mine. But sure.'

'You will come too, Nicky,' the rajah ordered. Then added suddenly, 'Have you seen Rukmani?'

Nicky reacted uneasily. The question was too direct, and he knew he could not evade it.

'Yes,' he said softly. 'She was at Sushila's.'

'Oh. Was anyone else there?'

'The usual,' Nicky shrugged evasively.

Any mention of his aunt would enrage his father. His father seemed satisfied, for after a quick word with Ian he returned to his other guests. Gunboat turned to look for Gertrude. She and Miss Hobbs had gone.

'You didn't tell me Ian was her son,' Gunboat said.

'Is that important?'

'Sure. Now I understand.'

◆

Gertrude was flattered. She had never met an English woman as attentive as Miss Hobbs. Mostly they ignored her or peered down at her, making her nervous and tongue-tied. Miss Hobbs, however, showed a genuine interest in her.

She now walked half a pace behind the bulk of Miss Hobbs with the awe of a child trailing a hero. The palace corridors were endless. Liveried servants bowed to their passage, unnoticed by Miss Hobbs, eyed nervously by Gertrude. If she had been alone, she would have turned and bolted.

'Is this as big as the palace in Tandhapur?'

'Oh no, my dear,' Miss Hobbs turned to smile at her. 'That one has seventy rooms and it's such a problem looking after it. Even though they are princes, we...' And she paused long enough to allow Gertrude to understand it was her that she was meaning, 'are more used to living in places like this than they are.'

'Yes, I know,' Gertrude said, pleased but unsure as this was the first time she had stepped into a palace.

'Here we are.' Miss Hobbs stopped, and selecting a key from the bunch that hung at her waist, she unlocked the door.

'It's so much quieter in here. I'll order one of the bearers to bring us lunch.'

She stepped aside. Gertrude entered, unsure what to expect. She imagined she was to step into a throne room. It was instead, small, cool, gloomy. She saw only shadows, and little furniture. Miss Hobbs switched on the light.

'Oh, it's beautiful,' Gertrude spoke softly.

The room was small but exquisite. The eye wandered, held an object, roved on. Silk-covered mattresses, raised a few inches high on carved ivory stands, covered most of the floor; huge silk bolsters were neatly arranged to support one's back. In the centre was a gold table. Gertrude was unsure whether it was solid or plated and Miss Hobbs easily read her mind.

'Solid,' she said. On top was a delicate and ornate gold egg sparkling with rubies. 'A Fabergé. He was a jeweller for the czars.' She opened it, removed a cigarette, and offered one to Gertrude, who refused. Miss Hobbs lit hers, sucked greedily.

'That's a Titian, and those are very rare Mogul miniatures.'

Gertrude followed the casual jabs of the cigarette. The walls, she noticed, were paneled with delicately carved sandalwood screens. The scent was delicate, lingering. The paintings hung in niches. There were a few statues too; small, precious, beautiful. A bookshelf was within arm's reach.

'All first editions. Dickens, Thackeray, Goldsmith. A drink?'

Gertrude nearly shook her head, but she'd not drunk from a gold goblet before.

'Gin and tonic, please.'

Miss Hobbs mixed. 'Damn. No ice.' She pressed a bell. A bearer immediately appeared. 'Ice. And bring lunch here.' She waved Gertrude down. 'Make yourself comfortable. The rajah likes me to use his room whenever I want. I quite like it here.'

Gertrude cautiously lowered herself onto a divan, then leaned back against a bolster. She felt, after a moment or two, strangely imbued with power as if by the mere act of occupation of the rajah's divan, she had absorbed his strengts.

'Comfortable?' Miss Hobbs smiled benignly down at her, before lowering herself next to Gertrude. The ivory stands creaked.

'Oh, yes.'

She tried to imitate Miss Hobbs's loll and languid arrogance. It was easy. It was then she noticed the incongruous object. It looked an ordinary dull grey tea set, placed at eye level. It appeared to have a pride of place. Miss Hobbs noticed her glance and picked up a cup and saucer.

'Here.' She handed them to Gertrude. They were frail and delicate.

'The set is hand carved out of granite. Hold it up to the light.' Gertrude did and saw the light filter opaquely through the stone.

'It is so light it'll float on water.' Then she laughed, coarsely. 'It took the fool forty years to carve that set after seeing one in a European's home. He gave it to the old rajah as a gift, and do you know—the teapot's spout is solid. He didn't know it was meant to pour. Typical of this country, isn't it?'

Gertrude didn't reply. She handed back the cup and saucer as carefully as she would have the sacrament, for strangely, and confusingly, she felt an unbearable pride and sadness for the craftsman who had carved the gift. She understood now why it was placed in this room.

Ice was brought. The goblet chilled and perspired in her hand. She felt herself studied and held her head averted.

Miss Hobbs spoke kindly. 'You must be related to Wild Tom Nailer. Aren't you?'

'I—I—think we are,' Gertrude said, grateful that someone should believe what her family always thought to be gospel truth. General Tom Nailer had been chief of the Indian Army.

'I thought so. There's a likeness. I knew Wild Tom when he was a mere colonel.' She laughed. 'He really had an eye for the ladies. The number of times I fought him off, I can't tell. Ah, but those days are past.' She sighed heavily and the stand creaked. 'It's a wonder you are still here.'

'We are hoping to leave.'

'Oh you should. There's no future here for us Europeans.'

The touch was heavy, and Miss Hobbs smiled as she saw Gertrude accept the compliment. 'Will you be leaving with Gunboat?'

'I'm not sure.'

'He's such a nice man. And he is in love with you. Of course, his leaving here depends so much on what he does.'

'What do you mean?'

'The prince will pay him only if he wins the fight. I felt that so unfair for Gunboat so I offered to pay the money whether the prince won or not.'

'How kind of you.'

'We have to help each other here. But Gunboat doesn't understand that. He doesn't need to waste his time on the prince anymore. He could leave tomorrow.' She paused. 'In fact you should ask him. You could leave tomorrow for England. Even America.'

'He didn't tell me.' Gertrude sounded wounded.

'He's a…well…peculiar man. You must know that.'

'Yes,' Gertrude muttered.

'You should discuss it with him,' Miss Hobbs said and quietly laid her hand on Gertrude's. It hid the small brown hand. 'I can arrange the tickets tomorrow.'

The silence lay as quiet as the hand. She removed it only to light another cigarette.

'I also heard your uncle was having some problems.'

'Yes.' Gertrude spoke quickly, sensing a friend who could help. 'Because he's Anglo-Indian they're denying him promotion. He should be a police inspector now.'

'Don't worry. I'll talk to the rajah. He knows the commissioner.'

Lunch came and Gertrude felt herself being waited on by two people, the bearer and Miss Hobbs. During the meal Miss Hobbs spoke about her own family, her life in Bombay, the wealth of the rajah's family. They finished with the kulfi, and after a polite belch, Miss Hobbs led Gertrude back to the main party.

It was breaking up, and Miss Hobbs kissed Gertrude goodbye and smiled conspiratorially. The rajah and Nicky shook her hand politely, and Gertrude was once more reminded of their distance. Cars waited to pick up the other guests and she and Gunboat were caught in the swirl of dust that floated after them down the driveway. Gertrude felt as if she were being banished forever, and when she looked back from the gate, the palace appeared silent and deserted, as if life in it no longer existed.

'Good time?' Gunboat asked.

'Oh yes,' Gertrude said enthusiastically. She stooped, squinting at Gunboat. It was warm, the dust tickled her nostrils, and the road felt hard and real under her feet. She sensed she had stepped out of a dream. 'Why didn't you take up Miss Hobbs's offer? We could leave tomorrow.'

He didn't reply immediately. They walked awhile and looked for a rickshaw or a hansom. A rickshaw was approaching.

'What did you think of her?' Gunboat asked quietly.

'She's a lovely person. She's so friendly and nice and kind. She's going to help uncle also. She made me feel—'

'Bullshit,' Gunboat said, still calm.

'Gunboat!' Gertrude was shocked by his language. A young woman should be given greater respect. 'She likes you and—'

'Crap. She's an evil witch. Be careful of her.'

'You're just stupid,' Gertrude said angrily. 'She wants to help you…us, and you think she's evil.'

'Listen,' Gunboat began to placate, wanting to explain.

'I won't,' Gertrude said and flagged down the rickshaw. The man perspired to a halt, lowered the shafts, and Gertrude scrambled aboard.

'You could use her help for our sake. Get us out of this bloody country. But you won't.'

'Stop being a child.'

'I am,' Gertrude snapped. 'And I don't want to talk to you ever again.' She ordered the rickshaw-wallah to pull, and he wearily began pulling her down the road.

Gunboat watched. Gertrude sat stiff and upright, fanning herself with a handkerchief. She didn't turn to look back and Gunboat felt a weary and enormous sense of loss. He slowly trudged up the road to the centre of town.

PART III

SEVENTEEN

Rukmani didn't return immediately to her father's house. She had Sushila's chauffeur drop her by Benson's, the provisions store on St Marks Road. He wanted to wait; she dismissed him and watched the car turn onto South Parade. She crossed the street to Koshy's restaurant, a branch of the one on Brigade Road, and stepped cautiously into the gloomy interior. It took time for her eyes to adjust. She saw Prithivi sitting in a booth.

'What kept you?' he half rose, petulant. 'I've been sitting here half an hour.'

'My grandmother kept going on and on.' She sat opposite, quite shy. 'I'm sorry. What are you drinking?'

'A beer. Want a taste?' She took one, grimaced, and asked the bearer for a sweet lime.

Prithivi reminded her of Raj Kapoor, the film star. He was handsome in a sleepy, somewhat spoilt way. His hair half covered his forehead and he had the endearing habit of brushing it back, only to have it fall forward again. He was four years older than she, and had begun working for his father. His family was wealthy landowners who were slowly moving into industry. She had had a crush on Prithivi since her schooldays, and they'd written each other passionate letters—full of innocence, quotes from Rupert Brooke, and hopeless unfulfilled longings. They met when they could. A quick phone call from her, and Prithivi would appear at the rendezvous. They had to be discreet, for dating was not permissible. Only chance encounters carefully engineered, quick glances in crowded parties, telephone calls, and those letters. Rukmani thought: it could never be as frustrating as this in the West. In the pictures you saw them dating, holding hands, kissing, jiving to the jukebox.

She listened to the Koshy's jukebox. The ballad was 'I Belong to You,' and she yearned to say that to Prithivi, but checked herself. He was looking worried, distracted. He stubbed out his Goldflake cigarette, lit another.

'Well,' she asked impatiently. 'What do you think about it?'

'I don't know,' even though she suspected he did.

They had talked for hours over the phone. She had told him her father's decision. She hated Gopi. It was Prithivi she wanted. He had been bold then, over the phone, promising to do battle for his princess. She wanted to elope with him. They would run to Kashmir or Nepal or Calcutta. India was huge, and one could get lost so easily. She had some of her jewellery, and he could find a job. He was, after all, an engineering graduate.

'What don't you know?' she asked, but already sensed the coming pain. Holding her breath did not stifle it.

'About running away. Our parents will get very angry.'

'Of course they will,' Rukmani said in exasperation. 'Mine more than yours. My father will probably disinherit me.' She leaned forward, touched his still hand. 'Please. I don't want to marry Gopi.' She shuddered dramatically, revulsion touching the pit of her stomach.

'I don't want you to,' he said fiercely, then softened. 'We must do this properly. Will your father change his mind?'

'No.'

It was surprising how, even in this faint light, she suddenly saw his handsomeness as weak. His mouth was too generous, his eyes would not meet hers. She knew she was losing. He would not defy his parents.

She would not cry; she would not bend. She was as stubborn as her father. At nineteen, not tempered by experience, unwary of heartbreak, Rukmani felt herself dying. She did not know she could feel this way. Her girlish love had been heady, exhilarating, so dashingly romantic.

It was the stuff she'd read of in poems and the romantic novels of Georgette Heyer, which she consumed as a schoolgirl. There was no end to loving; it burned in one's life right up to the moment of death.

For the first time, she saw how it could end long before death. Cruelly, abruptly, leaving one still alive, struggling for breath, struggling to escape the claustrophobia of one's heartbeat.

'Say no then,' she demanded, and discovered she was also angry.

'I can't,' Prithivi pleaded, wanting to hold on to her hand. 'I think we should wait. Your father will change his mind. He must. He needs my father's help.'

'He won't.'

She was angry. She pulled her hand away and stood up. From her height he now looked shrunken, hidden in the shadows of the shuttered room. Imperiously, she threw the end of her sari over her shoulder and walked out.

The sun hurt. The tears stung. The street and buildings danced as if she were in a mirage; blurred as if she were peering up at the sun from under fathoms of water. She hiccupped a couple of times, refusing to cry; only the tears trickled down. She felt so abandoned, so reduced from a proud girl to a sniffling child. She wiped her eyes with the corner of her sari; the kohl left a black streak on the orange cotton.

She walked awhile, wanting the misery to subside. She wished she could talk to someone. Sushila would be unsympathetic. Her relations with her seesawed: affection, dislike, distrust, affection. If her mother had lived, she could have turned to her for solace, possibly even for aid against her father.

Unlike Nicky, Rukmani could remember her mother when she made the effort. She had been five at the time of the death. The touch, the smell, the sternness, the loving, the spankings, they evoked a bitter anger, an unfathomable sadness at the loss. An amputation had occurred at five, and she knew the wound would never heal.

'What's up, Princess?'

Rukmani looked up, squinting into the sun at Gunboat Jack. He appeared to have been watching her for some time; even following her possibly.

'Nothing,' she said and tried to step around.

He had seen her. She had looked pretty, petulant, and yet so vulnerable. Her mouth curved down, like a stage mask, and she had been so deeply preoccupied that she'd not noticed his approach.

'Your father was asking about you at lunch,' he said. 'Nicky told him you were at your sister's.'

'Are you spying on me?'

'Don't get mad. No. Just thought I'd tell you.'

He wished now he hadn't greeted her. He would have walked on, but she appeared to assent to his company and they began to walk together down South Parade. On one side of the street were shops and cinemas; on the other, raised a dozen feet above road level, was a mud bund. There were benches and shady trees, and in the evenings the people would stroll up one side of the street, and then down the bund. It gave a view of those below. Gunboat and Rukmani crossed to the bund. At five in the afternoon there were few people around. They would wait until the heat had subsided before beginning their promenade. So for a while the bund was deserted. They walked in silence halfway and sat on the stone bench opposite the Liberty Cinema. It was showing *The Black Widow* with Van Heflin and Ginger Rogers.

Both remained preoccupied for a while. Then Rukmani sniffled.

'What's up, Princess?' Gunboat asked kindly.

She allowed the tears in her eyes to brim over. Then told him about Prithivi and Gopi and her father. Her sense of drama had been heightened by self-pity, but Gunboat remained attentive. He knew what it had been like. When you are young you have the recklessness of passion. As you grow older, the fears increase, the wisdom, the past pain, tempers one's courage. That is when you begin to lose.

'Maybe he'll change his mind.'

She sighed. The pain was almost visual. 'He won't.'

South Parade was quiet. A hansom cab passed below them. The horse was old and thin and moved painfully. The cab was patched and worn. A couple of chokras rode the stand on the back, and once or twice, in concession to the game, the driver flicked his long whip up and back. The crack would startle the boys and they'd jump off, laughing. Only to run after it and grab on once more.

Rukmani sat with an elbow on her knee, her chin resting in the palm of her hand. She had calmed. The sadness had begun to fade, and he knew soon she would forget this Prithivi. Never totally. No one ever does. A line, only faintly visible, would remain around her eyes, her mouth.

'What are you going to do?'

'Go to Oxford,' she said firmly.

'You're a bit young for that.'

'I've nearly completed my degree here,' she said indignantly.

'I don't mean that. I mean to go away by yourself. It gets...kinda lonely out there.'

Her head turned slowly, until it appeared her palm had pushed it out of alignment. For the first time, he sensed, she realized who had been sitting beside her.

'Do you think so?'

'Yes.'

She considered his reply. The word was so new to her, and she frowned as if trying to decipher its meaning.

'I never get lonely here,' she finally said. 'There are...so many friends.' She turned away, still frowning. 'Then you must feel very lonely here?'

'I guess so.'

He didn't elaborate, however. She would not understand until she'd experienced that herself. Here she was with family, with friends, a small human firmly and securely fixed in a hierarchy of relationships.

'I make friends very easily,' she said brightly.

Gunboat nodded. She was not to be dissuaded. She would need

to discover it all by herself, and he felt sad that she would soon be one of the wounded. Pretty princesses, he decided, should be preserved in lovely gardens. Someone needed to pass through life without being soiled by it.

He saw the limousine. It came slowly and stopped below them. The chauffeur got out and signalled. Rukmani stared at him a long time, and it appeared she was not to be moved. She stood abruptly when she saw her grandmother's face appear in the rear window.

'I will see you later.'

The only steps leading down to the road were fifty yards further along. She strolled, and the car crawled after her.

'Don't you have any shame?' her grandmother shouted the moment the car door closed on them.

'What about?' Rukmani asked. She thought her grandmother knew of her meeting with Prithivi. She needed time to marshal her defence.

'Sitting in the open with that man.'

'Oh,' Rukmani was relieved. 'Gunboat? He's a friend.'

'He isn't. We employ him. And you shouldn't be seen in public sitting and talking with him. Especially a European.'

'You don't like him,' Rukmani countered.

'That's got nothing to do with it. Everybody will think you're a loose woman now.'

'Let them,' she said defiantly.

She felt abandoned, careless not only with her life, but the whole future. It looked bleak; unworthy of her energy and thought.

'Let them.' For a moment, Rukmani thought her grandmother would slap her. The hand was raised, but it fell with a jangle of gold bangles back on her lap. 'You modern girls think that you can do anything you want,' she complained softly. 'You'll regret it later when you want to get married. You just wait and see.'

They rode in silence. Tense, harsh, angry. Rukmani wanted to weep once more. She wondered why families were so difficult, why they always fought each other. Bloody, bitter, revengeful. She knew her grandmother was only angry for her own sake. It was indiscreet to be seen alone with any man. She sighed. India was always so far behind everyone else.

'I'm sorry,' she whispered.

It was barely audible above the noise of the car. But it was heard. Her grandmother grunted and slowly relaxed. Her face was no longer fierce. At times she could look like a Punch caricature: the beaked nose, and the upbeaked chin. She patted Rukmani on the knee in acceptance of the apology.

The old woman stared out. It was darkening. Here and there a light appeared, weak and yellow, flickering a moment before being placed in a shelter. She recognized many things: a granite rock, the peculiar humped shape of a hill, the old temple set beside the fields, the sandy riverbed that changed direction constantly with each monsoon. Even trees were familiar. That banyan by the curve in the road. She remembered how small and puny it had once been—a sapling, erect and green and as young as she had once been. Now it was spread over a quarter of an acre, the roots from its branches driving straight down into the earth like stakes.

The first journey had not been as swift. It had taken a week to reach Tandhapur. She had been a child, a princess of ten on her way to her betrothal. The women had travelled in palanquins, slowly, stately. The guards and retainers on foot or prancing horses. They had been necessary in those days. The country was full of dacoits, and princesses were rich pickings. She had been with her mother and grandmother and many cousins. It had been an adventure, for she had no idea she was on her way to meet her future husband.

In those days the road had been a ribbon of dust and cart tracks, cut through the landscape. They would halt in tiny villages at dusk, and the servants would set up the tents for the women to rest in and then cook the evening meal. When they had reached within a day's journey of Tandhapur, they had been met by her future mother-in-law, the rani, and a small army of retainers. They had been escorted to the palace to the sound of conches and trumpets and tablas.

The old rani still remembered the first glimpse of her bride-groom. He had been a few years older, slim-straight, so fair-skinned and handsome. He had the family features: aquiline, thick eyebrows. He had sat a horse, watching calmly from a distance. Even when they sat side by side under the pandal in front of the priest on the auspicious day and auspicious hour, he had remained aloof. The marriage had been consummated five years later and in that time she had seen him only a few times. She had had to learn how to survive within his family.

He had never changed, and she had never understood him. He had not allowed her to, and that thought still made her feel bitter. She had always lived in the shadow of his life, never a part of it. He had, admittedly, been a complex and busy man. He studied Sanskrit, played every conceivable sport, composed poetry, developed the mines the family now depended on, passed reforms, built his schools, and plotted continuously against the British. However, he had not been a loving husband.

She had, finally, come to despise him. A lifetime of being ignored leaves a bitter deposit on the soul. It had reduced her to a meaningless jumble of days and years, of ceremonies and long dark silences and unanswered prayers. The birth of a daughter and the stillbirth of two sons had not lessened the divide between them. She was to blame for the lack of an heir to the throne, and he had never forgiven her for that. He had died in 1948, alone, with only the old servants at his bedside. She had refused to attend him, repayment as hurtful as she could make it for all those years of neglect. She doubted whether he even noticed her absence, for he'd not asked for her. Even to the end, he had triumphed.

If only her daughter had lived. She glanced at Rukmani, half hidden in the shadow. They looked so alike at times; they even behaved alike. Stubborn, capricious, often generous, argumentative. She couldn't help it but at times, if she woke from a doze suddenly, she would actually believe Rukmani was her daughter. Begin to call out, and stop when she realized she had dreamed. They had been so close because of the nature of their existence.

She had died too young, too early. They had not known she was a diabetic until it had been too late to save her.

It was a hereditary sickness. She had it herself and it puzzled her as to why her daugher had died from the disease, and not she. Not quite a puzzle, more an indescribable anger. The indecency of God to have deprived her of the only person she had truly loved. Her own time, she knew, was near. She had been warned to live on a special diet, take her insulin injections, care for herself as if she were a child. It was too late for that. She only wished to survive long enough to defeat that wretched woman Miss Hobbs, and keep the family intact. Once that had been achieved, the rest would be only the immeasurable boredom she had existed in for most of her life.

'Do you still want to go to Oxford?' she asked Rukmani.

'Yes.'

Change had to come. She saw it in the darkness outside. The electric poles spreading over the country, the tarmac road beneath the wheels of the car, the speed of their journey. Why not within? If Rukmani had been born in her time, she would have married whom her father had decreed. And led a life not that dissimilar to her own. She had a right to a happier life than an empty existence in some palace.

◆

The car sped through Tandhapur. Even it had changed. Once a village, now a prosperous small town. One day, it could become a city. Bearers came running the moment the car stopped. She would have liked to bathe and rest and eat. Often now, she had this painful hunger, a bottomless hollow in her belly.

'Come with me,' she ordered Rukmani.

They walked through the halls. Bearers ran ahead turning on lights. It had been gloomy moments before, now the whole palace blazed, as if a magnificent durbar were taking place within the walls.

The key to the vault was kept in a massive steel safe. It had been specially shipped from London by her husband. It was a grand contraption: steel inlaid with brass, and a huge keyhole. It looked impossible to open or move, and the family was proud of it. The old woman found the key, opened it, rummaged among the countless family documents piled inside, and found the other keys for the vault.

The vault had been built by her husband. It was part of the modernization of the palace: electricity, western flush toilets, showers, more rooms, the western furniture he bought on his travels in Europe. Prior to this, the jewellery was hidden in the old cellar. The cellar had an earth floor, and chatties filled with precious stones, gold coins, even money, were carefully wrapped in pure white linen and buried in the earth. He had rescued most; never all. For the wealth had passed through the generations, and some had been lost. In the palace grounds, long forgotten, would be these earthen pots filled with jewellery and gold. They could possibly be found, not by design but by pure chance.

The air in the vault was stale and humid. She wiped her face with the edge of her sari and began the inventory. There was an ancient ledger, leatherbound, gold-embossed, with stiff, fragile pages, but she had little need of it. She knew every piece by sight: gold belts studded with diamonds; ruby and emerald necklaces; bangles; gold chains; rings with diamonds, emeralds, rubies, amethysts; anklets; gold crowns embedded with diamonds; two gold sceptres; gold daggers and swords and shields. They filled the steel almirahs; some nestled in velvet cases, others were wrapped in linen. Here, in this small room, were two centuries of tithes and taxes paid by their subjects. Yet it was a trivial amount in comparison to the possessions of big princes: the nizam of Hyderabad, the maharajahs of Mysore, Jaipur, Baroda, Gwalior.

The old woman was systematic. She inventoried each almirah carefully. After an hour she and Rukmani were pouring with sweat, yet the metal was cool to the touch. The stones almost cold. Rukmani held the ledger. She recognized only a few of the pieces, and if it had not been for her grandmother's impatience, would have lingered over each and every one.

Her grandmother would also have liked to be more leisurely. The touch of each piece awakened memories. Other women remember their lives by events; she recalled hers by the jewellery worn. This for her wedding, that for the birth of her child; births, deaths, marriages, ceremonies, durbars, parties, namings. Each had been celebrated by the donning of one of these pieces.

She paused at an almirah. 'There's an emerald necklace missing.'

'Which one?'

'The one I gave your mother. It was a chain of gold roses holding emeralds. One in each bud.' She searched again. 'Yes. It's not here.'

'Maybe Sushila took it.'

'No. She has her own jewellery.' She closed the almirah. 'We must find out what that woman has done with it.'

She locked the vault. It was cool outside, and she sucked in the air. It didn't help. She felt as if someone had torn a hole in her stomach, too deep ever to be filled with food.

'Are you okay?' Rukmani asked.

Her grandmother looked weak, shaken.

'Yes, I'm okay. And don't tell your father about this. Not yet anyway. We have to find out what she has done with it first.'

EIGHTEEN

The four climbed the hill. It was early, and the earth was still cool. Gunboat recalled his climb with Gertrude. It seemed so long ago; much had changed.

The chauffeur accompanied the rajah, helping him on one side over the broken terrain. Nicky helped on the other. They had left early, predawn, so as to avoid the heat of the hillside. Above, they saw movement; the pilgrims had already arrived. Below, the Rolls-Royce was parked off the road, surrounded by admiring children.

There were around twenty people waiting to see the sadhu. As before, the men and women sat apart. The rajah, intent on revealing humility, sat with the men, Nicky and Gunboat beside him. The chauffeur remained at a distance. Gunboat sensed the other men would have also risen, but the rajah gestured them to remain. He could have removed them equally imperiously.

The youth emerged from the cave, beckoned a tall moustachioed man, and stood aside for him and the women, who also rose, to enter. They were inside about five minutes, and came out whispering softly to each other.

This time the boy called Gunboat.

'Go,' the rajah said when he saw him hesitate.

Little had changed. Even the sadhu appeared not to have moved. Gunboat sat in front of him. The eyes remained closed.

'The boxer,' he said and appeared delighted to have Gunboat visit him. 'The woman is not with you today, but be careful of her. She can do harm.'

'Like the other one,' he asked, not mentioning Miss Hobbs by name.

'Yes. You are in the midst of what I told you. The outcome depends on your courage.'

'In other words whatever I do, I lose out.'

'No. You can win only through courage.'

'Can't you tell the outcome?' Gunboat asked, impatient with the mystery.

He chuckled. 'That depends on the boy.' He reached out. Gunboat opened a palm and felt a faint pinch of vibudhi drop on it. The odour remained the same. 'Tell the rajah to come.' Gunboat blinked at the sunlight. He had no need to tell the rajah. The youth was already leading him into the cave.

The rajah ignored his surroundings, instead he focused on the sadhu ahead. He could feel the calm, the quiet, the serenity, and immediately namasted reverently. He sat at his feet, pleased to have found him. For a long while there was silence.

'You would like to be a sanyasi like me,' the sadhu said. 'But you cannot. You have your duty as a prince, and you must follow it. Be careful in whom you trust.'

'That is always the advice given to princes,' the rajah said petulantly.

'Possibly they need to be reminded often,' the sadhu said and opened his eyes. 'They are forgetful and neglect their duties. You do not wish to be who you are, but you have been born to fulfil your duty, and there is no escape.'

'None?' the rajah asked hopelessly.

'Possibly later in life.' He sounded amused. 'I saw you once, many years ago. I believe you scored a century that day against the British army. A marvellous inning.'

The change was sudden, unexpected, and for a moment the rajah thought he had misheard. His mind still remained on the sublime: this dream, this fantasy of revoking his princely life, like Siddhartha, and devoting it to the pursuit of God. He envied this man: the simplicity, the communing only with God, the purity of his thoughts. He had noticed at first glance the texture of the sadhu's skin. The soft glowing gold. It occurred only in the holiest of men.

'Thank you,' the rajah finally said, not wanting to pursue such a mundane achievement. 'I had not expected you to follow the game.'

'I did once,' the sadhu said. 'I never excelled in it the way you did. I believe you got your blue at Oxford and played for Glamorgan.' He sighed. 'A minor county, but still an important achievement for one of us.'

For the first time, the rajah listened to the voice. He noted the cadence, the pronunciation, the subtle hint of an accent that sounded so like his own. A change had occurred, yet nothing he could quite pinpoint. God had been abandoned for more earthly matters.

'You know quite a bit about me.' His humility had lessened.

'Who are you?'

'One Rajaram, sir,' the sadhu said, and he seemed to be mocking his humbleness in the presence of the prince. 'A sanyasi.'

'Before that,' the rajah commanded.

'I was one of the first Indians to be allowed into the I. C. S.,' he said, and smiled. 'The British were indeed magnanimous. They permitted us to believe we were fit to administer our own country. I was in Oxford quite a few years before you. I moulded myself into a brown sahib so as to achieve this great distinction that they reluctantly bestowed on me.'

'I may have heard of you,' the rajah said. 'Rajaram! It's familiar.'

'I doubt whether you have,' the sadhu said. 'That was my first and last achievement of any earthly merit. I resigned when I returned home, and became a sadhu.' He laughed. 'My immediate superior, one gentleman called Redhead, was disgusted by my behaviour and threatened to have me horsewhipped for my insolence.'

He closed his eyes. The silence lasted awhile. The amused smile remained on the sadhu's face as if he still revelled in the memory. The rajah listened to the hum of insects, the soft murmur of conversation outside, the almost imperceptible breathing of the sadhu. It appeared that he had been forgotten; even possibly dismissed.

'If you can, why not I?'

'I was not destined to be a ruler,' he said. 'You are.' He paused, as if trying to decipher a puzzle, then added: 'You wish to enquire about your death?'

'Yes,' the rajah said, though not surprised. In spite of the man's interest in cricket, he believed he was in the presence of a true guru. 'I'm not afraid of it. I wish to know if there is to be a rebirth.'

'No. This is your last life. You will not return.'

The rajah waited. Nothing more was said. He rose, bowed, and touched the hem of the man's dhoti. The sadhu reached out. Instead of placing the vibudhi into the waiting palm, he touched the rajah's face and pressed his thumb against the point between his eyes, above the bridge of his nose. He left a faint white spot there, and for a long moment the rajah felt an enormous sense of calm. It appeared to flow from the man's thumb, down through his heart and body, infusing him with a subtle energy he could never define.

He went out pleased and told Nicky what had occurred. Nicky listened uneasily. At times he did not understand the forces dividing his father. The need for sadhus—this Rajaram was one of many—conflicted with his stubborn refusal to attend the family temple. The god he pursued was one of the roadside, conjured up by materializations of one kind or another. It was as if he needed constant proof that worship and magic were one and the same.

Nicky was ready to leave, when he found that he had been summoned. He followed the youth. Possibly they were the same age. It was difficult to tell. The youth was scrawny, light, simply clothed. Nicky felt almost fat compared to him, and was aware of the gold trappings around his neck and wrist and finger. He wished now he had been more circumspect in his dress.

He sat at the sadhu's feet, staring and openly curious. He wasn't sure what to expect and had made a decision to ask no questions. If the man was as omnipotent as his father and Gunboat had said, he would know all. If not, he would know nothing.

'You have a difficult life,' the sadhu said. 'You are a prince, yet not one anymore. You are an Indian, yet not one wholly. Our past always haunts us. You are also involved in a conflict inside your family. The rajah is not aware of it, and you have to carry his burden. Listen to your friend, the boxer. He will give good advice.'

'Because he is a foreigner,' Nicky mocked.

'No. Because he has courage. You have it, too, but you have still to discover it. I don't mean the courage of a battlefield. That is mere bravery. It does not last. You hold to courage even when you are defeated.'

'And will I be defeated?' Nicky did not allude to the fight though it was what he meant. The sadhu would need to guess.

He did not get an immediate reply, and his attention wandered. The man was as spare as the youth, and his flesh appeared not much older. It was smooth, tight, unwrinkled. The dhoti was clean, though frayed and worn, and the cave appeared to be bare of any other possessions. If he ate, there was no sign of food; if he drank, there was no vessel. Life could be pared down to mere breath and a rude shelter. He could not imagine his own life being reduced to this mere necessity. It wasn't just ridding himself of the material clutter of palaces and servants and motorcars. That, in itself, was relatively easy. They could be squandered, sold, lost at the dice tables, bequeathed to the countless relatives who constantly plotted for what his family possessed. Mythology was filled with princes who had lost their kingdoms and died paupers on distant battlefields. It was the penance, the spiritual payment for past material possessions, that would be impossible to perform. This self-inflicted poverty that demanded not just the humility of the soul, but also of the mind and the body. Nicky knew as a prince he had been instilled with an ego, the necessity to succeed, to win, to manoeuvre. Here, each loss was victory over the exterior world.

Nicky returned his attention to the sadhu. He appeared still preoccupied, as if the question were beyond his grasp.

'You will win,' he said softly, 'because today you wish to. But one day you will discover that victory is a bitter ash and possibly...' he paused, smiled gently, 'you too could become someone like me.'

'It is possible,' Nicky said dismissively.

He doubted he would have the inclination. He rose. The sadhu put out his hand and placed the vibudhi in his outstretched palm.

'My prince,' the sadhu said quietly and opened his eyes to look at Nicky. He appeared to have known how he looked already for there was no curiosity in the glance. 'Guard yourself well.'

In the mere passing of an hour, the earth had become nearly intolerable. The soles of the feet burned and the glare was blinding. The four made their way down cautiously, trying not to touch the boulders, dancing from spare shade to spare shade. They met others, men and women, toiling up the hillside, indifferent to the heat, intent on reaching the top. They were villagers mostly, and they had dressed for the occasion, as if they were making a pilgrimage to a temple. The women wore their jewellery, and their best cotton or voile saris; the men wore clean dhotis and jibas. An ancient bus had stopped near the Rolls-Royce, and more people were climbing out. Soon, Nicky had no doubt, this hillside, nameless as yet, would be famous. The Hindu makes deities of men faster than they do the clay statues peddled at the temple gates.

'Why do they come?' Nicky asked his father. It was meant obliquely but his father understood.

'Because we need reassurance. We need the comfort of men talking to us. In the temples, with those corrupt Brahmins, we may pray, we may offer up our little offerings, but we do not know whether God hears. The counting of money makes too much noise. Here, we may believe that God has appeared in the form of a man who will converse with us.'

'An avatar.' Gunboat contributed his limited knowledge.

'Yes. Possibly he is that. But that isn't necessary. He is holy, and we can see that even we can become like him if we make the effort. God is available with a certain amount of sacrifice. It is comforting for those who cannot make it.' He climbed into the car and waited until Gunboat had settled in the front seat next to the chauffeur. Nicky sat beside him. 'Do you believe in him, Gunboat?'

'Not in. I believe him. He seems to know something I sure don't, and that's good enough for me.' He turned. 'You, Nicky?'

'I'll wait and see. He said I'd win the fight.'

Gunboat laughed. 'I could have told you that as well, Nicky. I'm your trainer.'

'Anything else?' the rajah enquired.

Nicky thought a moment. 'No...nothing.'

◆

Miss Hobbs listened. The palace was silent. The family had returned to Tandhapur, and only she remained. And Ian. But he was in a distant room. The bearers could occasionally be heard going about their duties. Cleaning and shutting up the rooms. When they had completed these tasks, they would hand her the keys. She would personally see to the locking of the liquor cabinet, the wine cellar, and the kitchen.

She had bathed and was now choosing what to wear. Her range of choice wasn't enormous. She had a few saris and half a dozen frocks. Those were out of fashion. It had been some time since she had worn a frock, and she stared at them as if wanting to make a choice from the small collection. None were suitable for the day. Two were black, a couple were silk dresses, and one was a ball gown, They were reminders of her past really, fragile symbols that she had once lived in a different world. Gunboat had reminded her of it. She had wanted to talk to him more about it; the nostalgia at times was almost overwhelming and she wanted to cry out, but he had not known what she'd meant. He knew of no officers' clubs or balls or shikars or polo on the maidan or pig sticking. He was a crude man, a boxer. They held their excitement in the ring, but once age stole their agility and strength they were shambling, weary men.

She thought often of the past, daydreaming of it and savouring the memories. It had been glorious being a European woman in India. You were greater than a maharani or a begum for, though you could not equal their wealth, you were courted by the men who held them in their power. You were with little effort a countess, a duchess, a princess; a pleasurable, parsasolled lady of leisure. You spent your childhood between Delhi and Simla and Darjeeling, the Indian dust washed daily from your bodies by white-saried ayahs, the Indian sun burning you a delicate pale brown, to be lost in womanhood for being pure white was so important, as fluent in the Indian tongues (though at times you pretended not to be) as the natives themselves. Your position in life had been predestined; you were part of hierarchy, a permanent order that had ruled India for centuries.

She remembered Charlie Potter so clearly sometimes. They had met in Calcutta. She'd gone there to spend Christmas with the Mitchells, old friends of her parents. She was nearly nineteen and the prettiest thing in the whole of Calcutta, and she honestly believed the compliments of all those officers. She danced and drank and flirted, under the watchful eye and chaperonage of Mary Mitchell, naturally. Charlie had come to their New Year's Eve party.

He had been such a handsome man: tall, broad-shouldered, with pale blue eyes that looked as dark as the Indian skies when set against his sunburned skin, and blond unruly hair. He had been a wild young man: a reckless polo player, good at shikars, flamboyantly generous with his gifts to her. He was a tea planter with Brooke Bond.

They married in the autumn of '36, after a six-month courtship. She had not made it easy for him. After all, the choice was almost infinite. So many young Englishmen needed wives. Even a pimply little mouse like Rosemary Collins could find a good match. No, she had not made it easy. Tantrums, sudden flights to the hill stations, mild flirtations with subalterns. He had persisted, and she capitulated. They were married in Saint Mark's Cathedral in Calcutta.

If the past is a dream, so are the nightmares. She discovered them in the hills of Assam. They had been there all the time: dormant, partially ignored in the way only the English can subtly not see. India could be lonely, desolate, frightening. The plantation was one hundred and twenty five miles from Shillong: a bare bungalow with countless servants, and the nearest companions eight miles away. You met the same faces each evening at the Rugby club: drank, ate, drank, flicked through two-month-old *Daily Mirror* magazines and *Tatlers*, drank some more. There were shadows too: deep, menacing. The nightmare of 1857 had never been forgotten, and it began to recur. Gandhi, the half-naked fakir, was gathering the forces (he should have been shot with many others), and there was a feeling that their private world was reaching an end. The war in Europe was distant; the war closer, familiar and frightening, deceptively calm, had begun to escalate. They all remembered 1857 and expected it to begin once more. India had taken its toll of them.

Those days were blurred. Her parents had died, Ian was born, Charles fought in the war. She had lived alone, nursing a child, working as a voluntary nurse, typist, anything to keep herself occupied. When the dream finally ended, she had separated from Charles and moved to Bombay. Ian was left behind. She couldn't raise him by herself.

Charles and Ian did not return home to England in 1947. Neither did she. They had no home. India was home and they remained, for this was a familiar land and people; the other was the alien.

Miss Hobbs chose a flower-patterned voile sari. The choice had been made a long time back: You couldn't remain English, although you were. Your blood was pure, you had aristocratic ancestors, you knew the viceroy. Those no longer counted. The world had changed; the order had turned to chaos. She was unskilled, the past could no longer be summoned to fill her daily life, and she had to survive.

She had no intention of remaining poor, unwanted. The job with the rajah was to be temporary, until she could marshal her forces. She had meant to remain a few months, until she discovered that the rajah needed her advice on many matters, apart from raising his children. She became, in effect, his resident, his prime minister.

Their wealth, their power, was hers, and she held to it. The opposition was only the grandmother and the rajah's sister, and over the years she had eroded that. He had quarrelled often with his sister, and it was only a matter of timing to ensure their distrust was made permanent. The grandmother was…well…a difficult woman. She was not to be banished, but Miss Hobbs had discovered her weakness: her hatred of her husband and the deep loss of her only child. Subconsciously, she blamed the rajah for the death of her child. He should have cared for her more, taken her to physicians, sensed the illness. Miss Hobbs knew it was also a matter of time.

Ian knocked on her door. She was ready.

'All packed?'

'Yes, Mum.' It sounded strange.

It had been a few years since they'd seen each other. Charles now was no longer capable of caring for his son. He drank too much and had taken up with a native woman. So Miss Hobbs had asked for Ian, and he'd been readily given. She had him change schools. From Darjeeling down to the Nilgiris, so he was closer to her. Soon he would be finished, and she had every intention of sending him away from India to return finally home to England. There was no future for an English boy here. For that she would need money; an adequate amount to pay his college fees and keep him in a manner that she felt he should be kept.

She carefully painted a tilak mark on her forehead, slid on a pair of gold bangles, and slipped her feet into chappals. She looked Indian now, except for her skin colour. It was as if the past had not existed. She appeared to have been absorbed by India, vanished almost without trace like all those previous invaders. It was what she wished others to believe which was why, privately, she clung to her past so fiercely. Her soul was inviolate.

'What do you think?'

'Okay,' Ian said. She still felt him a stranger, more so in her Indian costume. The distance between them was wide.

'You'll get used to…this. Now you have your ticket and the money?'

'Yes. It's really a bit more than I need.'

'You might need it,' she said. She knew she indulged him; it was a belated maternal affection. 'I'll get one of the bearers to put your case in the car.'

'I already told him.'

He was restless to leave the palace. Suddenly it felt so abandoned. He was uncomfortable in this opulence. School and the plantation bungalow were spartan, and he had grown used to that. He enjoyed the company of the rajah, Rukmani, Sushila, even the grandmother, but he was not part of them, the way his mother had become. An occasional holiday with her and them was all that was allowed.

'And you won't forget to send me a telegram the moment you reach your father's place.'

'I won't. I'll send it from Shillong if you want.'

'No. From his house.' He was to spend a couple of weeks with his father before returning to school. If he had not been so insistent, she would have refused permission. Charlie was a bad influence. 'I'll send your trunk on to school next week. You did make a list of what you wanted.'

'Yes,' he said stoically. It was the third time she'd enquired. They went out. Their footfalls echoed on the marble floor. The air was still; the dust, caught in shafts of sunlight, floated languidly, choosing a place to settle.

'Why didn't you let me spend my holiday in Tandhapur?' he asked as they stepped outside. The Humber waited.

'I thought you'd be happier here in Bangalore,' Miss Hobbs said. She had not wanted him to get enmeshed in the intrigues. By keeping him distant from the family, she made sure they tolerated him; felt him to be no threat. 'You had the club and there were a few girl friends, weren't there?'

'I suppose so.'

'Did you say goodbye to Trudi?' She was one of three pretty and feckless German sisters. Their father was a scientist working for the Indian Institute of Science.

'Yes. But she's going home soon, so I guess I won't be seeing her again.' He climbed in beside his mother. 'It would have been fun in Tandhapur.'

'Stop complaining so,' she spoke sharply.

They rode in silence. The cantonment station wasn't far, a ten-minute ride. The road ran past a maidan, Cubbon Park, and the new summer parliament being built. It was to be a massive structure and the surroundings were a hive of activity. Stonemasons squatted and chipped at the granite and marble in a chaotic click of sounds. The instruments were a cold chisel and a hammer. It would take years. The women carried the freshly mixed cement in pans on their heads and formed a long line to supply the builders. Already there was a shape to it, and already rumors of massive corruption. Lakhs, possibly crores, would be siphoned off by the contractors and the politicians and the clerks. Nehru, to give the south a sense of participation, had decided to make Bangalore the summer capital, and what he wished became decree. It was to be called the Vydhana Soudha.

There were many buildings going up on the road to the station: offices, homes, commercial buildings. One day the city would become a capital.

The road dipped and forked. In the middle of the fork was the government veterinary hospital. Its compound was, as usual, crowded with animals: buffaloes, cows, sheep, donkeys, dogs, even an elephant.

'I'm sorry.' Miss Hobbs broke the silence. 'I just thought you preferred to spend your holidays in Bangalore. Next time you can go to Tandhapur.'

'Thank you.' He was at least distantly polite.

◆

A dozen coolies rushed the car, each demanding to carry the memsahib's case. The driver chose one, and the others ran to the next vehicle.

'Don't loaf around at your father's,' she said as they climbed out and pushed through the crowds. The station was a small, single-storeyed building. There was a large hall and a couple of office cubicles at the sides. The main station, Bangalore City, was a mile west. 'I want you to train and get yourself fit for the boxing.'

'Oh. I'll win,' Ian said casually. He was eager to leave.

An Indian railway station is a place of suppressed excitement and adventure. It is a kaleidoscope of the country. Even here, Ian could recognize a dozen ethnic groups: Pathans, Gurkhas, Marwaris, Sikhs, Tamils, Parsees, Jats, Punjabis, Bengalis. He had acquired the Indian instinct to recognize even the subtlest differences in the people. The noise was overwhelming. Coolies shouting for passage, balancing cases on their heads; metal-wheeled trolleys pounding the concrete: hawkers shouting wares; bells clanged, whistles blew, people spoke countless tongues, a dozen monkeys chattered and scavenged on the platform. The smells were exquisite: purees, fresh-cut mangoes and oranges, fried spiced peanuts, vadas, idlis, sambar, urine.

His mother was saying, 'When do you have to come down here and box?'

'Against Nicky?' Ian said. 'I might not have to meet him. Depends if he wins his fights, I mean. He's not done this sort of thing before.'

'He's learning, so don't get too cocky.'

'So what if he wins,' Ian said indifferently. 'It isn't a matter of life and death.'

They were on the platform. She pulled him to a stop, spun him to face her.

'It is important,' she was so fierce, so angry that she mesmerized him. 'You must win. Do you think I'm sweating and slaving like a coolie for that family to have my son lose to theirs? They'll be cock-a-hoop to see Nicky beat you; they'll think themselves better than us. You don't know them the way I do. They are mean and spiteful, and that old rani is a witch. If you lose, I won't be able to work for them any longer, and that means I won't have the money to send you to university in England. You'll have to live here all your life, like an Anglo-Indian. Would you like that?' She had tightened her grip. It pinched flesh against bone, and he winced. She shook him. 'Would you?'

'No,' he whispered softly.

'Win for me, my darling.' Suddenly she softened, smiled, yet he felt there was little humour. 'Give me the time.'

'Why time?' He wished the train would come. He wanted to escape, to try to recall the pleasurable anticipation he felt a minute ago. He sensed he could never recapture it.

'Because then I can save up the money we need, darling.'

They heard the train whistle, and she let go. He rubbed his arm. Where she'd held, there was a yellow patch, slowly fading into his sunburn. The train came slowly. It puffed up the slight gradient, taking the curve. A surge of people pushed forward, gathering up baskets, holdalls, tiffin carriers, suitcases, metal trunks.

The locomotive was a steam engine, glistening-black, the brass and steel polished and gleaming. It threw out steam and smoke, which fell softly, darkly, on the gold mohur trees beside the track. As it drew alongside the platform, the driver opened a valve and they were bathed in damp warm steam. The first-class carriages were to the rear of the train, and the rajah's chauffeur found Ian's numbered seat and his bunk. He had the top one. The two below were taken by, he presumed from a glance, government officers on travel. The compartments were quite spacious: one bunk for each passenger. The windows had mesh and glass in separate panels. The mesh kept out the dust and dirt, but never effectively. The windows also had horizontal bars to prevent dacoits breaking in.

'Don't forget the telegram.' His mother kissed him and the train slowly pulled out.

◆

Tandhapur Mining (Private), Ltd. had a small office in the Ford building by the Cubbon Park roundabout. It was on the second floor, and Miss Hobbs slowly climbed the narrow stairs. The walls on either side were stained with fingermarks. She stopped, caught her breath. Since gaining weight, she found any exercise tiring. She remembered in her youth playing tennis, riding; she could do them all day. Now, even stairs tired her.

The door was frosted glass with the company name in black lettering. Inside, two young clerks sat at desks poring over ledgers and correspondence. Behind them were shelves piled high with files bound in red tape. Both men immediately leaped to their feet and stood to attention.

'Is Mr Sunderam in?'

'Yes, madam,' and one of the young men sprang to a rear door and flung it open as if heralding the passage of a goddess.

Sunderam was in his fifties. He was small, stooped, with a pleasant round face, plastered-down greying hair, and brahminical caste marks on his forehead. They were three vertical white lines that swept down from his hairline to join above the bridge of his nose. He was a Shivaite, and the marks represented the imprint of Shiva's feet on his forehead. The lines were neat, precise, and he always gave the impression he had just bathed.

He rose, namasted, and asked: 'Would madam like tea?'

'Yes, please.' Miss Hobbs spoke quietly, as if she wanted the man to know she respected him.

He ordered a clerk to fetch some and sat back down, rigid straight. Sunderam was the manager of the family's affairs. He controlled the day-to-day management of the mines, the family estates, taxes, payments, salaries, allowances, investments. He was steeped in the family's financial and political affairs. He had inherited the post from his father, and his father from his father. They were, in that respect, one and the same, and Miss Hobbs knew she had to move cautiously. His loyalty to the family was not questioned.

'And how may I please to help you, madam?' he was noncommittal in his politeness and she found it difficult to tell his exact opinion of her. She suspected he disliked her.

'How is your family?' she enquired. She had met only a child, never his wife.

'They are very fine, madam,' he said, and waited patiently, blinking owlishly.

'I was talking to the rajah yesterday,' she began cautiously, 'about the problem we are going to have to finance the mines' expansion.' She had deliberately emphasized the 'we'. He had no reaction, as if he hadn't heard. 'With Rukmani not agreeing to the rajah's arrangements, we obviously cannot rely on the loan we'd expected.'

'That is true, madam.' He waited once more, curiously birdlike.

'Have you approached the banks?'

'That is in hand,' he said.

The tea arrived and interrupted them a moment. She was ceremoniously presented with an old cup and saucer by the clerk. Sunderam drank his from a sparkling glass tumbler. She sipped; he sucked on the sweet, steaming liquid.

'What happens if Rukmani goes abroad for higher studies?' she enquired.

He thought a moment, frowned: 'Nothing.' As noncommittally as possible.

'She does control thirty-three per cent of the shares of the mine, doesn't she?' Miss Hobbs asked patiently. She knew he was not stupid. In fact, highly intelligent. He was obtuse only for her. 'The rajah suggested that I ask you how it will affect the operation of the mine.'

'I see,' he said gravely and carefully placed his tumbler down on the blotter. His tone didn't quite suggest disbelief, but he continued: 'She will have to grant the power of attorney to someone here.'

'And for her properties?'

'And for her properties,' he intoned.

'It should be granted to her father.'

'Yes, madam.'

'I'm glad about that,' she said and busied herself with her handbag. She drew out a neatly typed sheet of foolscap paper. 'These are last month's household accounts.'

'Thank you, madam,' he took them and carefully placed a glass paperweight over them. She knew he would check them carefully. He would find no mistake. He never did.

'Could she grant the power of attorney to the old rani?' Miss Hobbs asked casually as she rose.

He stood too and bobbed his head. 'Yes, madam.' He namasted politely.

On the drive back to Tandhapur, Miss Hobbs thought, the old rani is going to be the most dangerous. She detests and distrusts me. At first I suppose it wasn't personal. She hated the British because they dethroned her husband, demoted her to the ex-rani in favour of her daughter. When I entered the household, I became her target. But as long as I am closer to the rajah than she, I can outmanoeuvre her. It is important that Rukmani grants that power of attorney to her father. The remaining shares were owned by Sushila and Nicky. Sushila might cause some problems, but since she'd moved from the household, she'd also removed herself from the family problems. She had her own in her new family. That leaves Nicky. He is young, and still manageable.

She brooded awhile on the old rani. She felt some unease; she hadn't seen her for days. The old witch could be hatching a new threat to her. When she returned to the palace she would ask the servants. They were the best source of information. Never directly. Just gossip which could be overheard in the corridors and kitchens.

NINETEEN

For Gunboat the daily routine began at daybreak. Mohan woke him with a cup of tea. He dressed and met Nicky in the garden. The yuvaraj was never late. The Labrador had dropped out of training. Only the fox terrier accompanied them eagerly on the daily run.

They would then spend an hour in the ring. Nicky stopped dropping his left; he punched straighter, harder; and on the occasion when Gunboat tested his fierce temper with a quick flick to the head, the boy kept control. He would duck behind his guard, eyes watering, and remain there until he saw an opening. He moved quicker now, and surer, and when Gunboat took him to three rounds, Nicky had the stamina to keep pace.

'You know,' Gunboat said over breakfast. That had also become routine. The prince, it seemed, preferred his company in the mornings. 'I think we should have you fighting someone your own size.'

'A sparring partner?' Nicky asked, pleased with his expertise.

'Yeah. It will give you better practice than fighting me.'

'I could get one of the village boys,' Nicky said airily and turned to Swami as if he were about to order a soft drink.

'I don't think that's a good idea, Nicky,' Gunboat said quickly.

He was amused by the way of princes. If a chopping block was required, some poor son of a bitch could be brought in.

'We gotta get someone who will fight you.'

'I see.' He appeared disappointed. 'Who can we get then?'

'I know a couple of boys in Bangalore who aren't bad boxers.' Gunboat measured Nicky against memory. 'About your height, maybe not the same weight. But they're pretty good.'

'You train them?'

'Not in the way I'm doing you,' Gunboat said. 'I gave 'em a few tips. Peter would be the best.'

'Peter?' Nicky's nose wrinkled.

'Do you object?'

Gunboat controlled his irritation, acutely remembering Gertrude. They were all truly an abandoned people; discarded, almost forgotten and not needed. The Indian had the delicate social antennae of a mating ant.

'No,' Nicky said softly, aware that he had offended Gunboat. He, too, remembered the girl. 'I would naturally like to give them some emolument for their services.'

'Naturally,' Gunboat said. 'We'll figure that out when I fix it up next week. When do you get back to school?'

'End of next week. The boxing starts about five days after that. So I haven't too much time.'

'We're doing fine. You don't want to peak too early before the fight. Lots of boxers overtrain, and by the time they fight, they're tired and bored with all the training and sparring.'

Nicky rose, understanding. 'When will you teach me to fight dirty?'

'Soon,' Gunboat said noncommittally. It didn't satisfy Nicky. He remained until Gunboat added, 'Next week. You really do want to win?'

'Yes. Don't you believe I can?'

'Yeah. You got what's needed. Hunger. A real belly hunger.' Gunboat stood and they both went in. They passed two other guests, both middle-aged men dressed in slacks and shirts, who immediately greeted the yuvaraj before continuing out. 'Businessmen, our new princes,' Nicky said laconically.

There were many guests who came to stay a few hours, a night or two. The guest palace functioned with the lazy efficiency of an old and elegant hotel. Gunboat had come to feel at home in it now, treating it as his possession. It had lost its sense of lonely foreboding. The ghosts, he suspected, had accepted him as one of the more permanent tenants.

Gunboat gauged Nicky's mood. He sensed the boy had become closer to him, though at times the aloof arrogance would suddenly resurface as if it were a warning for him not to overstep his position.

'It's her you're fighting, isn't it?'

'Yes,' Nicky said. He hesitated, and Gunboat thought he would withdraw, turn imperious. 'It is the only way I know how. I'm still a minor in family matters, and there is little else I can do.' He mounted the stairway with Gunboat, head bent in thought.

'I was young when she entered the household,' Nicky said, as if the past were that distant and only faintly remembered.

'I was raised by my sisters and my grandmother and my aunt, and countless cousins. They were all women and I was,' he smiled and corrected himself, 'I am spoilt as you see. There was a great deal of affection, never a moment of loneliness or need, but there was never any love. But I was pretty happy, I guess. I was eight when my father hired her. She persuaded him I should go to a public school in England. After all, the sons of all the princes went abroad to study. Nehru is an ex-Harrow boy. So I went. When I returned there was little that remained of my family.'

'Why did your father permit that?' Gunboat sat on his bed, stripped off his sweat shirt, and switched on the fan. The breeze was warm, but the movement was enough to cool him.

'He was preoccupied with the state. India was changing and we all needed to adjust to our new roles. He had to spend enormous time in Delhi with the Concorde of Princes arguing with the government about status, our privy purses, our compensations. Countless problems. The new government was scaling our privy purses according to the number of gun salutes the British had accorded us. We had three, so we all haggled like merchants in a bazaar.'

Nicky paused, wondering whether he had spoken the truth. He was young, and it was difficult to judge his father's action from such a close range. The preoccupation sounded plausible though, possibly, not forgivable.

'It was simple,' he continued. 'The British practised the art so well: divide and conquer. They took India like that, and she took this family.'

He squinted out into the garden. Sunlight flooded the room, turning all it touched near white with glare.

Nicky turned, called, 'Mohan.'

Mohan came running. He had been within earshot. Nicky gestured, and Mohan undid the knot holding the bamboo tatty and let it fall. The gloom lit at its edges with glare, took time to adjust to, and it appeared the room grew cooler.

'Yes, I want to win that fight very badly,' he added, remembering how the conversation had begun. 'I am depending on you for that.'

'I'll do my best,' Gunboat said.

'What will you do when it's over?'

'Catch the first boat out of here to New York,' Gunboat said. The prince remained in the doorway, his back to the over-bright garden, his face as dark as the shadow. Gunboat sensed he was already being missed by the boy, and wanted to add something. A consolation, a joke, but before he could think of it, Nicky had gone.

◆

Nicky knew he would miss Gunboat's company. In Tandhapur he had no friends. None of the boys were equal in rank, none as privileged, and though in childhood he had played with the children of syces and the malis and the estate managers, they had grown apart. It was not so much his fault as theirs. They lost their innocence and acquired a watchful deference and false humor. He had learned to distrust excessive laughter.

It was only meant to please the prince.

His grandmother waited for him. She sat in the cane-backed reclining chair, a small table in front of her, and a line of playing cards. If alone, she whiled away her time playing patience; if not, she commanded that Nicky or Rukmani, anyone, play whist or blackjack or bridge. Though she carried no purse, a new deck materialized wherever she went. He suspected the servants constantly carried one to satisfy her sudden whims.

Swami stood peering over her shoulder, kibitzing. Once, impatient at her slowness, he reached over and moved a card. This familiarity with the old rani didn't surprise Nicky. Swami had served in the family all his life and was as much a part of it as the son and daughters. What did surprise him, however, was her lack of reaction to this interference. Usually she scolded him, and then they whiled away fifteen minutes arguing. Instead, she accepted his move passively and continued playing.

'Are you okay?' Nicky asked.

She nodded. She looked preoccupied but also, to Nicky's eye, tired. The lines of exhaustion around her mouth were deep, almost separating her cheeks from her mouth; the eyes were reddened. There was a pinch to her face, as if she were in some pain.

'Are you sure?'

'Yes, I'm sure,' she said. 'Now get changed. I don't have all day.'

His clothes were laid out on the bed. He stripped to his underpants. As a child he had been raised, bathed, dressed by her, and now there was no shyness.

Swami carried a fresh towel and stood out of water radius as Nicky bathed. He looked worried.

'She isn't well,' he finally said. 'For the last few days she has been quiet. You saw, didn't you? Normally she would get angry with me.'

'I know,' Nicky said. 'Maybe she's just thinking about something. She does get like that.'

'No.' He was adamant. 'Maybe she should see a doctor.'

'Tell her then,' Nicky said and stepped out from the shower.

Swami towelled him dry.

'You tell her,' Swami said. 'You are her grandson. When I suggested it, she told me to shut up.'

'I will.'

Nicky waited for his clothes to be brought in, and dressed. He took time. He studied his face. He had begun shaving, not regularly but once every three days. He still looked smooth, and he wished the growth would hurry so he could do it daily. Carefully he oiled and combed his thick black hair. Wet, it obeyed the comb's path. Once dry it would curl and turn unmanageable. He slicked it down the best he could. He inspected his trousers, white cotton, and accepted them; he refused the shirt and sent Swami to fetch another. Though he had not shaved he slapped on Yardley's cologne.

The old rani continued with her cards even when he finally sat beside her.

'Have you seen a doctor lately?' Nicky asked.

'Yes,' she said, and finally gave up on her cards. Swami gathered them up, and slipped them back in the pack and dropped it in his shirt pocket.

She leaned back slowly, as if her muscles and bones were reluctant to take that rest. She revealed no inconvenience, yet Nicky sensed the pain. The flesh tightened and quivered as if the old woman was determined not to allow herself to lose control.

'What did he say?'

'I'm tired. I need a rest. Maybe I'll go to Badrinath,' she said more to herself. It was a famous place of pilgrimage in the Himalayas. 'Or Tirupati,' cutting back her ambition as if aware she had not the time. Tirupati was much nearer, a hundred miles south of Madras.

He had been there once as a child, with his mother. He remembered vaguely the terror of having his head shaved, and the ochre liquid the barber used to cleanse the shaved skull. He still remembered having wept bitterly, but then he had been comforted by his mother. Myth had it that Vishnu had rested on the flat rock where the temple now stood, before continuing his celestial journey across the universe.

'Maybe you should,' he conceded, and made a note to check their family doctor. He would forget, and remember too late.

'She took a necklace,' she said abruptly.

'Which one?'

'The emerald one I gave your mother,' she said, and added, 'the cheeky bitch.'

'We should tell Father.' He rose.

'No,' she said, commanding him down. 'All that will happen will be her saying it is lost, and then one day it will be found in some drawer. That will prove nothing. We must find out where it is now. With which moneylender.'

'There must be thousands,' Nicky said.

'No. She would not go to a bazaar lender. He would not have the funds and can't be trusted,' his grandmother said.

Obviously she had given it some thought. 'It will be one of the big Marwaris. There are not many of them. I will get the police commissioner to make me a list and visit each one. But I cannot go alone.'

'I will come with you,' Nicky said.

'No. It can't be another one of the family. I need a witness when I find the necklace. Someone your father will believe. I am not saying he will disbelieve me, but our minds are such that she could possibly persuade him to think I had planned the whole thing.'

'But the Marwari can tell Father.'

'So I bribed him to lie.' His grandmother smiled for the first lime. 'It is easily done too. I thought of that as an alternative,' she conceded. 'I know one who owes this debt. At the moment, I don't need to.'

'So who do you want to go with you?'

'What does your father think about your friend?'

'Gunboat.' Nicky shrugged. 'They seemed to get on.'

It was difficult to judge. His father's sensibilities were not fully Indian. They were partially British. They judged a man, not by caste so much but more on his ability to play with a straight bat or else, under stress, to comport himself as a gentleman. He expected of men (women never entered the reckoning) that they be honest, trustworthy, and truthful, and was constantly surprised that they never were. He was miscast and misplaced, not only in time, but also in race. Gunboat had never held a cricket bat, in which case his character was greatly diminished. However, his father believed Gunboat a gentleman, forgiven for being an American, and just possibly acceptable.

'I knew we shouldn't have sent you to that British school,' the old rani scolded. 'What do you mean "get on"?'

'He seems to be friendly,' Nicky said slowly, trying to articulate his thoughts. 'He even went to see this sadhu Rajaram with Gunboat.'

She grunted. 'With your father, that is an important concession. Send Gunboat to me.'

She struggled out of the chair and rose into the muted light coming in from the east window. Standing straight she reached Nicky's shoulder, and though they were equally lit, it appeared as if she was in a barely visible shadow that darkened her face. Nicky would have helped her, but she pushed his arm away and slowly walked out.

'Go with her,' Nicky ordered Swami.

◆

Miss Hobbs saw the old rani pass. A few feet behind, soft and silent, came Swami. Neither saw her for she stood behind a pale marble screen. It was half an inch thick, intricately carved and so delicate the light came through the very stone. She waited to check their direction, and stepped out in the corridor.

◆

The old rani lived in a distant wing of the palace, impossibly far from the rest of the family. She had moved there on the death of her husband in the Hindu rite of banishment. It was a scandal that she still led such an active social life, and an interfering one in Miss Hobbs's opinion.

The rajah's family lived close to one another. Rukmani's suite of rooms was halfway down the corridor from Nicky's. Miss Hobbs knocked on the door. A servant woman opened it and allowed her in. Rukmani was at a desk, absorbed in writing a letter. She was a prolific letter-writer and diary-keeper. Her diary was locked in her almirah, and in that trait she was no different from any other girl in the world. When she saw Miss Hobbs, she carefully placed the letter under her blotter and turned her chair.

'To Prithivi?' Miss Hobbs asked confidingly.

'No,' Rukmani said.

It was to him. A letter of remorse, of the bitter sadness of falling out of love. Or was it infatuation? She wasn't sure. All she felt was a deep pity for herself.

'I have talked to your father about him,' Miss Hobbs said, sitting down. 'He just refused to change his mind. I'm afraid the old rani advised him on that. I told him you were a grown woman, and not living in the nineteenth century. You are westernized, and quite capable of making your own decisions, but,' she sighed as if it were beyond comprehension, 'I suppose old traditions die hard. I am trying my best to help you, you know that.'

Rukmani didn't reply immediately. She studied Miss Hobbs warily. She remembered when Miss Hobbs had first entered the palace. It was as nanny and housekeeper. The three children needed upbringing, tutoring, and in the rajah's opinion, an amount of westernization. It was important at that time, because of the centuries of British rule, that the children of the rich ape those habits and characteristics of their rulers. Miss Hobbs was not there in the role of a schoolmistress, but rather as a status symbol. Most of the princes hired British teachers or nannies to care for their children.

At the beginning, Rukmani thought she liked Miss Hobbs. She was a child, and Miss Hobbs was an excellent storyteller and told her all about her exploits in the hills and in Bombay and in the viceroyalty. Gradually, however, in the manner of all women as they grow wiser, a certain distrust crept into the relationship. The young princess was growing into a very pretty woman, Miss Hobbs into an older, weary one, and with each passing year their animosity had increased.

'Yes,' she finally said.

It was calculation on her part. She needed, for now, an ally. Miss Hobbs was admirable for the part. She could intercede with her father.

'Do you really want to go to Oxford?' Miss Hobbs asked with kindness, and answered her own question. 'Ah, at your age I wish I'd done something like that, but we were not expected to, you know. Young women were expected to be genteel, none too bright, and be good wives. University had nothing to offer us or so we were told by our parents. You'll have such a marvellous time there, I just know it. A princess at Oxford. Boating, balls, champagne parties. I heard so many stories about the social life—'

'I am not interested in that,' Rukmani said primly. The wound was fresh and permitted no joys. Only cares.

'Oh, you'll get over Prithivi soon,' Miss Hobbs spoke with understanding. 'One day, surprisingly, you won't even remember who he was. Of course,' she conceded, 'we're hoping you are going to study as well, and get your degree.'

'I'm going to get a first.'

'That's even better than your father,' Miss Hobbs said. 'He got a third, but that's because he was too busy playing cricket.' She fell silent; allowed the silence to remain a while. Rukmani dreamed of escape from the palace confines. 'Of course, it is going to be difficult.'

'I know,' Rukmani sighed. 'They're both so old-fashioned.'

'That can't be helped, my dear.' Miss Hobbs was placating. 'They were both raised that way and they're doing what they think is best for you.'

Time passed. Crows cawed outside the window, answered by the angry chatter of squirrels. The palace itself remained silent, drowsing in the heat. 'I'm fairly sure I can change your father's mind, but... it depends on how much you will help me.'

'How?'

'I'm only looking after your own interests, you know.'

Miss Hobbs was once more kindly. 'That was the reason I took the job in the first place, to look after you children. That's why I'm remaining, instead of returning home to England. When you go abroad, you know, you'll have to grant the power of attorney for your control in the mines, and your properties, to someone.'

'You?' Rukmani said abruptly.

'Not me.' Miss Hobbs appeared astonished by this suggestion. 'I'm not a member of the family and don't want any part of it. No, I think you should give it to your father.'

'Why not my grandmother?' Rukmani asked.

'I thought of her too,' Miss Hobbs conceded, 'but she isn't on your side, is she? Apart from that, I think she's closer to Sushila than you. And when you're away, it's quite possible, I'm not saying it is going to happen my dear, just possible, that she might be of more help to Sushila than to you.'

'How can she do that?'

'She will have the right to sell, make deposits, draw money for various things…' The rest remained unsaid.

The silence returned. Minutes passed softly, unnoticed as the ray of sunshine creeping across the marble floor. Dust gathered, fell, settled. Rukmani glanced at the desk. An edge of the letter showed, smudged with ink. The desk was antique: mahogany, leather-topped, the drawers inlaid with mother-of-pearl.

Rukmani glanced back. Miss Hobbs sat comfortably, patiently, her hands folded on her belly. She chewed betel, reddening her mouth. A question had been asked implicitly; an explicit answer was expected. Rukmani circled, probing for an advantage to Miss Hobbs by this action. She saw none. It was only a matter of days before her grandmother found the moneylender who held the necklace. Then Miss Hobbs would be out. If it took longer, and that was possible, she saw little harm in aligning her needs with Miss Hobbs. She could discard her later.

'Okay,' she said. Miss Hobbs sighed and rose. 'But I'll sign the power of attorney on the day I leave for Oxford.'

'Naturally, my dear,' Miss Hobbs indulged her. 'I didn't expect any different.'

Miss Hobbs understood Rukmani's strategy. The girl was young, the calculations transparent. The loss of the necklace had been discovered. The servants had informed her that the old rani and Rukmani had spent hours in the vault. Now, the old rani would have to discover the moneylender, and that would take time. Miss Hobbs felt confident she could raise the money to reclaim the necklace and have it found in Rukmani's, or better still, the old rani's cupboard. She stopped, laughed, and the sound carried down the deserted corridors.

TWENTY

Gunboat dozed. The fan's breeze ruffled the pages of a paperback, flicked his hair, held perspiration at bay. He had lunched well, in the company of a minor government official from the Department of Mines in Delhi. The official hoped to make a study tour of America in the near future, and was curious about not only the country but Gunboat. He had asked impertinent questions, the way all Indians do. At times, Gunboat thought as he parried, they can be as inquisitive as a government form. Age, marital status, if not married why not, earnings, family background, education. Their curiosity, like children's, could never be satisfied, and Gunboat had long since taken to giving evasive answers until they tired.

He dreamed of America. Peculiarly, this time it wasn't of the land or the people. He dreamed of food. The lunch, with a cold beer, had been chapattis, half a dozen curries, yoghurt, rice, pickles. Delicious yet inadequate. Possibly it was why his dreams stirred of food. He would sacrifice an arm or a leg for a pastrami on rye with mustard, a dill pickle, and cole slaw. He knew where he would get one. It was in a small deli just off the Grand Concourse Boulevard, half a block up from the subway station on 164th Street. It would be his first celebration. A buck on the counter, a pastrami on rye, and a cold Bud. He could almost taste it now. He could smell the odour of steam, frying chicken, cheeses, stale coffee; people, men of bay rum, woman of Woolworth perfumes and lavender powders. The windows misted; outside the snow and cold. He missed cold, real cold, the breath's smoke, the cheeks flushed by swift cruel wind. 'Gunboat.'

Gunboat woke. The ceiling fan remained a blur; his face was damp with perspiration. He wiped it, then remembered he had been called. Johnny stood at the foot of the bed, dusty, crumpled from travel.

'What are you doing here?' Gunboat sat up.

'You didn't come to Bangalore yesterday, so the mountain came to Mohammed,' Johnny said. He looked tired, uncertain. 'You know, this room is as big as my house.' He walked around it as if it were a museum to be inspected and never touched.

'Hey, man. This bed is bigger than mine.' He propped himself up. 'Why didn't you come?' Johnny asked from a distant corner. 'I missed you.'

'I'm sorry,' Gunboat said. He had forgotten what it felt like to be missed. One day it would be permanent. 'I didn't have a good reason to return to town.'

'Gertrude?' Johnny returned to the bed. 'I saw her on South Parade outside the Plaza on Thursday.'

'With anyone?'

'Bunch of them.' Johnny spoke as if they were crows. 'What were you doing?'

'Training the prince,' Gunboat said. 'Was there a skinny guy with slicked-down hair with her?'

Johnny frowned. 'I didn't see him. She saw me and turned away.' He would have called her name, but stopped. 'Is it finished with you both?'

'I don't think so. We had a row. I wrote her a couple of days back. Maybe she'll reply.'

She was like a child still, unaware of hurt, testing the limitation of her female power. One day she would cross the boundary, and only then be touched with that painful comprehension that she, too, was mortal. She too would be wounded and weep.

'That's all.' Johnny sounded disappointed. 'I thought there'd be a huge tamasha on here.'

'It's quiet here.'

The quiet lay on the surface; the deceptive stillness of old and ancient and ordered things. This feudal family appeared as permanent as those granite rocks and the harsh baked earth. He sensed the frailty beneath. He was told little but observed the unease in the members of the family. They were waiting, breath held, but he did not know for what.

The old rani had summoned him the night before. Mohan had come, awakened him just as he had fallen asleep, and told him to accompany him. They'd softly crossed the garden, not to the palace but to a gazebo beyond the fountain. It was surrounded by mango trees, somewhat derelict. It had been raised to be a splendid symbol of leisure, possibly for the palace band, if there had been one, to entertain the family and guests. Six steps led up to the octagonal floor, the concrete cracked and chipped from the years of rains; the tile roof was barely intact. The old rani sat on a garden bench, staring into the darkness. She did not invite him to sit. Mohan remained in the deep shadows of the trees.

There was no light. All he saw was the shine of teeth, the glitter of gold in the pale moonlight that slipped through the leaves.

'You were asleep?' she asked.

'Nearly.' He lit a cigarette.

The flare caught her by surprise. She looked so weary; but she straightened, still in control of the flesh.

'I like you,' she said as if she had been studying from afar. 'You don't talk much. Europeans never stop talking. They are a tiring people.'

'Thank you.'

'How is the yuvaraj doing?'

'Learning fast.'

'Will he win?'

'You bet.'

'He must win.' She was fierce. 'It is important for us. If you need anything…'

'Everyone keeps offering,' Gunboat laughed. 'I seem to have hit the jackpot.'

'Are you taking?'

'No.'

'You are a fool,' she said with amused kindness. 'Is that an American trait?'

'I suspect it's my very own,' Gunboat said.

'The British accused us of corruption, but they were the past masters of the art. They robbed and cheated us and grew enormously rich off us. We learned too much from them,' she mocked. 'Including democracy and equality and freedom. None of which they themselves possess.'

'You hate them.'

'Yes.' It came as a hiss.

She fell silent. The night was no quieter than day. The garden was raucous with crickets, frogs, shadowy movements that rustled the fallen leaves. Far away he thought he heard the cough of a predator. Deep, menacing, momentarily silencing lesser creatures.

'I didn't bring you here to discuss them. I would like you to accompany me to Bangalore in a few days. Could you?'

It was no command; a polite request. 'Sure. What's it about?'

'I am searching for an emerald necklace. When I find it, I would like you to be present as a…witness.'

'Where will you look?'

'Among moneylenders,' she said. 'Will you, please?'

Gunboat thought she had charm when it was a necessary implement. It sat well with her. Her request made him feel favoured, as if he'd been granted a reprieve of some sort.

'Sure. Why me?'

She laughed: 'We have the unfortunate trait of not trusting each other. So we turn to…she hesitated, 'strangers.'

'Sure,' Gunboat repeated, hesitating whether to question her further. He decided not to. She would tell him in her own time. 'Good night, your highness.'

She nodded; watched him go, accompanied by Mohan. The night

was cool, moist, and she savoured the air. Her life had been spent in this garden and she wondered whether it had any worth. She had been given in marriage to a prince, and her life had ended there, not begun. Time had been squandered, slowly, painfully slowly. She had been a bauble, like those jewels in the vaults, neither more nor less precious. She knew it had been less and wanted not to think of that. It would only make her feel worthless, and this was no time for that. She was nearing the end, and she knew it.

She was permanently tired now, but sleep became more difficult. Minutes snatched in a doze, then snatched away in sudden, frightened wakenings, as if reminders that soon she would never waken.

Sometimes, as on this night, she speculated whether life had held alternatives. Possibly. Probably not. She would have been given to a different prince, and it would have been little different. She dismissed the musings. It was too late, and depressing. She accepted this destiny. The sum total, she calculated, was this final effort to protect the family from that woman. It had led here; not to another place, another position in life. She accepted that and dozed off on the bench. In the shadows her servants waited for her to summon them.

◆

Johnny washed his face in the bathroom and returned, wiping it with a square linen handkerchief. He folded the damp cloth and tucked it back in his trouser pocket.

'You could have used the towels,' Gunboat said.

'Thank you,' Johnny said politely, as if he'd not noticed them. For a moment he brightened. 'I'm holding five thousand chips as bets on the fight.'

'What odds?'

'They haven't changed.' Johnny smiled. 'You think the prince will win?'

'Jesus, if one more person asks, I swear I'll throw a punch at him. Yes, yes, yes.' Then feeling the confidence fade. 'He should with all the training I'm giving him.'

'Good,' Johnny said. 'I keep telling bettors, the prince could lose. You know I'm not being definite. If he wins we'll clear up a...bundle?'

'Yeah. Bundle. What brings you here anyway? It's a long bus ride.'

'Long? It took all night and day. I had to change buses three times to reach here.' Fastidiously he patted his clothes. Some dust rose. 'I'm in love,' he said shyly, and sat down.

'Yeah?'

'Yes.' He appeared despondent as if afflicted by an incurable disease.

'So you should be happy. Congratulations.' They shook hands. 'Let's have a toast to the lucky woman.' Gunboat poured a whiskey in two shot glasses. There was no ice and it tasted bitterly warm. 'I'll ring for some beer.'

Johnny was impressed. 'You can? Do it then. I've never been served beer in a palace.'

Gunboat crossed to the door and pressed the buzzer in the door jamb. It would take time for a bearer to make his way to the room, if he was awake and not sleeping away the hot afternoon. They sipped, grimaced, and put the glasses down.

'Who is she?'

'She's just finishing her B. A. at Maharani College,' Johnny said. 'She is absolutely beautiful and likes me a lot. We've talked a bit, not much. You know how it is.'

'Yeah,' Gunboat agreed.

'She is of marriageable age, very fair, and I want my parents to meet her family. She is also a Brahmin, and she has a good dowry.'

'You'd ask for that?'

'Sure.' Johnny was surprised. 'Why not? That is the custom. It will be about ten, maybe fifteen thousand rupees.'

The bearer interrupted, still drowsy. Gunboat gave the order. 'That will be enough to start us off. Except...' He faltered, dabbed at his perspiration with the damp handkerchief. 'I haven't got a job. I must meet the yuvaraj. It's very important.'

'I'm seeing him this evening,' Gunboat said. 'What kind of a job?'

'Anything,' Johnny said in relief. Then curtailed his magnanimity. 'Preferably with Hindustan Machine Tools or Parry's. Paying around two hundred fifty to three hundred rupees a month. A trainee manager possibly, so that there is a chance for promotion.'

'Anything else?' Gunboat enquired politely. The gentle sarcasm was lost.

'No. Even Bharat Electronics is okay.'

'And how is the yuvaraj going to do all this?' Gunboat was genuinely curious. He'd expected a request to work for the family mining company.

'These princes know everyone,' Johnny said. 'All he has to do is make a call to the manager or chairman and they'll issue orders to hire me. You see, the rich here all stick together. Same club, same school, same games, same friends. My job is only a minor favour to them. For me, it is my whole life.' He reached into his top pocket and carefully drew out a clean, white envelope. 'Here's my curriculum vitae.'

Gunboat took it. It was a spare life. Birth, schooling, university; little else.

'I thought you were a revolutionary.'

Johnny laughed. 'I told you. We poor can't remain that forever.'

◆

Gunboat enjoyed the evening workouts. The shadows were long, cool, and there was some breeze. Nicky would skip for fifteen minutes, punchbag for another fifteen, rest, and then spar three rounds with Gunboat. He was thinking like a boxer now. Strategizing in the ring, working Gunboat into corners, making him come out, tiring him with a chase.

'Okay, Prince,' Gunboat said at the end of their second round. 'I'll show you how to fight dirty.'

Swami wiped the sweat off Nicky, gave him a silver tumbler of ice water.

'Will the referee ever see it?'

'Depends on how good you get, Prince,' Gunboat said. 'Only the best fighters can slide in these punches without the ref noticing. The bad ones...they're gonna lose anyway.' They met in the centre, their shadows joining, immensely tall on the ground. 'Gene Tunney, one of the best we ever had, fought good dirty. A ref never saw some of his punches, but the guys he fought sure felt them. Here...' He pulled Nicky to him, tapped him on the side, just over the kidneys. 'The rib cage is a clever protection. It don't let you get a good punch into the kidney with your closed fist. So what you do is use the edge of your palm. See?' He tapped. 'It just fits into that opening there. Hit hard, and you can just reach the kidney. Do it in a clinch. Chop in with your palm. Hard. That was a Tunney trick.'

Nicky tried. He had to reach up and around. The blow delivered was awkward and hit only the rib cage.

'It's got to be someone your size. See, when you clinch...'

Gunboat bent at the knee, held the prince, gently tapped at the opening with the edge of his palm. He felt the prince do the same, except harder.

'What else?' Nicky asked. He looked pleased, as if he'd been initiated into an ancient cult.

'Jesus. You're gonna be one hell of a dirty fighter. A mean one, too.'

Gunboat pushed out a fist, separating the thumb from the clenched finger. 'When you jab in the face, point your thumb at the guy's eye. Do it fast, just before you land, then close it back in again. He'll scream fucking murder. Then you gotta act innocent. Kind of "who me?" Fighting's also acting. You gotta put on a show.'

'You ever win that way?'

Swami stripped off their gloves. He towelled the prince. Gunboat wiped himself, drank ice water from the bottle. He had to lean back to hold the opening an inch above his open mouth and pour the water down his throat. It was unclean to place one's mouth to the opening.

'No,' Gunboat answered. 'And I've never wanted to. Sure, I've done it once or twice, but that's in retaliation. The other guy would try it first. Once he knows you know the same tricks he stops.' They walked slowly back to the palace. 'It's never worth it to win that way.'

'I know,' Nicky said gently.

He was the chela to this fighter, the way that skinny boy was to that sadhu. You learned from your elder, not only the craft, but also the morality of living.

'I need a favour,' Gunboat began awkwardly.

It wasn't necessary. Nicky appeared pleased to grant it. It gave him an opportunity to be a prince, a patron to his friend.

'Sure. What?'

'It's for a friend. You met him in that jail with me.'

'Swaminathan?'

'Yeah. Johnny. He's planning to get married soon, he's fallen in love, and needs a job. He'd like to work for Hindustan Machine Tools or Parry's or Bharat Electronics. Trainee manager, he suggested.'

'What is his education?'

'A bachelor's in chemistry.' Then he added, 'a third.'

Nicky kept silent. They stopped by the palace steps. The evening light was fading rapidly. A few stars, faint as tinsel, were scattered in the sky; the moon was pale, weary.

'Okay,' Nicky said. 'I will do it.'

'You can?' Gunboat said in surprise.

'I don't see why not. I think we know the chairman of both companies. They are government-owned, but that shouldn't cause problems. Does he have a C.V.?'

'Yeah. He's visiting me at the moment. Do you want to meet him?'

'That isn't necessary,' Nicky said coldly. 'It is a favour to you. I shall get my father to arrange the interviews.'

'Do you mind if he stays the night?' Gunboat asked. He couldn't conceal his irritation. Nicky's abruptness was patronizing, the dispensation of favours without involvement.

'No. He is welcome,' Nicky said, then added: 'You are his friend,

Gunboat. I can't be his. He is older, poorer, and is now...beholden to me.'

'You could say hello.'

'Possibly,' Nicky said, turned, and ran up the palace steps.

◆

Johnny lay on the bed reading a Trollope paperback. He'd bathed, changed, and had a drink on the table.

'This is a fantastic hotel,' Johnny said. His old enthusiasm had returned. 'Ask and it's given to you on a silver platter.' He studied Gunboat a moment, as Gunboat stripped off his sweaty track suit. 'Did you talk to the yuvaraj? Will he see me?'

'He won't see you, Johnny,' Gunboat said gently, and Johnny's face fell. He looked as if he would cry. 'But he'll get you the job. I'll remind him again in a few days, so you'll be able to get married soon.'

Johnny leaped from the bed, grasped Gunboat's hands with both his, and pumped them up and down. He was in tears. He embraced Gunboat too. 'Thank you, thank you.'

'I've done nothing,' Gunboat said, uneasy with the effusive emotion. He disentangled himself and escaped into the bathroom.

◆

Miss Hobbs's suite of rooms was furnished very differently from the rest of the palace. Her drawing room resembled a gracious, if somewhat unfashionable, English parlour. Pretty lace curtains hung over the doorways and windows, a comfortable sofa scattered with cushions faced an artificial fireplace. A couple of uncomfortable straight-backed chairs, elegantly Victorian, were placed on either side of the low coffee table. On the walls were many photographs. They were oval-shaped, sepia-toned, of people: her parents, grandparents, her marriage, her British friends standing by stylish old motorcars, many portraits of her as a young and pretty woman. On a sideboard was a Telefunken wireless, tuned to the BBC World Service. Beside it were three piles of magazines: *Field & Stream*, *Tatler*, and the *Daily Mirror*. Against one wall stood a bookshelf crammed with novels from Foyle's literary book club.

It wasn't so much the furnishings as the air of orderliness about the room that made the visitor feel he had been transported to an English flat. Nothing was out of place; no Indian ornamentation intruded except for a couple of morahs that served as footrests.

Her bedroom was little different. The dresser was covered with English perfumes, colognes, powders, lipsticks, and the bed had a pleasant floral-patterned coverlet. The mosquito net was a concession to the bothersome flies.

Miss Hobbs sat at a small desk tucked into a corner. She had completed her daily accounts and entered them neatly in a fine legible hand with a Doric pen into a school exercise book. She always felt a certain satisfaction at completing this daily task. It was a very private exercise in which the complex world was reduced to accurate amounts of money for tangible objects: meat, poultry, vegetables, eggs, fruit, flour, oil. The quantity was prodigious for the small household, but guests and servants had to be fed well.

She glanced at the small carriage clock by the bedside. It had once been her father's. It was late, ten-thirty, and time to make her visits. She slipped a flower-patterned robe over her nightdress, locked the accounts in a drawer, and went out. Her rooms were opposite the rajah's. She entered without knocking.

His rooms were surprisingly bare. He had two reception rooms, little different from those in other parts of the palace, and his bedroom contained a massive four-poster bed, two armchairs, a desk, and little else. His wardrobe was kept in a small anteroom. She had heard that the nizam of Hyderabad, reputed to be the wealthiest man in the world, slept on a charpoy in a tiny room no larger than that single and simple rope-strung bed.

The rajah was reading a file of papers. He held a Parker pen absent-mindedly, and his reading glasses were on the edge of his nose. He noticed her presence only when she leaned over and kissed the top of his head.

The relationship between Miss Hobbs and the rajah had begun four and a half months after she began her employment. It had been deliberate on her part. She noticed his vulnerability, his loneliness, the need not so much for a family as for sexual companionship. She had initiated the relationship slowly, for there was time. After-dinner talks: first about the children, then about his dead wife, about the state, and finally about himself. The intimacy was easy, natural, she listened well, and he succumbed. She did not share his bed nightly—that would have been too obvious—just often enough to ensure that she could influence him when necessary.

'What are the papers?' She took the file from him and sat opposite.

'Business,' he said, rubbed his eyes and leaned back.

He enjoyed the discussions with her. She had a mercantile mind that understood the intricacies of the state's financial problems. Simply put, the privy purse from the government was not adequate to support the palaces, the horses, the family style, the taxes; the mine was antiquated and needed an infusion of capital to make it more efficient. He could, if needed, sell the lands, sell the jewels; but they were an inheritance to be passed on to Nicky and he could not make that decision. The land was not a mere possession; it was a feudal identity. He waited until she'd completed her study of the files.

'I think we'll have to mortgage the Bangalore palace and the mine to get the finance we need.'

'I know,' he said. 'But I am going to need the children's consent.' He fell silent, stroking his fingers gently. The papers rustled in the fan's breeze. 'They might not give it. Sushila can be very uncooperative.'

'What if the other two agree?'

'Then, it is possible, but Rukmani is angry with me and will cause problems.' His long sigh meant he no longer understood his children. They each pulled in different directions, heeding only their own selfish needs.

'I was thinking,' Miss Hobbs began slowly as if an idea had just occurred. 'Rukmani really wants to go to Oxford. I know Nicky also will one day, but wouldn't you be proud to have a daughter at your old university?'

'She should obey me and get married,' he said stubbornly. 'Her grandmother agrees with me...for once,' he added.

'I know, I know,' Miss Hobbs placated. 'But she's an old woman, and times have changed. India is changing, and so is Rukmani. She is not a princess in purdah. She's a modern westernized girl.'

'I wish she weren't,' the rajah said. 'She is too independent, and this westernization is an excuse to defy me. She is a Hindu girl and should obey her father.'

'You cannot go back to the past,' Miss Hobbs said shortly. She had expected him to be easier and was losing patience. 'You wanted your children to have a more westernized outlook. Now you want them to be good traditional Hindu children. They cannot belong to both worlds.' She softened, allowed her words to be mulled over. 'I'd suggest you let her go. It's that or allow her to marry Prithivi.' She knew it was a gamble.

'No.' He sighed once more, gently, painfully. He felt a loss, a sense of failure at not being able to control his daughter. Miss Hobbs's suggestion was the only action left open to him. He was not a man to impose his will, if he sensed that in the end it would alienate his daughter totally from him. 'I suppose that is the best, if she wishes it. Then there's the finance.'

'That will be easy,' Miss Hobbs said, not wanting to sound eager. 'She will give you the power of attorney to control her share in the mine and her properties. With Nicky's share as well, you will be able to arrange the mortgages.'

'Sushila...?'

'She will obey her brother. Or at least listen to his reason, and I'm sure he will not let you down.' She paused, allowing him to understand the simplicity of the moves. 'And once you have that control you can easily raise the capital and finance Rukmani's years at Oxford.' Then she couldn't resist adding, 'We could make this family one of the wealthiest in India. Equal to the Tatas or Birlas. They are today's maharajahs.'

She knew it would appeal to his feudal vanity. Few of the princes had the business acumen to make the transition from feudal wealth to the more secure industrial one. If he could be the exception, that would make him feel superior to the others. It took time. It appeared as if he had not heard, but he still caressed his fingers. It meant he was deep in thought: weighing the suggestion, trying to probe its flaws. She had the will to remain still; indifferently patient for him to accept her advice. If he controlled the mine and the lands, it meant that through him she would also, and she was sure she could arrange the necessary loans from her business contacts. They were eager and she could be generously rewarded, enough to last a lifetime if she decided to ever leave this family's employment. However, she intended to remain. If the family grew rich, so would she.

'It's a good idea,' he finally pronounced. 'I will tell Rukmani tomorrow she can go.' He hesitated. 'She might decide to give it to her grandmother.'

'I doubt it,' Miss Hobbs said confidently.

She spent another half an hour discussing the details of the financing. She often felt she had been miscast in life. If only she had been born a century back, a man who had come to seek his fame and fortune in India. Playing one prince against the other, growing richer by the day, until the time came for him to return triumphant to England and live the rest of his days as a true nabob.

The rajah was pleased. At the end he rose and moved to sit on the bed. He was dressed in a dhoti and jiba both pure white and neatly pressed.

'You have relieved my mind of so many worries. If only I had thought all that before.'

'You did,' she said, and kissed him on the cheek.

◆

The moon was bright, the garden silvery. The shadows and silhouettes of the palace were clear and sharp; it appeared to float up and out of mortal reach, with the moon impaled on a minaret. The gravel was crisp underfoot, and the trimmed hedges damp to touch. They left delicate drops of moisture on Miss Hobbs's dressing gown as she passed close. She heard a low growl and stopped. The terrier came to investigate and would have followed. She whispered to it to remain, and it reluctantly obeyed, quivering with inquisitiveness as she slipped under the trees.

She had to halt once more, blend into the shadows as one of the palace guards sleepily patrolled past. There were six on night duty. Four at the gates, the other two on patrols.

The doors to the guest palace were open. She climbed the staircase. There was adequate light. It shone ephemeral and glistening through the arches and the trellised windows, touching on marble and wood and granite to make them appear of the same material—old silver.

Gunboat slept. On the bedside table were two empty glasses and a half-empty bottle of Black Knight whiskey. She looked around. His friend had been given a tiny room at the rear of the palace, though his effects still remained here. She woke him, and waited until he sat up.

'How are you?' she asked.

'Sleepy,' Gunboat grunted.

He peered at his luminous watch. It was past midnight. He lit a cigarette and waited. Her hair had been combed down, as if she were prepared for bed. Her face still wore make-up, especially the mouth.

'Would you care for a drink?' She could have been presiding at a garden party, and her Englishness made Gunboat smile.

'Why not?'

She took the glasses, rinsed them in the bathroom, and returned. She poured out a measure in each. As they toasted, Gunboat remembered their first meeting and wondered what she had come to offer him.

'You're not a very wise man,' she began.

'Nope.'

'I made you a very generous offer, and you accepted it.'

'That's true. You dropped the money and left it here. I figured I'd hang on to it until you asked for it back. Do you want it back?' He swung his legs off the bed.

'Not immediately,' she said. She took his cigarette, puffed twice, and returned it. 'I smoked forty a day once. I thought boxers were expected to remain fit.'

'Not this one,' Gunboat said.

She left a deep slur of red on the tip, and he stubbed it out. She watched his deliberate action.

'I've come to renew my offer.' She had decided to abandon the politeness. It didn't work on such a crude man. 'If you consent to leave immediately I will give you a steam ticket to New York, and an adequate sum to keep you for a week or two.'

'Generous,' Gunboat commented.

'I'll even give Gertrude a ticket to New York.'

'Yeah,' Gunboat said. 'I figure she doesn't want to go to New York.'

'Oh, she will.' Miss Hobbs was quite complacent. 'I talked to her at that lunch. She'll be grateful to anyone who will help her leave the country. She likes you still, except she sees no future in you.'

'So she marries me for a steam ticket?'

'That's up to you. I didn't mention marriage.' She sipped, savoured, and added, 'Or else you can remain in this country for the rest of your days.'

She said nothing else after that. The quietness after their voices was sudden and still, and it took time for other sounds to make themselves heard.

'She said that?' Gunboat asked. Miss Hobbs nodded.

Gunboat dreamed of that girl. It was the dream of men with

spare lives, haunted by loneliness and abandonment. Gertrude was all he had, all he'd possessed in these past years. She had graced him with her body; more important than that, with her youth. He believed her to be a child who'd never age, never lose the suppleness of that body, the mesmeric smoothness of skin. If he lost her, he knew he'd never find such a woman again.

TWENTY-ONE

She allowed him silence. Only once did she move, and her gold bangles tinkled prettily. She guessed his thoughts though his face was averted and in shadow. He imagined his room, small and shallow, and imagined a life to be spent surrounded by those boundaries. She knew he also longed for the girl: a skinny bitch, pretty in a pinched way. She could not account for the taste of men, though admittedly Gunboat had had little choice. He was a poor white in a society that calculated its members by colours, castes, and cash. He was the right colour for a people who revelled in the fairness of a person's skin, but the wrong bank balance. Gertrude was right for him. She, too, hovered in the shadows of the unwanted, and Miss Hobbs was sure Gunboat would hold onto her. Old men were foolish in the presence of young girls. They believed youth to be infectious, and those nights in bed fornicating were contagious.

'No deal,' Gunboat finally said and felt pity at his own self-destruction.

'I think you underestimate my influence.'

'I don't.' He was weary of her, of himself, and wanted to return to sleep. 'I never take a dive.'

'What does that mean?'

'Lady, in boxing terms, that means I don't break my word. I gave it to Nicky. It stands.'

'I meant with Gertrude,' Miss Hobbs said softly. 'I could influence her to return to you.'

'If I can't hold a woman by myself, it's best to let go of her.'

She stood, peering at him down the length of her nose. Her grey eyes were hard, chilly as the evening sky before the rains. She hated Gunboat and it wasn't tinged with any respect for his honour. She had suspected him a fool; now she believed it. He was a badmash, a madman, and those cannot be touched by rational offers. They were controlled by their own madness; touched if not by the devil, then by God himself.

'You will never leave India,' she said, and it sounded a prophecy.

He knew he had lost and felt bleak sadness, for somehow her conviction made him feel she spoke the truth. The sadhu had warned him and he'd not listened.

'Tell me,' she added. 'Will Nicky win his fight?'

'Yes,' Gunboat said. He fetched the cash and returned it to her.

◆

That satisfaction had to last him for all his life. He drove the prince harder, remembering his own ambitions, his own hunger for winning. The cold morning hours of roadwork, the long afternoons and evenings spent in the gymnasium on Thirtieth Street and Eighth Avenue. The stench of sweat, of exhaustion, of excitement, as he tuned his young body and mind to fight until he fell or was bloodily defeated. That was the time he had known the complete meaning of life: to battle and be victorious, to hear the crowds, to feel and deliver pain, to be so physically alive that the body hummed like the taut string of a violin. There were gods to reach out for and tear down: Louis, Marciano. But they weren't meant for him. Grosse meant him for the tank towns, the small mean bets, the preliminary fighter who played to empty ringside seats. Then it became too late, and the pain too much.

They ran longer now in the mornings. The full circumference of the garden, and that was five or six miles. They passed a new landscape: a village of palace servants who bowed and drew aside as the prince passed; undergrowth as thick as the jungles beyond the fencing, and, in a far corner, a graveyard. It was neglected, overgrown with weeds and brown alfalfa grass. The headstones leaned at angles, worn smooth by the heat and rains. There still remained a faint division down the middle, a narrow pathway, just discernible.

'Who are they?' Gunboat asked.

'Dogs and Englishmen,' Nicky said, and laughed. He was fit enough for that, and it pleased Gunboat. He understood the irony. While the British ruled, many places were prohibited to dogs and Indians. 'Palace dogs,' Nicky continued. 'Fathers, grandfathers, and great-grandfathers. They used them to hunt.'

'And the Englishmen?'

'Only two. One called Collins, the other Morehouse.'

In the ring, Gunboat pushed Nicky harder. His punches, still controlled, stung more. The prince would wince, but he would continue circling, jabbing. His own punches came swifter and harder.

'You've got to hit a lot harder,' Gunboat goaded Nicky. 'Move faster, but don't lose balance. If you can't get at the head, hit the heart. Hit it with all your strength. That can stop a fighter cold.'

They went three rounds. There were faint bruises on the prince's arms, shoulder, chest, and cheeks. 'You dropped your guard a couple of times,' Gunboat said while Swami towelled the prince. 'I could have knocked you out.'

'Why didn't you?' Nicky asked.

He was panting and looked worn. The pace was telling on him, and Gunboat felt some sympathy. He was taking his anger and ambitions out on the prince.

'I don't want you scared,' Gunboat said. 'When a fighter gets knocked down, he doesn't like to come up again. But that depends on the guy.'

'You think I'll stay down?' Nicky asked. He looked cold and angry.

'No. But I don't want to test that yet.' They walked away from the ring, tired, letting the evening breeze cool their sweat. 'I'm going to Bangalore with your grandmother tomorrow. I'll fix up a couple of sparring partners. That don't mean you can take it easy. I want you to do the roadwork and punchbag and skip.'

'I thought you said you don't want me to peak before the fight,' Nicky said dryly. He leaned against the wall, feeling the warmth of the granite. It would take all night for the stone to lose the day's heat.

'You won't. When do you get into town?'

'Wednesday. But I won't be at the palace. I'll be in the school.' He sighed like any schoolboy at the thought of losing his freedom. 'How will we work out there?'

'Can you get permission to get out for a few hours in the evening?'

'I suppose so.'

'You can do your roadwork in school,' Gunboat said. 'In the evenings we'll spar and punchbag.'

The prince looked doubtful. 'It's the start of the cricket season. I'll have to do nets.'

'Skip the cricket,' Gunboat ordered.

'I can't,' Nicky said. 'I'm in the first XI. Opening bat.'

'You have to do one or the other.'

'I could spar in the mornings.'

Gunboat considered, and was placated. 'Okay. I'll fix that.' He turned and would have left, but Nicky held his arm.

'You're angry with me for the last two days.'

'No. I just want you to win.'

'It's more anger. If not at me, someone else.' He looked out at the shadows approaching them. 'Miss Hobbs?'

'Yeah.'

'What did she offer?'

'Steamship tickets, if I quit tomorrow.'

'The same as before. Unimaginative.' He stopped, listened again. 'Tickets? Who was the other one for?'

'Gertrude.'

'Would she go with you?'

'So I'm told,' Gunboat said.

'I cannot match that.' He would have sat on the bottom step but a bearer came running with a rattan chair. Nicky appeared not to notice as he sat on it, and the bearer retreated. He spoke carefully. 'Do you wish to...leave with her?' Gunboat made no reply. 'I've learned a lot from you. I will not hold you any further, if that is what you want.'

'Do you think you will win without me?'

'Possibly.' Nicky considered further. 'Possibly not. But I do not wish you to lose the woman.'

'Listen, kid.' Gunboat sat on the steps by the chair. 'You know nothing about women. Let me make the decisions. Okay?'

'Sure. So you will stay?'

'Yes.'

'Tell me about women then.' Nicky settled in his chair, prepared to remain all night if necessary.

Gunboat laughed. 'I ain't that dumb. Each one's different, but they are all the same. They like games, especially when they're young. That is their power. To withhold their bodies, and watch you crawl for it.'

'You can always buy a prostitute,' Nicky suggested.

'It's never the same. Buyin' and gettin'. You'll learn that difference. When you're buyin' all you get is body. When they're givin', you get a kind of madness. Part soul, part heart, part animal, all body. And I mean all. And that's when they have you by the balls.'

'And she has you by them?' Nicky asked. He bent forward, studying Gunboat curiously as if he were a rare specimen.

'Yeah,' Gunboat said. 'It hurts. But I'll live.' Just barely. God, how he longed for her to reply to his letter. The days and nights had become unbearably heavy.

They fell silent. Darkness came, the palace lights went on one by one. They threw great white patches onto the lawns and the drive, silhouetting Nicky and Gunboat. Two bearers waited in the shadows, silent and still.

Nicky nodded, as if understanding. Gunboat puzzled him. He was the flaw in his theory on human nature and he suspected the flaw to be a dangerous one. If you cannot purchase men, power ceases to exist. Power, in Nicky's limited world, was offering men what they wanted most, and in their taking, they came under one's control. And all men succumbed.

'What would happen if I fired you?' Nicky asked.

'You can't,' Gunboat said. 'We agreed to a sum and an objective. You cannot break your word, Prince.'

'Why not?' Nicky asked. 'I can do what I please.'

'Your word is all you live by. It is your private morality. Once that is twisted, you got nothing.'

'You already have nothing.'

'I don't have palaces admittedly,' Gunboat said. 'But I worry you because of the way I behave. Right?'

'Right.'

'That's something.' Gunboat laughed and stood up. 'I can worry princes.'

'Where did you learn this?'

'From...he hesitated, 'my father.'

'Was he a boxer too?'

'No. He was a stevedore, and worked the waterfronts in New York for a starvation wage. He came across to America during the potato famine.'

'Did he give you your name?'

'No,' Gunboat said. 'I got that from an old coloured fighter who taught me to box.'

'What is your real name?' Nicky stood up, waited expectantly.

Gunboat laughed. 'You know something—I've forgotten.' He clapped the prince on the shoulder and began to move off.

Nicky watched him. He had not expected an answer to that question.

'I talked to my father about Swaminathan,' Nicky called after him. 'He'll get a job.'

'Thanks, Nicky. I'll tell him when I see him in Bangalore.'

Nicky walked through the palace rather than go around to his private entrance. He jogged down the long, deserted corridors, remembering how once, in his childhood, the palace had been so full of noise and life. Countless cousins had lived here and he'd had the company and laughter and games of so many children. His father had wanted the family westernized, and the cost was the dispersal of the larger family. Westernization was independence rather than the interdependence of his feudal past, and survival was for the individual rather than family. Nicky wasn't sure the move had been wise, but it had been inevitable and he could not set the clock back.

He passed Rukmani's room. She was playing her gramophone records, mostly American and English popular tunes which could be heard daily on the Binaca hit parade broadcast by Radio Ceylon. He knocked, and heard her call. Rukmani was lying on her bed, reading a romantic novel. She threw the book aside and scrambled off the bed.

'I've been looking for you,' she said.

'I was training,' Nicky said and sat on the edge of the bed. His sister looked excited, clutching a secret that delighted her alone. 'What's up?'

'Guess.'

'You're marrying Prithivi?' Nicky said.

She dismissed this with a toss of her head. Nicky presumed love was forever and wondered how she could recover so quickly when only a few days back she threatened tragedy.

'Take another.'

Nicky sighed. 'You're going to Oxford.'

'How did you know?' She was disappointed.

'It was one or the other,' Nicky said. 'Father has given permission then?'

'He came in an hour ago, and said he'd made all the arrangements.'

She danced around the room, once more the child that he remembered, full of mischief and joy. It was an adventure, an escape into freedom. She was leaving and had no thoughts for what she left behind.

'I will miss you,' Nicky said gently.

He would be alone now. Rukmani would be the last childhood friend. Once she was gone, he knew he had lost all his youth and could never return. They had been close. She and Sushila had cared for him as a small child, spoilt him, loved him the best they could in their own childlike ways. There were many memories.

One: She had built, with the help of a cousin, a treetop house in the banyan tree. It was an enclave of only the female children, a secret place way above the earth that was reached by a rope ladder. He had been the only male child privileged not only to visit but to spend a night there as her special guest. It had been so much more comfortable than the palace.

Another: At their sister's wedding, Rukmani had stolen a tin of Goldflake cigarettes. While the wedding ceremony had been in progress in the palace, Rukmani had taken him and two other cousins to the farthest end of the garden, near the small cemetery, and shown them how to smoke. They had all become ill, and Rukmani had been thrashed by the old rani for daring to harm the yuvaraj.

'Oh, I will miss you too,' Rukmani said, but he knew she did not quite mean it the same way. She had already left.

'Why did he change his mind?'

She stopped dancing. 'I don't know,' she said too guilelessly, and continued.

He watched awhile, feeling she had not quite been truthful. He knew her well enough; she would not divulge what she knew unless it convenienced her.

'Are you sure?'

'Sure,' Rukmani said, and collapsed on a chair.

She was breathless, her sari falling from her shoulders. Perspiration spotted her forehead and she fanned herself with a magazine. She looked pretty, spoilt, sensual.

'Was it Miss Hobbs who talked to him?'

'Of course not,' Rukmani said, then she giggled. 'I can handle her.' She made it sound conspiratorial.

'Be careful of her.'

'Oh, I am,' Rukmani said. 'She's not as clever as she thinks.'

'What does that mean?'

'You'll see,' Rukmani said, and refused to elaborate. She just laughed, enjoying a private joke.

The door suddenly opened. Chandra, the oldest family retainer, stood panting. He looked near collapse. He was an old man, near his seventies, and had been the old rajah's personal valet. He was Swami's father and now worked, when he felt like it, for the old rani. Most times, he would hobble in from the village just to gossip with her. He had an elephant leg, his left, and was stooped and frail.

'The old rani,' he panted, 'is dying. Go quickly.' He was in tears, for she was more friend than ruler.

Nicky was the first to the door. Rukmani ran after him trying to put on her slippers. She hopped, finally gave up, picked up the hem of her sari, and followed.

'Tell the rajah,' Nicky ordered.

'Where is he?' Chandra called after him.

Nicky looked at his watch. 'In his meditation room.'

'Can I disturb him?'

'I am telling you to.'

They ran. The news had travelled quickly. He heard the whispers, the hurrying of servants. With death the palace awoke. The breath of movement was towards the old rani's quarters; it felt as if the palace had tilted in her direction and all things slid to be present at her dying. Ghosts and spirits, long-forgotten princes and princesses, the very dust that had lain dormant in the shadowy corners came to life.

A great sigh of expectation echoed down the marble corridors; doors and windows appeared to open and close by themselves as if people, invisible, had passed through them, all hurrying towards her bed. Lights came on and off, shadows appeared and disappeared, the great reception halls stirred with the hurry, like long-sleeping beasts awakened and told to be prepared. The vast durbar hall, full of dust and moulding paintings and peeling gilt and faded velvet curtains with frayed gold tassels, came brilliantly alight. The Venetian chandelier, an inverted mountain of glass drops that once graced a Hapsburg palace, had been lit. Nicky and Rukmani threw long black shadows that raced and overtook them and then fell back as they passed into the corridor.

◆

A small crowd stood at the doorway of the old rani's apartments. Some had entered; most remained peering fearfully in. Nicky pushed through. His grandmother lay on a vast bed, small and alone. She appeared to have shrunk; her face was as pinched as a squeezed orange, and for a moment he thought how swiftly death had robbed her face of its fullness. Then he realized she had removed her false teeth, and with dying her cheeks had puckered increasingly in, as if she had not the strength ever to puff them out again. Her white pillows were spattered with blood. Her blue silk, gold-bordered sari was wrapped loosely around her, protecting her as would a shroud. Her wedding chain fell loosely from her neck onto her left shoulder. She appeared asleep, too deep a sleep to be awakened from.

'Send for the doctor,' Nicky ordered.

'I have,' Swami said. He too was in tears. 'I sent the car five minutes ago. She should be here soon.'

Nicky and Rukmani sat carefully on the edge of the bed. She was in tears, sniffled, fluttered helplessly as if wanting to waken the old rani. She touched her grandmother's hand; it didn't respond. Nicky took it, held it. The flesh was barely warm, breath scarcely raised her chest. He too wanted to waken her, as he had done so often. Shake her, so she could rise and care for him.

The rajah pushed through. He had been raised from his meditation, as if from a deep, deep sleep, and still wore his tranquility. He had dressed hastily, in jiba and dhoti; the dhoti had been tied unevenly. For a minute, as he stared down at the old rani, he retained his serenity, as if he had not been told why he'd been summoned to her bedside.

His appearance gradually changed, as he comprehended the event.

'The doctor—'

'She has been sent for,' Nicky said.

The rajah stepped forward a pace. He was opposite Nicky, looking down, the concern starkly visible that changed to sadness, and then, suddenly, terror. He shook, trying to look away, trying to break some awful spell that so frightened him and forced him to keep looking down on the old rani. He aged swiftly. The lines around his mouth grew deep, his skin puckered and lost colour. It looked like unwashed sand. Memory consumed him.

'She looks...his whisper was broken, coarse with distance, '...like your mother did.' He spoke through nightmares. 'She has the same illness. She...'

He did not finish. With a huge effort he turned and pushed back through the small crowd of retainers. He did not go far; only to a corner of the room to sit heavily on a reclining chair, head bowed in his hands.

Nicky had not seen his mother die, nor her body. He tried to match that photographic likeness of youth and beauty against the face framed on the pillow. There was some resemblance, but death itself was a prism that shifted the focus of his eye. He saw only his grandmother. He glanced to Rukmani. She had been older, and her memory awakened, for she too had that same terror. She wept openly now and Nicky understood that it was the living that needed comfort; the dying could never ever be given enough.

He released his grandmother's hand, took Rukmani's, and led her away from the bed. She stumbled after him, uncaring, and he took her to sit by her father. He looked back from this distance: the old retainers wept, Chandra loudest and near collapse. The young ones looked curious as if viewing a drama of which they were not part. They did not know the old rani, had not given their lives to her.

His father's personal assistant had also been fetched. He came to the bedside, grave and respectful, then came to stand by the rajah.

Nicky realized he was waiting for instructions. The rajah had yet to lift his head.

'You must send telegrams to everyone,' Nicky said quietly as if he did not wish his father to hear him. 'Telephone Sushila and my aunt. They must come immediately.' He would have continued, but stopped. He had no idea what other instructions could be prepared for the dead.

'Yes, your highness,' the assistant said and withdrew, back to the door, facing the bed.

As he reached the door, he turned and stepped aside. Miss Hobbs entered. Her head was bowed, she was barefoot, and there was an air of solemnity about her as if it wore a heavy cloak and she could scarcely bear the burden. The retainers parted. She was a good head taller than they. They appeared so frail beside her. She looked down at the old rani for a long while, as if she were trying to remember what the old woman looked like, and then turned and went out. From his distance Nicky could not tell what she had been thinking.

Time passed. The rajah sat back, eyes closed, weary, fighting memories. Nicky sat by him, glancing now and then to the bed, going up to examine his grandmother. She had not changed. The retainers squatted on the floor, silent; the men to one side, women to another.

The doctor came as Nicky peered down. She was a tubby woman, having some family resemblance. She was a distant cousin, his granduncle's wife's sister's daughter. She had once lived in the palace, and when no longer welcome by Miss Hobbs, she had moved to a little estate she had, around one hundred acres, fifteen miles on the way to Arcot. She practised her medicine on his family, and on all those villagers his family cared for. Her practice was simple: births, measles, smallpox, chickenpox, broken limbs, farming accidents, wife beatings, malnutrition.

Nicky watched her through her paces: stethoscope, pulse, tongue. She broke a phial, sucked the liquid out through the syringe, and injected the old rani in the arm.

Gunboat Jack

'What is it?' Nicky asked finally.

'She's in a diabetic coma,' Dr Vasanti said. 'It could be too late. I gave her insulin.' They both watched as if expecting the old rani to suddenly waken and sit up. Nothing occurred. 'I warned her to take treatment and I prescribed a very strict diet for her. Did she obey it?'

'I don't know,' Nicky said, and felt foolish at his ignorance.

'She never told us she was ill.'

'She wasn't ill,' Dr Vasanti said. 'She could have lived for many years if she had cared for herself.' She sighed and sat on the bed. 'Your grandmother never listened to anybody. Always thought she knew best.' Then she added unnecessarily, 'Your mother died of the same illness.'

'I know,' he said and thought how irrelevant that was.

Death was a constant, the manner of dying like a shuffled pack of cards. By chance mother and daughter had drawn the same card. It could quite well have been different.

They sat quietly. Occasionally Dr Vasanti would check his grandmother's pulse, then her heartbeat. It was about an hour before her death that his grandmother stirred. He felt her weakly squeeze his hand, as if wanting to hold onto him and stop the slide down into darkness. He held tightly, probably causing pain but she would not have noticed it. Her eyes opened, just a glimmer of dull shine in those brown eyes. She lay that way a long while, trying to comprehend where she was. This familiar room could have been a strange place, for she appeared not to have the feel of recognition. She glanced slowly aside and saw Nicky.

'She was here, wasn't she?' she whispered and Nicky bent forward to hear. Her breath, surprisingly, smelled of betel nut.

'Who?'

'That woman.'

'Yes.'

'I saw her looking at me,' she continued very slowly. She spoke in her mother tongue now. Telugu. English appeared to have been forgotten. 'She is very pleased.'

Nicky didn't wonder how she could have seen Miss Hobbs. He expected that in death all magic is revealed. That last secret that has escaped the living all their lives and all their searches is granted to those who are dying.

'Nataraj,' she said, 'you must not let her win.'

'I won't.'

'Promise.' She caught her breath, as if wanting to preserve it forever.

'I promise,' Nicky said.

She tightened her grip with what strength she had. It was little. Her palm was dry and smooth, and the hand in his tiny. He had always considered her a much bigger woman.

'Rukmani knows what you must look for,' she whispered. 'Take that friend with you. He will look after you. Promise me you will win.'

'I promise,' Nicky repeated.

She closed her eyes and Nicky thought she had slipped back into the coma. Her grip still held him. Silence. All held their breath, sensing the moment had come. No one moved, no one coughed or sniffled. Even tears had stopped flowing. It was as if this silence was necessary to make her passage from life to death that much easier. A noise would jar the soul and send it ricocheting out into deep cosmos to wander forever, lost and abandoned. Nicky had no awareness of time. It went, swiftly or slowly he wasn't sure. She was awake, for without opening her eyes she said, 'Ram, Ram, Ram…I pray not to meet my husband again.'

It was the last she spoke.

◆

Gunboat woke in darkness. He washed and dressed and waited for Mohan to bring him the tea. No one came. The darkness lessened. Pale rays of light moved purposefully across the sky, gradually revealing the hidden details of the garden and the palace. Gunboat went out to await the prince. The sky was pink, like diluted blood, the sun a clear washed gold. Gunboat noted the silence. The palace was quiet;

the lights glowed. There were no malis, no servants sweeping the drive. The garden appeared to have been hushed, for he thought he could hear no birds. Even the terrier had not kept its morning appointment.

Two cars raced down the long driveway a minute apart. They slid to a halt and from one jumped Sushila; from the other two women he did not recognize. Gunboat knew the prince would not come. He sensed a dread urgency in the movement of the women, and turned back to sit at the empty breakfast table. He waited, forgotten and abandoned.

The sun grew warmer, brighter, creeping over the stones towards him. The palace had come to life, as if the sun had revived it from its torpor. Retainers appeared busy, hurrying here and there but not performing their tasks. Others formed outside, waiting to enter. Now cars began to arrive, a procession that appeared never to end and slowly formed a jam in the driveway. The men and women who climbed out were of all ages; all quiet and subdued, namaseing each other, deferring to elders. The men wore white dhotis and jibas, the women silk saris. Three Brahmin priests walked slowly, solemnly down the driveway, followed by a procession of silent musicians. They held their instruments in their cases.

Mohan came at ten. He looked sad and drawn and weary. His eyes were reddened.

'The old rani is dead,' he said quietly. 'The yuvaraj wishes you to attend.'

Gunboat had known, and he rose and began to move towards the palace.

'No,' Mohan said. 'You must bathe and wear fresh clothes.'

They went up. Gunboat found his bath had been prepared, and a clean pair of white trousers and a shirt lay on the bed. Mohan waited while he prepared himself and then led him across to the palace. The lights were still on, the chandeliers still blazed.

The old rani's body lay on a simple bed in the durbar hall. Her ancestors, faded with age and by damp and neglect, stared down at her from the walls. The bed was on a dais at the far end, where the throne on which the rajah sat in the long-forgotten past once stood.

Gunboat noted a painting as he moved slowly through the aisle of people. It was of Nicky's grandfather, perched as a young boy on the throne. Turbaned and jewelled, surrounded by courtiers. To his right, simply dressed, stood an Englishman. He wondered whether it was Collins or Morehouse.

Carpets had been laid with a pathway to the bed. On the right sat the women, on the left the men. Gunboat approached the bed alone, aware of being watched. The old rani had been bathed, her hair, well-streaked with grey, which she normally wore in a kunday at the back of her head, had been oiled and spread, as if blown by a pure breeze, on the pillow. A rose garland circled her neck. She wore her jewellery, and she looked far younger in death than in life. Others followed him, looking down in that distant way in which the living examine the dead.

Nicky gestured, and Gunboat sat carefully cross-legged beside him. The rajah sat separate, sad and burrowed still in memory. Nicky was dressed as the others, in pure white. He too looked withdrawn and burdened. Opposite, in the women's half, were Rukmani and Sushila and, separated by a few rows farther back and alone, sat Miss Hobbs. She did not appear awkward or alien, but a part of this ritual, part of the people she had spent all her life with. There were also children, here and there, restless and fidgety with the silent vigil.

A priest murmured; camphor and incense burned. The air was sweet with their odour, sour with the rising decay of the old rani's body in the heat. Hours passed. Soft drinks with some sweetmeats were served by the retainers.

'It won't be long now,' Nicky finally said, sensing Gunboat's discomfort. 'She wished you to attend.'

At three in the afternoon a bier was brought in. It was made of palm leaves knitted together, resting on two poles. The old rani's jewellery was removed for the last time, and she was carefully laid on the bier. The musicians started playing. There were three tablas, two clarinetists, two flautists, and two men who blew into conches. The sound of the conches—a long-drawn sad wail that rose and fell and left their echoes long after—haunted the procession that slowly wound out of the durbar hall, down the driveway and out onto the highway. The rajah and the prince were immediately behind. Behind them came Rukmani and Sushila and their aunt and the old rani's sister.

Gunboat lodged himself midway. The sun was a blinding glare; the heat rose off the tarmac and the earth in visible waves. Ahead, cymbals clashed, the tablas were drummed to a frenzy, and the conches called the mourning over the vast hilly landscape. Some men danced in front of the procession and hurled dust grabbed from the roadside on each other. Tandhapur had come to a standstill. The road was lined with mourners who waited for the procession to pass before falling in behind.

It wound through the town, past the small temple, and then into the countryside. Gunboat guessed they were heading for the river, a tributary of the Godaviri. It took an hour.

The river was down a few feet; the water glittered like knives and flowed softly, with hardly a ripple, down to the seas. A space had been cleared and obviously was used often, for it held the remains of charred wood, empty coconut shells, and stacks of ashes. The pyre was prepared: a stack of wood flat on the surface on which the body was carefully placed. The priest chanted his prayers, poured ghee over the wood, anointed the face with vibudhi, and circled the pyre chanting.

A torch was lit. The rajah took it and with the priest's guidance held it to different parts of the pyre. Flames took slowly, and an assistant of the priest carried a heavy burned rock and placed it on the old rani's chest to prevent the body from sitting up in the fierce heat. The fire gradually took hold, the flames almost invisible in the hot sunshine. The noise was continuous: tablas, conches, flutes, clarinets, chants, the crackle of wood burning. The odour of roasting flesh, sweet and acrid, nauseous. Gunboat felt exhaustion. He had been suddenly immersed in an ancient ritual—a noisy, colourful, kaleidoscopic pageant—and thought he was suffocating through all his senses. He shifted away from the crowd, seeking relief. Others too were moving away, some to return to their duties. Miss Hobbs stood at a distance, alone and separate. She looked at him but made no acknowledgment of his presence.

By the time the fire had finally consumed the body of the old rani it had become dark. The embers glowed, bright sparks jumped high and faded suddenly, to fall back as ash on those who still remained. The priest began to sift through the ashes, gathering hers, mingled with wood, in an urn.

'Let's go,' Nicky said softly, and they both turned away and began the long walk back to the palace.

TWENTY-TWO

Both palaces were ablaze with lights, hurrying shadows, murmurs of conversation, music. The driveway was still jammed with cars. The garden too was alight. Lamps had been switched on, trees lit, and chairs placed on the lawn. Many of the guests sat out, drinking fresh lime juice, absorbed in talk, slapping away mosquitoes.

'It was like this once,' Nicky said, 'every night.' They walked in silence.

'I will miss her. She is...was...good fun.' He laughed. 'Oh, there were times she could be very autocratic—I got thrashed a few times by her—but she was fun. Did you know she was an expert on diamonds? She was. She taught herself, and she became so good that even the big jewellers would come to her to authenticate their evaluation. She also taught herself English. She didn't speak a word until she was twenty, and then when she found that her husband thought her ignorant, she crammed all her studies into a year. She spoke it well, didn't she?'

They reached the fork in the driveway and stopped. People passed, bowing to the prince, some approaching to murmur their condolences. He greeted each politely, yet kept them distant as if he wished to be unattainable.

'She gave me many presents,' he said between interruptions. 'Expensive ones too, but the one I remember the most was a green bicycle when I was eight. It was a beautiful machine with a cushioned seat and a three-speed gear. A Phillips.' He looked around, puzzled, as if it lay somewhere in the garden. 'I wonder where it is? I must look for it.'

They stood on the edge of a bright patch of light. His eyes

glistened like an animal's in deep darkness. His cheeks held a single streak that appeared to scar his face.

Gunboat stepped back in the shadows. The prince followed.

'It was time for her to die.' Nicky wiped his face with his loose sleeve. 'The world has changed too much for her. At least she had been a rani. I am no prince.'

'You are,' Gunboat said.

'Because I was born one?' Nicky mocked.

'Partly,' Gunboat said. 'But also because of what you've made of yourself. You would have made a good ruler.'

'And now what do I make of myself?'

'Something pretty good, I'd say. Whatever it's going to be.'

They stood in silence. The prince appeared to be mulling over his words.

'You're okay, Prince,' Gunboat softly added.

'Yeah,' Nicky said, in close imitation of Gunboat. 'Let's eat. But you better change first.'

They ate in the state dining room. The centrepiece was a massive rosewood table that gleamed in the bright chandelier lights. It must have been able to seat fifty. Gunboat had no time to count. He was led to the top by a servant and placed beside Nicky. Only the males sat at the table, and Nicky introduced Gunboat to those nearest. They were all relatives, of varying closeness.

A silver thali was placed in front of him, and in the large high-rimmed plate, four silver bowls. Bearers filled each with various curries, placed a large mound of rice in the centre, and pickles. All the dishes were vegetarian. Gunboat looked down the length of the table. Everyone had been served similarly, and in front of each was a silver tumbler with ice water. The bearers moved from person to person, ladling out the food. Others stood by with silver pitchers of water. Gunboat was famished. He had not eaten all day, and he dug into the food with his fingers, as the others did.

They strolled out into the cool night after the meal, chewing betel nut and paan leaves. The men were sitting on the lawn, the rajah in the centre, surrounded by people. The women were not to be seen, and Gunboat presumed they had now gone in to eat. Nicky chose a chair near the shadows, away from the others. In silence he studied the palace and the surroundings as if seeing it all for the first time.

'Do you gamble?' he finally asked.

'A bit,' Gunboat replied, thinking of all the money he had won and lost at the Bangalore races.

'I've thought often of the odds that I was born into this house.' He gestured, diminishing the grandeur to mere bricks and tiles. 'Five hundred million to one or two...depending on our population. I could have, by a greater chance, been that servant who carries around the tray or the child in a gutter.'

Gunboat had no reply. It was a bald statement, expecting none. It was as if the prince, in the mood of mourning, had an intimation of his own mortality. Possibly the thought had just occurred; possibly it had haunted him many years. It was not so much a recognition of luck as an awareness of the pain that lay beyond the boundaries of these walls.

'We will leave tomorrow,' Nicky said abruptly. 'I would like you to accompany me, as you promised, for my grandmother.'

'Fine,' Gunboat said, and Nicky rose. 'I'll stay awhile.'

He lit a cigarette and looked hard at all around him. It was the last time he would be here, and in a way he was glad he could remember the palace so full of life. It evoked some of its past extravagance, though he knew it to be muted by the circumstance of the gathering. He did not sit long. Others were leaving to sleep, and he did not wish to be the last for he would then see it empty once more. As he strolled back to his room, Gunboat thought of Tiger in that small, steaming room in Calcutta. The rituals, if not the circumstances, were the same.

◆

He had not known then what to expect. The house had been in a narrow lane. Mean with open sewers and skinny pie-dogs and thin children with large eyes. He'd stopped and entered. The small hall was full of people, all men. An old man, dressed in a clean white dhoti and jiba, rose. His eyes were red. His hair was white, yet the dark face was unseamed. He looked like Tiger too. The handsome face was touched with age and sadness and some understanding. He'd namasted and silently led Gunboat to the next room. Tiger lay in clean white clothes, a garland around his neck. Death was silence, Gunboat thought.

The room smelled of camphor. The walls were covered with photographs of Tiger. There had been such strength, such vitality. A fighter was a man completely alive, feeling the power of his own body. A small cabinet held the trophies. Gunboat sensed movement from behind a door and turned. A young woman wearing a white sari watched him. She was young, not more than eighteen or nineteen. Her face was heart-shaped, fragile. Her brown eyes were unblinking in her study.

'I'm sorry,' Gunboat said softly.

She made no reply. There was no anger, just a bewildered acceptance. She turned away quickly, and Gunboat saw the child holding on to her legs. The child was curious. It saw a large white man standing beside the physical presence of his father.

'It couldn't be helped,' the old man said.

Gunboat had wanted forgiveness, yet not this easily. They should have begrudged him it, touched him with their own bitterness. He would have preferred that, for now he felt that he had committed no terrible sin. The death of a man, a son, a husband, a father, was of no important consequence.

'I would like his widow to have this.' Gunboat drew out an envelope and held it out. It was his full purse, less a hundred.

'It isn't necessary,' the father said.

'Please.'

The old man took it and placed it unopened in the cabinet.

Gunboat would have liked to give it to her, but she was hidden behind the door, and he could not enter.

He joined the men in the veranda. They made room for him on the stone bench running alongside the wall. His back was to the street. He felt himself covertly studied, yet no stare remained long. The eyes slid away. The old man returned with a cup and saucer of coffee and a plate of sweetmeats. Gunboat took them. The silence was almost continuous. Now and then the men would join those on the veranda. The women would disappear inside.

'Was he your only son?' Gunboat asked the father.

'I have another. He is in government service and doing well. He's been posted to Madhya Pradesh, but he'll be coming soon. It takes a long time by train.' He studied Gunboat carefully. 'You must not blame yourself. The doctor told me my son had a tumor. If it had not been you, it would have been another man. I did not like what he did. It wasn't secure, but Thakur was happy.'

'Thakur?'

'Tiger. He liked that name.' He spoke haltingly, groping for the unfamiliar words and half-listening to his own careful mispronunciation. 'The Tiger is a noble animal. Fierce. Strong. Quick. No?'

'It is. He was good.'

'I am happy you think so. He admired Joe Louis muchly. He wanted to be like him.'

'Who wouldn't.' Gunboat noticed the others drank coffee from small cheap glasses. The cup and saucer was his privilege and it made him awkward.

'Imagine something so big,' his thumb pressed against the very edge of his small finger, 'could kill such a strong man.' He still seemed in wonder, rather than in bereavement. Death was always a surprise. 'It is God's doing.'

'Yeah,' Gunboat said. He finished his coffee and rose.

The other men rose as well. They namasted, and the old man saw him to the door.

Nicky and Gunboat left mid-afternoon. Nicky had to say goodbye to all those who remained as guests and performed prayers at the temple for his grandmother in the company of his sisters and aunt and grandaunt.

'Do you drive?' Nicky asked as they were about to enter the car. It was a '54 Ford sedan, spacious and roomy. Its boot contained their suitcases.

'Yes.'

'Do then,' Nicky said, and told the driver to sit in the back.

Miss Hobbs watched the car speed up the driveway, trailing brown dust, and turn onto the Bangalore road.

'Where is Nicky going?' she asked the rajah.

They were in his office. There were no supplicants waiting this day in deference to the old rani's death. He looked fatigued and fretful. The papers did not occupy him, and he was staring into the distance, the way a man does when mesmerized by his ill luck. The rajah did not answer, and his silence irritated her. She proudly considered herself a truthful woman, and an unsentimental one. She did not mourn the death of the old rani. She was relieved by it. She knew that the rajah had not been particularly fond of his mother-in-law, and yet he behaved as if someone deeply loved had passed away.

'Where is he going?' she repeated loudly.

'Who?'

'Nicky,' she said patiently.

'Bangalore,' he said and would have retreated into his solitude.

'The palace is closed,' she said. 'And school only starts day after.'

'He is staying with Sushila.'

She allowed him this time to retreat. She suspected he brooded more on his wife, and the more preoccupied he remained the better. She called for a car, and packed a small suitcase. There was little doubt that Nicky had gone to look for the necklace. One of the servants had repeated word for word the old rani's wishes.

♦

Gunboat and Nicky reached the outskirts of the city as the light was waning. It was not quite dark enough for the street lights, and the city was shadowy. Gunboat slowed, mindful of the unpredictable nature of Indian pedestrians and cyclists and cows.

'Where now? Straight to your sister's?'

'No.' Nicky pulled out a neatly folded piece of paper. On it were half a dozen names and addresses. 'Head for Basvanguidi. Do you know the way?'

'Not well.'

He stopped and changed places with the driver. Nicky gave quick instructions and they set off.

'What's the list?'

'Moneylenders. My grandmother obtained it from the police commissioner.' He looked back. Gunboat did not understand. 'We have...lost a very expensive piece of jewellery, and my grandmother thought it might turn up at one of these Marwari moneylenders.'

'And you would like me to be there when it's...found?'

'Yes.'

Gunboat laughed. 'Okay, let me figure this out. Someone stole it. Right?'

'Yes,' Nicky said politely.

'And that someone is possibly Miss Hobbs?'

'Possibly.' He appeared reluctant to admit her guilt and Gunboat allowed him time to explain. It came as they passed the traffic circle at the top of the long hill. 'My grandmother thought so. She could be right but...'

'You'd like to believe her innocent first. Wise boy.'

♦

The car dropped Miss Hobbs on the corner of Brigade Road and South Parade near the taxi rank. She ordered her driver to continue on to the palace and wait for her there. She climbed into a taxi, an old rusted Chevrolet.

'Commercial Street,' she ordered the driver.

◆

Johnny was standing in front of Koshy's Coffee Shop with Ram Singh and Lakshman. The three were holding hands, in the familiar gesture of friendship, watching the pretty college girls promenade past and exchanging low lewd comments. Ram Singh was astride his scooter, the other two beside him, giggling at each other's boldness.

'Listen, boss,' Johnny said as they began to tire of their evening ritual, 'give me a lift to Commercial Street.'

'What for?' Ram Singh asked, and giggled. 'There are no dames down there.'

'I...want to buy something,' Johnny said reluctantly, not wishing to elaborate. It was to be a gift for the girl he'd fallen in love with.

'Buy it around here.'

'I can't afford to. Come on. Give us a lift. You can have a free drink at Gunboat's.'

Ram Singh stroked his beard. The evening had begun to quiet down; the girls were going home. 'Okay. But I'll only drop you off.'

'Thanks,' Johnny said and mounted the scooter.

Commercial Street was a small, narrow thoroughfare, still in the cantonment area, yet crowded with stores selling everything from cloth to black-market French perfumes, American cigarettes, and English record players. There was no sidewalk. Pedestrians negotiated the street between cars, cows, cyclists, and a narrow gutter, regularly breached by planks or granite stones that led to the shops.

◆

The taxi dropped Miss Hobbs midway. The shop lights, long strips of bluish white neon, were coming on. The dark faces under them took on a sort of purple hue. The crowds of shoppers allowed little room to walk freely. Each step needed two sidesteps, and it took Miss Hobbs a good ten minutes to work her way up the street. Apart from the strolling shoppers, she was constantly assailed by shopkeepers trying to tempt the memsahib into buying their wares. Silks, satins, voiles, cottons, laces, Kashmir shawls, and lingerie from Paris were offered to her for exorbitant prices. They expected her as a European to know no better.

She checked her progress, found the narrow staircase that led up to the offices above the toy shop, and climbed slowly. The stairs led directly into a room. On the walls were paintings of Lakshmi, Lord Ganesh, Gandhi, and Nehru. They appeared equal in their importance and it was easy to see how the Hindu confused men with gods. In mythology they were often one and the same, and in reality the lines had become equally blurred. There were no chairs. A thick carpet covered the stone floor, and spread around were divans with huge bolster cushions to recline on. In a corner was a massive steel safe, not dissimilar to the one in the palace.

Three men, dressed in jibas and dhotis that instead of falling freely to the ground were tucked up under their legs, and fastened at the back so they looked half pants, reclined on the mattresses. They all wore turbans, not like a Sikh, neat and pointed, but rounded instead with some of the material falling back like a pigtail.

They were respectful. They did not rise, but namasted. She returned their greeting and slowly settled herself in front of the eldest man. He had a round, fat face, a neatly trimmed moustache, quick eyes that never remained too long on any person or object, and the kind of quietness that comes from long calculation. The other two resembled him, though much younger, and the board outside the room did mention Bagri & Sons. One was sent to fetch her a soft drink; the other remained seemingly absorbed in his ledgers, though he glanced up at her often.

'It is a great pleasure to see you again, memsahib,' the old man Bagri said, and waited.

'I've come to reclaim the necklace,' Miss Hobbs said abruptly and noticed him flinch at the quickness with which she got down to business.

He had not expected that of her, for in spite of her Englishness, she had a good Indian mentality. She was one of the few European women, for instance, who spoke such fluent Urdu with him, and he had been delighted with this discovery. She said she had learned the language in the streets as a child, but he suspected she had also studied it for she didn't speak vernacular but a more classical version of the language.

'Of course,' he said politely, and ordered his son to fetch the patta, the document of loan signed by Miss Hobbs and him.

The youth went to the safe, opened it, and riffled through the papers until he found what was wanted. He handed it to his father with his right hand and returned to his place. The old man studied it, quickly calculating the interest. The sum charged was extortionate. It was 50 per cent, compounded. For her it had been a concession. He had been known to charge 101 per cent.

'That will be fifty thousand rupees, including the full amount of the loan, memsahib,' the old man said politely. He noted her intake of breath, a common reaction, and knew by that that she didn't have that sum. It would now come to pleas and prayers, invocation of gods, and mercy. He would listen patiently, and then claim the money or the object.

She surprised him. She did not speak awhile, as if she were making her own calculations, and he was ready to inscribe his on paper.

'I would like the necklace on loan then, for two weeks,' she suggested. She rummaged in her purse and pulled out a sheaf of notes. They were the same she had taken from Gunboat Jack. 'Here is part repayment of the money.'

'What about the fifty, the original sum?' he asked.

He took the money and passed it to his son. His other son returned with a cool drink and a straw. Miss Hobbs took it but did not drink.

'I will repay the whole sum in...two weeks,' she said. 'I will be able to, I know that. There is a business deal coming up very soon and I shall have control of it.'

He considered the proposition. He had little to lose. He had her patta, some of the money, and no doubts she would repay the remainder. He wasn't ignorant of her identity, although she had pointedly not told him. A matter of a few questions. The necklace had the maker's mark, an old and established jeweler, Bapalal. The maker recognized it, and remembered to whom it had been sold. He had then sent one of his sons by bus to Tandhapur to verify this information.

'Memsahib,' the old man said mournfully, dramatically, 'what can I say? Whatever you wish from me I will do. If you want the necklace on loan, it is yours. I trust you. Inder, give the great memsahib the necklace.'

The son went to the safe, rummaged once more, and drew out the necklace reverently. It was a beautiful and intricate piece of work. It weighed at least eight sovereigns. The stones were perfect, quite priceless. He passed it to his father. His palm warmed the chilled metal and stone.

'You will not mention this transaction to anyone?' Miss Hobbs asked. She took it, placed it carefully in her purse, and struggled to her feet.

'I will not,' the old man swore. 'It is important to have discretion in my business, memsahib.'

◆

Johnny wandered slowly up Commercial Street. He was not sure what he wanted to buy the woman he loved. Something exquisite, something beautiful. He sighed. Something inexpensive. He had only forty rupees. He gazed in the shops, watching the brilliantly coloured bolts of silk spread out for customers, the shiny radios and tape recorders, the dull-glowing gold and silver jewellery. He stopped in shops, examined, haggled, moved on. He decided on a silver bangle. She would wear it so everyone could see. He peered into a small silversmith's. The shop was beside a narrow stairway leading up to a moneylender.

'Come, sir. I have what you are searching for,' the shopkeeper said. Johnny stepped up and squatted in front of the cabinets.

Johnny had seen what he wanted: a delicate silver bangle, drawn and twisted like rope. It was now a matter of price. They had haggled and reached fifty rupees. Johnny stuck to forty. Suddenly, the shopkeeper called out: 'Memsahib, memsahib.'

Johnny turned. A large European lady, dressed in a sari, had stepped out from the moneylender's doorway. It was unusual to see a European in this part of the town. She did not look towards the shopkeeper but moved purposefully down the street.

'Chuthia,' the shopkeeper said good-naturedly. 'All right. Forty rupees.'

He placed the bangle in a box and handed it to Johnny. He was delighted. Now he had only to pluck up the courage to present it to his love.

◆

The Ford stopped outside Gunboat's compound. The chauffeur ran around, opened the door, and ran to the boot and took out Gunboat's small case.

They sat awhile, weary. Headlights from passing cars picked up their silhouettes, moved them rapidly from one side to another, returned them to darkness. The list had been unhelpful. They'd rushed from one address to another and not one of the moneylenders recognized the necklace or Miss Hobbs.

Gunboat glanced at Nicky. The prince sat in a corner, chin cupped, brooding.

'What next?'

'We'll try others tomorrow,' he sighed. 'There must be a thousand in this city. A couple of million in the country. They're leeches. They hold people totally in their power. Some of my subjects never ever get out of their debt.'

'Why don't you lend them the money?'

'We do, when they ask us,' Nicky said. 'All don't. They prefer to go to the moneylenders. Sometimes they have no choice. Their father got them in debt, and they are then bound to the moneylender.' He sat up. 'But that doesn't solve this present problem. I will send a car tomorrow to fetch you.'

'What about our training programme?'

'You set up my sparring partners and tell me where and when. I have only a week left, you know.'

'I know.'

He took the case from the chauffeur and walked down the dirt track. Jockey Rosen sat in the veranda, glass in hand, puffing a cigarette fiercely. Gunboat climbed the steps.

'Got a drink for a thirsty man?'

'Gunboat.' And he appeared delighted to see him. 'I've missed you, old friend. No one to sit and talk to about this bloody country.' He got up, fetched a glass from the interior, and poured a measure. 'Family's out visiting friends.' He saw the case. 'Back for good?'

'I guess so.' The drink warmed him, and he coughed. Indian whiskey had strong alcohol fumes. 'The prince gets back to school day after.'

'How's the training?'

'Goin' good. You betting?'

Jockey Rosen remained silent awhile. His glasses glinted in the light when he moved his head. For the most part he remained still, as if he had not heard the question. It was his fourth whiskey, and he felt sad, maudlin. He cocked his head, listened: the spare traffic, the call of hawkers, the bell of a sweetmeat cart, the rise and fall of voices, a breeze rustling the leaves.

'I really don't want to leave,' he began apologetically. 'I've been happy here and I've made a good living. Made a few good friends too, you know, mate. I've been treated well by them…by this country. It's my son.' He stopped abruptly as if he had admitted a betrayal. 'He's got to have some future. A degree from St Joseph's isn't worth the candle for the lad. He'll be better off in Sydney. You understand, don't you?'

'Yeah, I do,' Gunboat said.

'Otherwise I'd stay,' he said forcefully as if Gunboat had disagreed. 'I swear I would.' He poured himself another drink, swallowed it in one gulp, and stood. He swayed, and Gunboat reached out to steady him, but with the courage of the drunk the small man drew himself upright and straight.

'I bet a thousand on the prince,' he said suddenly, as if remembering now the question. 'I hate the poms here. Always have, I guess,' he muttered to himself as he carefully negotiated the even floor to the doorway. 'With you training him I might even win some money, but who the hell cares. It's the least I could do. Bet a thousand on an Indian against a fucking pom.'

Gunboat heard him fall on the bed.

The room was, once more, claustrophobic. He prowled it, three strides across, four lengthwise, and finally fell on the bed. It smelled disused, yet clean, like a freshly dug grave. He could not remain long in the dark silence.

Brigade Road was not quite deserted. A few shows remained open, there was a small crowd of college students hanging around outside Koshy's, the cinema house car park was packed for the nine thirty show. There were no promenaders. A few regulars remained in Gunboat Jack's. They stopped playing for a moment to greet him and shake his hand. Johnny sat at the bar and Gunboat slipped onto a stool beside him.

'Hi, Johnny.' Gunboat was pleased to see him. 'Got news?'

Johnny nodded. He appeared, to Gunboat, to be carefully sober, as if he were guarding a secret.

'I have an interview tomorrow with Bharat Electronics.'

He glanced at Gunboat, glanced away; restless eyes that seemed incapable of settling anywhere. Finally, he swallowed the remainder of his beer and would have left if Gunboat hadn't held him.

'What's up?'

'Nothing.'

'The girl tell you to drop dead?'

'No.' He remained forlorn. 'Her parents refuse to give their consent until I get the job.' He shivered. 'What if I am not employed? I feel ill.'

'Don't worry. You'll get it.'

He knew there was no other advice. Here, love did not come before, but only after marriage. After the carefully calculated social, economic, and astrological conditions.

'Who knows?' Johnny whispered fatalistically. He fell silent and then shyly took out the box and showed Gunboat the bangle.

'It is beautiful. For her?'

'Yes.' Johnny sighed. 'Will you give it to her? From me, of course.'

'C'mon, Johnny. You gotta give it yourself.' He wished he could cheer up his friend. 'I'll let you tell me a joke.'

'You will?' Johnny looked suspicious, then pleased. He had hundreds.

Gunboat nodded and waited. Silence.

Johnny screwed his eyes shut in thought. Gradually, they opened, puzzled.

'I can't think of one. All I can see is her face.' He was near to tears at this lost opportunity. Gunboat would never ask him again.

'Next time then.' Gunboat slipped off his stool quickly. 'See you around, Johnny.'

Johnny held his hand the way a woman would, fingers intertwined, palm to palm. Tightly. 'Wish me luck, Gunboat.'

'I do,' Gunboat said and prayed also for his own as he left.

PART IV

TWENTY-THREE

The school in the cantonment sprawled over fifty acres. The focus from which the school and playing fields radiated out was a granite two-storeyed structure of classrooms and dormitories. It also had a five-storey tower, like an English battlement, with a clock. There were a dozen other buildings scattered over The grounds and in a far corner, shaded by gold mohur trees, was a chapel. There were four playing fields for the four XI's, and depending on the term, they were used for cricket, football, or hockey. There was also a swimming pool, a gymnasium, two tennis courts, and a large assembly hall.

Bishop Walsh, named after its founder one hundred twenty years back, was a public school run on the exact lines as an English one. There were three houses: Clive, Hastings, and Elphinstone, named after English heroes. Each had different colours, house songs, and dormitories. The masters wore gowns and mortarboards. Once it had been the exclusive preserve of English boys, but now there were only a handful left. Nicky's father had been the first Indian permitted to attend the school and that was a rare privilege to be accorded even to a prince.

One day before it had been deserted and forlorn. Now it resembled a railway station. Cars drew up depositing boys of every size on the steps of their dormitories. They were dressed alike: khaki slacks, white shirt, dark green ties, yellow blazers with green piping, the school crest with its Latin motto on the top pocket, and peaked yellow caps. Some had tassels and these were the prefects. The smaller ones wept at their parting; the older ones embraced each other, renewing old friendships and enmities. Nicky's car pulled up by the clock tower. The chauffeur unloaded his luggage and climbed the stairs behind him as he led the way to his dorm. It was in the west wing; Nicky was captain of his house, Clive, the same as his father's though the rajah had never risen to captain, and had a corner bed with a window on either side and a larger storage locker. The dormitory was spartan. Each boy had an iron cot, mattress, mosquito net, and locker. The shower rooms were in the centre of the dormitory.

The younger boys deferred to him as he passed; the older ones greeted him with affection, but with noticeable reserve. He was popular rather out of excellence than likeability. Nicky was aware of this, and at times it served him well; at others he felt envious of those easy companionable friendships boys made and preserved through their school years. He had lived with these same boys for over four years, yet felt no closer to them than when he had first joined the school.

There were many things to be done: lockers filled, boys inspected, younger ones comforted, housemasters to be met (his was an Englishman due for retirement at the end of the year. His whole life had been lived in this school, and he was a bachelor. This made for many rumors about his homosexuality though nothing had been proven by the boys); class schedules copied and the games master consulted on the coming boxing matches and the cricket season.

The games master was also an Englishman, also due for retirement. His name was Allenby, and in his youth he had played hockey for India, as a goalkeeper, with the legendary Dhyan Chand. He had since grown plump, and flushed, as if he indulged in too much port.

They met in his small study overlooking the first XI field.

'Been practicing, Nataraj, I hope,' Allenby asked.

'Some, sir,' Nicky said.

'Good, good. We have to win the trophy again this year.'

He was proud of his cricket team. Three of the boys, including Nicky, were potential state players. They made up the continual strength of the side. His favourite game, however, remained hockey.

'I would also like to box for the school this year, sir,' Nicky said.

He stood, as no master invited a schoolboy to sit.

Allenby was surprised. He cocked an eyebrow and sniffed, as if disapproving. He also measured Nicky as if he were a racehorse.

'That's unlike you.'

'Yes, sir.'

'You know, if you win your bouts I'd say you'll be fighting…' he ran another measurement…Ian Potter.'

'Yes, sir.'

'He's won all his fights against us. Good fighter.'

'Yes, sir,' Nicky repeated. 'He's also played us in football, sir.'

'I know that. A strong fullback.'

'Yes, sir,' Nicky said.

The two schools played each other in every sport and annually held an athletic contest as well. The rivalry had been continuous for nearly eighty years.

'So be it,' Allenby pronounced, and made a note in his pad. He was pleased Nataraj had enrolled in his boxing team. It was difficult to get boys, and rumour was that this could be the last year for boxing. Indian parents disapproved of the sport. 'Isn't he somehow…connected to you?' Allenby looked up, frowning.

'Yes, sir. His mother tutored my family.'

'Well, as long as it doesn't interfere with your cricket, you can box,' Allenby said and dismissed Nicky.

◆

At the end of the school day, the car returned to pick up Nicky. As a house captain and senior prefect he did not need permission to leave the school ground for a few hours. He was expected to be present for the eight o'clock roll call in the dining room.

Gunboat had arranged for the use of the boxing ring in the army's gymnasium off the Hosur Road. It was a practice ring, as professional as he'd ever seen, and well maintained. Nicky changed in the dressing room with his sparring partner. The boy was an inch or two taller, a blond-haired, blue-eyed Anglo-Indian who lived in the orphanage on St John's Road. His name was Peter Baldwin and he was quiet and shy.

'Okay, you two, I just want you to take the first round easy. I'm going to referee.' Gunboat climbed into the ring with them. 'When I say break, break, and if you fall, wipe your gloves. Peter,' he turned to the boy in the corner who was shuffling and shadow-boxing. He looked strong and practiced. 'Block his punches, and pull yours a bit this round. In the next we'll see how you both do.'

The boys circled. Peter came forward, jabbed, and was blocked. Nicky imitated him. The blow was shrugged off with the glove. Baldwin crouched low, weaved, shuffled, making himself a difficult target. His punches came upwards, from below face level. Nicky learned to lower his head, to keep level and hold his guard up.

It felt good to be sparring with someone his age and height. He danced forward, jabbed, stepped back for the return. It swung past his head. He jabbed quickly but Baldwin's defense was as fast.

'Fine.' Gunboat stepped in between. Both boys poured with sweat.

'How long was that?' Nicky asked.

'A full three minutes. Towel off.' The boys returned to their corners.

'Nicky, you have to keep moving forward. You're letting Peter take control. This time, play it a bit harder, but not too hard. Just remember he's only a sparring partner, and I figure he could lose control and hurt you.'

'That would do me good,' Nicky said quietly. 'I'd know how it felt.'

'Leave that 'til tomorrow.'

Again they circled. Nicky followed his instructions, forcing Baldwin to backpedal continuously, jabbing to keep Nicky at a distance. Baldwin backed into a corner, feinted, ducked, and in the next moment Nicky found himself trapped and held there by a quick hard barrage of punches. He took them on his arms and gloves, well protected from real damage. He lurched out, clinched, and pushed Baldwin back into the centre. He heard Gunboat call 'break,' and they parted.

'Great,' Gunboat said and stepped between them. 'How you both feeling?'

'Fine,' Baldwin said quietly.

'Bruised,' Nicky said. 'He's a good boxer.'

'You bet he is,' Gunboat said. 'He could have taken you a couple of times. You dropped your guard, and you're still swinging a bit. Straight I told you. Straight and hard.'

He accompanied them back to the dressing room, giving both instructions. He was proud of both his protégés, though he identified more with Baldwin. The boy was smaller and thinner than Gunboat had been at his age, but for him boxing had the same meaning. It was a way out of poverty, and a large mean anger drove the boy to fight hard. It had been difficult for him to control himself with the prince. Tomorrow Gunboat would allow him to hurt Nicky.

'How are you feeling?' Gunboat asked as they walked to the car.

Nicky shrugged, then his shoulders drooped. 'I still haven't found that moneylender.'

'We will.'

'When?' he asked angrily as if Gunboat had the answer. 'I feel I'm failing my grandmother, my family, myself.'

'That's a heavy load for a kid. Just concentrate on the fight. You can't climb into the ring with all that. You'll lose for sure.'

Gunboat was worried. He'd not seen Nicky so close to despair. If the prince lost, so did he. His life would be forever here. Alone.

'I—I won't, Gunboat.' Only half-believing, preoccupied as he climbed into the car.

◆

Miss Hobbs glanced at the clock. It was nine p.m. and she laid down the magazine, a two-month-old *Tatler*. She rang for the bearer, signed the chit for her two gin and tonics, and asked him to call a taxi.

She was alone in the reading room of the Bangalore United Services Club. It was a pleasing room, with matching chintz curtains and sofa cushions and a rack of English magazines. She picked up her leather bucket handbag. It was heavy with carefully collected objects, and she held it tightly. There were half a dozen men in the club's main room and a couple greeted her. The room was generous, fashioned on the lines of an exclusive English club. There were a dozen deep leather armchairs, a couple of antique writing desks, and on the walls ancient muskets and the mounted heads of animals. Beyond it was the men-only bar: a wood-paneled room with high leather stools and a teak counter.

It was a spacious and exclusive club. Once only the British military used it, and the list of past presidents on the board, starting in 1860, consisted of either generals or colonels. Now its members were wealthy Indians and the difference was barely noticeable. The ballroom was across the sweeping drive, and beyond that the swimming pool and a couple of tennis courts. At the rear were the squash courts and rooms for out-of-station members.

The taxi stopped under the porch, and Miss Hobbs gave the driver instructions. The palace car remained parked under the tamarind tree.

It was a twenty-minute ride to Russell Market. The sprawling bazaar, with the still odours of fresh meats and vegetables, was shuttered and silent. The narrow lanes leading off the square were crowded with carts and rickshaws and the bodies of tired men and women. Here and there a tea stall still remained open, but soon they too would shut, for the bazaar opened early.

The taxi dropped her off at the southwest corner. She paid generously for it to wait, and trudged carefully through the day's garbage of rotting fruit and spoiled vegetables and rotten meat. She held a handkerchief to her nose to ward off the stench. A stranger, in this darkness and silence and menace of poverty, would have been afraid to take to these narrow, winding lanes alone. She was seen and noted—the bright pinpoint of a sucked beedi, the shift of a lounging body, the growl of pie-dogs—but she strode with the authority of one who had once ruled. None would molest her.

She checked her location, carefully stepped over a gutter, and knocked on the door of a tiny single-storey house. It was jammed between a cloth shop and a tea stall. There was a small wooden plaque on the door: Jayaprakash, BA, Consultant for the Occult.

A woman opened the door, her face hidden by the edge of her sari. She led Miss Hobbs to a tiny, stuffy room. A single folding chair faced an altar and a formidable array of carved gods and goddesses. The centrepiece, a foot high and made of some dark stone, was Kali.

'Madam, it is indeed a very great honour to have you visit again.' The man who spoke was dark as the statue and blended in with the shadow thrown by the single oil lamp. The flame was still, straight. The man was bare-chested, with a dhoti around his waist.

'I need...help,' Miss Hobbs said. She took the chair and sat.

'Of course. That is why so many people come to me. I give help.'

He sat at the altar. He was a slim man, quite ageless and with expressionless eyes. They appeared not even to shine in the lamplight, and revealed no sadness, no joys. They observed with utter detachment. He gave no impression of evil except when he smiled. Then he revealed pink gums in an obscene grimace.

'You have brought what is necessary, madam?' he asked and began preparations.

Lighting incense, camphor, arranging paan leaves and the bell to summon the spirits he prayed to. It looked no different from any prayer room, for a belief in God and goodness necessitated a similar belief in God and evil. He bestowed either impartially, depending on his summoning. One could not exist without the other and God, Brahma, the ultimate power in the universe, made no human judgement or differentiation between the two forces.

'Yes,' Miss Hobbs said.

She laid out neatly, from her bag, fruit, camphor, coconuts, incense, money, and Nicky's sweat-stained polo shirt.

Jayaprakash took the money first. He counted the ten-rupee notes, fifty in all, and placed them in front of the altar. He took her other offerings too and arranged them in a neat row, to be picked up as the prayers were spoken. The shirt was last.

'Could you not have something more personal, madam?'

'It was difficult. You know.'

'Yes,' he said regretfully. 'We Indians are so superstitious. We never will catch up with the West.'

It was spoken with no irony. It was a mere observation on the habit of many people to burn their hair and nail clippings within moments of cutting. Nicky's grandmother had always carried out this task, and he had yet to forget the habit.

'It has not been washed?'

'No.'

'Good,' he said and placed it on a brass tray. 'You wish for ill luck and troubles? Death?' He savoured the word, sounding pleased.

'Death!' She savoured it too. She shut her eyes, imagining: In another age she could have chosen poison, an assassin's dagger. 'No. I just want him defeated.'

He lit a small fire, held within a square of bricks, opened a book, and began the ceremony. Miss Hobbs watched, mesmerized by the flames, the musical cadences in his voice, the heat of the room.

The ritual took two hours. A piece of the shirt burned; the remains were packed tightly in a plantain leaf and placed in a mud pot. Both participants were sweating and Miss Hobbs's handkerchief was soaked, as were the edges of her sari. Jayaprakash scraped together a part of the shirt's ashes, placed them in a scrap of newspaper, screwed it up, and handed it to Miss Hobbs at the end of the ceremony.

'You will place this among his personal effects, madam. Something he uses daily, an almirah or a drawer. Even a book will be sufficient.'

He wiped his body and face with a small towel and rose tiredly.

'Thank you.' She took it.

'He has not,' Jayaprakash said quietly, as if a thought had occurred, 'performed a homam himself, has he?'

'I do not think so.'

'Find out. If he has, this will not have effect and I will have to perform another ceremony.'

'An excuse for more money.'

'Madam.' Jayaprakash appeared shocked by the suggestion. 'I would never consider that. But I will wish you to verify the matter.'

'Why?' she paused at the door. The night appeared no cooler.

'Because it is possible. As I said, we are superstitious and we take precautions.'

◆

Nicky examined the swelling. It was on his top lip, dead centre. There was a faint red streak on the inside. Baldwin's punch had hurt, and momentarily Nicky had nearly swung wild in fury. He had remembered Gunboat's advice: when hurt, backpedal. He had. Baldwin had followed too quickly, and Nicky had jolted him with a short right to the ribs. At the end of the session, both boys respected each other's ability to hurt.

'What happened?' Gobind asked, peering into the mirror. He was a year junior to Nicky, and one of three brothers. 'Bee sting.'

'Balls,' C. K. Reddy said, also studying the swelling. He was an Andhra from Hyderabad and Nicky's opening partner in cricket. 'Looks as if you were trying to smooch and she bit you.'

'Looks like that,' Gobind said judiciously.

'Who was it? Hema? Nargis? Or that English girl, Sally? Oh God, I'd like to climb up her legs.'

'Bee sting,' Nicky repeated.

'Don't lie,' C. K. said and they followed him to his bed. Theirs were next to his. 'You've gone out every evening. Must be heavy, boss.' They looked wistfully envious. Girls were beyond reach, and even to hold the hand of one promised to be a heavy experience. 'You in love?'

'No.' Nicky laughed and got into bed. It was nearing lights off. The housemaster would soon be on his rounds.

'And it's not a girl. Worse luck.'

He thought of the prostitute, considered telling them of the rare experience, and decided against it. He felt faintly ashamed of the episode and a longing to return.

'Who are you fighting tomorrow?' Gobind asked.

'Raghu.'

'And if you win?'

'I'll win,' Nicky said. 'Shetty.'

'Then you'll get Potter. That chuthia white skin will kill you,' C. K. said mournfully.

'Balls,' Nicky said. He couldn't resist the chance. None of the other boys had trained or been taught. They went into the ring unschooled, with Allenby's only instruction: Don't butt. 'Want to bet?'

'Five rupees,' Gobind said quickly.

'Five to one then,' Nicky suggested.

There was silence. Gobind calculated his pocket money. 'Okay. C. K. You want to split it?'

'Why not?'

'Lights out,' Reynolds called from the doorway. Boys scrambled to their beds and tucked themselves in as the housemaster made his way down the room. He held a package in one hand. 'Your driver left this for you, Nataraj.'

He dropped the package on the locker, next to Nicky's pillow. It looked like a book, and Nicky recognized Miss Hobbs's neat handwriting.

'I didn't ask for it.'

But Reynolds had returned to the door. He surveyed the loom and switched out the lights.

Nicky thought of dropping the unwanted parcel to the floor. He felt too weary, and despair still clung to him. He and Gunboat, after the sparring match, had visited another three moneylenders and drawn blanks. He felt Miss Hobbs slipping out of his grasp, twisting and dancing away, laughing uproariously. She was too clever for him. He tried to sleep but the night was warm and stuffy. He tossed and turned, restless in a strange unease.

TWENTY-FOUR

The ring was on the stage. The padding in the corner and the tape on the ropes were in the school colours. The assembly hall, a cavernous building, was filled with boys and masters. The walls were paneled, and inscribed in each, dating back to the beginning, were the names of champions: Victor Laudorums, school captains, cricket, hockey and football and boxing captains, athletic record holders, clever scholars. From the rafters, hung school and house flags.

Gunboat was not allowed in Nicky's corner. Two classmates were his seconds: Gobind and C. K. He remained in the wings, and once the two boys understood his presence they sensed the small fortune slipping from their grasp. The bet could be lost.

The younger boys fought first. They flayed at each other, wearing gloves too large, holding on to their pants. They went three rounds of a minute each, and Gunboat was amused that they behaved like champions when they won: clasping gloved hands, embracing the loser, accepting the towels thrown over their backs like racehorses being led from the course.

Gunboat said nothing to Nicky, except to wish him luck. The boy he fought was his height, a couple of pounds lighter, and untutored. Nicky jabbed and punched and drove the boy against the ropes. There he hit hard and untiringly, drawing blood from the boy's nose.

Gunboat was not surprised by his cruelty. He had every intention of annihilating his opponent, and no quarter to be given. Allenby stopped the fight in the second round and raised Nicky's hand with that nervous look that gentler men give to others who unleash such destructive violence.

'Take it easy with them,' Gunboat said when Nicky joined him. 'Save it for Potter.'

'How did I do?' Nicky asked, not listening.

'Good,' Gunboat said. 'You did what I told you. Except the kid wasn't much good.'

'That was his problem.' He wiped the sweat from his face and chest. 'I have to fight hard, you know that. If I take it easy this time, it will be more difficult against Potter.'

'Yeah, I know.'

The next day Gunboat saw Miss Hobbs sitting in the last row with the masters. She was deep in conversation, a solicitous kind, with Nicky's housemaster, Reynolds. She stopped when Nicky stepped into the ring. He passed the word to Gobind who whispered the information to Nicky. He nodded, not bothering to look, but he appeared to stand straighter, his face grew harder. He repeated the previous day's performance; if not drawing blood, swelling and blackening his opponent's eye.

'You think I've lost my punch,' Nicky asked Gunboat. 'I didn't draw blood.'

'Maybe he don't bleed as easy,' Gunboat consoled him. 'Potter's going to be a lot harder than these two.'

'I know,' Nicky said. He held out his hands. Gobind undid his gloves.

'You think I should have another session with Baldwin?'

'No. You've only got a couple of days left. Take it easy, relax. Forget about the fight.'

Nicky waited until his seconds had moved out of earshot. 'Maybe I should visit that woman again?'

'Nope,' Gunboat growled. 'That's the worst thing you can do.'

'Even at my age?'

'Any age. Never before a fight especially. It drains you.'

'You sound like a yogi.' Nicky laughed.

'Not too much, I hope,' Gunboat said and thought wistfully of the nights with Gertrude. She had written a polite note in reply to his love letter, and now his pride prevented him from calling on her. He prayed she would come to him.

◆

They went out, Nicky still in shorts and vest. The shadow of the assembly hall stretched long over the first XI field, wavering in the fading light. Small boys approached Nicky gravely and congratulated him on his fight. He appeared not to notice. They accepted this, and one or two bolder ones patted him tentatively as if he were a precious statue. The others remained in awe.

Miss Hobbs sat on the stone parapet on which the boys gathered to watch first XI matches. Gunboat fell back a step as Nicky approached. He was polite, friendly, and she was the same.

'Why don't we walk?' she suggested, and they started off across the field towards his dormitory. She looked back. Gunboat followed.

'Is he always there?'

'We have to talk about my fight with Ian,' Nicky said, without turning.

'You're fighting well,' Miss Hobbs said, betraying no resentment. 'It will be quite a match with Ian.'

'It should be,' Nicky said.

Lights were coming on in the dormitories as the boys returned to shower and prepare for their study. He remained silent, knowing she would talk first. He had to wait until they reached the steps.

'Did you get the parcel?'

'Yes, but I didn't ask for any book.'

She smiled coyly. 'It's just a present. A first edition of Gibbons's *Rise and Fall of the Roman Empire*.'

'Thank you.' Nicky was surprised.

'Keep it safely in your locker.' The small screw of paper from the black magician was in the spine of the book. 'Near you.'

'I will.' Nicky stirred, restless. 'I must change.'

'Of course,' she said, and studied the small silver cylinder hanging from his neck. It was entwined with a gold chain. She knew what it was.

'You shouldn't box with that,' she said gently. 'You could get hurt, if you're punched there.'

'It hangs down the back when I fight.' He touched it. 'My grandmother told me never to remove it.'

'It's dangerous still,' she said insistently. 'You must take it off for the fight.'

He shook his head stubbornly. She remembered the head movement; it was a long time ago. He was small, only seven, spoilt and stubborn. The years in the English public school had done him some good but had not changed his character. Nicky turned and jogged away to his dormitory. Gunboat began to follow and she stopped him.

'Nicky could get hurt fighting with that silly thing around his neck.'

'He believes in it,' Gunboat said. 'And that's good enough for me.' He wished her good night and strolled after Nicky.

Miss Hobbs watched them, eyes half closed, calculating how she would get Nicky to rid himself of the protection. She signalled the car, climbed in, and sank back with pleasurable anticipation. At this very moment Rukmani was with the family lawyers, drawing up her power of attorney in favour of the rajah. And soon, Miss Hobbs knew, she would have complete control of the state's finances.

TWENTY-FIVE

That morning he had awakened afraid. He had not understood it at first. He'd lain minutes before the wake-up bell rang, trying to understand. It was a rare occurrence, not sensed since his childhood. It was still dark, and he could see little outside the netting. The other boys slept. The first birds had begun calling; they sounded alone, like him. They reached out and heard each other. He had no one. The fear didn't take any visible form. He did not sweat or tremble. It was in the hollowness of his belly, the almost unsupportable weight on his heart, as if it no longer had room to pump. He felt a revulsion at this weakness, as if he'd soiled his bed, but he could not control it.

It remained with him all day: at chota hazri, morning net practice, classes. It felt as heavy as the books he carried from locker to classroom and back between each class. The hollowness seemed contagious for, at the end of the school day, by three-thirty, he felt it had spread down to his thighs and the calves. He jogged to try to get rid of it, but when he returned to shower it was still embedded in him like a piece of metal that could not be removed.

At tea, he had sat beside Ian. The four boys from Sherbourne had arrived the previous night and were using the junior dorm of Hastings House. Ian had appeared calm, even indifferent, to the coming boxing match. He was cheerful, making jokes and playfully sparring with his pals.

'You're a lucky chap,' Ian said, and stretched for the marmalade.

'Why's that?' Nicky felt he could eat nothing.

'It's only going to be a one-round match,' Ian laughed. 'You'll be back in your dorm before I even get to the station.'

'I might keep you a bit longer.'

'I told you, you prince-wallahs aren't terribly good at this sort of thing.'

'And you English are?'

'Not all the English. Only me.' He placed his arm around Nicky. 'Don't worry. I won't hurt you too much.'

'Neither will I. Maybe you should catch your train now…before you get hurt.' They both laughed. 'How is your mother?'

Nicky had not seen her since their meeting and felt some unease. She had not returned to Tandhapur but remained in the Bangalore palace, ominously quiet. He had asked his driver what she did with her days, and he had replied, 'Nothing.' She sat in her room or else on the balcony looking out on the garden; in the evenings she walked for an hour or so in the garden. She appeared to be waiting for something to occur, almost, he sensed, silently willing it. The intensity of her quiet was unnatural, and superstitiously he touched the thayethu around his neck.

'Fine,' Ian said noncommittally.

In his short life Ian had not known her well. She had been a photograph on the table in his father's bungalow for years, and when she had materialized to claim him, he suspected with the intuition of the child, that it was for the saving of her soul rather than for his well-being. He wished now his father had not relinquished him so easily.

'You have to win, you have to beat him tonight,' she would say fiercely. 'To a pulp. You can win, you must. Do you hear me?'

Then she would fall silent, not listening to his mumbled assent. He could not harbour the same implacable hatred of Nicky. He had wondered what had occurred, and when he'd asked, not once but repeatedly, she had told him to shut up. He had remained an hour, fidgety and restless, incarcerated in her room, listening to her silences and outbursts. When he stood finally to leave, she begged him to remain. They were both alone; they had to stick together. She had embraced him then as if he were a lover, and suddenly frightened, he had struggled to escape her arms, her kisses, her odours of perfume and powder and perspiration.

She had released him then, stared coldly, and announced: 'You will win.' As if it were an edict. 'For my sake.' And this a prayer.

'I'll try' was all Ian could promise as he left her.

As the shadows lengthened and began to fade, the guests began to arrive. Most were parents, old boys too, for this was an annual event, and many onlookers. Nicky stood by the window, and looking through the branches of the trees he caught glimpses of the cars arriving.

'How are you feeling?' Gobind asked. C. K. stood by him. Both looked professional in tracksuits with towels around their necks. It was a dramatic job being a second.

'Okay.' He saw Gunboat. 'I'll see you there. And have the twenty-five rupees ready, boss.'

They met by the warden's office and went to sit on the stone bench where Miss Hobbs had sat.

'I'm just hoping you remember everything I taught you, kid,' Gunboat said. 'I know you're feeling kinda scared. Every fighter has that feeling, a sort of sickness in the belly as if you want to throw up. Even Louis never shook it, because once you climb into that ring you're all alone. There's nothing anyone can do to help you. You got to do it yourself. I know you can. You're good, real good. And you're going to win.'

'You will be nearby?'

'Yeah,' Gunboat said. 'Just near Gobind and C. K.'

They sat silent. The visitors passed, talking, laughing, their faces deep in shadow now for dusk had become darkness. 'I'll win.'

'You better, Prince. I got all my money riding on you.'

'What odds?'

'Five to one against.'

'I should have put down some money as well.'

'No, that's never a good idea. You get to start thinking on it. When you get in there, you quit thinking about everything except the fight.'

The visitors were down to a trickle. It was nearly seven and the first fight began in a few minutes. Nicky glanced back to the drive.

He saw Gertrude approaching and nudged Gunboat. Gunboat rose and kissed her. She looked shyly down at Nicky. He hesitated and then stood.

'Best of luck…Nicky.'

He sensed she wanted to kiss him, but they were too distant for such familiarity, although he wished it. Instead she shook his hand.

'Thank you, Gertrude.'

'I know you will win.'

'I hope so.'

'I'll see you after the fight,' Gunboat said, and they both watched her walking towards the hall.

'You back together?'

'Yeah.'

Gunboat had been in bed, unable to sleep. From inside the mosquito netting the view was blurred. It allowed him to imagine he still lay in the palace bed. The past sometimes is difficult to believe, Gunboat thought, when the present remains perpetually the same. There was a gap in my life, when I didn't exist in this room. I lived somewhere else, in another life, in another time, and now I'm back. This is my only reality.

The darkness, the night sounds were familiar. He listened and wished it were the monsoon season. He liked the sound of the rain and the harsh winds against the sides of the house, and the sweet cleansing smell of washed earth. He heard footsteps, light, hesitant. They came round the house, paused awhile. Then a soft knock on the door.

'Who is it?' Gunboat asked.

'Gertrude.'

When he opened the door, she stepped past him, wispy, perfumed; whirled in the centre, frock afloat, filling the room.

'Hi.' Gunboat spoke first to close the silence.

She stood, conspiratorial, and he sensed her laughing. She took a step, kissed him softly on the mouth, as if not wishing to waken him from his dream. He heard the zip, and the frock spilled to the floor. She unhooked her brassiere, tossed it afar, and slid under the net and into bed. She laughed.

'Come on.'

He didn't wish to question the dream and climbed in. He had forgotten how she felt: slim, warm, with silk skin, and a mouth tasting of cloves and lipstick. They made love hurriedly, silently, as if neither wanted to awaken. He drove into her hard, cruelly, wanting to erase that past pain, infect her with it. She accepted it, pulling him down, holding with each thrust until it was over. She sighed and let her head fall on his shoulder. They were damp with sweat, so slippery it seemed they could have become one body.

'You for real?' Gunboat asked, peering down through the glow of a cigarette.

'Yes.' She didn't lift her head. 'I missed you.'

'I thought you were being consoled by Malcolm?'

'Him.' She spoke in regal dismissal. 'He's only a silly boy.' She snuggled closer. 'Why did you have to go away and leave me like that? You know I can't be left alone.'

'What about you leaving me?' he countered.

'I didn't. You went away.'

'Yeah!' He thought of going further, refrained. He wanted to accept her, forgive her.

'Yeah!' she said. 'I thought of...' she hesitated, deciding to leave it unsaid. 'Malcolm is just a friend. I've known him since a baby. That was all.'

'Aren't you going away with him to England? Your mother wanted that, you know. I'm not much of a catch.'

'She doesn't know anything. She'd like me to have an arranged match like an Indian girl.'

'To an Indian.'

'Of course not,' she said indignantly. 'I mean good prospects, fair, my...community too.' She chuckled. 'When are we leaving for the Bronx?'

'Suppose I don't go?' Gunboat whispered. 'He could lose the fight.'

She sighed. 'We'll stay then, won't we. The prince will look after you.'

'You think he will? He's just a kid, you know.'

'A rich one. And with some power. We could find a small flat in Richmond Town...' She prattled on, arranging their lives neatly, as if the past had not occurred and this was continuous dialogue. She stopped suddenly. The silence was so noticeable, bleak, desolate. 'You do want me, don't you?'

He thought of his anger, and his dignity. They lay dormant, unable to be recalled. She was still a child, unchanged since they'd last made love.

'Yes, I want you.'

◆

Apart from the assembly hall, a distant hum of noise, the school looked deserted once more. Nicky kneaded his stomach; the fear remained. It had become familiar now, though it had not lost its terror; he understood why it was there. He wanted to talk to Gunboat, listen to additional comfort, but there was nothing more left to say. He was alone once more, and felt as if it would remain with him for the rest of his life.

'Thank you,' Nicky finally said to Gunboat.

'You're welcome.'

Lights swept the playing field, and two cars raced up the drive. The rajah and Miss Hobbs climbed out of the Silver Cloud. In the other Sushila and his aunt and grand-aunt and two cousins. A distance separated the progress of the rajah and Miss Hobbs from his family. Nicky stood when they reached him. Miss Hobbs nodded and continued walking, shrouded in a strange serenity.

'How are you feeling?' his father asked, and placed a hand on his shoulder.

'A bit wobbly,' Nicky said.

'I would like you to win. If you don't, it isn't important. There are other things.' He kneaded his son's shoulder, and Nicky felt the affection. 'It's a pity it is against Ian.'

'Yes.'

He looked around with a familiar eye. 'When I was here,' his father said, 'it was so difficult. They made me change my name. Victor, they called me; even in their school reports. I couldn't use our name.' His eyes continued their examination of the school. All that could be seen were silhouettes against the bright night sky. Nicky had heard the story before; his father even had the name tattooed on his forearm. 'We were expected to be exactly like them, otherwise they made your life…difficult. Everyone who rules moulds his subjects in his own form. They did that to God, why not us too. I suppose I did imitate them, but I had to be better than they as well to succeed. You know, I was the first Indian to ever make this school's first XI. I would practice and practice and practice, until I was better. There was a chappie called Wright, I remember…' He paused, turned to look at his son. 'I took his place, and he hated me all his life. They wounded us all. Not all. Only those of us who came in contact with them, and that changed us; and in turn we changed those we touched. Like a disease, I suppose. The past cannot be exorcised; we have to learn to live with it wisely. I wish it could have been that at the midnight hour it had slipped away. But it remains and it is too late, and too distant, for us to return to a time when they did not rule us. There is no chance for that. Nehru has decreed that the temples of tomorrow are to be the industries, and he's forced us to face west once more as if it were Mecca. Silly man, but how else would he have become prime minister if they had not recognized him as a gentleman. They passed the reins to one of their own. He now rules, with Prasad and Menon and Desai. We have to now remould ourselves in their images, otherwise we will not survive.'

'I know,' Nicky said, and waited in the silence for his father to continue to re-examine their lives.

The rajah hesitated, then held Nicky, tightly, quickly; then stepped back as if he had not moved. 'Best of luck.'

The others had held back. They now surrounded him. Two were male cousins, and they pumped his hand. The women patted him on the shoulders and arms, the nearest they came to embracing him. He could smell the odours of attar and sandalwood and kholi, feel the crisp rustle of their saris against him, and hear their soft voices, accompanied by the musical chink-chink of bangles, exhorting him to win.

From the assembly hall came a roar and the echo of Allenby's voice over the loudspeaker.

'I must go,' he said and they accompanied him to the hall. 'Where is Rukmani?'

Gunboat walked a few feet ahead.

'As usual she wasn't ready,' Sushila said in disgust. 'She'll be coming soon.'

Nicky hoped she would make it in time.

Their attention wandered and Nicky was glad to leave them for the dressing room. The first fight was over. Sherbourne had won, and the small boy who had lost was being consoled by Allenby. In the opposite wings of the stage, the winner was being cheered softly. Nicky caught a glimpse of Ian, stripped to shorts and singlet, already laced up; Anderson was conferring with him. The second fight had begun.

Three judges—one from each school, the third a test cricketer—sat at desks at the rear of the stage. They also were the referees.

Nicky peered through the faded red velvet curtain. The hall was packed. The first twelve rows were filled with guests. In the first was his father, with Miss Hobbs, and three rows behind he saw Gertrude, sitting by a small, bespectacled European man and woman. Gunboat was crouched, talking to them. Beyond them were row upon row of exuberant noisy boys, cheering, booing, chanting.

'You better get ready.' Allenby said. C. K. and Gobind took Nicky's tracksuit and laced up his gloves.

Nicky sat, looking but not seeing the two boys flailing at each other. He wanted to coil himself, protect and harden the deep interior of his soul from the coming loneliness and pain. He wished for silence rather than the welling sounds; darkness rather than stage lights.

'You'll be fine,' Gunboat said quietly. 'Just remember what you can, and do it.' He kneaded Nicky's shoulders, rubbed his arms. C. K. and Gobind worked on his calves.

Time must have passed, for Gunboat suddenly stood up. 'Okay.'

Nicky looked. Allenby climbed into the ring. He was dressed in a white-jacketed dinner suit and trailed a microphone.

'The next fight is the flyweight division. Representing Sherbourne is Ian Potter.' He waited as Ian climbed in the ring. 'And for Bishop Walsh is T. Nataraj. Potter weighs one hundred twenty pounds, Nataraj one hundred sixteen. The fight will be five rounds of three minutes each round.'

Nicky climbed in. Allenby called both to the centre and instructed them quickly. They shook hands and returned to their corners.

Nicky rested against the post, arms outstretched along the ropes, feeling one of his seconds massaging his neck. Smith, the Sherbourne teacher, was about to strike the gong. With that small movement Nicky felt a calmness, a release from the fear that had ridden him all day. He pushed away from the ropes, arms upraised. Then stopped.

Ian was whispering to Anderson. They both glanced quickly at him, then Anderson stepped across to the judges. Smith's hand stopped. He listened and they all looked at Nicky.

Smith spoke, gesturing with his mallet: 'Nataraj, remove that… thing…from around your neck, please.'

TWENTY-SIX

Nicky glanced involuntarily down at the thayethu, shook his head, and advanced to the centre of the ring. Ian lolled against the ropes.

'I insist you remove it,' Smith said. He was a compact, neat man with a lean face and a vague military bearing. 'It could do an injury to both of you,' he added with kindness.

'I can't,' Nicky said.

He looked at Smith, then Ian. Turned to his seconds and Gunboat as if needing support. They remained still, helpless. He could see little of the crowd; he only registered the long and sudden silence. The front row remained in his line of vision, in the edges of the glare. His father looked concerned, as if noting for the first time the appendage attached to his son. Next to him, Miss Hobbs leaned forward, as if straining to hear a distant and whispered dialogue. From the back of the hall, he sensed the boys whispering and fidgeting.

'In which case I cannot permit the fight.' Smith lowered his voice so it carried only to Nicky. 'I will have to declare Potter the winner.' His mallet gestured regretfully, as if understanding the dilemma.

Nicky sensed fear: a boy's terror of descending darkness, the visitation of phantoms and demons and misshapen spirits clutching for his heart. There was no escape and he knew he would be consumed, piecemeal, separated, trapped in the guilts of these damned. He blinked, near to tears. Ian smiled. Nicky understood that he knew what he had done: brought defeat without a blow. He turned, wanting to reach out, and saw Miss Hobbs. She had leaned back, arms folded, complacent. The rajah appeared puzzled, and from around the vast, bannered hall Nicky heard the whisper: 'What's happening?'

'Natarajan!' He heard Smith from a great distance calling.

'One moment.'

It was Gunboat this time, and he responded, turning. Gunboat slipped through the ropes, taking permission from the judges with a glance.

'I know what your grandmother said, Nicky,' Gunboat whispered. 'You better take that off.'

'How?' Nicky asked, puzzled.

He dare not disobey her authority. And what warrior fought without a talisman for protection? Arjuna, Bhima, Rama, a pantheon of heroes, had entered battles with potions and amulets and herbs and prayers and even gods riding at their shoulders for, unaided, they would have fallen at the first arrow, the first thrust of the sword, the first swirl' of attacking evil.

Gunboat reached out. Nicky stepped back.

'Nataraj,' Smith called impatiently.

'We can hang it in your corner. On the post,' Gunboat whispered.

He followed Nicky's glance. Miss Hobbs appeared anticipatory, almost delighting in the removal of the talisman. In another time and place Gunboat knew he would not have understood the prince's fear; instead impatiently snapped the thread. But over the last decade he had inhabited a world that stretched far beyond the surface reality of existence into shadows and corners and infinite darknesses.

'Did she give you anything, Nicky?'

The prince appeared not to hear. He was mesmerized by Miss Hobbs. She loomed large, an approaching zeppelin filling his vision.

'Nicky! She give you anything?'

'Yes,' Nicky said softly. 'A book.'

'Where is it?'

'In my locker, by my bed.'

Gunboat crossed to the referees, leaned over the ropes, placated them. He returned and led Nicky back to his corner. He touched the thayethu, felt the shiver, and consciously touched his own. His destiny too lay in her hands, and he needed the protection. He felt no envy for Nicky. Carefully he lifted the thayethu off Nicky's neck, and watched, and hung it around the post.

'C. D. Run—and I mean run—to your dorm. In Nicky's locker there is a book. Still wrapped.' Nicky nodded. 'Take it out and burn it. Like now. Go.'

C. D. turned and ran.

'We're ready, ref.' Then in a whisper: 'Don't be afraid. Just remember what I taught you.'

Nicky nodded. He was afraid, he was vulnerable to his own imagination, to a past he could never escape. It clung not just to his soul, but to his mind. He shook his head, wanting to clear it, to rid himself of centuries of gods and spirits and magic and, finally, servitude. He heard the gong in the distance. In the dining hall it summoned silence; now it summoned him to fight and he felt leaden with his terrors.

Ian waited in the centre. Nicky trudged forward, uncomprehending the weight, wishing only to lighten himself, dance as gracefully, eagerly, destructively as Ian.

'You prince-wallahs are all the same,' Ian whispered, understanding the self-destruction, knowing that victory as always would be easy.

They touched gloves. He snapped a quick left at Nicky's head. Mere reflex, made it glance off his cheek.

Nicky peered past his raised gloves, past Ian's. The bunched leather masked his face. The eyes were familiar. Like Miss Hobbs's. Grey, now malevolent; mesmeric. The nose, the mouth were dissimilar, stolen from another face. Too late! He felt the punches slide in, low, hard. One to his ribs, the other to his face. It caught his nose, stung. No rage; only bewilderment, a puzzlement at his inability to move, to retaliate. He felt the others; some to his arms, others to his chest and head.

'Back away…back away.' Gunboat spoke from some distance. He couldn't.

Gunboat held the ropes. 'Back away…goddamn it.'

He winced, wanting to leap over and protect the prince from the pounding. Or even stand by his shoulder and whisper instructions, sweat his own sweat into his blood.

'Move...move ...'

His feet appeared nailed down; his arms moved of their own volition, protecting the best they could. Yet Gunboat understood what was occurring. In the ring, in battle, you were finally alone, shed of all companionship, muffled by violence.

'Oh Jesus.'

He could sense not pain but numbness. That comforting cold that sapped and finally robbed the body of all feeling. Nicky was swaying. A tremor. The legs would then buckle, and finally the body topple. He didn't have long to last. He looked to Smith. The mallet was half raised, still time to go. He looked away. The rajah's features were stone; frozen in concentration, willing the yuvaraj to battle. Miss Hobbs leaned way forward; mouth apart, relishing, even, Gunboat suspected, orgasming at the violence. God, she was familiar.

'Where the hell's C. D.?' Gunboat asked Gobind.

Gobind didn't hear. He was shouting Gunboat's advice to Nicky. Once or twice he covered his eyes and peeped through his fingers.

'Oh God,' he whispered over and over, 'he'll never beat that bastard.'

The gong sounded.

Ian stopped, contemptuously turned his back, and returned to his corner. Anderson clapped his shoulder, knelt to whisper.

Nicky remained swaying.

'Get him,' Gunboat ordered Gobind.

Gobind carefully, as if treating an invalid, led Nicky to the stool and sat him down. He bathed his face, wiped off the sweat. The vast hall was silent; not a whisper, as they watched these administrations.

Gunboat knelt. His mouth near Nicky's ear.

'Listen, Nicky.'

He received a distant, weary response. There was blood on his mouth from an internal cut. Gobind dabbed it away. Gunboat moved closer, his mouth caressing the ear.

'Listen, you son-of-a-bitch prince. What the hell are you doing? Trying to make a fucking horse's ass out of me? You dumb bastard. Someone takes a cheap piece of tin from you and you turn to jelly. You still believe in all that Stone-Age crap. Listen, I taught you and I taught you good. There are no goddamned gods looking down on you; you're fucking alone in this world. Believe you me. All you got to work with is your own fucking self and those fists. Any gods there are, believe me, they are playing pinball with the universe and don't give a shit about you down here in that ring. And the same goes for the devil.'

Nicky's head turned. The eyes were narrowed, peculiarly cold. Another man would have felt the chill.

'Why are you getting mad at me for? He's the son of a bitch pounding the shit out of you for Christ's sake.' He softened. 'No. It's her, isn't it. She's got you whipped, boy. She's sitting down there giving you the evil eye and you don't have your goddamned little ju-ju to protect you.' He ripped his own off, hurled it back. 'They've been giving you the evil eye for three hundred years, and you got so that you believe they got this special power. Horseshit. They got nothing. You're the one who let himself get conned. You're a prince, Nicky. What did you tell me that first time? You're Kshatriya: a warrior. You got your duty. Not to her. You got duty to yourself, your family. You got to believe that duty, and that's to beat the shit out of that guy across the ring. And listen, you son of a bitch, you got a duty to me. You owe me nine grand. That's my ticket out. I've done my duty to you, teaching you the best I could. Your duty is to win the goddamned fight for me.'

They stared at each other for some time. Neither retreated. Nicky loathed Gunboat at that moment. No one had dared use such coarse language with him. He would have struck him except he still had a fine sense of hierarchical propriety. He was a Kshatriya. Gunboat was a crude boxer. He wouldn't soil himself. He had forgiven his imperfections because of their friendship. Now he couldn't. He was betrayed. But that was the common lot of princes.

'Mad, Prince?' Goading. 'I'm a Kshatriya too I figure. I'm a fighter; not a goddamned quitter like you.'

The gong was struck; Nicky turned away. Ian had risen. He appeared fresh, unmarked. Nicky ached around his ribs, chest, forearms. Gobind helped him stand, pulled away the comforting stool.

◆

Rukmani slid into the empty seat next to Sushila as her brother advanced to meet Ian. She saw him touch his temples with his gloved right hand, a religious gesture as familiar as the sign of the cross. He looked not so much afraid as cautious, even weary.

'What's happening?' she whispered. She noticed now that Sushila had her eyes tightly shut. 'Is he winning?'

'Winning?' she peeped with one eye, warily. The two were circling. Ian looked lazily confident, dabbing the way a beast would, knowing it can kill. 'That...that...bitch's son is beating Nicky up.'

'Don't use such language,' her aunt ordered. She was ignored by both. The only authority they had recognized was their grandmother's.

'The bastard.' Rukmani straightened. 'Go on, Nicky. Beat him, hit him, kick him.'

'You can't kick,' her aunt said mildly.

'Why not?' Sushila asked.

'It's the rules.'

'Damn stupid rules. Kick him,' she shouted.

'We should go up there and do it,' Rukmani said. 'We'd show him.'

But she too shut her eyes when Ian suddenly darted in and hit her brother in the face.

Nicky felt it, tasting the blood in his mouth. His rage, still directed at Gunboat, shifted fractionally away—towards Ian. He wanted half-heartedly to leap at him, as he would have without training, but he knew Ian would just take him.

He heard Gunboat call, 'Back away.' And momentarily refused the instruction. A prince could not be a coward. A second punch, short, sweet, grazed his right eye, stinging, and he took a couple of steps back.

Nicky needed to think, to recall all that he'd learned. He wished, briefly, he had seen Gunboat fight. He would have had a model then, imitated the same moves. Now, he only had the words, instructions; some experience, yet not as much as Ian. Ian smiled. Nicky knew he thought as a boxer should within the rope walls of the square. He was manoeuvring Nicky into a corner.

Yet, he could not be Gunboat. Could not be Ian. He needed to understand the enemy, instead of blindly imitating him. Lull him, lure him, outmanoeuvre him. Nicky backed. His arms scraped the ropes. Ian moved quickly to the left first, to block the escape, and then to the right. Square in front. He hit. Nicky covered; the blows came into his forearms, shoulders, gloves. They were coming in a barrage. One or two scraped the top of his head, unable to reach his face, brushed his ears. He suddenly stepped forward, embraced. He smelled the sweat, its stinging bitterness in his nostrils; sliding against the bare flesh, silken in contact. Ian struggled.

'Break,' Smith called.

Nicky held. Ian's frustration at not finishing him made him struggle more violently, tiringly.

'Break.'

Nicky pushed violently. Ian stumbled a step back. Nicky flicked out his left. Straight. True. It stung Ian's nose. Nicky heard the first cheers, thought he could even distinguish the voices of his sisters. Ian blinked rapidly to clear the involuntary tears.

He was vulnerable; only just. Nicky stopped that thought. How could he not be? He was no *deva*; no gods rode his shoulder and made him immune to defeat. It would take time, strength, and bravery. To inflict pain, he would have to suffer the pain himself. Absorb it, turn it around; unleash it at his opponent. He had never experienced pain or suffering before. Life had come too easily to him. Here, it wouldn't. The ropes were a pit. He'd entered voluntarily and now would have to discipline his mind and body to win this fight. How? Deception. Deception was the better part of valour. He doubted he had all the skills or strength to defeat Ian outright. Ian was too practiced in fighting, too determined to win. Deception! Allow him to believe in his victory before it had been achieved.

They circled, Ian wary. The slight punch had stung, not hurt, and he kept his distance. Nicky backed, allowing Ian to come forward, a step at a time. Ian threw a jab; Nicky allowed it to slide off a glove. He thought now, when he allowed his body to follow the training, it did so as if it belonged personally to Gunboat. The moves were programmed. He would not worry much about whether it always came right. Ian feinted to the belly with his left. Nicky allowed him to think that he believed, and when Ian swung the right to his head he rode the blow. Moving with it, knowing it appeared he'd been badly hit. The sound of leather to the flesh was a frightening sound; it echoed in the silence of the old hall. The collective intake of breath frightened him more. Ian believed what he saw, stepped in fast, and brought his left up in a jab to the heart. Nicky stepped back, taking it, turning fractionally to let the fist slide under his arm. He held and clinched.

'Let go,' Ian whispered fiercely.

He punched into Nicky's sides, ineffectually. Nicky only panted, allowing Ian to carry his weight as they shuffled around the ring.

'Hang on,' Gunboat whispered fiercely. 'Hang on. Tire out the son of a bitch. You're getting to think finally.'

In the heat, in spite of the whirling fans, the two fighters sweated. Winning would depend on stamina; not so much on skill.

Gunboat knew what it was like when you were battling yourself. Entering a ring was a ritual act that demanded a mental cleanliness. If you stepped in, burdened, the fight became nearly impossible. Like struggling in molasses. He had told Nicky that the fight depended on himself, not some piece of silver shit. He hadn't quite believed that himself. Everyone needed protection, from wherever, whatever. You needed the gods on your side in i his life; a piece of luck to float you past those hurdles. Without luck, you got nothing. All he had needed was a piece of luck, and today he could have been a titleholder, an ex-contender, his name in *Ring* magazine, his name on some tarnished silver trophy; remembered in those smelly gyms loud with the sounds of pounding leather. Fighters always needed charms, magic, tricks. He knew fighters who could not fight without kissing their locker doors; one, he grinned in remembrance, even carried a lock of his girl's pubic hair strapped in a small velvet bag around his waist.

Nicky had entered totally vulnerable, robbed of all belief. He knew the anger wouldn't last; no passion could, even in a ring. It got spent, distracted by pain, by thoughts of mortality. There comes a time of lull. The opponents measure each other, renew their courage. Ian and Nicky circled, keeping one another at a distance. Ian threw crisp straight lefts that always flicked fractionally to the left or right of Nicky's head. Nicky threw slower, shorter punches that appeared to have been summoned from the last reserves of strength.

Ian was experienced. In four years he'd not lost once. He understood the ring, the toll it took on strength and courage; the outer limits of pain, and the test of patience. He knew his worth; he was a champion. He had stepped into the ring with complete confidence; more habit even, knowing that shortly he was to be victorious. He had no doubts of the outcome. How could he? He knew his opponent: delightful, charming, bit uppish but lacking in the essential strength to win. Nicky, he had no doubt, would fight well, but once given a few short hard jabs, his enthusiasm would wane. Pain is an acquired strength. Nicky did not have that capacity.

He jabbed at the head. Nicky swayed back. Ian dropped a quick short right in his ribs. The first was blocked by an elbow; he suspected by chance rather than design. He pulled away, as if stepping back, and then drove in to the same sweet spot, a fraction below the ribcage.

He heard the grunt of expended breath.

Ian had no doubt he was superior. He had been surprised by his mother's insistence he win. As if he could lose? He knew she did not know him; they would forever remain strangers for he had little liking for her. It was hard to forgive her early desertion. It had hurt, even destroyed, his father, and embittered him. He would win here not for her, but for his own sake. He suspected this would be his last fight in India.

He drove Nicky against the ropes and put up a barrage of punches. Nicky was well insulated by his gloves and arms, and Ian dropped back, momentarily tired. He caught a glimpse of the thayethu hanging on the post. He had insisted on its removal, not because of his mother, but because of a genuine wish not to hurt Nicky. One punch to the metal cylinder could have embedded it in Nicky's chest,

They were in the centre. Ian stood his ground, conserving strength, only feinting, jabbing out. Nicky circled, only lightly touching Ian's defences. Ian sensed Nicky's concentration wavering. It always happened. The mind couldn't be disciplined for long. He waited, and saw the opening. Nicky glanced towards Smith, and Ian hit the unprotected face.

He stepped back as Nicky fell away and down.

TWENTY-SEVEN

'Defeat, yes, defeat,' Miss Hobbs whispered.

In the silence she almost thought she had spoken aloud, and glanced at the rajah. He had not heard. He was crouched as if he would spring to the stage. He could not see her pleasure. She felt it an auspicious time, sensing a complete victory. For a moment, she appreciated her son. He swaggered now, the way Potter did, crowing at his feat of strength. He had the same careless handsomeness; the easy-natured flesh that, through age, would weaken and fall. Unlike her. She would not fall. She indulged herself in little except the finest of calculations, and now she was to be given her reward. Wealth. Unlimited.

She heard the cheer, a roar of encouragement. Nicky propped himself up, pushed himself to a kneeling position, facing Ian.

She heard Gunboat call: 'Watch the bell...wait for it.'

Smith's hand was poised. He looked concerned, as if wanting to hurry the second hand to save the boy.

'Stay, stay,' Miss Hobbs whispered, wanting him, if not to die immediately, to be defeated.

'What?' asked the rajah, relaxing.

'Nothing.' She fell back in her chair as Nicky stood.

Smith struck the gong, and Nicky's second leaped in to lead Nicky back to the stool.

'Ian fights well,' the rajah conceded.

He was attuned to excellence in sport, appreciated it with the detachment of the aesthete. If his son was defeated, he knew the boy would accept defeat with grace. That was the true sign of a sportsman, to be gracious in both victory and defeat.

'I think he'll win.' She couldn't help herself.

'Possibly,' he said softly and turned fully to examine her as if she were a stranger. 'But it isn't over as yet.'

'No, it isn't,' she agreed amicably. She knew when not to disagree.

'Are you okay?' Smith knelt by the stool. Gobind squeezed a sponge over Nicky's face, delicately wiping away the water.

'I'm fine,' Nicky said.

'You want to continue?'

'Yes.'

Smith hesitated, then returned to his official position.

'What the hell you look at the bell for?' Gunboat demanded.

'I thought it was time,' Nicky said sullenly. He was still angry with Gunboat.

'I told you. Time stops in there. You fight until you hear the bell; not a second before.' He rubbed Nicky's arms, kneaded his shoulders. Gobind worked on his calves.

'How am I doing?' Nicky asked softly, almost reluctantly.

'Fine, just fine, until you turned your goddamned head. You had him believing you were tiring. You're okay, aren't you?' He thought suddenly he could have misread his fighter.

Nicky grinned. 'Sure. You liked that dive, huh? Good as you?'

'I never took a dive.' Gunboat laughed. 'But I did take a few rests on the canvas. You're getting good. But don't get too cocky.' He turned serious, knowing Nicky needed more than just praise. His anger evaporated.

'He's a flat-footed fighter, Nicky. He can't move as fast as you can; make use of speed. Get in and out fast. He fights square, so you got a bigger target to hit. Give him your profile, so he doesn't get much to hit at. And remember: He cocks his fist when he's going to jab his left. He's done that every time, and he drops it...not much...a couple of inches—when he's gonna follow with the right. Watch for that.'

Nicky nodded. He hadn't noticed, but his training had been

inadequate. You need to have totally absorbed the skill to work strategies. He turned to check: The thayethu still hung on the post. At least it protected his corner, if not him.

Gunboat noticed.

'Just remember what your grandmother asked on her deathbed,' he said softly.

'To win.' Nicky stopped. He felt lost, burdened. He was losing here, and in spite of his efforts he'd not located the moneylender. Miss Hobbs had defeated him there.

'Don't think of anything else,' Gunboat read his mood. 'Just win this fight.'

As the gong sounded Nicky stood, danced to the centre. Ian came in quickly, crouching, watching to finish the fight. His fist cocked and dropped a fraction. Nicky sidestepped the charge and hit low and hard into his solar plexus. He felt satisfied at the grunt, and the glimpse of a yellowy pink-tinged stain. He kept on his toes, moving constantly. Ian sullenly kept turning, facing, catching his breath. Nicky slid in a couple of lefts, if not damaging, at least ruffling Ian's confidence.

Nicky kept Ian distant, snaking out straight lefts. They did no damage, but kept the defences occupied while he probed for an opening while warily eyeing the cocked fist. It moved. He waited fractionally, ducked, and felt a left brush his ear. He dropped, hit hard at the heart, and stepped way back to avoid the hesitant right. Ian sucked air, wiping perspiration with a bare arm.

It was lonely in the ring, lonelier than any sport he'd played. His only companion was an enemy wanting to hurt, to defeat him. His friends, his advisors, remained beyond the boundaries of the ropes and could not be summoned to help if he fell. It was no different outside, he realized. From now on, he would be as lonely as he was in the ring. Power demanded it. The rajah had understood that, accepted it; but on the death of his wife had reached out blindly for companionship and given it up to Miss Hobbs. Nicky had no one. Gunboat was already in the past; he'd been outgrown. He had taught what he could and could reach no higher.

Nicky wanted Ian in a corner. It was impossible to drive him from the centre. He was planted, turning like a faintly puzzled buffalo, his left scratching air. Nicky lowered his guard, visibly wincing at the weight of his fists. Ian came forward, cautious. Nicky stepped back, still on his toes. Ian prodded, swung a right, hitting Nicky's glove. They moved further back. Nicky sensed the ropes and dropped his right further, his face unmasked. Ian cocked a fist, jabbed, and threw his right, trying to reach from a distance.

Nicky came against the ropes, dragging Ian forward. He overbalanced. Nicky twisted away and punched to the temple. Ian backed against the ropes, his left jabbing out, short, hard, constant. As it neared his face each time, Nicky noticed the thumb. It pointed, separate from the fist, only to be enclosed again on its return. He feinted left. The fist followed. He stepped quickly to the right, dropped his guard, and drove at the open face. The punch felt good. Ian shook his head, as if sweat blinded him, and swung wildly. The thumb caught Nicky's nose, gouging, spurting blood over Ian's glove.

◆

Gertrude winced. Nicky's mouth and chest were bloody.

'It's only a nosebleed,' Jockey Rosen said consolingly. He patted her hand.

'Isn't that enough? I feel ill.' She looked over at Anne. She had her eyes half closed. She opened them fully when she heard the gong and saw Nicky taken to his corner. 'He's going to lose, isn't he?'

Jockey Rosen nodded solemnly. 'Seems like it. I figure he hasn't won any round yet. And only two to go.' He sighed. 'It would have been nice to have left winning my bet on him.'

'When do you leave?' Gertrude asked wistfully.

'End of the month.'

She wanted to enquire what Australia was like, then didn't. It was futile. The whole world would be a distant place to her now. And to Gunboat. They would remain here, if not forever, for many years, and by then it could be too late. She could have lost the urge, the hunger to escape, and become satisfied with this new India.

'Who do you want to win?' Jockey Rosen asked softly.

'I don't know.' Gertrude twisted at her handkerchief.

It puzzled her. First it had been Ian. He was of her race, her culture. Now Nicky. Not because of his agreement with Gunboat. Well, there was a mercenary interest. But Nicky was part her too, deeply rooted. And she had sensed he wanted her to kiss him good luck. It was as if he was trying to change, unbending towards someone like her. He was no more yuvaraj; like her he was stateless and trapped between the past and an uncertain future. She doubted whether his world would change so much that she could be considered equal; there were too many barriers, and too much past. At least he had made the gesture, the effort to be touched by her.

◆

Gunboat dabbed the nose, then touched it with iodine. Nicky didn't flinch.

'He's going to keep on that nose,' Gunboat said. 'Blood always makes referees nervous.'

'Don't let them stop the fight.' Nicky sniffed. His nose felt swollen.

'I won't. Keep moving. You did fine in that last round, but you got cocky and let him get through with that roundhouse. Keep your guard up.'

'It was his thumb,' Nicky protested.

'I know,' Gunboat said quietly. 'But you got to deal with that by yourself. Don't bitch. You know the game.'

'I do.'

C. D. ran in and knelt panting by Gunboat. He was drenched in sweat; his eyebrows were singed and flakes of black ash clung to his clothes.

'Where the hell have you been?' Gunboat asked.

'Burning that chuthia book,' C. D. said indignantly. 'You try to do that with just a match. I had to get petrol from one of the cars and douse the fucking thing.' He patted Nicky's arm. 'It's gone, boss.'

'Thanks.'

Nicky felt released, as if a fine web had been suddenly unravelled, freeing his arms and legs. He knew it was foolish, but the past beliefs could not be flicked aside that casually. He glanced ringside. Miss Hobbs sat, arms folded, implacable. Her eyes never appeared to leave his face.

Without turning, he spoke: 'Remove the thayethu.'

'You sure?'

Nicky nodded. He sensed movement and saw Miss Hobbs's eyes follow it. She revealed no emotion except to unfold her arms and lean forward. The new intensity of her study would have unsettled another person. Nicky stared, then turned away as if she were no longer worth his attention.

He saw Ian stand, circle away to his right. Nicky moved right too and felt Ian's eyes fixed to his nose. It felt conspicuous. Nicky touched, but through the glove could detect no swelling, only a throb that expanded over his whole face. They circled the full ring, and both felt the impatience of the crowd; a sigh of disappointment. Ian decided. He moved to the centre, trying to draw Nicky to him. Nicky circled.

Ian was surprised. He had expected by now to have won. Nicky remained: accepting punishment, accepting pain. Ian knew the nose hurt; it had swelled, and one more punch would split it. He would go for that. Nicky would quit then; but he was no longer confident of that. He had seen the amulet removed from the corner post. A deliberate gesture, as if Nicky knew he was alone and would have to fight alone. It made Ian uneasy.

He stepped in quickly, jabbed hard with his left. It was blocked. He saw an opening to the stomach and threw a right. Nicky dropped his guard, blocked it, and stung Ian's face with a left.

Ian backpedalled. It had been a good punch, nearly full strength. He needed caution; yet that nose beckoned. It had been an unfair punch, but that was the sport. He wondered if Nicky had noticed. The prince-wallah had changed. He had stomach now, the grit to remain to the end; he was not in awe. He did not believe Ian unbeatable; he expected, in fact, to win, and that was a disturbing notion. It removed Ian's edge, cut him down to Nicky's equal,

Nicky became bolder. He remained on his toes, moving around, throwing lefts. Ian blocked them, noting their straightness, their accuracy. They could wear him down. He had no doubts of Nicky's strength; only of his heart. Ian feinted a punch to the head, dropped it fractionally, and went for the chest. Nicky rode the punch and slid in under the extended arm to jab him in the side. There were welts, an increasing number, appearing on his skin.

Ian stopped, momentarily. When the amulet had been removed Nicky had been staring ringside. He suspected now that Nicky fought not him but his mother. He had no doubt she wielded influence with the family, and with that would come the inevitable enmity. Nicky was her enemy. It had to do with the removal of the amulet and, he guessed, something beyond. They were the opponents. He was only the physical reincarnation of the spirit Nicky would have preferred to battle. Ian recalled not having any wish of luck from her, only the demand for victory. Nicky's defeat would consolidate her hold, extend her empire. For her the past still held its thrall. Ian was determined to win; not for her, for himself.

Ian had a better sense of timing than Nicky. He could measure the three minutes and know there was less than a minute left. The seconds passed. He jabbed, again and again to the face; each time Nicky stepped fractionally out of range. The nose remained untouched. Ian gambled. Quite suddenly he crouched, swung to the midriff, and moved in quickly. He would take everything thrown to reach the nose. Nicky backed away. Ian dropped his guard and took two savage jabs to his mouth. He tasted blood for the first time, but he saw that Nicky's guard had dropped as he swung his right. Ian punched straight. The nose burst blood. Nicky backed, dazed, and Ian went in.

'Stop!' Smith ordered. He halted the clock. 'Nataraj, come here.'

Nicky approached. Blood dripped down his chin, staining his shorts and the bare floorboards of the stage. 'I think we better stop this fight.' He turned as if he were about to declare Ian the winner.

'No, sir. I want to continue. He hasn't won yet.'

Smith hesitated. He glanced to Gunboat. Gunboat shook his head. Smith knew the rajah was in the front row and glanced down and across, not questioningly but seeming to look for some signal. The rajah had his arms folded.

'I'd stop it,' Miss Hobbs whispered.

The rajah turned, as if noticing her for the first time, sensing a different motivation than concern for his son.

'Let him go on,' the rajah said.

Seeing his son hurt, that ghastly blood dribbling down his chin and chest like vomit from a senile man's mouth, made him feel nauseous. It had taken willpower to command the fight to continue. He doted on his son, not merely because he was the yuvaraj. The boy was the final memory of his wife, a precious, parting gift which he'd raised himself.

He also understood in a peculiarly detached English part of him that this spectacle was sport. He had been imbued with the understanding that within a game, within the rules and rituals, one could be harmed, even cause harm, and yet emerge bearing no ill will. It was a strange anomaly that the English understanding of sport should be so similar to the Bhagavad Gita's understanding of life: that victory and defeat were to be accepted as one and the same. He was proud that he had taught Nicky to understand this essential ingredient. It gave one a sense of balance, of justice. If Nicky could have become a rajah, he would have ruled well and wisely.

Gunboat gently touched Nicky's nose. The fight had continued another thirty seconds before Smith struck the gong.

'I think it's broken,' he finally pronounced. The blood had dried partially, some dripped. He dabbed with iodine generously, and Nicky's face turned yellow.

'Yeah?' Nicky sniffed.

'Don't sniff. You'll draw in blood. Breathe through your mouth.'

C.D. towelled Nicky; Gobind pressed his legs and arms. There was a sense of defeat to both, their actions were casual, almost perfunctory. They knew Nicky was tired, also weakened, not so much by the loss of blood as by the shock of pain.

'Well, kid, you've got to give this one all you got.'

'I know.'

And he wished another could take his place in the battle, even briefly, so he could gather his strength. He wanted to ask how? What? But knew Gunboat would not have the answers.

He felt someone paw his arm, turned. Johnny stared, peered at him, trying to focus.

'You winning?'

'No.'

'Ram...Ram. I have three hundred rupees on you, Yuvaraj.' He swayed, and bumped the rope.

'Jesus,' Gunboat said. 'You smell like a distillery.'

'Want a drink?' Johnny proffered the battered silver hip flask to Nicky. 'It's Napoleon...or is it Wellington...one of them...brandy.'

'Don't give that to him,' Gunboat said sharply and snatched the flask from under Nicky's nose.

'You have a drink then.' He leaned his head on the rope. 'Why aren't you winning, Yuvaraj? You are a Kshatriya. I am a humble Brahmin. You are the defender of the people against the enemy. But you failed three centuries ago; you let them defeat us.' He sighed deeply as if remembering, then brightened. 'I was given the job, Yuvaraj—now I can marry. I have been celebrating my good fortune.'

Nicky glanced to Gunboat. It was a command to remove Johnny. Gunboat took Johnny's arm. He stumbled, swayed, and stood with some effort at dignity. He peered at the audience, squinting, and focused finally on Miss Hobbs. 'Oh...that white memsahib. I saw her on Commercial Street, coming out of a moneylender's office.'

'What was the name?' Nicky commanded.

Johnny struggled, but his memory slipped. He gestured vaguely and then stumbled back into the wings to sit on a bench.

'Get it,' Nicky said and rose.

'Please shake hands,' Smith said, and the two boxers touched gloves and stepped back.

Nicky sensed, if not complete victory, an escape from defeat. He felt elated. He could fulfil his grandmother's last wish. She would reach out from beyond and pull down her enemy. He sensed an urgency. It had taken too long to locate the moneylender, and he supposed he should be grateful to that drunken clown. In three minutes he could be gone, snatching the emerald necklace from under Miss Hobbs's nose. Yet if she had already reclaimed it, and possibly she had, returning it to the vault, there would have to be some proof that she had stolen it. The moneylender would have to be persuaded to give evidence to his father, though he did not wish that. It would embroil the family in a battle. His mind wandered. If only somehow he could persuade Miss Hobbs to leave, gracefully, of her own accord.

Nicky knew Ian had won the four rounds. He had the air of victory as he circled, wanting to avoid trouble, squandering the precious seconds. Each time Nicky advanced, Ian stepped back, dodged away. Nicky felt he had little chance.

Except one.

It had to work. It was within the rules that Ian had altered. Nicky came down off his toes. He needed the balance; the act of implanting his feet on the boards gave him strength. He followed Ian around the ring, waiting. Ian noticed the change in strategy, puzzled, wondering what Nicky would do. Possibly he had thrown in the towel and would, like him, avoid the battle and lessen the pain until the bell. He smiled. Nicky suddenly rushed him. Ian clinched, feeling the weight, confident of no harm. He felt himself turned away from the judges and suddenly felt a gagging agony in his left side. Nicky had chopped at his kidneys, reached them with practiced accuracy. He struggled to remain upright, to hold on for dear life, but Nicky was sliding away. Ian doubled, needing those vital seconds to recover. Nicky hit the unprotected face as hard as he could, again and again. Alternating now with the belly.

Ian had never been struck with such savagery. His lip split open, and he felt a sharp, brutal pain in the side of his jaw. He lifted an arm to protect his face and exposed his belly once more. The breath was driven from him, and he felt himself falling to escape.

'Stay down,' he heard Anderson command.

He couldn't. He would never stay down to Nicky. He stood, felt himself hit against the ropes. He slid, held, slid. He needed space, seconds. He tried to stumble away. Nicky followed. Punching at his head, his face, his body. Each blow took its toll; each appeared to have a greater impact than the next. He fell.

He heard Smith order Nicky: 'Go to your corner.'

And the count began. He waited for five, rose to his knees. By seven he was on one, straining to straighten and stand. By nine, he nearly made it, then slipped.

He felt Anderson gently lift, and now, too late, he managed to stand.

'Shake hands,' Smith ordered and Nicky approached.

He felt not so much elation as pride in his victory. He lifted his arms to his school, and saw the boys jumping up and down in their places. He saw their happy faces, sharing his victory. Heard them chanting: 'Nat-a-raj...Nat-a-raj.' His father stood, clapping for him; Miss Hobbs was not in her seat.

They shook hands, embraced. 'Perfidious Indian,' Ian mumbled softly, humourously.

'Perfidious Albion.'

'I think you broke my fucking jaw, you bastard,' Ian said, and stepped back.

Nicky understood ritual: 'And what about my fucking nose?' They embraced; stepped away, hurt and weary. Nicky climbed out of the ring and felt himself snatched and lifted as if he weighed as much as a small child.

'You were great.' Gunboat laughed. 'You were great, Prince. I'll make you a contender if you want.'

'A...crack? At the title?'

'Sure. We'll make the Garden together. Even the Polo Grounds for the title fight.' He sensed Nicky wince and placed him down tenderly.

'Hurts?' he asked, and answered, 'but it's a good hurt.'

'Yeah.'

He was hugged by C. D. and Gobind. One wiped his face and body gently; the other unlaced his gloves. He felt someone thrust through his protection and force a vessel to his mouth.

'Have a drink, Prince,' Johnny demanded. 'We're all celebrating.'

Nicky sipped, winced at the burn, and spat. He pushed the flask away, but gently, knowing the intention. Small boys now crowded him, touching with reverence. And beyond, he saw his father. Nicky needed his praise, his embrace more than the others, and pushed his way through. The rajah touched his face, as if wanting to heal the bruises and erase the blood, then held him tightly.

'It was a good fight, and I am pleased you won.'

He ruffled his hair, then looked across the ring to the other wing. Nicky turned. Ian sat, tenderly touching his jaw. The rajah crossed the stage. Nicky saw him talking quietly to Ian. Miss Hobbs was not to be seen.

The only women on the stage were his sisters. They pushed through, brushing boys and men aside dismissively, until they reached him. They both examined his face.

'He looks better,' Rukmani finally announced, hiding her worry.

'I don't think so,' Sushila said. 'He looks as if he's been stung by bees. Like he was when he was five.'

Rukmani considered. 'I suppose so,' she conceded reluctantly.

They both patted him, affectionately, proudly.

'When Miss Hobbs saw you won, she left.'

'Like a bullet,' Sushila said with satisfaction.

Nicky turned, looking for Gunboat. He saw him, sucking the brandy from the flask. 'I better change. Gunboat and I have something to do.'

'I nearly forgot,' Rukmani said. She drew out a thick manila envelope from her gold chain purse.

'What's that?'

'My power of attorney,' she said. 'I made it out to you and Sushila.' And she appeared inordinately pleased with herself.

TWENTY-EIGHT

Nicky lounged against the cushions, partly in the street light coming through the small window. The shadow of the bars fell across his chest. Gunboat sat upright by him. The old man Bagri ignored Gunboat, as he had done for the last half-hour, and concentrated on the boy with the swollen, misshapen face.

'I cannot help you on this matter, your highness,' he spoke diffidently, with just an edge of insolence. 'It is a private matter between me and Miss Hobbs. That is, if the lady was ever here.'

'She was seen,' Nicky repeated patiently. His voice sounded blurred, nasal.

'Not in this room. Possibly outside. That doesn't mean she came here.'

Nicky straightened. He studied Bagri distastefully. They had fenced; now he was weary of this plump little man. Bagri met his stare; his eyes gradually wavered and flicked away. Only to return to the same cold stare. It was as if the boy had become stone, hard, and unforgiving. He made no effort to break the silence, allowing it to grow heavier by the moment.

'I am busy,' Bagri finally said, and picked up a ledger.

It did not move the prince. Bagri could feel his eyes, even the insolence of the boy. He had no respect for elders. The silence became claustrophobic, coiled as if, when it broke, violence would be unleashed.

'I will pay for her patta,' Nicky finally spoke in a surprisingly gentle voice. He was in pain and tired, and wished the meeting over.

Bagri considered, looked up. The prince continued the silence, not expanding his meaning.

'How much?' Bagri asked.

'Its value,' Nicky said.

'I think—'

'Its value,' Nicky repeated, allowing no negotiation.

Bagri nodded. It had crossed his mind that the European lady might not pay. Europeans were poor now, not the power they had once been. The yuvaraj was the reality. He gestured. His son fetched the document; Bagri held out his hand to Nicky. It was looked at as if it were unclean.

'The money will be sent this evening.'

'You expected me to trust you,' Bagri said in astonishment.

'You have no choice,' Nicky rose. 'You lent money on a stolen piece of jewellery.'

'How am I to know it is stolen?' Bagri shrugged away the menace.

'Who will the police commissioner believe? You or me.' And again made no effort to elaborate. 'My office manager will deliver the money.'

'Give it to him,' Bagri said in disgust and dismissively. Nicky signed a receipt for it and dropped the patta in his deep side pocket.

Nicky was elated. He laughed as they walked up Commercial Street to the car. He looked like a boy who had just passed an examination he'd expected to fail.

'I did well, didn't I?' he asked Gunboat with obvious pleasure.

'You sure did.' They reached the car, got in.

'You going to show it to her now?'

'No,' Nicky said. 'She will find out for herself, and that is always the best way. The most subtle.'

'How will she?'

'Bagri will send someone to inform her,' Nicky explained carefully as if it were that obvious. 'Not to help her; to harm me, if possible. I will have to get him the money by this evening.'

'I thought you had that sewn up.'

Nicky laughed. 'No. It's a lot. I will have to ask Sushila.'

Miss Hobbs had just completed her accounting when the bearer told her Madan Bagri waited outside. She had returned late at night to Tandhapur. The palace had been dark on her arrival, but as she moved through the empty rooms, the lights blazed on ahead of her. It was a feeling of almost mystical power that before her advance lights and servants eddied back and forth. She appeared to be the centre of the universe; it was she who gave life to this monstrous pile. Food had waited if she had needed it. She did not. She bathed and slept.

In the early morning, when it was cool, and the dogs lay at her feet and the garden was raucous with awakening life, she settled to her accounts. It gave satisfaction to pull the figures into a controlled, regimented order; the world outside had spun out of her control. Miss Hobbs knew the small meanings of power and kept Bagri waiting while she changed her sari. He would report back to his father of her affluence.

'Where is the rajah and Rukmani?' she asked when she was ready. She had no wish for them to see him.

'They have not returned,' the servant said.

'Tell the man to wait in the...' she hesitated, 'in the library.'

The young man was sitting on the edge of a leather armchair when the servants threw open the door and she stalked in. He stood, and she kept him standing while a bearer mixed a drink and brought it to her chair.

'Yes,' she said, decreeing him to speak once the door closed behind the bearer.

Madan Bagri told her what had occurred and she was glad she had taken a drink. It held her steady, something to help focus her concentration.

'And did he send the money?' she asked finally.

'I don't know,' Bagri said. 'I left by bus last night. My father wished you to know.'

'Commendable,' she said dryly. 'I thought he would have had more integrity.' She received no reply. The young man merely looked uncomfortable. 'You may go,' she said and rang the bell. 'How did he find out about…us?' Saying it as if it were a delicate love affair.

'Someone saw you,' Madan said as he was let out.

'The wretched little boy,' Miss Hobbs spoke softly to herself. 'The little bastard.'

She poured another drink. The necklace had been returned to the vault; now she had to deal with the yuvaraj. The old rani had been easier. She had been distant from the rajah. The yuvaraj was close, and it would be difficult to divide them. The rajah doted on his son. She sat awhile, sipping, considering, discarding. The yuvaraj was invulnerable to her; and she had little time left before he showed the patta to the rajah. She felt, finally, her time had come and sighed in regret.

◆

Nicky arrived at the palace in the late afternoon. The malis tended the garden; those nearer stood and bowed as the car swept down the drive. There were no shadows; the sky was dark, serrated with heavy still clouds. The monsoons approached; magically, with the touch of rain on the trees, the grass would turn instantly rich green.

He made no enquiry of Miss Hobbs and felt the curious glances of his servants as he moved through to his room; he caught their whispers, their sighs of sympathy. His nose was in plaster, and adhesive tape battened down the protection. Parts of his body ached and he moved cautiously, breathing only faintly. He and Ian had both spent the night at Willingdon Hospital, his reason exhaustion, Ian out of necessity while they set his jaw.

Over the years he had grown to know her routine. He stepped out in the late evening. It was gloomy, and cool; the wind swayed the tops of trees, making them sound like the quiet roar of the seas. The lights were on: along the drive, in the palace throwing long, sharp blades of light. The dogs were by her as she returned from her walk in the garden, and they left her side to greet him.

Miss Hobbs sat on the stone bench by the fountain and waited until he stood before her. She studied him carefully, noting the face with some satisfaction, before acknowledging his presence with a curt bend of her head.

'Ian's well,' Nicky said.

'Yes. I spoke to him over the telephone. It was a terrible line.' He was silhouetted against the palace lights and she could not see his face that clearly. The dressing camouflaged him too well.

'You have my patta?'

'Yes.'

'Are you going to show it to your father?'

'No,' Nicky said. 'The necklace has been returned?'

'Yes.' She bent and stroked the terrier. 'He will miss me.' She gestured to the empty palace, and beyond to the hills fading into the darkness.

'I know.'

She sensed his hesitation and pushed. 'And you can carry that burden?'

Nicky looked back at the palace. The lights were brighter, but the silence was almost unbearable. Now and then the shadow of a retainer passed an open window. He turned back, as if wanting to relent.

She mocked: 'My, what a strong little boy you are.'

'He will find someone else.' Then he added more confidently, 'You know him. He will not forgive betrayal. He is fond of you, and I don't wish to start a quarrel. I will win it, no doubt, but it will hurt us all. I would like you to leave. Go home. I will arrange for two tickets. But you must not mention this to my father.'

'Home?' she echoed as if testing out a new tongue.

'Home,' Nicky repeated. 'You can keep what money you borrowed on the necklace.'

'I did it for Ian,' she said as if it were an acceptable defence.

'I know.'

'Home,' she said again, and Nicky imagined he saw terror. It passed, an illusion of the shadows.

Gunboat Jack

'You always talked about home.'

'I did, did I?' And she wondered whether she ever had.

Above, a lone crow, cawing, hurried east. The sky was dark, familiar as the earth she stood on, and she wondered how it looked from an English garden. The palace grounds were deserted. Beyond the high walls came the occasional faint sound of a motorcar.

Who was there to go to? She vaguely recalled a couple of cousins, and thought she must write. Who else? No one. She imagined at this time of the year England must be cold. It would be raining too, no doubt. She heard it always did. It was strange: She knew everything about that country, yet nothing. Here she knew nothing, yet everything. You could live all your life, even generations, yet never have it as home. What would she do? The thought of housekeeper or tutor saddened her. Another year or two, and she could have returned a nawab with a cottage in the country, a couple of dogs, and idleness.

'Yes, home,' she spoke suddenly, buoyantly as if it were a warm and familiar word. She had dreamed of it; now it was hers. 'Yes, we will go home. We'll find a nice flat and a good school for Ian. Then he'll go to Oxford.'

'Of course,' Nicky said softly, wishing now to leave, but she was completely absorbed.

'We'll have a marvellous time. I have a third cousin who is a baronet, you know. I shall write to him today and most probably we'll stay at his country seat until I'm settled. I spoke about him, didn't I?' She looked directly at him expecting a response, some confirmation that she existed, too.

'You did,' Nicky agreed.

He watched a mongoose dart around a patch of cannas, then scurry away. The evening had darkened, almost turned night. The sky was a soft, deep grey, lit at the very edges of the horizon by the pale washed moonlight. He sniffed, smelling rain at some distance. He wondered vaguely whether the aristocratic family existed. His father had humoured her because of her insistence, and often he'd watch her thumb through her collection of photographs and papers. How families fell.

'...most probably Ian will finish off at his old school.' She caught his attention.

'Which one?' He remained polite.

'Eton. Or was it Harrow?' She abruptly rose, peered at him through the deep shadow. She wanted to pluck the dressing from his nose, but he stepped back instinctively.

Her artful softness turned hard. Her control was such that the hatred—cold, cruel, unforgiving—remained only in her eyes. The grey was stained with such darkness that he could see no shine; her eyes were still as pebbles on a dried riverbed. He understood now that loving and hating were the equal vulnerabilities in a human. They revealed not only the heart, but the brain and the soul as well; only emotional neutrality was impenetrable. She hated now with this vulnerability and he tried to match her stillness, cloaking the fear he had to feel, a terror that came with the knowledge he had such an enemy, with controlled indifference.

She spoke and lost: 'I curse you. I curse you to loneliness, I curse you to despair, I curse you to wander the way I now will, I curse you to poverty all your life.'

Nicky rose, wanting not to reveal his superstitious fear, wanting only to remain the prince.

'I always knew you English were such graceful losers.'

He turned and strolled back to the palace. He felt no elation, no sense of victory. Only sadness at her betrayal of his father, his family, himself. The harm he knew now was irrevocable; the past could not be recalled or changed.

TWENTY-NINE

The white liner filled the eye. The grey seas licked its side, almost in reverence of its size and strength, and gave it the appearance as if by its weight alone it held the seas still. Beyond, the flat sea, specked here and there with soft foam, stretching out to the horizon, looked almost insignificant.

The liner towered above the crowded dock: a noisy chaos of stevedores and coolies and passengers and visitors and mountains of luggage, giving men the capacity not merely to dream of adventures but a belief in themselves and their capabilities to conquer the limitless seas. The sun struck it with such brilliance that it appeared to illuminate the tiled dark customs shed and bathe each and every person, brown and white, with a special glow. On the decks, those passengers who had already travelled some immense distance on this liner—from Ceylon and Singapore and Bangkok and Sydney—leaned against the rails peering down and up, away across the harbour towards the city of Bombay, with the nonchalance of seasoned dock watchers. Carelessly, for their own amusement, they threw coins overboard for the chokras to dive for and break the still surface of the water gleefully holding cheap treasures.

Nicky and Gunboat and Gertrude stood by the gangplank, straining their heads upward. The liner rose above them like a cliff pocked with portholes and many heads. Gertrude walked to the edge and tentatively touched its metal sides as if it were a dormant beast she was afraid to waken. Then, on a childish impulse, she placed both hands and tried to push. She laughed when nothing happened.

She returned to their side to fidget, wishing she stood on the vessel's decks like those other passengers, wishing she could look out on India from the safe detachment of the height and superior distance of an ocean liner.

'Don't you think we should get on board?' She broke the silence between her two companions. 'It's nearly twelve.'

'You go,' Gunboat said gently.

She hesitated, wanting not to appear unseemly, then nodded and laughed. She took a step towards Nicky, and he held out his hand. She ignored it and threw her arms around him. She felt him stiffen, then relax and hold her as tightly as she held him. She kissed his cheek; he hesitantly, softly, hers, and she knew he had not kissed women before. It was alien to him. Nicky smelled the powder and the faint perfume and softness of Gertrude.

'Thank you…Nicky.' And she stepped back.

He smiled, and gave a short, almost formal bow. 'Have a good voyage. And I wish you all the happiness.'

It sounded rehearsed, but he could think of little else to say. In many ways she was and had always been a stranger, remaining beyond the periphery of his vision. He could not now be expected to feel the sadness of parting.

They watched her first walk, then hurry up the gangplank as if she were afraid the liner would leave. She needed its safety. Then she was lost in the crowds standing at the rail. The passengers now were down to a trickle. An officer, splendid in white and gold braid, checked his watch. Gunboat turned to Nicky.

'Well, Prince…I'll see you around.'

Nicky laughed. 'I'm no longer a prince, Gunboat. You must remember that.'

'That's one thing I shan't.' He looked up. The sun was overhead, a blur behind a passing cloud. In the distance other clouds had gathered.

They had moved swiftly since the fight. The prince had kept his word, and beyond. He had purchased the steamship tickets on the P & O flagship the S. S. *Strathmore,* and to make the sailing they had flown from Bangalore to Bombay. Gunboat had little to pack; Gertrude had filled a suitcase, and had cried on leaving behind all her childhood things. Her mother had promised to ship them over. She would miss everything; Gunboat would miss only Johnny and Jockey Rosen. And Nicky.

'When is Miss Hobbs leaving?' Gunboat asked to make conversation. He sensed an ending when there is no more to be said.

'Soon, I'm told. She is staying with some friends in Ooty. She'll leave when Ian finishes his term.' He stopped, lost in thought, and then abruptly changed the subject. 'How long will you spend in England?'

'Couple of weeks. Gertrude wants to visit relatives. Then we'll catch the liner to New York.' He savoured the sound of the name. It felt good to be so near.

'You are happy to return home?'

'Yeah.'

They fell silent, accepting the end. It had been part friendship, part servitude; but over their time together the distinction had blurred. Within minutes they would move apart, re-entering their different worlds. It was like a love affair. Some affairs lasted, others ended at sunrise and could never be rekindled. They both thought that in the distant future they could possibly meet. In New York? They would drink a glass or two, savouring the memories. Like loving, some friendships were capable of lasting the distance.

The officer struck a silver bell three times and stevedores approached the liner.

'Gunboat—Gunboat...' They looked up at the faint voice. Gertrude hung over the rail waving her scarf. 'You're going to miss it.'

They laughed, and were happy that there was this excuse for them to part. They had reached a point of awkwardness and now they could embrace, touch each other on the backs, and walk away from each other.

'Goodbye.'

'Goodbye.'

By the time Gunboat had reached Gertrude's side on the deck, Nicky had gone. Gunboat knew that as always a car waited outside for him, to take him where he wished.

Gertrude lost patience with the slowness of the boat and went away happily to explore. Gunboat remained. It took time for the land to recede, and for a long while he watched the Gateway of India grow smaller and fainter. As it grew dark, and the brown earth became part of the night, and the lights behind him grew brighter, he moved away from the deck and went below.

AFTERWORD

When I was a schoolboy in Bishop Cottons, Bangalore, in the 1950s, there was a character called Gunboat Jack who intrigued my teenage imagination. It was a fantastic name, Gunboat Jack, evoking all kinds of adventures. I assumed it was a real name and heard that he was American. He was dark, not 'black' or 'African' or 'Negro', to describe him. The only Americans I saw in the movies were all white—Humphrey Bogart, Errol Flynn, Alan Ladd—a dark American was never in a movie or a part of my experiences.

Gunboat existed on the periphery of my life and my vision. Once or twice, I even saw him at a distance, usually in the evenings, when cycling down Brigade Road. Dusk shaded him from my getting a clear view of his face. He was tall, wore cowboy boots, a black coat and a Stetson. We would pass each other in a flash, allowing me only a quick glimpse of him. I never met the man nor heard him speak. He lived in another world than the schoolboy, constrained by studies and that daily routine.

But we had something in common. I heard he had been a champion boxer and I boxed too in my school, though I was no champion. Boxing was compulsory back then, like other sports in my school. I fought boys my age, and weight, three rounds, and found it an exhausting sport. There were also inter-school boxing matches. My opponents sometimes were Anglo-Indian and there were even a few English boys. All of them were waiting to go 'home', and I never knew what they meant then.

I finished my schooling, left the city and left the country, forgetting Gunboat Jack. Later, on a quick visit, I heard that Gunboat Jack had returned to America. When I decided to write the novel, Gunboat at first was not even a character. I wanted to write a novel about a princely Indian family, its internal conflicts and how Independence had changed their lives. There would a boxing match between the Indian boy and an English boy, as a sort of a metaphor of both the conflict and the ending of empire in India. I needed a character to teach the Indian boy to box and that was when Gunboat Jack shimmered out of my memory from those schooldays.

If I were to be faithful to that real life character, whom I had never met, he would need to be that 'dark' American. I would need to accurately reproduce his speech pattern and the sounds of his voice from the 1950s. As I was living in America at the time, I knew black Americans spoke differently from the white ones—tone, texture, jargon, slang. I could not even describe Gunboat's features. I knew nothing about Gunboat, apart from his being an American and a boxer. As I could not do justice to both the language and his character, I changed him to a white American. Also, I did not want to introduce a third race, and its bleak history, into my novel. I believed then that Gunboat's fame was confined to Bangalore. There was no Google to check on his background and few people knew his origins. My editor at Simon & Schuster accepted Gunboat as white, as did the reviewers.

Years later, an American writer working on a book, contacted me. Christine Lewis had found my novel, *Field of Honor* (the original title of the novel), listed in the biography section of Gunboat's official boxing record. She loved the novel but pointed out that Gunboat Jack was a black American. Why white? I told her about my difficulties writing on black culture. Christine sent me faded clippings and posters from the 1920s. His real name was Wilson Colzie, also known as Gunboat Smith then. Gunboat was arrested for a hold-up in 1919 but the judge let him off. One poster was of 'Gentleman Jack' listing all his fights in Lawrence, Mass., another from March 1931 of a boxing match in White City (Island grounds, Madras) between Gentleman Gunboat Jack (10 stone, US) and Robin Neil (10.8 stone, Calcutta).

In the early 1960s, Gunboat's sister wrote to the US Ambassador to India to help her get her brother back home. The US embassy found him and sent him home, where he died.

As mentioned, this novel was first published as *Field of Honor*, but the current publishers of the novel, Aleph Book Company, suggested that the title be changed to *Gunboat Jack* to give the book a new lease of life but also to link it to the real-life character who once thrilled the citizens of Bangalore with his exploits. I hope the man who was an inspiration for the character in this book will come alive for a new generation of readers. As for me, my epitaph for him is his famous quote: 'I like three things too much. I like drinkin', I like women and I like music.'

Timeri N. Murari
Chennai
February 2019